Praise for Extreme Romancing in Idaho

"A delicious, high-stakes adventure with delightful twists and characters that will steal your heart."
—KayLynn Flanders, author of *Shielded*

"Extreme Romancing in Idaho is brimming with charm, tension and characters who leap off the page. Pierson is skilled at writing sweet romances with layers of depth that aren't afraid to touch upon life's heavier moments. A beautiful reminder that no matter what we're going through, there is always room to fall in love."
—Jackie Khalilieh, author of *Something More*

"Absolutely delightful. The wit, the romance, the heart--I was there for all of it."
—Jessica Heileman, Amazon best-selling author of *Plotting Summer*

"This enemies to lovers is a slow burn, with lots of playful banter, a great storyline, and characters you wish you knew in real life."
—Lisa-Marie Potter, co-author of *Men in Books Aren't Better*

"Extreme Romancing in Idaho is a laugh-out-loud, enemies to lovers romance with an engaging competitive twist. I loved watching the chemistry between Angie and Remi, and how their rivalry compelled them to one up each other, while simultaneously pushing the other out of their

comfort zone. This story has everything I love in a romance!"
—Amanda Nelson, co-author of *Men in Books Aren't Better*

"If you're looking for a sweet, and humorous read, this is it! Bonnie Jo delivers a multi-layered story, skillfully weaving the interplay between loss and love. *Extreme Romancing in Idaho* will have you cheering for Remi and Angie to go the distance and find their happily ever after— as well as make you want to experience the beautiful scenery of Idaho first hand."
—Lindsay Maple author of *Holly Jolly July* and *Not Your Basic Love Story*

"*Extreme Romancing in Idaho* is sweet and funny, with irresistible characters and such a charming setting—everything I'm looking for in a romance! You can't help but fall in love with Angie from the first page; yet the smart and funny banter between Remi and Angie made me want to root for both of them equally, chapter after chapter. This book was an absolute joy to read!"
—Heather Dixon, author of *Last Summer at the Lake House*

"Remi and Angie's story was SO fun. I absolutely loved the idea behind it. And I loved watching how tortured Remi was with every single thing that happened. Remi's growth throughout the book was so satisfying. The sexual tension was delicious. The romance was slow and deep, just like I like it."
—Sally O'Keef, author of *Every Breath*

Extreme Romancing in IDAHO

BONNIE JO PIERSON

RISING ACTION

Text copyright © 2024 by Bonnie Jo Peirson

Cover Illustration © Nat Mack
ISBN: 978-1-998076-83-3
Ebook: 978-1-998076-90-1

FIC027270 FICTION / Romance / Clean & Wholesome
FIC027020 FICTION / Romance / Contemporary
FIC027250 FICTION / Romance / Romantic Comedy

#ExtremeRomancingInIdaho

Follow Rising Action on our socials!
Twitter: @RAPubCollective
Instagram: @risingactionpublishingco
Tiktok: @risingactionpublishingco

To my Emma Jo. Go take on the world.

Extreme Romancing in Idaho

Chapter 1

Angie

*W*orld traveler. Check. *Loves kids.* Double check. *Collects skulls of small animals?*

I read the last line again on Theo's eHarmony profile. Why would anyone admit that, let alone put it on their profile? But this guy had such a darn sexy body. Too bad he was going to be the next Ted Bundy, and I'd be safer on a date with a rattler.

I swiped left.

My green hospital scrubs caught on the stiff fabric of my chair. I glanced up from my phone, arched my back, and rubbed along my lumbar spine. A couple of flight attendants gabbed as they rolled their bags to security. The server at the café wiped an already clean table nearby.

"Good morning," she beamed when she caught me looking.

"Thanks. You too," I said through a yawn. Ugh. Morning people. I would never understand them.

The air filled with the scent of freshly brewed, dark French Roast, and I glared at my empty disposable cup sitting on the floor beside my foot. I'd consumed four cups to get through my shift at the NICU last night, and at some point, I had to cut myself off.

Only three flights a day came into this airport: six a.m., noon, and six p.m. Why couldn't my parents have been on the six p.m. plane? I arrived here before the sun got out of bed, which should be illegal. This morning was the most abysmal one yet. I flipped from eHarmony and re-read my parents' text strand.

> It's not good. Stage four.

Mama tacked on a sobbing emoji to her last sentence.

> What's our next option? Another round of chemo? We can still fight this.

I'd written that message knowing this type of stage four cancer equated to a death sentence. I hadn't wanted to give up on a miracle.

Papa's responses gutted me.

> No more treatments ... I want to be home ... Sorry, Muffin. Looks like I won't be able to be there on your wedding day after all.

By wedding, he meant a hypothetical wedding in the distant future, one we'd been joking about since elementary school—the wedding where the groom was yet to be found.

I couldn't deny any longer that his colon cancer had come back like the Terminator dragging itself from underneath the hydraulic press. Only in Papa's story, the robot was going to win in the end. We were headed into the world of hospice care.

Hospice was worse than mornings—and coffee didn't make it better.

At the onset of his cancer diagnosis, we'd made a deal with each other; he'd fight this Terminator inside him and be a survivor to walk me down the aisle. It was one of his greatest dreams, that and meeting his grandkids.

Given the few months estimated time frame, I couldn't make the second happen. But I could make the first a possibility. I was a doer. My other half existed out there, and come hell or high water, I'd find him before Papa left this Earth. So, I jumped headfirst into online dating, creating profiles on every dating app imaginable. Tinder—before I knew it was for casual hook-ups. Learned this the hard way—eHarmony. Bumble. Match. Hinge. Coffee Meets Bagel. Plenty of Fish. And even FarmersOnly.com, because city folks just don't get it. All of which led me to some epic no-good-very-bad dates.

Dates like Fart Boi at the driving range. He literally let one go with every swing. Then the guy who Facetimed with his mother during dinner on our first date. I live with my parents, and even I couldn't handle the Oedipus vibes oozing off him. Oh, and how could I forget about Pee Pee Pants McGoo, who was so drunk he wet himself while trying to make out with me?

The past year, Papa had been in remission. My drive to find someone had slackened, believing my dad would be with me for at least another decade. But now, time was running out.

What would I do without Papa? Who would envelop me in a hug, let me cry into their chest, and make this lonely wasteland of a world bearable? Sure, I had other friends and family, but it was like I was trapped in a desert surrounded by people offering me salt water, and Papa was the only one holding the clearest spring water out to me.

My eyes burned. My thoughts drifted between the real world and the dream world until the rumble of the jet engines rattled the airport. Instead of curling up on the chair and falling asleep, I opened my newly downloaded dating app: ExtremeSingles, a place where lovers of extreme sports looking for long-term relationships could meet. With the failures of the other dating sites, I was becoming desperate. I needed a fresh pool to fish in. Never mind that I hated anything extreme.

With a swipe of my thumb, I scanned over the next potential Mr. Angelina Johnson.

Daniel Smoot. Loved dogs. Lived in Boise. Favorite extreme sports: climbing, rappelling, and BASE jumping. I shuddered at the thought of doing any of those things. This guy also played guitar and piano. Believed in love at first sight, and he was looking to settle down!

Boom. Drop the mic. Someone on the hunt for a committed relationship wouldn't be opposed to a quick marriage. Perfect! Minus the extreme sports hiccup, but I could make it work.

I went to swipe right, but I stopped. I gnawed at my thumbnail. He could be a total loser like my last three online heartthrobs. But who was I to call anyone a loser? A thirty-five-year-old woman still living with my parents? I raised my eyes enough to see the plane's wheels touch the ground.

But I would never find true love if I wasn't willing to take risks. I chewed a loose chunk of my thumbnail off, spit it on the floor, and swiped right.

You are a match flashed onto the screen.

Holy kittens in a kaboodle, Batman! We matched.

I read his name again. He had blond hair, sun-tanned skin, and great fashion sense. I couldn't wait to smooch that Smoot.

Who was I kidding? This guy must swipe right on everyone since someone as active as him would never have swiped on my profile pic. I'd intentionally replaced my filtered picture with one before I'd lost weight, hoping it would discourage douchebags.

My picture still displayed my long blonde hair arranged in a nice braid and showed off my next best feature, my blue eyes. Mama said she was always jealous of my lashes and complexion, but I only saw the double chin and monthly forehead pimples.

I tapped into the chat.

> Good morning. Speaking of mornings ... Are you a morning person?

I stared at my phone waiting for a response as the plane taxied and came to a stop.

Nothing. I took that as a no.

Switching to my messenger app, I typed a quick text to my brother, Jared.

> Mama and Papa arrived safely. I'll keep you updated with Papa's cancer.

It was hit and miss whether Jared responded. He was basically nocturnal, living his best musician life.

Workers in bright-yellow vests towed the ramp to the plane and lined it up with the open door. Dropping my phone in my purse, I looped it over my shoulder and threw my empty cup in the trash. I strode to the window. Mama stood in the doorway beside the flight attendant, waiting to be let off.

Passengers flooded from the plane. They'd slowed to a trickle by the time my parents exited. A flight attendant opened a wheelchair, and Papa, wearing his favorite red flannel jacket, climbed into it. I frowned. He hadn't been in a wheelchair a couple of weeks ago when he'd left to go to the Cancer Institute, which apparently sucked at treating colon cancer.

They made slow progress down the ramp and onto the asphalt. Mama's short, red hair tousled in the wind; her shoulders hunched toward Papa. He'd lost more weight, and his hair had become as white as snow.

Mama turned to talk to someone behind her. That was when I saw him. My perfect ten—short black hair, well-kept, trim beard, tall—wearing a full-on backpacking backpack with an outdoorsy helmet hanging off the side.

Armed with a bright white smile and the ability to use it, Backpack-Helmet Man took Mama's bag and pushed Papa's wheelchair down the gangway while the passengers rushed past them. I melted where I stood. He got sexier with every step he took.

I pressed my nose to the glass. He said something that made Mama laugh. Great. He was one of those people who possessed easy-going superpowers, the ones who diffuse the tension around them. Simply watching him made a bit of the stress from my crappy week slip away.

Backing away from the window, I relocated closer to the metal detector. Other passengers were already walking into the side of the airport where liquids of more than three ounces were allowed. My parents came into the building, still assisted by my dream man.

In times like these, I enacted the Golden Chris Standard, in which I used four of the most exquisite male movie stars, all named Chris, as a comparative measure for the guys I met.

His face had a similar structure to my personal favorite of the hot Chris's. Chris Pine. This guy had the same kindness etched in his features that I examined anytime I watched Chris on the big screen. Of course, I was projecting, as I'd never met Mr. Pine in person, but I imagine he would never make fun of someone for having a body that fits into plus-sized clothes.

Rex and Wendy shouted greetings to my parents. Tall, dark ... and completely bald, our mayor and his shorter, pale, and platinum-blonde wife were perpetually traveling. Being from a town as small as Clear Springs, we couldn't go anywhere without being sucked into a conversation, even at the airport in the 'big' city. It was like being part of a perpetual high school reunion.

"Oh, honey. I missed you so much." Mama finally reached me and enfolded me into a squishy hug. The tears I hadn't let out all morning rested on my bottom eyelid. I blinked, and one fell. I wiped it away before Papa saw it.

"Hey, Muffin," Papa said.

I studied the blue and yellow lines crisscrossing the deep red of his flannel. I'd never liked the nickname he'd given me as a child, but I loved him more than a lifetime of jelly-filled donuts.

"Thank you, Remi." Papa looked at the man, who was at least a couple of inches over six foot, and then held out his hand to me. "This is our daughter, Angie. The one we were telling you about on the plane."

Where was some sand so I could plant my head in the ground like an ostrich? They'd talked about me and probably attempted to set me up with him. I couldn't get more desperate than that.

"Remi was such a help to us on the plane and so nice during the flight." Mama leaned next to me and whispered, "And there's no ring on his finger."

Remi's eyes locked on mine. I didn't normally notice the color of someone's eyes the first time I met them, but his were striking. Deep and rich like the Idaho soil, encircled by thick, dark lashes, and they held such fierce life in them, as if he hunted for joy each moment he lived.

"Remington James the Third. Nice to meet you," he said with what sounded like a practiced country-boy twang. He held out his hand to me, grinning like he'd found buried treasure.

I expected a wave or a nod—not a handshake. And definitely not the whole 'The Third' intro.

"Nice to meet you, Remington James the Third." I laughed as his cheeks grew a little red. I assume he'd been named for his father and his grandfather before him. I'd been named after Angie Harmon, the actress for Abby Carmichael on Law & Order, not one of my relatives. Nope, a TV star. After the first episode aired a few months before I was born, my parents became superfans. I didn't tell him all this of course. "I'm just Angie."

I slid my fingers into his hand. He held mine with a strong grip and shook vigorously. Goosebumps raised the hairs on my arm as I studied him. His soft, businessman's hands were manicured, yet his clothes matched that of a mountain climber ... or one of those people who went to every national park.

Maybe Smoot and Remi had figured out the secret ingredient to happiness: extreme sports. Too bad I had the courage of a gnat.

Mama scooted behind Papa's wheelchair. "We'll head over to baggage claim. Meet you there." She winked and mouthed, *Get his number.*

I rubbed my forehead, certain a trace of a blush dusted my cheeks.

Remi adjusted the straps on his backpack. The helmet hanging from it thunked against its metal frame. "So, have you lived here your whole life?"

"Yep. Small-town girl. That's me. We don't even have a stoplight."
Stop talking. Just stop talking. I squeezed my lips together. The farthest
I'd been from my town was this airport. "Where are you from?"

"Uh—Texas." He tilted his chin down.

Hence his Southern accent with a Texan twist.

"If you've lived here your whole life, then you've been to the Perrine
Bridge," he said.

The bridge? It spanned the Snake River Canyon. "Yeah. I drive over it
almost every day."

"*No way.* My buddy and I are going to BASE jump it."

I took everything I saw in him back. He was nuts. Jumping into a
chasm with no guarantee your 'chute' would open? No, thank you. At
least three BASE jumpers died every year catapulting into the canyon.

Smoot couldn't be *this* extreme.

"Are there any good places to eat around here?" He shrugged his
backpack on his shoulders and smiled at me.

"I really like eating at Elevation 486."

"That's how tall the bridge is. 486 feet!" He bounced onto the balls of
his feet. For a second, he may have actually left the ground.

Yikes. He acted like I was the most blessed thing on this earth to have
the privilege of having a close relationship with the sacred structure.

"Sorry." He cleared his throat. "You must think I'm … intense."

"Just a little bit." I held up my thumb and pointer finger with only a
small gap between them.

He let out a burst of laughter like a kid on a carnival ride. If only I
could hop on the same ride with him.

"It's just … I've been waiting my whole life for a chance to take on
this challenge. My enthusiasm kind of takes over." He shifted his weight.

"So, what do you like to do for fun? Jump off bridges?" Sarcasm wove in between his words.

Between finishing nursing school, working, caring for Papa, and running the farm, I didn't have much time for fun. What would it be like to travel around the country with a helmet strapped to your bag and do whatever the heck you wanted?

It would be heaven. Except I would do other things, like soak in hot springs, lay out on a sandy beach, get massages, and ... soak in hot springs some more. "No way would I do something as stupid as jumping off a bridge."

His shoulders dropped a little with my answer.

"I guess I like to ride my horse," I continued. I glanced away for a second. My parents had their bags but didn't gesture for me to leave. Sly devils.

"You actually ride a horse? Not the kind you put quarters into?"

Merriment twinkled in his eyes, and, despite my bad mood, I laughed. Darn his superpower.

"I'm impressed. I live in a city. People don't ride horses there." He stepped closer, giving off a scent of fresh air and clean laundry with a hint of cedar.

I didn't do dangerous stuff like meeting a man in person. The apps were safer. With the online chat, I could get to know them a bit, choose if I wanted to give them my number, and *then* set up a date in real life—layers of built-in protection. Popping straight into the 'in real life' meeting always ended badly. Like what happened with Troy, my most recent ex. He cheated on me with Melissa Kesler, the high school counselor, and they eloped to the UK.

"Well, my parents look like they're ready to go," I said, then sped over to Mama and gathered their two rollie bags.

Remi followed me.

"Here, let me help you out to your car," he said.

"Isn't he the most considerate man?" Mama looked at me while she asked her question.

Yes, he was. He was also way out of my league. My search for a match started and ended in a pool two levels down from Remi. Men living in my realm proved to be more considerate.

I pushed my way out the door. The wind blasted into me on the way to our old Dodge truck. I bent to lift the bags into the back, but Remi beat me to it. He made those bags look as light as a piece of straw. I caught myself staring at his muscles and shook my head.

It would never work. I would fall in love with him in, like, five minutes, then what would happen? He'd ask me out for drinks, then dinner, maybe a movie. Perhaps we'd make-out at the back of the theater, I'd invite him over to hang out with my parents, and we'd talk all night. Inevitably, when he was done with me, he'd discard me and move on to the next vulnerable girl. I might as well spare myself the heartache and stop the progression here and now.

Besides, spring planting season loomed before me. My scant extra time would be spent with *the* one. Possibly with my match, Daniel Smoot.

My phone buzzed against my thigh in my purse. I pulled it out, and indeed, there was a message from Smoot.

> *Hey! So excited you messaged me. Not a morning person. Haha. What do you do for fun? Love that your profile says adventurous.*

My heart lifted. He messaged me back! Okay. Maybe I stretched the truth a bit when I'd put adventurous in my profile. Adventure for me was watching Netflix instead of Hallmark on my days off.

Here was a good, solid option for me. Fun, fairly cute, and, from his profile and message, had a great personality. I peeked over the edge of my phone at Remi. Farewell, tall, handsome Remi with the softest eyes I've ever seen. Goodbye, heaving biceps and taut pectorals. It would have been nice to touch you.

He slammed the tailgate closed, setting his helmet to motion once again.

My mind churned through all my failed dates this past year. I couldn't be boring old me if I wanted to snatch a soulmate like Smoot. No. I had to reinvent myself. Become more interesting ... like Hot-Back-pack-Guy-the-Third. If Smoot wanted adventure, I'd give him adventure.

Without thinking, I typed my response.

> Hi. Full-on night owl here too. And I love to jump off bridges. With a parachute. For fun.

I hit send and threw my phone back into my purse with my heart in my throat.

Without much control—I blamed lack of sleep—my eyes found Remi again. He stood next to Papa while Papa struggled into the cab, not offering too much help or making him feel dependent.

Ignoring the gravitational pull tugging me toward Remi, I yanked my door open. The hinges creaked louder than the howling wind. Mama sat beside Papa in the back of the truck, and I scooted behind the wheel.

"I'll take this inside for you." Remi gestured at the wheelchair. "It was nice meeting you, Mr. Tony and Ms. Nora, and ..." He paused and locked eyes with me. "You too, Miss Angie."

Miss Angie? Who talked like that? Shoot me now and bury me in my grave. Second thoughts weaseled into my resolve.

I slammed the door on them and his beautiful face. Through the long years of being the chubby kid through my adolescence, I'd learned that boys like Remi were never an option.

Jiggling the key into the ignition, I turned it. The truck chugged to life ... and died.

Chapter 2

Remi

I tapped on Angie's window. Her head bobbed up and down as she manually cranked it open. People still owned cars with manual windows?

"I'm fine. It'll start." She tried again, but her attempts ended with the same results—a dead truck. "No. No. No."

"Give it another try, Muffin," Tony said.

Muffin? He'd called her this in the airport too. The flush in her cheeks and the way she shot me a quick glance told me Angie didn't especially love it.

"And press on the accelerator while you do it." Nora pointed at the pedals on the floor.

Angie didn't say anything to them and kept trying until turning the key only resulted in a click. She leaned her head on the steering wheel.

"I can give y'all a ride if you need one," I offered. I didn't exactly know how I was getting home, but I'd figure it out. My co-conspirator and best friend, Myles, mentioned he might be able to pick me up, but if he didn't show, I could call an Uber since the rental car place wasn't open. If they even had Uber drivers out here.

Nothing but empty fields surrounded the airport. No hotels. No restaurants. No houses. Just vast emptiness, making me feel exposed to the constant wind.

"No, we're fine," Angie said.

"That would be lovely." Nora leaned over her daughter.

"Great."

Angie narrowed her eyes at my one-word answer and started rolling up her window. I didn't know what I'd done to earn her reticence.

"Y'all stay out of the wind in the truck. I'll be back after I return this wheelchair." The window closed before I finished speaking.

I smiled at her through the glass while she pretended I didn't exist. Stubborn woman. How hard would it have been for her to say thanks? It wasn't like she had any other option.

If only I could take away the glimpses of sadness I'd seen in Angie's eyes. It was no surprise her expressions were tinged with misery. Nora and Tony hadn't said much about his health, but I caught the words hospice and cancer.

In one plane ride, it wasn't hard to figure out that the Johnsons were nice and genuine. Why did such awful things have to happen to good people?

I scrubbed a hand down my cheek. Nora and Tony talked the whole way from Salt Lake about Angie. They told me how she supported them, how she'd worked the farm when Tony's health had deteriorated, and she'd also managed to be the first in the family to graduate with a bachelors. My curiosity about her, which had burned as hot as a Texas summer, cooled in the face of her disinterest in me.

I probably should have skipped all the bridge talk, but I was within miles of a once-in-a-lifetime experience, an unforgettable adrenaline rush.

The wind gusted and nearly took me with it. I turned to roll the wheelchair inside, but it was no longer next to me. My head shot up. The rolling chair blew across the parking lot at record speed like a ghost propelled it.

I sprinted after it. My backpack forced me to run like an awkward college freshmen with a billion books in their bag. I looked back at Angie—she was all-out laughing at me. With the spectacle I made of myself, I wasn't surprised. I picked up my pace.

A car honked as I ran in front of it. It slammed on its brakes, and the driver got out. I didn't even pause. The possessed chair was closing in on a black Mercedes, and I couldn't let it mar the gleaming paint. My fingers closed on the left handle a couple of seconds before it broadsided the sports car. It whipped to a stop, the footrest slamming into my shin.

"Ow!" I yelled and hopped on one foot.

"Hey, Remi."

Myles? Torrents of air blasted past my ears, making it hard to hear anything. I gripped the wheelchair and faced the driver of the car that'd nearly hit me.

"What are you doing chasing a wheelchair through the parking lot?" Myles wore sweats and a hoodie with his shoulder-length hair pulled back. He stood on the footboard with the door still open and leaned over the roof of the small red car. His door flexed in the wind.

Pushing the wheelchair in front of me, I moved closer to him, so I didn't have to yell. "I'm returning it for a friend I met on the plane."

"Sometimes you are too damn social!" Myles yelled and sat back in the driver's seat. "Let me get parked." He closed the door and veered into the parking spot to his right. He shut off the car and came to my side.

We clasped hands, and he gave me a one-armed hug around the steel frame of my backpack.

"Dallas isn't the same without you." I hadn't seen him in months.

"Yeah. Well, it's been rough here too. Sorry I'm late."

In looks, Myles was my opposite. Straight blond hair. Lighter complexion. Light green-blue eyes. I'd known him since elementary school. After he'd saved my social life all through my growing up years, I'd made sure he had a very comfortable living doing what he loved most. My mom always lectured me on what a proper employer-employee relationship looked like. I was surprised she didn't call him *the help*.

I successfully maneuvered the wheelchair to the ticket counter, exchanged pleasantries with the sparse airport employees while Myles remained quiet by my side. He'd been like this since Samantha had broken his heart a couple of months before he'd come here.

"Hey, remember the people I was too damn social with on the plane?" I asked on our way to the parking lot. The automatic doors slid open, allowing the wind to pummel me again.

"Yeah." Myles' chin-length hair fell out of his man bun and stuck to his whiskers. He brushed it behind his ears only to have it wisp around his face again.

"Well, I kinda offered them a ride." I pointed to the truck, the bed loaded with their luggage and the cab still packed full of Johnsons.

"You never change." He gave a soft chuckle. "I don't know how we'll fit."

"We'll make it work." I slapped his back.

"I've missed your optimism."

"And I've missed your sarcasm."

I walked over to Angie and her parents while Myles brought the car alongside their truck. Taking the two carry-ons from the pick-up bed, I introduced the Johnsons to my oldest friend. Both suitcases fit in the compact car's trunk with ease. I slid my backpack from my shoulders and carefully placed it on top of the two bags. It only had one change of clothes in it, my toiletries, and my Stetson hat my father had given to me the day I started working for our company.

Making sure the case my Stetson rested in wouldn't be crushed, I lowered the trunk until it latched.

Nora had already helped Tony into the front seat and climbed behind him, leaving Angie and me. I moved to sit on the middle hump seat, and at the same time, she leaned into the car. We bumped shoulders and wedged into the opening.

"I'm ah—" I started.

"I'll sit ..." she said at the same time. "Hold on."

We both squeezed our way out of our predicament.

She held up a hand. "I'll go first." She folded herself into the car, and I piled in next to her.

Being six foot two inches had its advantages. Fitting into the backseat of small cars wasn't one of them. It took me three tries to get the door to shut. My whole right side touched her. I tried to set my hand down, but it brushed her thigh, so I held it next to my chest.

"You two situated?" Myles looked at me through the rearview; his laughter tacked on every word.

Angie's chuckle joined Myles's. "You do know it takes forty-five minutes to get to our house, right?"

My bare upper arm touched her soft skin. I could think of worse ways to spend forty-five minutes.

"On second thought, we'll find another way home." Angie shifted, and the side of her breast touched my arm.

My lips lifted into a crooked smile, and I swallowed. The fun meter for this company trip notched upwards by two more marks. Who said business couldn't be mixed with pleasure?

"At this time in the morning?" Myles backed the car out of the parking spot and sped out of the lot, not giving her a choice. "I'm your best option."

Angie leaned back against the seat. *Thank you, Myles.*

"I, for one, am grateful for the ride," Nora said, glancing toward Tony, who'd finally gotten situated in front of her. The level of effort and the amount of pain it'd taken him to simply climb in the car was a reality I never wanted to live.

The trip had worn on him. Even I could tell the difference in him from when we'd first taken our seats on the plane.

"You are more than welcome," I answered for Myles and me. The car wobbled in the wind. "Does it always blow like this here?"

"In the spring?" Angie laughed again. "Yes."

Nora leaned over Angie to talk to me. "We used to tie a sheet to her ankles and wrists and watch her get blown around the yard. She loved it. Didn't you, Angie?"

Angie braced her forehead in one hand and shook her head. If she could beam out of this car, I had no doubt she would.

"I'll have to try that," I said with what I hoped was an understanding smile.

"Better use king-size sheets when you do," Tony said from the front seat.

"And take pictures. I'll look you up on Instagram when I get home." Nora nudged Angie, and Angie sank lower in the seat.

The longer this drive went on, the more I loved this family. I couldn't help but wonder about the son they mentioned on the plane. Would I like him as much as I did the rest of the family?

I might end up running into him since I was here for *as long as it takes,* according to my father. Some of the real estate deals I'd worked on had taken over six months to come to an agreement. With Idaho being an outdoor enthusiast's paradise, I didn't mind the time I'd spend here getting this job done.

First, I'd BASE jump the bridge. Then I'd go to City of the Rocks to rock climb and rappel. Or I could rent an off-road vehicle and drive up a mountain.

"Y'all ever been to City of the Rocks? Myles and I were going to try to go there next week." I couldn't resist asking the Johnsons about the lesser-known treasures in this valley.

"We were?" Myles eyed me in the rearview.

I half-grinned. "I hadn't told you yet."

"It's one of my favorite places in the whole world." Angie spoke so quietly I almost didn't hear her.

"We camped there as a family once or twice a year. Maybe we should head up there next week too. What do you think, Angie?" Tony looped his arm over the seat.

His face tightened. Even such a small movement caused him pain. Angie must have also noticed.

"I don't know if I can, Papa. I have a lot of shifts," Angie said.

Her comment sat in the car's silence for a good ten minutes. Both Nora and Tony dozed, and Myles focused on the road. After struggling with my pocket, I pulled my phone out and took it off airplane mode.

It immediately started vibrating with a dozen text alerts. Names flashed across my screen under numbers I hadn't saved to my contacts. *Hey, Remi it's Kathryn/Mindy/Taylyn/Crystal*... the texts would end in some variation of "I had a great time last night." The rest of the messages were from my parents and brother checking up on my trip progress.

Too late, I shielded my screen from Angie, having no idea how many texts she'd already seen. After typing a quick response to my brother, Matthew, I tucked my phone back in my pocket, pressing against Angie even more, and bumped my head on the ceiling of the compact car.

"What kind of work do you do?" I kept my voice quiet so I wouldn't disturb Tony and Nora, who were doing the sleepy head bob. She shifted against me again, and I had to restrain from outright admiring her cleavage.

She overtly rolled her eyes and angled away from me as best she could but answered me anyway. "I'm a nurse. I work in the NICU."

"You save little babies' lives?" I was surprised by how attractive I found this information.

"When I can. On the good days."

"That's pretty amazing," I said. And then I did the unthinkable. I tucked one of her stray hairs behind her ear.

This never worked in my playbook, which had a ninety-five percent success rate.

Step one: draw her interest, then walk away, forcing her to come to you.

Hadn't I learned this most basic rule after years of practice? But I'd never felt this kind of instant chemistry with a woman.

She stiffened and turned her wide eyes to me. In her stare, I could tell she felt what was going on between us too. Our faces were mere inches apart. All I had to do was tilt my head toward her and my lips would touch hers.

How wonderful would that feel? It'd compare to the rush of jumping off a bridge, especially if it progressed into my bedroom.

"Where do you live again?" Myles asked, ending the moment.

Angie leaned closer to her mother.

Dammit, Myles.

She rattled off her address. The numbers she'd said sounded vaguely familiar. I rested my hands on my knees. Myles turned onto the small yet well-kept street a few miles west of Main Street. We passed the groomed gardens around the neighborhood sign *Mountain Meadows.*

Oh. Hell.

Nora lifted her head and opened her eyes. "We're home." She smiled. "Sorry you couldn't have seen our farm a few years ago. It used to be surrounded by endless fields."

"Then some jerk-off company bought every farm touching ours and planted these ugly houses here." Tony wrenched his thumb at the identical houses lining the freshly asphalted streets.

"They want to buy our farm too. But we'll never sell." Angie's voice came out as hard as stone.

The car drifted off into the weeds lining the driveway. Myles corrected and rolled back into the center of the lane. His gaze reflected off the rearview mirror and scalded me. My grip tightened on my knees.

I was here to buy a centennial farm that neither the kids nor the parents wanted to sell.

I was here to buy Angie's farm.

Chapter 3

Remi

Stacks of Levi's lined the wall next to the Carhart jackets and coveralls in the local farm store. I thumbed through them with my ears tuned to the conversations around me in the Monday morning rush.

Idaho was a goldmine. Everyone and their parakeet wanted to move from their over-priced lofts to the open fields and lower cost of living. I'd tipped my father off to its potential—and why wouldn't I? That was my job. Plus, I'd always dreamed of being a part of one of the most rugged states in our country.

Scents from the numerous feed bags piled on shelves mixed in the stagnant air, creating a unique, veterinary-office-meets-Target smell.

Myles flicked through a rack of clearance clothes to my right, the metal hangers scraping against the hanging rod. "You sure this is the best place to—"

"Gather information," I interrupted, still half-listening to two farmers in the chicken aisle bellyaching about a dog attacking their flock. "Yes. Trust me. This is where the action happens. Not only is this store owned by the mayor and his wife, but it's also the only gas station in town."

Myles leaned his arm against the freestanding clothing rod. "James really agreed to give us our seed money if you get this deal done? As in two *million* dollars?"

Although I shared a name with my father, he went by our middle name, whereas I much preferred our first. Anything to be different. "Yes. He is desperate to get this property. Nobody has ever told him no like this. And he can't resist the challenge the Johnsons present, making him an easy target to get whatever I want."

"How did you arrange to sit with them on the plane?" He ran his hands along the hoodies with Idaho splashed all over them.

"I didn't. Crazy, huh?" Lady Luck was once again on my side. I'd been my normal charismatic self on the plane and now they loved me. "I didn't put two and two together until we dropped them off at their house."

I could kiss Tony, Nora, and most definitely Angie for standing up to my father but seeing how they were my problem now, made me conflicted.

"What did the Gucci Bag Rampager have to say about the two mil?"

Myles's nickname for my mother never failed to put a smile on my face. Once, in our early teenage years, we sneaked into Mother's closet and tried to count the number of Gucci and Louis Vuitton bags she owned. We didn't get through half of them before we were caught. It was one of the many times Mother banned me from seeing Myles.

The more she pushed me to stop hanging out with him, the more I needed a friend like him in my life. Myles lived in the real world. He went to public school, ordered cheap Chinese take-out, and consumed SPAM, a canned block of supposed meat, regularly.

Without Myles, I would have never seen the inside of a thrift store ... or a Wal-Mart. I'd be out of touch with reality like my parents and Matthew, which was why I succeeded where they failed. I spoke both billionaire and pauper.

"She wasn't happy. But she'd never dream of going against James."

Much like her endless Gucci collection, I couldn't count the number of times I'd begged my mother to hold me on her lap and read me a story or do something corny, like play a card game or video game with me. She never did. It was the one deal I'd never been able to close.

A wide smile split across Myles's face. "Texas Bros, here we come." He held up his hand, and I high fived him. "What's your plan?"

Myles and I had started dreaming about Texas Bros—a store to fit all your extreme sporting needs—in college. But here we were, years later, still in golden handcuffs by the wages and even better perks of working for Cockrell Development Co. which I'd nicknamed the CDC.

Communicable diseases aside, working for the other CDC, Center for Disease Control and Prevention, would be a vacation compared to being a puppet for my brother and father. I even toyed with the idea of creating a badge for myself: Remington James, special agent, CDC.

Yesterday when we'd dropped Angie and her parents off, I'd told Myles to circle around to the back entrance of the neighborhood. We were staying in the model home in *Mountain Meadows*, a house appearing to be ostentatious and fancy, yet, upon closer inspection, it was as cheap as quarter-machine jewelry.

If I headed the company, our houses wouldn't be garbage builds, but I didn't want the responsibility of being CEO. I didn't enjoy my job, yet I couldn't leave. Getting out was harder than leaving the mafia. Let me rephrase. Sure, my dad would let me quit, but without a penny to my name. I'd be disowned. Cut off. With a few phone calls, he'd make sure I wasn't hirable and that no bank would give me a business loan. He had the personal cell phone number for the Pope himself. His reach was global. And more than my dreams were riding on my success.

Buying this farm was my one and only way to a future I wanted to live.

"I'm assuming you have a plan," Myles said.

I was interrupted in replying when the bell above the door rang, and three guys in greasy, dark-blue coveralls walked in.

"Hey, Myles," the one with short brown hair said with a wave.

He was flanked by a tall, muscly, curly-headed dude who could be on a calendar cut-out for working mechanics, and a shorter man with black hair, bronze skin, a thick mustache, and rockin' a dad bod.

Grabbing the nearest Carhart jacket, I walked to Myles. "You have friends," I muttered under my breath. "Perfect. This'll speed things along."

"I always make friends, you dumbass." Myles spoke through his smile and then returned the man's wave. "Mornin' Blake." He amped up his Texas twang, then nodded to the other two men. First to the tall, shaggy-headed one, then to the shorter one with the wicked Tom-Selleck-worthy mustache. "Chuck ... Pedro. This is my friend from Texas I told you about, Remi."

Blake took my hand and shook it.

"Dude, did you really BASE jump the Eiffel Tower?" Pedro asked on his way to the fountain drinks.

All three men stared at me, waiting for an answer. The rest of the store quieted as the two cashiers behind the register stopped mid-conversation and eyed me.

I looked at Myles. "You told them about that?"

"What can I say? I was one too many beers in."

"You really did it?" Chuck grabbed a king-sized bag of peanut M&Ms and set them on the counter. "I thought Myles made it all up to impress us."

It was our graduation trip from college—a jump years in the making. We'd been worried security would grab us before we had a chance to take the leap. They hadn't. They'd taken us into custody after the jump of a lifetime, eventually releasing us after confiscating all our gear. It didn't matter. We'd lived through it, and I'd do it all over again.

"Yeah," I answered. "We jumped from the second platform and got some wicked footage."

"You have to show it to us!" Pedro hollered while he filled his jumbo refillable container with Dr. Pepper.

"Next bros night out," Myles promised.

"You have bros nights?" Endless locations. Countless community developments, and not once had Myles been incorporated into friendships like this.

"Yeah. At Tractor's Bar and Grille."

I'd like to say I wasn't jealous. Yet I started strategizing ways to sabotage them, their standing in this town, and their mechanic business. First and foremost, their relationship with Myles.

Okay. So maybe I was a bit ... overprotective. Myles was literally the only authentic friend in my life. Since elementary school, he'd been the one person grounding me to the real world. The rest of my family hated him. Yet, I'd managed to get him hired on as my project manager in charge of overseeing every job under my umbrella.

My life was a perpetual chess match.

"You want me to add a package of Reese's for Maddie?" the older woman cashier asked.

"Oh yeah." Blake walked to the shelf and grabbed the peanut butter cups. He slapped them on the counter. "Thanks, Wendy. She would have been so upset if I'd forgotten."

Her name, coupled with her vague familiarity, helped me place her. "You're the mayor's wife." I stifled my chuckle at how in a town this small, the mayor's wife ran the cash register at the local gas station. Wendy's curly hair was pulled back into a messy ponytail, and she wore a button-up flannel shirt and leggings. I couldn't resist comparing this woman to the glittering social sphere of the mayor's wife in Dallas.

"That's right. I saw you with Nora and Tony yesterday. Remington, right? What has you coming here all the way from Texas? You work with Myles?" She bagged the candy and other snacks Pedro had set on the counter.

Verified. Word traveled faster than a scalded cat in small towns. "No," I lied. "I'm looking for work. You know anyone hiring?"

Blake swiped his card in the decades old card reader. "You know Tony and Nora really could use help."

"You got any farming skills?" Wendy slid the receipt into the sack and handed it to Blake.

Chuck grabbed it from her before Blake had a chance while Pedro dug in the bag, grabbing the M&Ms.

"Hey, those are mine." Chuck reached for the candy Pedro held away from him.

"See you outside. I'll finish filling the gas cans," Pedro called on his way out the door with Chuck hot on his heels.

This conversation was going exactly as I wanted it to—the power of grifting. Mention Tony and Nora and "job" in proximity. Bada-bing-bada-boom. Their minds went right where I wanted them to.

I met Myles' eyes over Blake's shoulder before responding to Wendy's question. Myles shook his head. I ignored him. "I've got loads of experience."

I couldn't pass up the opportunity to thread myself into the Johnsons' everyday life. The direct approach had failed both my brother and father. I needed to find a backdoor to close this deal, an edge I'd only discover if they didn't suspect my motives for being here.

Blake moved to the door. "See you later, Myles. Nice to meet you, Remi."

I waved, and Myles leaned against the counter.

"Without her dad I don't think Angie will be able to manage things on her own," Wendy continued. "I'd start there."

"Perfect. You mind helping me with a wardrobe? I pack light."

With my comment her eyes lit up, likely seeing all the dollar signs at her disposal. She walked out from behind the counter. "Agnes, Joe, Mitch!" she hollered at her employees. "You want to help this man get everything he needs?"

Though all three had been pretending to stock shelves, they responded quickly enough that I had no doubt they'd been listening the whole time. Agnes had glasses thicker than the bottom of beer bottles, Joe could be Paul Bunion reincarnated, and Mitch was the opposite, small enough to be a jockey.

"You sure you know what you're doing," Myles muttered under his breath.

If I failed, I'd be cut off. No more stipends, fancy vacations, or access to the money in the business accounts. My father's greatest desire was for me to become a soulless, money-grubbing man ... exactly like him.

Last I checked, my soul was still intact, and I wanted to keep it that way.

"Trust me. In two weeks, we'll be shopping for storefronts." I smiled.

One wardrobe and some boots later, I stood on the Johnson's front porch. My feet creaked against the chipped, dark-blue-painted boards. I looked over my shoulder at the view behind me. Tall Sawtooth mountains jutted into the sky, their peaks covered in clouds. The view stretched on forever unhampered by skyscrapers. No wonder they wouldn't sell.

Angie's farm consisted of a little over 500 acres. Fitting five single-family homes per acre, our business stood to make upwards of half a billion dollars on her land.

The lots would sell as fast as Tesla stock in the early-2000s.

Wind chimes lined the front railing. Their jumble of harmonizing chimes rose and fell with the gusts. Light sprinkles of rain blasted against the back of my neck like shards of glass. The Carhart jacket I'd just purchased kept that part of my body warm, but my cowboy hat did little to warm my head and ears. Mentally, I added a beanie, thermals, and gloves to my list of things to buy. I already missed the warmth of my home state.

I lifted my hand to knock on the door, and my phone buzzed against my leg. Slipping it free, I looked at the notification.

It was Kathryn. *Hey, don't become a stranger ...*

Her text indicated she thought of herself as someone special in my life; like a girlfriend. Typically, I didn't have this issue. I was always upfront and honest about everything when I engaged in any type of activity involving a woman. Kathryn and I had hooked up a couple of times, and we'd had a ton of fun, but I'd made it clear I didn't want any commitment.

I'd met her at my brother's office.

My first big mistake.

Tucking my phone back in my pocket, I knocked on the door. The porch light turned on—even though the sun had fully risen, dark clouds blocked its rays—and Nora opened the door.

Her eyes widened when she saw me, a soft smile breaking over her face. "Remi?" She tightened her knit sweater over her chest. "What brings you here? Oh, where are my manners? Come in. Get out of that weather."

I stepped into the entryway, and she closed the door behind me. The old oak floors groaned underneath my weight. Warmth filled the small space, and I began to sweat. The smell of homemade bread combined with the scent of the old stuff in the rest of the house, like an antique store was hosting a baking competition. The acrid aroma of Tony's medical supplies added tension to the otherwise cozy feel in the home.

The TV echoed down the hall; faint snoring accompanied the sound. An arched opening led into a formal living space to my right, where a large window framed the view of the mountains. Stairs angled upward on my left, the wall above them covered in family pictures and images of little Angie, and a boy I assumed was her brother. The only light in the room came from a lamp on a table that stood against the half-wall supporting the stairs.

"If I'd have known you were comin' over, I would have tidied up a bit. Or at least I would have run a brush through my hair." Ms. Nora fluffed a flattened section of her short, red hair, gathered a stack of mail on the entryway table, and tucked it under her arm. "Travel knocks us out these days." Shifting in her slippers, which looked like loaves of French bread, she stopped talking and waited for me to speak.

"Don't be frettin' over me. You look lovely." I smiled.

"Oh, hush." She flicked her wrist at me, waving away my compliment.

"I overheard someone saying at the Country Store you're looking for a farmhand."

"Wendy." Nora shook her head. "If you're ever wondering what's happening around town, spend ten minutes there." She laughed.

Her laughter came so easily that I guessed she did it often despite her husband's current health problems.

"I'd like to take the job," I said, even though she hadn't said anything about a position being available.

She eyed me up and down. "You?" she asked. Then she laughed again.

I frowned and tugged at the end of my jacket. Maybe Agnes, Mitch, and Joe had led me astray with my wardrobe. Did I not look the part?

"I'm sorry." She covered her mouth.

"Look. Even though I currently live in Dallas, I've worked on land my whole life." I stuck to the truth even though I'd stretched it like a snake sunnin' on a rock. I'd worked on purchasing and developing land since childhood, not actually ever putting a shovel into dirt. "But still, I want to experience Idaho farm life while I'm here. I'll work for free."

Nora waved her hand again. "We don't accept any charity. You'll be paid a fair wage. Ten dollars an hour."

I didn't react to that number. I hadn't made so little since elementary school. Obviously, coming up with a wage of any kind would be a sacrifice for them. "Sounds good."

"Angie's out in the field," Nora said, pointing through the front window, where a tractor kicked up dust in the broody weather. "Why don't you head out there? Use our truck. The keys are in it."

"Thanks, Ms. Nora."

"Nora's fine. Angie's going to love this."

Her laughter gained strength as I opened the door and stepped outside.

Chapter 4

Angie

I was buried in a cowpie up to my neck, and the only way I could get out of it was to lie my ass off. But then that kept me securely in the manure. Countless people lied when they dated online, yet I'd never actively participated in catfishing.

That was what I was: a filthy, bottom-dwelling catfish. When I'd told Lili, Gabby, and Ryan on shift at the hospital, they'd busted a gut and instructed me to lighten up. It was easy for my friends to get entertainment out of this situation when they weren't the ones performing fabrication acrobatics.

My tractor hit a rock, and my head bounced into the ceiling.

"Ouch!" I yelled over Garth Brook's voice coming from the speakers.

Smoot knew his stuff. Apparently, he and his buddies were BASE-jumping fools. He also paraglided, rock climbed, rock-crawled, sky-dived, kite-boarded—whatever the hell that was—and zip-lined in the rainforest. He'd even rappelled down Lincoln's face at Mount Rushmore during his stint as a park ranger.

Currently working as a skydive instructor, he lived and breathed extreme sports. He also owned a cabin in Pine. Smart. Motivated. Successful. More than ready to settle down. These were all things I'd been searching for in a prospective partner, so I couldn't let one teensy thing, like my fear of anything remotely dangerous involving heights, ruin our potential future.

Far out of my comfort zone, I couldn't keep pretending much longer, either. I didn't know the lingo, the necessary gear, and, most importantly, I didn't have the experiences to back up my lie. Normally, I'd ghost him. But what if he was *the one*, and I let him go because I was a coward?

Old Angie would back away. New Angie did research and talked about barrel racing and rounding up the cows as much as possible. He found that fascinating, but already he was asking to FaceTime. Could I be this fabricated woman without the aid of Google?

Remi, the guy from the airport, popped into my mind. The helmet strapped to his backpack and his carefree attitude said it all. He lived for extreme sports ... and women. I still couldn't stop memories of his tight body, and the way he'd helped my parents, from sneaking into my thoughts.

Why would I waste time thinking about him? His true colors shined as bright as a neon sign. All those texts from different women? I stuck out my tongue and made a puking sound. Men like him who toyed with women, who used them solely to satiate their needs, were the scum of the Earth.

It was like two different men resided within him. The kind man who helped the elderly, and the devilish douchebag sitting in the car next to me. The caring man had to be fake as a plastic plant.

Shoving Remington James the Third out of my thoughts, I neared the end of the row and slowed the tractor. The bouncing tires jolted my seat. In one sweeping motion, I U-turned, dragging the plow in the opposite direction. A giant cloud of dust billowed behind me like I was vacuuming the field.

The water was going to be turned on in a couple of weeks. My favorite day of the year was when the canals filled. With it, the valley shook off the dust of winter and sparked back to life.

Yet before the floodgates opened, the plowing, fertilizing, and planting in all our fields needed to be finished. I'd be working the farm every minute I wasn't at the hospital. Then watering would begin, and I'd disappear into fricking early mornings, working until long after the sun dipped below the horizon.

How was I going to do this without Papa? And keep up with my nursing job?

At first, I'd gone into nursing to help Papa when he was first diagnosed with cancer four years ago. But when the time came to pick my specialty, I couldn't work on the cancer floor. Day in and day out, watching patients live through what I was going through at home. No. Emotionally and mentally, I'd break.

So, I'd picked babies—fresh, new lives full of endless possibilities. Of course, I also knew a hell of a lot about cancer, especially the colon kind. Colostomy bags and chemo—weight loss—pain—we'd been through it all, and now it was back.

I lifted my chin and stretched my back as I slowed the tractor for another turn. We'd beaten it once, and we would beat it again. I didn't care what those doctors in Salt Lake said.

With the tractor facing our house once again, I saw our pick-up truck bouncing toward me through the field.

Papa? Had something happened?

I slammed the tractor to a stop, pulled the parking brake, and threw myself out of it. I hit the ground running. The truck slowed next to me, but Mama wasn't the one driving it.

Remington? The perfect ten from the airport? My previous thoughts came together into the apparition in our farm truck ... only he was real.

The womanizer had returned.

I skidded to a stop in the soft, plowed dirt and put a hand to my chest. My heartbeat knocked against it.

He opened the door.

"What in the hell are you doing out here?" My shock at seeing him came out abruptly in my question. I sucked in air through my nose and slowly let it out through my mouth. Thinking before speaking had never been one of my strengths.

"Well, I—uh—heard you were lookin' at hiring some help—"

"No." The word flew out of my mouth before it'd been fully formed in my mind.

"Your mom offered me a job. She told me to come out here and have you show me where to get started."

Mr. GQ himself, Mr. I-can-get-any-woman-I-want, was coming to work on my farm.

Turd in a bucket! How much was Mama paying him? I'd fought her about hiring help. We couldn't afford hiring a high school kid, let alone a full-grown man with brand new clothes and enough money to fly here to go BASE jumping. I tilted my head at him, looking for a tag on his crisp Wranglers, bright-white shirt, and brown Carhart jacket zipped to his mid-chest.

When I finished with him, his shirt wouldn't be white. And was that a Stetson on his head? Hats like his cost well over a thousand dollars. What the hell was a man who could drop that kind of money on a hat doing here, in my field, asking to buck hay and feed slop to the pigs?

For once, I didn't speak.

He slapped his hands together. "Where do I begin?"

"You ever worked on a farm before?" I asked.

"Sure. I'm from Texas."

Like being from Texas qualified you for farm labor. "You can drive a tractor?"

"Yes sirree."

"Buck hay? Feed chickens?"

"Yep."

"You know how to milk cows?" I asked, even though we didn't own a dairy. We ran beef cows on our land; milking day and night wasn't something I'd choose to do with the rest of my life.

"Uh-huh. But I may need a refresher course on that one." He held his pointer finger in the air.

I kicked my boots lightly in the dirt. If we were playing Bullshit, I'd write a big BS on his forehead. "Okay. Get in that tractor and drive it to the end of the field." If he could get it in gear with the implement running, I'd strip off my shirt and jump in the ditch.

"That tractor. Right now. The big one." He took a few steps toward my John Deere.

"I don't see any other tractors." I held my hands out, palms up, and swept them in all directions.

He laughed. "No. I guess not."

He approached my Deere slower than my Grandma Anne and placed his foot on the step, giving me a pleasant view of his butt in those tight jeans. Dang. I bet I could break a board on it.

I closed my eyes and refocused. He climbed into the driver's seat and looked around at all the levers. We'd bought this tractor before the cancer, back when we had good harvests and plenty of money to invest in the farm. It was fully equipped and as confusing as hell to someone who didn't know anything about farming, like stepping into the cockpit of a plane.

He pulled on the door. It didn't budge. "The door won't close. It's stuck."

"You have to pull on the lever under the—"

He moved his hands over the glass. "What?"

"Here let me!" I yelled over the running engine and marched over to him. "This lever. Right here."

"Oh, yeah." He smiled and went to close the door but paused. "Look!" he shouted. "When I said I could drive a tractor, I meant more like a lawn tractor."

And there we had it. The truth. "Here. Let me shut it off."

I stepped onto the bottom step and leaned over him. I'd done this hundreds of times with Papa—stretching over him to grab my drink, or car keys. It wasn't until my chest pressed against Remi's toned thigh that his scent—clean sheets and cedar—penetrated my senses.

This wasn't Papa. I turned and looked at him. He met my eyes with a level of heat I wasn't prepared for. We were within an inch of each other, and despite my best intentions, an awareness of this proximity sent chills zinging through me. I breathed in short intakes of air to keep my chest from touching his.

I turned off the key, pulled back, and climbed to the ground. The increasing wind caused a sprinkling of rain to dot my dusty arms. This path only led to heartache for me. Sure, Remi possessed an unnatural level of attractiveness, but beauty only ran skin deep, and attraction didn't equate to kindness.

I'd be no better than those poor women texting him, dying for one drop of attention. I'd been in that position before too, and I'd never allow myself to go there again.

"This is a little different than a lawnmower." I looked up at him. The brim of his hat blocked the bright sun. "Are you really here to work for us?"

"Yes, but I know nothing about farming."

"Then you're fired. We don't offer any severance packages, but I'm sure Mama will give you a jar of pears on your way out."

"You can't fire me."

He challenged my gaze, and I lifted an eyebrow at him. He had no idea what I could and couldn't do. Mama surely would come to understand my reasons. On the other hand, I would be passing up an opportunity to make his life a living hell.

I smiled. "Fine. You can stay, but only on probationary status. Why didn't you tell me the truth earlier?"

"Technically I've fed my dogs. And I have no idea what bucking hay is, but I've gone on a hayride, so I figured it was close enough." He quirked his mouth in a sideways grin, maneuvered down from the tractor, and closed the door.

He was masterful at twisting the truth to suit his needs, a skill he probably acquired while tricking women into falling into his bed. I narrowed my eyes. "Mama hired ... *you*?"

"I think I convinced her to take me on with my winning personality."

"I think it had more to do with your good looks."

He tucked his bottom lip under his teeth, his eyes dancing. He glanced at the ground before he looked back at me. "You think I'm good-looking, huh?"

"Yes." Think *before* talking would be my new mantra. "But your pretty face isn't going to get the pigs fed."

He laughed.

"Come on." I motioned for him to follow me to the truck. "Mama will have lunch ready. I'll give you a rundown of the daily chores. You can start tomorrow morning."

"Will you teach me to drive that?" He pointed back at my Deere.

"Baby steps. Tractor lessons only start after you prove you're worth my time." That and I couldn't be locked in the cab with him without jumping him.

Chapter 5

Remi

I'd never been more drawn to a woman than when Angie climbed out of her massive tractor yesterday. The thing was as big as a house with tires taller than me.

There sure wasn't any slack in her rope.

Pulling up my collar against the early morning cold, I braced my legs against hay bales on the flatbed trailer being towed behind Angie's ancient truck. She jerked the truck to the right, and I struggled to stay upright so I didn't go spilling into the pasture riddled with cowpies. Eighty cows trailed behind us, mooing and trampling the soft ground; mud and shit splattered their underbellies. Some of them flicked their heads and sprayed froth all over their friends.

What if we humans behaved this way?

I could see foam spraying out of our mouths over our meals and splattering onto each other. Myles would go for that at dinner tonight. *Excuse my foam, your food is that good.* Yuck.

Angie was an independent, capable woman, and I found myself in the rare position of being intimidated by someone else. Yesterday she'd given me all the expectations she had for me to fill in for her father, and I doubted my decision to take this job.

However, this was my only window into the family who'd managed to stonewall my dad for years and find a weak link to break their refusal to sell. As an added benefit, I got to be closer to this enigma of a woman—who was as friendly as a fire ant.

She presented a challenge I'd never come across, and I couldn't resist trying.

The truck slammed to a stop, and I flew into the stack of bales behind me. Hay covered my hair and my clothes.

I sneezed.

My first stop after this morning would be the pharmacy to buy Allegra, Zyrtec, and a whole gallon of Flonase.

Angie popped out of the truck. "I'm sorry. A calf darted in front of me."

"I'm good." I lifted a bale of hay with the two strands of thin orange twine binding it together and used my knees to throw it off the side of the truck bed. Now I was entirely acquainted with the term 'bucking hay.' I literally had to throw my hips into it to get the rectangular bales off the trailer. When Angie had demonstrated, she'd made it look easy.

The cows descended on the fresh hay.

"How many more bales do we have back there?" Angie asked, still hanging out of the truck.

I counted: one, two, three, four—"Seven more. You want to use all of them?"

"I'll drive to the end of the field, keep throwing them off every six feet or so," Angie said.

I gave her a thumbs up in my now-dirty, new leather gloves as she sat back in the driver's seat and closed the door. The truck crawled forward over boulders and through divots. I managed to remain on my feet and throw hay off as she stopped at the end of the row.

One more bale was left on the trailer. I could see Angie's eyes on me in the rearview, and I wanted to make this one real impressive. I bucked that bale as hard as I could, but when I pulled my hand back, it didn't listen. My fingers were looped tight under the twine. Where my fingers went first, my body followed.

After being suspended in the air for a few seconds, I crashed to the ground. The impact dislodged me from the twine, and I rolled free through pile after pile of cow shit. Trying not to think of the excrement sticking to my new jacket and jeans, I stopped.

Angie's brake lights glowed in the morning mist, the sun bright on the horizon. I'd give anything to pull a chain or flip a switch and shut off the dawn light so I could slink my way back to the flatbed unnoticed.

She strolled over to me. "You okay?"

"Yep." I rolled onto my back and breathed in. My side and shoulder hurt where I'd first connected with the ground. For sure, I'd feel the consequences of the fall tomorrow. "I'm fine."

I thought she'd come over and help me up or sit next to me, but she didn't. At first, she let one laugh escape and then another slipped through her nose until she was doubled over.

As embarrassed as I was, even as pain filtered in every muscle I moved, my shoulders shook as I laughed with her. I stood and tried to dust off what I hoped was mud on my pants. That was when I noticed the cows had closed in and were looking at us with their glossy eyes. Having never been this close to a large animal, I took a couple steps back.

"You afraid?" Angie's smile bordered on cruel enjoyment.

"This ain't my first rodeo." I plastered a confident smile on my face. Why was I such a moron? Ain't my first rodeo? Where the hell had that come from?

I blamed Texas. Being raised by the son of a Texas rancher-turned-real estate tycoon hadn't helped either.

"You just can't stop with the lies." She shook her head. "Go on then. Rub her head."

"You want me to touch the cow?" At her nod, I continued, "I don't see why this is necessary."

"Believe it or not, genius, sometimes the cows get sick or injured, and if I'm at the hospital, I'll need you to handle it."

She gestured for me to proceed forward. I straightened my shoulders and walked toward the smallest group of them, locking eyes with the one I'd selected to pet. Its breath puffed into the air as it snorted and tossed its head. I almost backed away but held strong, placing my hand right between her eyes.

I looked back at Angie. Lifting my chest as I took a deep breath, I challenged her with a raised eyebrow. I could do this.

Another cow chose that moment to kick its leg back and hit my crotch. Breath whooshed out of me, replaced by agonizing pain pulsing from my balls into my stomach. I dropped to my knees and dry heaved. I leaned back onto the ground and stared at the brightening blue sky.

What am I doing here? My brother and father wouldn't have expected this of me. Why was I torturing myself?

Angie's laughter grew louder, and she leaned over me. "Never approach a cow from behind. Especially not a mama cow." She continued to chuckle. "Wanna give up yet?"

At the sparkling hope in her eyes, I knew I couldn't let her win. I wasn't about to extinguish the fire and call in the dogs on the first day. The cows, who'd at first dashed away at my knees hitting the ground, now dipped their noses close to me.

Strands of hay hung out of their mouths. I couldn't read their expressions, but I knew what they were thinking. *Classic. Stupid humans...* and *This hay has the right amount of weed in it.* I imagined cows thought of little else beyond food going into their stomachs.

Finally, I wordlessly shook my head at Angie.

"Took you a hot second to decide." She stuck her hand out to me. "I'll drive you to the house so you can get an ice pack."

The sun rose behind her, shining through the blonde strands of her hair pulled back in a loose ponytail. She wore no makeup, and her natural beauty was irresistible. Damn, she was gorgeous—and in one day, I'd learned to proceed with caution around her. I took her hand and stood, walking bow-legged.

"I'm fine."

"Suit yourself," she said, throwing me a knife. "Cut and gather the twine from the bales. I'll wait for you on the canal road."

She walked back to the truck, swung into the driver's seat, and drove off.

The quiet morning closed in on me. Shuffling and mooing cows became background music. Carefully avoiding their backsides, I cut the orange strands, pulling them free from the bales. In between each bale, I took in the scenery surrounding me.

The rolling green pasture edged by the Snake River Canyon with its snow-capped mountain peaks behind gave this place an almost fairytale feel—like I lived in a landscape painted by Monet. I'd seen his *Haystacks* at d'Orsay the first time I'd visited Paris.

The pain, still throbbing to the tips of my toes, disrupted the picturesque setting. This was a hard land, and only the people strong enough to tame it could live on it.

I smiled even as anxiety clamped down on my throat. How long would I have to do this job to close the deal? A week? A month? Assuming I could survive that long.

Angie looked at me like a porcupine in a nudist colony, lying in wait to find new creative ways to inflict pain. I tempered my scowl as I approached the truck and tossed the bundle of twine in its bed.

Through the open driver side door, she leaned against the truck's bench seat. Her phone pinged, and her eyes briefly met mine. She tucked her lip under her teeth and slid off her glove to check her notifications. I leaned over to peek at her phone. The little parachute notification from the ExtremeSingles app popped up along the top, but then she turned her shoulder and held her screen close to her chest.

Hold on one hotfallutin' minute. Angie? Online dating? On the extreme sports site? "ExtremeSingles." I didn't bother pretending I didn't see her notification. "What happened to 'I'd never do something as stupid as jumping off a bridge?'"

"I still won't."

"Then what are you doing on this particular dating app?"

She looked me up and down, then said, "You won't understand."

Pretending to be scandalized, I pressed my wide, splayed fingers against my chest and gasped. "Bless my soul, Miss Angie, are you ..." I lowered my voice. "Catfishing?"

"No," she answered too quick. "Maybe. Only halfway."

I chuckled at her obvious terror at being even slightly dishonest. How cute.

She narrowed her eyes at me and returned her attention to her phone. "I'm just trying something new."

Based on the look on her face, she really liked the person who'd messaged her. How could she be more attracted to a man she met online than me, a nicely formed, flesh-and-blood specimen standing right next to her?

"So, do you like him?"

"How do you know it's a him?" She glanced over her shoulder at me with a raised eyebrow.

All the good ones were lesbians. But, good news, it explained why she was so indifferent to me. The world made sense again.

She laughed, presumably at the face I must have been making. "I'm not gay."

The vice around my chest eased. "Cool. I mean, I'm good whatever your sexual orientation is." I leaned against the truck, but my glove slipped against the slick metal, and I lurched to the side. I hid my stumble by slapping my glove on my leg.

She paused, looked at me, opened her mouth to say something, but then closed it again. Turning from me, she typed furiously on her phone, pressing send ten times in less than thirty seconds.

"Hold on there, tiger." I snatched her phone, quickly glancing at her messages.

"Hey!" she yelled. "Give it back."

"What is this?" I flicked through the rest of her messages and read them out loud in my most feminine voice. "*I can't believe you've hiked Kilimanjaro. I would die for an opportunity like that.*" I snorted. "*What are you wearing right now?*" My voice dropped into my normal octave as I read how ridiculous her last message was.

"Shut up." She grabbed her phone, and I let her take it.

"You're never going to get this guy if you keep sending messages like that. You're coming on too strong."

"What do you know? Dan's nothing like you."

She cradled her phone against her chest like she thought this man was a soft and gentle baby animal.

"He's a man, and men want one thing." I held up my pointer finger in her face. "Sex," I mouthed.

"You. Are. Disgusting."

"I also happen to be a man. Keep going on like this and you'll chase him away faster than greased lightning."

"Greased lightning? What are you—"

"How many times have you been ghosted after you matched?"

"That's none of your business."

"Oh, this is worse than I thought. All of them dropped you, didn't they?"

The slight sag in her shoulders and the way her chin dipped down a notch gave me the answer I needed. She had all the goods but none of the game.

"No." Her denial was too adamant to be true.

I gave her a look that told her exactly how much I believed her.

"This time, it's going to be different." She changed her tune.

"No. It isn't. This dude is a text message away from running."

She was giving away too much too soon. If only she'd let me teach her my ways, then she'd have men four states over begging to be with her. Every instinct in me told me this land deal hinged on Angie. If I got her to agree, then her parents would follow; therefore, the closer I got to her, the better. "The only way this guy will stick around is if I help you."

"Whatever. You're barely competent enough to feed cows."

"Would you rather end up with cows or men?"

Just as she was about to spew another quick retort, defiance leeched from her eyes. "You know all about the extreme sports scene, don't you?"

"Lesson one. When you say stuff like 'scene' you sound like you're eighty."

"I don't know why I even tried." She rubbed her temple in circles and started to walk away. "Forget it."

"Yes. I dabble in extreme sports." As in, I've done everything: skydiving, kiteboarding, motocross, canyoneering. You named it. I'd done it.

Pausing mid-stride, she turned back to me and took a breath. "All right. I might need your help." She said this like she'd swallowed vinegar. And then the dam broke. Words spilled out of her faster than I could catch them. "... I mean, this guy knows everything ... even rappelled down Lincoln's nose ... extreme sports, and I kind of told him I did ... big fat lie, and there's only so much I can Google. Besides, I hate heights. I'm scared of pretty much anything that could result in my death. Honestly, I don't know why more people aren't terrified of these kinds of things. I mean, white water rafting. You could get sucked under the water and never come back up. Who would do that? And don't get me started on BASE jumping—"

I grappled with the words lost in the jumble and tried to piece together a request. "You want me to take you BASE jumping?"

"That's not just a no. That's a H-E-double hockey sticks no." Her teeth tugged at the nail on her middle finger. She dropped her hand away from her mouth. "I simply need you to make me sound more authentic. Teach me the lingo, what type of gear you use, that kind of stuff."

"You want me to help you lie to him."

"Kinda. Not really—Yes." She stood and started pacing in front of the truck as she kept talking. "I want you to help me be more interesting to this guy. Like, keep his attention. You know?"

She—a woman who cared for her parents, ran a farm on her own, worked in the medical field saving lives, had a sense of humor, and on top of all that, had a face and body with curves that went on for miles—wanted *me* to make *her* sound more interesting.

However, she did a horrible job presenting herself.

"Why do you want this guy so much? Why not break it off and try again?"

"I don't know. I really like him. We connected."

I'd trained for years to spot a lie, and Angie lit up like a red flashing light. "Liar. Try again. The truth this time."

Pink rose in her cheeks. "Fine. I want to get married before Papa dies, and this guy shares my same goals."

"You want to get married to this guy in a matter of months?"

"What's wrong with that?"

"So many things, but let's start with the obvious. Marriage."

"Let me guess. You don't believe in it."

"Hell no. I believe in it. It just doesn't work." The majority of social structures in the animal kingdom were built on one male to many females. Forget penguins, swans, and the rest of the mating-for-lifers. "I'll never get married."

She flapped her lips together. "I doubt you'd ever convince anyone to marry you."

"Oh. I could. You underestimate my powers of persuasion."

"You'd have to use them to convince any woman to hitch themselves to ..." She gestured with her hand palm up from the top of my head to my toes. "... all that."

What? I was a gorgeous man. Women flocked to me. But I had to admit I was intrigued that Angie wasn't one of them. What was it about me she found so repulsive? "And yet you're asking for my help."

"I'm only asking for your expertise. And maybe a smidgeon of that persuasion."

Straightening my shoulders, I stretched my neck and kicked my legs out into a wider stance. I'd found my leverage. "Why would I help you? What's in it for me?"

"My appreciation."

"Nope. Not good enough."

"A Christmas bonus? I'll kill the fatted goose." The silliness of her statement hardened in a sludge of sarcasm.

"Let the goose live." I laughed. "I'll help you, but I have some conditions ..."

"I shouldn't have even asked for your help," she muttered under her breath.

I ignored her. "One: you have to stop trying to hurt me."

"That's a vague condition, princess. And besides, how am I supposed to stop a cow from kicking you in your jewels?"

Once again, I plowed on ahead without acknowledging her comment. "Two," I paused to make sure I had her full attention, "you can't fire me."

"How about you help me, or I tell my parents you lied, and that you've never worked on a farm before?" She sent me a glare hot enough to fry an egg on a sidewalk.

"Go ahead. Tell them." Nora was half in love with me, and Tony already treated me like a son. Though I liked to think of myself as a genuinely nice person, I had a knack for getting people to do what I wanted them to do, which made me so good at my job ... and picking up women. "Your mom won't care, and you know it."

Her fierce look eased into a frown, then she crinkled her lips to one side.

"Three: you have to do everything I say."

She held up her hand. "I'm not going to jump off a bridge without a parachute if you tell me to."

Like I would purposefully get her killed or maimed in any way. "I, in turn, will ensure your safety."

"I feel like I'm making a deal with a Loki."

I smiled in my best Tom Hiddleston impression. "I guess you're going to have to trust me." My impression of Loki was spot on. I kept going, "Four:" To be honest, I was making up these conditions on the fly. "You have to teach me how to drive your big tractor."

"That's like a half million-dollar risk—"

"Those are my conditions," I interrupted and stuck out my hand for her to shake it. "Deal or no deal?"

She scrutinized my hand like I had a communicable disease. Taking in a short breath, she agreed in one word. "Fine." She gripped my gloved hand, not even shrinking away at the cow excrement dotting the new leather.

"Then let's get to work." I released her hand, and, yanking off one glove, I held my open palm to her. "Give me your phone."

She hesitated. I'd bought my way into a cushy couple of weeks. No more getting kicked in the nuts.

"What's this guy's name?"

"Daniel Smoot."

"Smoot? His last name is Smoot?" I couldn't hide my reaction. Surely, with a name like that, she couldn't be considering a relationship with him. I mean, if all went well, assuming she'd choose to take his name, her end game would give her the name Angie *Smoot*.

She didn't respond and lifted one perfectly groomed eyebrow at me.

"I get it. His name is off limits. Your phone." I wiggled the fingers of my still outstretched hand.

She unlocked her cell and placed it in my palm.

I snapped a picture of the view, typed one sentence, and hit send. "For the record, I don't think you can pull this off." I tossed the phone to her.

She caught it in the middle of her angry huff. "I can too, you skunk ass."

"Skunk ass is the best you can do?"

"Papa and I have this thing about being creative with our swear words, and a skunk ass is far worse than jackass, in my opinion."

I laughed.

"Finish feeding the cows. Don't forget to lock the gate." She jumped in the truck, but when I went to climb in, she clicked the locks. "You can walk back," she called through the open passenger window and drove off in a puff of dust.

I cut the last twine and whistled on my way to the farmhouse.

Let the games begin.

Chapter 6

Angie

The gravel path to the pigpen wound its way around the barn; Remi followed. I ignored him while I pointed out the chicken coop, the barn, and horse pasture, all places Remi would be well acquainted with once I unloaded his full list of duties. Booster the Rooster crowed as we passed him and his harem.

The sun sank low in the sky. Pastures, still cloaked in the yellowing leftovers of winter, contrasted with the freshly plowed fields adjacent to the neighborhood. I hugged my sweatshirt closer to my body in the cool air. This was my paradise—the one secure place in the world where I could be myself without judgment. Maybe that was why Remi's presence here made me so uncomfortable. Remi was the alien invading my home planet.

A gust of wind carried the scent of the sprinkling we'd gotten this morning. Not enough rain to make me happy, but at least it was something to fill up the reservoirs and keep our canals running. I rubbed at my upper arms, trying to keep myself warm in the chill air.

"You cold?" Remi scooted next to me, set one of the slop buckets on to the ground, and started taking off his crisp jacket.

Detergent and fabric softener permeated the air every time he came close to me. He must have washed it after rolling in cow crap yesterday morning. I glimpsed well-toned muscles under his shirt. Once again, he'd worn another tight, white T-shirt. Had he bought those shirts in bulk when he'd applied for this job?

Taking a step back, I said, "I'm good." But I couldn't help softening a little toward him. In all my online and real-life dating, I couldn't think of one time a man offered me his jacket.

Remi hung his coat on the fence. "Oh, I wasn't giving it to you. I'm just starting to break a sweat." He picked up the slop bucket, stepped past me, and dumped it for the pigs.

Scratch that. What a cocky son of a camel.

His immature behavior gave me more drive to break him. He'd do all the dirtiest, most strenuous jobs while I took my joyous time sitting in the tractor, listening to audiobooks while I prepped the fields for planting. He'd spent most of the day clearing the furrows in our gravity-irrigated fields, not a super difficult job if you had a tractor. But, of course, I made him do it without one.

Bracing his hands on the top board, Remi leaned over the panels of the pig pen and watched them eat.

"Don't get too close to Ham, Pork Chop, and the Bacon Bits." I pressed close to his side. "A couple years back, old man Peterson passed out in his pig pen. They ate him, bones and all." I gave him a push toward the pigs.

Though he tried to hide it, he flinched and jerked back from the pen. I bent over and placed my hands on my knees, laughing at him. Hashtag: worth it. This was too easy.

"Go on." I leaned against the wood-paneled fence. "Dump the other slop bucket in."

Stepping forward, he tipped the bucket's contents to the pigs, glaring at me the whole time. "I don't believe you."

I wiped tears of laughter from my eyes and moved into the barn. The crunching gravel behind indicated Remi stayed close.

"Fine, don't believe me. Ask Google. The story made national news." I glanced over my shoulder at him and strolled to my favorite outbuilding.

Four wood and wrought-iron stable doors stretched above my head to the left and right of me. All were empty save one, the one with Mae in it, my quarter horse mare. We'd sold the rest of the horses to cover some of Papa's medical bills, but I couldn't bear to part with her. Her stable connected to the green pasture, so she could choose to go in and out as she pleased.

Remi's cell rang at the entrance. Despite the glow from his phone screen, a shadow passed over his features. "I've got to take this. Be right back."

He strode a good distance from me, well away from the pigs. He kept his eyes trained on me. I stayed in sight for a bit, but then I moved into the dark interior, acting like I was straightening the harnesses. Once inside, I traipsed through Mae's stable, shushing her on my way past. She plodded alongside me until we came to her pasture's gate.

"Sorry, girl." I slid through the opened gate, then closed it behind me, cringing at the small clanking noise the latch made.

I sprinted through the grass until I heard Remi's low voice. With his back turned to me, his shoulders rounded over his phone like he created a cave of protection around his traitorous smart device. He turned in my direction, and I ducked behind a post.

"... quarterly dividends ... profit margin ..." His voice drifted through the wind. "... fair market ... Yeah ... great ROI ... Don't go there. Matthew will loop you in ..."

Leftover rain droplets blew off the fence and smacked my skin. The edge in the stiff breeze should have frozen me, yet I broke into a sweat. Who the hell was he talking to? What was he talking about?

"... too aggressive of a timeline ... I'm having to square the circle on this one ..."

Curiouser and curiouser. Not one of the snippets I caught between the gusts computed with the man Remi presented himself as. He was hiding something from me. Maybe his presence had something to do with the companies circling like vultures around my land. Could Remi be a corporate spy?

I shook my head.

My latest psychological thriller audiobook must be going to my head. Corporate spies exist in a glittering world far too fancy for my farm. But if not espionage, then what could he be doing here? Why my farm? Why now? I was so lost in puzzling over him that I almost missed Remi ending the call and pivoting toward the doorway—my last known location.

I bolted to the barn.

Managing to race back to the bridle wall just as Remi meandered inside, I hefted Mae's saddle from the bench to disguise the reason for my heavy breathing.

"Here. Let me." Remi jogged to me and took the saddle. Its weight didn't even cause him to strain. "Sorry about that. It was one of my exes."

Without responding verbally, I gestured to the rack on the wall, afraid if I said anything, I'd accuse him of lying to me. In this case, my best play would be to stay silent, gather more evidence, and then confront him.

He placed it in the empty slot and rubbed his hands together. "What next?"

Narrowing my eyes, I stalked past him to my horse. As usual, she chose to be where I was. She padded to me, leaned over her stall, and nudged me with her nose.

"This is Mae. She's a sweetheart. I'll be taking care of her mainly, but you'll be mucking out her stall." I walked to the wall and pulled a pitchfork from the rack. "There's a wheelbarrow over there." I pointed to the other end of the barn and shoved the handle at him.

Mae's ears flicked forward at Remi's intruding presence. Her eyes dilated and she straightened her neck, examining him.

"You want me to do this now? With the horse in the stall?" His eyes widened as he looked at Mae.

"Sure. She's good about staying out of the way."

"She's too big to stay out of the way." He rubbed the back of his neck. "How often am I supposed to do this?"

"Every evening. Would you want to sleep in your own urine and manure?" Criminy, what kind of operation did he think I ran here? My animals were my top priority, especially Mae.

"No. But I'm housebroken, so I don't think you have to worry about that." He quirked his eyebrows at me.

Determined not to reward him for his joke, I cleared my throat, stifled my laugh, and took on a nonchalance attitude while digging through the tack box.

I froze.

There ... in the corner of the box ... was the beginnings of a wasp nest. Two wasps with their wings in line with their body clung to black hexagonal pockets with their spikey, spindly legs. My knees weakened, barely maintaining the ability to hold my weight.

Skin tensed along my spine, and the phantom pain of multiple stings struck me, reminiscent of the time a wasp had gotten stuck under my shirt. I jumped backward.

"What are you doing?" Remi asked.

"Wasps," I managed to squeak, pointing to the small hive. "Your job includes eradicating these useless insects whose only purpose in life is to inflict pain."

"Hm." Leaning into the handle of the pitchfork, he scratched his chin. "Have we stumbled on another one of your fears?"

I tugged at the bottom of my shirt. "You're confusing fear with respect. I respect they're devils sent here to torment me, and they respect I will kill them on sight."

His face cracked into a smile, and he shook his head. "What do you need in there?"

"A bottle of deodorizing dust."

Exhibiting bravery as I'd never seen before, he reached his bare arm past their glossy eyes. After a moment, he pulled a bottle out from the box and held it out to me. "Is this it?"

"Yes. Sprinkle the damp spots. You don't have to clear out the straw every day, just the soiled parts of it and refresh it with more if needed. Once a week, take it all out and lay down new bedding."

He looked from the stall to the pitchfork, to the bottle, to Mae, and back to me. "And where do I get more straw?"

"There's a stack outside, under the tarp. If you need a shovel, it's hanging on the rack on the wall." My phone pinged, and I hustled toward the barn door.

"Wait." He dropped the deodorizing powder and stopped me. "Is that Smoot?"

I tugged my phone out of my pocket, knowing it was Daniel before I looked at the screen. "Maybe." I smiled as I read his message.

> *I can't stop thinking about you. Am I sending you too many messages? I don't want to chase you off.*

We'd been messaging almost constantly since we matched, although Daniel's interest increased when I used Remington for his expertise. Whenever Remi wasn't in my immediate vicinity, I'd safely steer our conversations away from extreme sports to my more well-versed subjects.

> *Haha. I'm worried I'll scare you off with all the talk I've been doing about farming.*

> *Let's FaceTime tonight.*

Dan's reply lit up on my screen as if he'd been in tune with my thoughts.

I stopped walking and took a sharp breath. My cursor blinked, waiting for my typed response. I couldn't put him off again, or he'd for sure move on to someone else. Remi took advantage of my hesitation, snatched my phone, and ran to the far end of the barn, typing the whole time.

"Hey, give that back." I chased after him.

"This is part of our deal."

His thumb stopped moving across my screen in one decisive movement. I jumped, stretching for my phone, but Remi stood on his tiptoes, holding it out of my reach.

"Really?" I stopped trying to get my phone and put my hands on my hips. He was more annoying than Jared. Considering, I grew up with my brother constantly torturing me, that was saying something. "You're so childish." How could one human drive me this crazy?

"Relax." Remi returned his attention to my screen, scanned it, and began typing again. "Do you think I'm going to sabotage your relationship?"

"I wouldn't put it past you."

Remi was as persistent as the scum in the grout lines in my shower. No matter how hard I scrubbed, I couldn't get rid of it.

"There. All fixed." He handed me my phone.

I skimmed through the messages. "Wait. We can't FaceTime until Friday? Why?"

"There are a few reasons for my madness."

Here we go again. I shifted my weight to my other foot.

"Number one: Men are more attracted to unavailable women. If you always make yourself free, he'll lose interest."

On the flip side of that, if I never became available, he'd find another woman more willing to be with him.

Remi continued to list. "Number two: We'll have time to prepare for the first face-to-face meeting."

Like I needed that much preparation.

"Number three: You have to go on at least one extreme sports adventure before you talk to Smoot. The best way to lie to someone is to make the lie a truth."

"Then it's not lying."

"Exactly."

"Do you always make lists when you talk?" I lowered my eyebrows at him.

"The reasons I make lists when I talk are—Number one: It lessens miscommunication ..."

Balling my hands into fists by my sides, I jerked my thumb at the stable. "Whatever. Just clean the stall."

Mae swung her head between Remi and me. She tossed her tail up and down and whinnied while Remi droned on.

"Number two: I get to emphasize my words with my fingers." He held up two fingers.

I picked up the pitchfork he dropped, walked until I stood in front of him, and stabbed it into the ground.

He gripped the handle, meeting my narrowed eyes. "Number three: Lists help me stay on top of ..." His gaze traveled the length of my body, searing into me. "... things."

I shook my head at him and his seedy implications and dug into my pocket for my slip of paper. "Here's a list for you." I shoved the list of chores I'd made for him into his palm, then left him with the opportunity to become intimately close to my horse's manure.

Chapter 7

Remi

"Number four!" I yelled at Angie's retreating back, crumpling the paper she set in my hand, and shoving it into my pants pocket.

I laughed to myself. Getting under her skin like a burr on a hog's hide brought more joy to me than I should admit. The smile dropped from my lips as I faced her horse.

Mae had stuck her head out the stall, and her big, glassy eyes stared into my soul, pupils so wide only a sliver of brown circled the black. Maybe I could leave the stall dirty for one night. But then Angie would have the satisfaction of knowing that I was terrified of this massive animal.

Plus, I couldn't lose sight of my goal. Anything was worth getting out of the family business and gaining my freedom. One final job. I wouldn't let a few farm chores—or a horse—get in the way of my goals.

With as much stealth as I could, I slid the stable door open, stepped inside and closed it, keeping my eyes locked on Mae. The mare threw her head up and down and pawed at the ground when I invaded her space. Visible clouds of hot air puffed out her nostrils with each of her snorts and whinnies.

"Relax," I told her. "I want to be here about as much as you want me here."

I held the pitchfork out in front of me. Up to the moment Angie handed the pronged torture device to me, I'd thought they didn't exist anymore, only used for movie props. Surely, people didn't still use them—like in real life. Of course Angie did on the daily, her world far separated from mine.

That woman could start an argument with an empty house. She drove me nuts. Thankfully, I didn't think she'd overheard any of the conversation with my father. Given he'd called during an after-hours international meeting, I had to take it. Every answer I'd given him about my progress here far from satisfied him. Didn't matter. Matthew could deal with him.

I tightened my grip on the pitchfork.

The horse moved back and forth in front of the exit to the pasture, refusing to give me the space I needed to get my job done and get out of here. Guaranteed Angie was somewhere out in the open air enjoying herself while I faced off with a horse—who'd just dropped a fresh pile of manure.

"Whew." I waved my hand in front of my nose and gagged on the scent in the air that was as pleasant as an overfilled porta-potty. "What's in the hay you're eating? It does *not* agree with you."

Mae whinnied and tossed her head at me. Apparently, she didn't appreciate my humor. Staying as far away from Mae as possible, I worked my way to the closed gate leading to her pasture, opened it, then, with my back pressed against the wall, I side-stepped my way back to the pitchfork.

"You should try eating that fresh springtime grass in your pasture." I waved my hand, shooing the mare away from me. "The sunset is beautiful tonight. Wouldn't want you to miss it."

The exasperating horse didn't listen. She stopped prancing back and forth and planted herself in the middle of the stall. I was living in an alternate reality, far from my salaried staff and pool house livin' days in Dallas. My mother would be appalled to see me like this.

Come on, Remi. Don't let your fear show.

I straightened my shoulders and scooped the first pile of manure, only to look around for the wheelbarrow I'd left outside the stall. Tossing the poop and the pitchfork in the corner, I slid the door open, and at that precise moment, Angie's horse chomped down on my left butt cheek. I yelped and tumbled forward onto the ground.

I struggled to my knees and flipped around to look at the horse in the eyes, but she didn't spare me a second glance as she trotted past me and out the barn door. In retrospect, I probably should have closed the door before I'd opened the stable.

"Shit!" I stood and sprinted out the door. Getting Mae to go back into the stable would be about as easy as pissing up a rope.

I scanned the area. Good, Angie wasn't anywhere around. I could get the horse back in the stall, and no one would know I'd let her out. By the time I caught sight of Mae, she was already in the yard, nibbling on the grass and the budding bushes. She didn't wear a bridle or a rope that I could use to grab and lead her back to the stable.

"Hey!" I yelled at Mae. She lifted her head and blew out a puff of air with almost a grunt. "Why do you have to make me look bad?"

The horse pawed at the ground and then returned to eating the budding leaves on the shrubs. I moved closer to the horse's position—but not *too* close—and waved my arms.

"Go on. I promise I'll have your accommodations up to a five-star standard if you go back to your home." Making sure I remained in front of Mae, I took a few more careful steps in her direction.

Looping my arms around her neck, I wrapped my fingers in her mane. I dug my heels in the ground and pressed back with all my weight, trying to get her to move forward. In one fluid movement, she sat on her haunches and tossed her head, sending me sprawling onto the flat of my back. Closing my eyes against the blinding sun and fluffy white clouds in a sky that went on forever, I lay on the damp, prickly grass.

Mae put her face in mine. Her hot breath rustled my hair, and I opened my eyes. Her snout, silhouetted against the sun, dripped onto my face, but I was beyond caring—until she nibbled on my hair, giving it a good yank.

"Ouch!" I bellowed and rolled to my feet.

Damn horse was a few sandwiches shy of a picnic and as mean as a mama wasp. A clip from *Sleeping Beauty* came to my mind. Specifically, the part where Prince Phillip fell from his horse and denied his horse some carrots.

I'd gone through a phase where I'd been obsessed with that film, and I still maintain it had a badass ending with a dragon and a magic sword.

Mae lifted her head from the bush as I ran to my truck, threw open the door, and retrieved the baggy of my salvation from my lunch cooler. Closing the door, I returned to the backyard.

Four orange carrots lay in my palm, contrasting with my yellow glove. I extended them to Mae, and she inched toward me, glancing behind her as if to see if this was a trick. I took a step back, and she quickened her pace, picking the carrots off my palm with her lips.

"Ah, you like those, do you?" I dumped the rest of the carrots into my hand and backed toward her stable at a more rapid pace.

She plodded along with me as I walked into the barn and through the stable door. I resisted doing a victory dance. Now all I had to do was get her to walk through the gate at the back, connecting her stall with her private pasture. She paused with three feet in her dirty straw bedding and only one in the grass.

"I guess I'll eat these if you don't want them." Selecting the cleanest carrot, I stuck it in my mouth and chomped down.

Mae whinnied and trotted toward me. When she reached me, I dropped the carrots on the ground and raced past her to the stable.

I closed the gate between us. "Ha! I got you." I pointed my finger at her, but she only flicked one ear toward me while rummaging through the early spring grass for the carrots.

I cleaned the stable in peace and pulled out my list to see what was up next.

The chicken coop. Oh joy. Something I'd always wanted to do.

Chapter 8

Angie

W hat had possessed me to stray from my safe, boring life? I clung to the splintering, wooden telephone poll, unwilling to go any further. The green grass wavered beneath me in my tunnel vision, so I squeezed my eyes shut. I'd gotten myself into this.

I never dreamed the day would lead me here. After I woke up from my nap and worked for a half day on the farm, Remi insisted we come here to the ropes course at the community college. My list of things to do this spring season perpetually grew even though I worked hard every day to make it shrink. I didn't have enough hours in the day to accomplish what I needed to, and yet I'd let Remi convince me to leave the farm and come here, to my worst nightmare.

Heights.

Remi's idea for helping was to get me to do everything I'd lied about doing in my conversations with Dan. In effect, he was making an honest woman of me. I hated him for it.

Find your happy place, Angie.

I was on Papa's lap driving the tractor for the first time, riding Mae through the grassy pasture on an imaginary tropical island with the sound of the waves in my ears, not the Idaho wind buffeting them with me suspended more than fifty feet above the ground. I gulped in air and tightened my grip on the metal posts they'd stuck into the side of the pole to use as a ladder.

I'd managed to finish planting the corn field today, tomorrow I'd cut the north hay field, have Remi check the gated pipe while it'd been flooding the peas—

"Angie, the fastest way down is up," Remi called from underneath me.

"I hate up." I glared at him from under my borrowed helmet.

He'd reserved the ropes course at the college for the two of us to use this afternoon and evening. We had three hours here, and I'd frozen on my first attempt. All I was supposed to do was climb up this pole, jump, and catch the trapeze bar suspended in the air above me. Remi had made it look easy, climbing without hesitation and leaping to successfully catch the trapeze. This was a child's playground to him and Mount Everest to me.

"Remember our conversation in the car?" He kept his hands on the rope that supported me. The college kids let him take charge once we'd gotten here. I had no idea why. "The best way to keep up your charade is through experience. But I guess if you want to give up and tell Smoot everything, you can climb back down."

Steely determination shot through my spine as I straightened and opened my eyes. I knew what he was doing, goading me further into my stubbornness along my path of self-destruction. I glared down at him as I lifted my hand off one peg and moved it to the next one. I followed the motion with my foot, my harness shifting with me every move I made. And the next thing I knew, I was standing on the tip of the wooden post no bigger than a dinner plate.

Waves of paralyzing tingles pulsed from the tips of my toes to my forehead, and with each pass, my body was doused in cold sweat. The whole course, tight wires, and dangling ropes lay before me, looking much more intimidating than it had from the grass. Peaks of rooftops were visible beyond the treetops. A stiff breeze, carrying the scent of grilled meat from the restaurants across the street, caught the rope tethered to my harness and caused the pole to sway. A short scream shot out of me.

"You're okay. Now, all you have to do is jump." Remi's voice carried to me, but I didn't look at him. The red-headed college kid said something to him; I didn't hear it with my ears ringing.

"The air is thinner up here." I gasped. One tip in any direction, and I'd fall.

Would the rope catch me? I could be the exception to the thousands of people who'd done this course safely. How could I trust the college kid had tied the knot properly? Perhaps I had a defective harness. Crazier things had happened.

"Would it help if I counted to three and you jump?" Remi asked.

"You start counting, and I'll punch you once I find my way down!" I shouted at him.

His laughter floated to me and calmed some of my fear. Shoving my doubts to the back of my mind, I bent my legs and shoved off the pole. For a moment, the thrilling sensation of being weightless caught hold of me. Nothing pulled me down. Nothing could hurt me. Nothing touched me but the gentle caress of the early spring air and the warm rays of the evening sun.

In this one moment, I could do anything, conquer anything, but then gravity found me. My outstretched fingers barely grazed the metal bar before I swung toward the ground. The rope snapped against my harness, jolting my body back into the anxiety which had encased me before the leap.

I clenched my eyelids together and screamed as I swung back and forth, only stopping when my tennis shoes brushed the ground.

"You can open your eyes." Remi's voice next to my ear made me throw my eyes open and jolt upright.

My head connected what I guessed was his chin and sent him stumbling backward. I flipped around to face him. Shivers flowed along one side of my body, spilling over me like a warm liquid where his whisper still lingered. I covered my mouth with my gloved hand. "I'm so sorry. You shouldn't sneak up on me like that."

"Ow." He groaned and rubbed his chin. "Do I need to remind you of condition number one?"

"Stop. It was an accident." I walked close to him. "Here, let me see."

Removing my gloves and tossing them to the ground, I pulled his hand away to get a better look. The point of impact was already swollen and red. Instinctively, I ran my fingers along the injury, but it wasn't until he locked his eyes on mine that I remembered he wasn't Papa or a patient.

Laid bare for me in his deep-brown eyes was a yearning like I'd never seen before. His scalding gaze told me he wanted to kiss me ... to do more than kiss me, which didn't make sense. He made it clear he disliked me, and I found him repugnant.

Yet, more than anything, I wished for the courage to tilt my lips toward his and give him a taste of what he wanted. But just as gravity couldn't be ignored, neither could reality. He did this to countless women. He probably trained in a collegiate school for womanizers. I wouldn't be another hashmark on his list of conquests. Besides he couldn't be interested in me with my ample love handles and the confidence issues that came with them. Yes, I loved my body and all that, but the love I had for myself wouldn't change what others thought about me with barely concealed judgment. The taunts from my high school days still haunted me.

He cleared his throat. I took a couple of quick steps away from him, and the look in his eyes disappeared. "I'm thinking of terminating our agreement."

Panic raced through me. I couldn't do this without him. Not with Dan's FaceTime call looming. Remi's lips quirked into a half-smile, and I scowled, hating he saw exactly how much I needed him.

"Promise not to hurt me anymore?" His smile grew across his face.

"Promise not to sneak up on me anymore, you creeper?"

He shook his head and rolled his eyes.

"And I don't want to do that again." I pointed to the tip of the telephone pole.

"The first leap is always the hardest." He waved his gloved hands in a wide arc. "You can do anything now ... and we have the whole course to get through before sundown."

Mr. Redhead Testicles-have-barely-dropped came up behind us and pointed to the next obstacle where another college student looped a rope through her harness. "Let's try the next one. Both of you have to do it."

"I think I've had enough for one day." I picked up my gloves and moved to hand them to the college kid.

"I thought you'd give up this easy. I made a bet with Myles." Remi untied his rope and looked up at me through his too-damn-long lashes.

I ground my teeth. He had me in checkmate. Without a word, I tugged the knot free on my harness and stomped to the next high adventure course. Two wires stretched around seventy to one hundred feet in the air like a V while the college kid explained what we were supposed to do.

Apparently, we had to interlock our hands and lean against each other from the narrow part of the V to the wide end. Like some extreme trust exercise.

With the comfort of the ground under my feet, my legs shook as I looked up. I didn't want to climb a pole ever again, but Remi gestured to the obstacle as if he were saying, "After you." I didn't have any other option. I couldn't let him win, so I started climbing.

Instead of me handing him a list of chores, he was shoving a whole gallon of impossible things at me. But I'd started this, and I wouldn't back down.

Sooner than I knew it, I was on the top, standing on the platform facing Remi.

"Relax. Trust your harness. Trust in your safety net. Trust me," Remi said.

Trust him, my ass. My face must have reflected the turmoil I'd tried to keep hidden. Remi's gaze met my eyes, and I calmed a little—until I looked down again. I gripped the rope tethered to me and took short breaths.

"That's easy for you to say, Mr. I-jump-off-bridges-for-fun. I'm afraid of heights. Like epically." My legs wobbled as I teetered on the platform.

Remi maneuvered closer to me and took one of my hands in his, cupping them together as the instructor had demonstrated. Oddly, my world became more secure now that I was connected to Remi's sturdy form. He wasn't shaking or wobbling or showing any signs of fear. He was stalwart and confident, and I wanted to be more like him, at least when it came to sports.

"It helps if you breathe in your nose and out your mouth." He smiled at me and squeezed my fingers.

I did as he instructed, almost feeling like the moms I helped coach through labor—even though I'd never been through childbirth. All the training videos had the hee-hee-hoo breathing pattern, but I'd probably pass out if I started breathing like that up here.

Remi took my other hand, easing my grip from the rope one finger at a time. Brief panic encased me as my pinky slid from the rope and into his solid grip, but then it was replaced by something else. His grip became more reliable than the rope and certainly warmer. Though we both had gloves on, the contact between our hands transferred heat from the tips of my fingers to blossom in my cheeks. I forgot about the ground and the smallness of the wire and focused on our connection—on Remi.

The guides yelled something from beneath us, but I didn't hear it. They sounded like Charlie Brown's teacher on the phone—*wah wah waw ah.*

"You're going to have to lean fully on me to get through this." When Remi spoke, the timbre of his voice bound me to this world.

I nodded even as my chest shook with every breath I took. Carefully, slowly, I shuffled both of my feet onto the wire, letting go of Remi's gaze to find my footing.

"Good job. Now focus on me, nothing else. One step at a time."

Several retorts came to my mind—one step closer to a heart attack—one more step closer to death—time. I didn't have much of it left because my heart was going to stop, but the sensations that made my toes curl had crawled their way up to my jaw and kept it clamped shut. So, I did as he said and burned him with my stare.

We took another two steps along the V together, our bodies growing slightly further apart.

"Nice. Now concentrate on your breathing and try to slow your heart rate."

The wire swung back and forth under my weight. "Ah-ahh." My heart did the opposite of what Remi wanted it to do: it beat even faster. Two more steps had us fully leaning on each other. "I can't do this."

"Then give up and let me win." He squeezed my hand painfully, drawing my attention back to our grip.

I frowned at him. My mind couldn't come up with a clear thought. "I can do anything you can do." Sheesh. I sounded like a kindergartner.

I looked back at his eyes, knowing they had never left me. My abs tightened as I let go of my fear and leaned fully into him, forced to trust him to catch my weight and keep me in place.

Our bodies became almost completely flat. I kept my eyes locked on Remi even as I felt my feet slip and my body start to fall. I managed to contain my scream until I lost contact with him and the wire. I slammed against the harness as it caught me. Once again, I didn't stop screaming until my feet touched the blessed grass.

The rope went completely slack, and I laid down face-first on the soft carpet of green. Remi stooped next to me and laughed.

"Maybe the reason I grow stuff is because I love plants and the ground. I think I should stay on it." I rolled onto my back, flopping my arms open. The lowering sun heated my skin, and the wind calmed, but I still breathed hard.

"Does this mean you give up on Smoot?" he asked with a tilt of his eyebrow, challenging me to accept defeat.

"Not a chance." I moved from my safe and comfortable position.

He laughed again, grabbing my hand. He pulled me up. "Come on. You've earned yourself a banana split."

Oh! I hadn't eaten a banana split in years. The thought of the decadent hot fudge, caramel, and strawberries topping the mounds of creamy goodness with fluffy clouds of whipped cream—a few cherries and a touch of peanuts—turned on the sprinklers in my mouth. How did he know my weakness?

"Your dad mentioned it was your favorite dessert." He tilted his chin down and half-smiled.

Hot fudge and biscuits! He was as irresistible as my favorite dessert during time of the month. "I can't—I mean, I can't eat a dessert like that. Do you know how many calories are in a banana split?" I continued without letting him answer, "About a thousand. That's more than half my allotted caloric intake."

His eyes widened, and they traveled down the length of my body. "With a body like yours, I'm surprised you're so worried about calories."

I took a couple of steps back from him, opened my mouth to say something, and then closed it. I repeated this action a couple of times. A body like mine? What did he mean by that?

The two college kids had finished winding the ropes and asked us for our harnesses. Remi unbuckled his and stepped out of it. I followed his actions with my mind still adjusting to a reality where he might think of me as attractive.

"You act like you don't know you're a beautiful woman." He shook his head and took my harness, handing both to the smiling college student.

"I'm not a woman. I'm a farmer."

My comment set Remi into a fit of giggles. "The most attractive farmer I've ever met."

Heat crept into my face once again, and I covered my cheeks with both my hands.

He motioned to the parking lot with his head. "I'm taking you out for dessert because you are living a more adventurous life, remember? I'll even take the hit and split those calories with you." He winked.

"Fine," I agreed, but not because his wink sent butterflies flittering all which ways in my abdomen. No. I'd conquered my fear of heights today, and I'd be FaceTiming Dan tomorrow. I deserved to intake each and every one of those calories.

Chapter 9

Remi

The day had finally arrived for the highly anticipated FaceTime call. And Angie was a mess. She'd allowed a brief break in our day for this and had taken time to shower, but she worked tonight. She'd scheduled FaceTiming Dan during her only chance to nap. I still had on my farm clothes, and they weren't the cleanest.

Hot rollers covered Angie's head, making her look like she walked out of a sitcom from the fifties, and after a heated debate over 'less is more,' her makeup was finished. The last task to tackle: wardrobe. Wrapped in a bright-blue robe, Angie held an emerald, flouncy shirt for me to inspect. Though the shirt would pull out the flecks of green in her eyes, Smoot would be thinking with his other head the moment he saw her breasts spilling over.

"Nope. Neckline's too low. Not a bad option, but not on the first call." I took it from her and tossed it on top of the growing pile on Angie's bed. "Think of yourself as a gift. You want to wrap yourself up, layers if you can, so he can imagine uncovering you in his mind."

"Ew." With her back to me, Angie continued to shuffle through her closet. "All men aren't like that."

"Last time I checked, I'm the one with the penis in this room."

"You're so gross."

"You think penises are gross? No wonder you're having issues."

"You know what?" She turned and pushed her hands against my chest, attempting to shove me toward the door. I dropped one foot back and remained where I was. "Forget it. I can do this on my own."

"And how will you avoid looking like a gaper when he tells you about a splitter morning in the epic pow, perfect to send into a gnarly jump, bro?" My guess was he'd spray all over the conversation like the conceited jerk I envisioned him being. No one climbed Mount Rushmore without an ego the size of Lincoln's nose.

She stopped pressing against me and held her hand, palm up, toward her closet, then to the clothes on the bed. "Fine. Why don't *you* pick something out for me?"

I'd told her to stay in her T-shirt and pajama bottoms for the call, but she'd refused.

Angie turned her back to me and walked out of her room.

My phone buzzed in my pocket, and I pulled it out, my eyes instantly scanning the screen.

Thinking of you. Hope your trip ...

Damn. Yet another text from Kathryn.

Swiping the notification off the screen without reading the entire message, I grabbed a casual but fitted crew-neck tank from Angie's closet and some jeans. I followed her into the bathroom. Whoa. This bathroom could be in an episode of *I Love Lucy*, as it was complete with mauve floral wallpaper, beige carpet, a kitty clock over the vanity, and a pink toilet, sink, and bathtub. The brass fixtures left the bathroom with an elegantly dated touch.

It smelled of old electrical heating elements and pine air freshener. Standing in front of the vanity mirror, Angie unrolled each of her curlers and placed them back into the ancient relic they came from.

"I'll only have like forty-five minutes for this call." A clip fumbled out of her hands and clattered on the floor. She bent to get it and smacked her head on the edge of the vanity. The last roller in her hair came undone and skittered onto the counter. "Ow. Ow. Ow."

"You okay?"

She shoved her hand where she'd hit the counter and pressed. "Shit. Shoot. Shit."

I couldn't help but chuckle at her lackluster attempt to swear.

Removing her hand, she turned to me. Blood poured from a gash in Angie's head.

My ears started ringing, my world swayed, and I tightened my grip on her clothes in my hand.

"How bad is it?" She glanced down. "Shoo-it. It's bleeding."

The tips of my fingers tingled while black ate at the edge of my vision. Blood was okay as long as it stayed where it belonged, but once it escaped, I became sick as a dog passing peach pits. I took a deep breath through my nose, let it flow through my teeth, and leaned against the wall.

"Remi." Angie's voice was muffled through the continuous whooshing sound lodged in my ears. "Remi? You look pale."

I risked a glance at her. In her concern for me, she'd let the blood continue to flow. It streaked down her forehead and onto her cheek like she'd secured a lead role in some slasher flick. I shut my eyes and placed my hands on my knees, on the verge of passing out.

I'd passed out once when Myles got a bloody nose while we were playing basketball. I shoveled out all this advice about extreme sports and how to get a manly man to Angie, and yet here I was on the brink of unconsciousness over a minor head wound. I couldn't do anything about it now, with my weakness exposed for her to exploit as she wished.

"I think you need to sit down." Her gentle touch rested on my shoulder, yet she firmly pressed me toward the bathtub's edge. Obediently, I sat on its rim. "Now put your head between your legs."

I did as she instructed with my eyes still closed. If I didn't see any more of the red fluid, which shall not be named, pooling out her wound, I stood a chance at staying lucid. Sounds of the faucet running and toilet paper rolling against its holder penetrated my cocoon of hot and cold sweats.

"Did you cover it?" I squinted at the plush, pink toilet rug. The hem of her blue robe swung into my vision, exposing the long length of her smooth legs. I opened my eyes wider, appreciating the view she offered me.

"It's safe to look."

No, it isn't safe to look. I told myself. *Not at all.*

My wooziness eased, and I was hard-pressed not to rub my hands along her inner thigh and pull her onto my lap. I breathed in deeply again, for an entirely different reason.

No. I wasn't going to act on my attraction to this woman. She tortured me daily, and she needed my help to keep a man on her line. Although, right now, she was the most alluring thing I'd ever seen.

I sat up and shoved her clothes at her. "Get dressed. Call's in fifteen minutes."

"I'm gonna need your help—"

"What?" No way in hell. I only had so much restraint. "I'm not helping you get dressed."

She laughed. "You wish." She pulled the toilet paper away from her injury along her hairline. Once again, my blood fled from my face to my extremities. "This'll need a butterfly bandage."

I was shaking my head before she stopped speaking. "I can't do it. I don't do blood." With the mention of a butterfly bandage, I focused on the imagery it created, of bright and vibrant butterflies dancing with the wind.

She laughed even harder at that. "You, an extreme sports expert, can't handle bandaging a small cut."

"You saw me practically pass out at the sight of it, and now you want me to touch it?" I'd tried to pinpoint when I'd developed this reaction to blood, but I'd never been successful. It must be genetic. *Takeaway, I'm no nurse.*

"If I can jump off a telephone poll, you can help bandage my wound."

"Can't we get your mom to do it?"

"And interrupt Law & Order: SVU?" She gestured to the stairs with her free hand. "Be my guest."

I glared at her and thought back to our conversation about having a penis. If I was tough enough to jump off bridges, I could do this. "Fine. What do you need me to do?"

Keeping the toilet paper pressed to her cut, she shuffled through the cabinet under the sink and pulled out a first aid kit. Did she stash these in all her bathrooms? How often did she get hurt?

She unclasped the plastic buckles and grabbed the few items she needed while I gave myself a pep talk. Come on, Remi. I'd jumped off the cliffs at Navagio Beach in Greece, skydived in the Himalayas, hiked to the top of Machu Picchu, and surfed with the sharks in Australia. I could handle touching the edges of flappy skin and fatty tissue.

One glimpse in the mirror showed me how pale my face was even while Angie kept the tissue pressed to her head. She struggled to open a bandage with one hand.

"Here." I took the slip from her. "Let me." I pulled the bandage open and set it on the counter—a white oblong thing with no butterflies on it. Boring.

She handed me a bottle of super glue with raised eyebrows. Without needing further instruction, I tugged off the top.

"All I need you to do is keep my hair free of the cut. Can you manage that?"

I nodded but didn't say anything and stepped closer to her. Aside from the ropes course, I hadn't been this close to Angie in the week I'd worked for her. I kept my distance and did my job while we bickered about something I'd done wrong.

She smelled of hairspray and whatever coconut shampoo she used. Carefully, I gathered her hair, my hands brushing her neck just behind her ear, some strands still warm from the curlers. My eyes dipped to where her pulse thudded against her throat, to where I loved to tease delicate skin. What would Angie do if I bent and touched my lips to her neck and checked to see if she tasted of coconut?

Oblivious to my thoughts, Angie leaned closer to the mirror and pulled the tissue away from her gash. The blood flow had slackened, but only slightly. I slowed my breathing and focused on containing the golden strands of Angie's hair.

She ran a bead of glue along her broken skin and took in a sharp breath. "It stings."

I swayed on my feet and dropped my gaze to the counter, the black in my vision becoming stronger. I refused to pass out. Angie would never let me live it down.

"What am I supposed to do in this call again?" Angie asked as she held her skin together.

"You're going to answer, but then fifteen to twenty minutes in, tell him you've got to go," I said, grateful to have something else to think about.

"I still think that'll make him think I'm not interested." She narrowed her eyes. "Darn. My makeup is ruined. Hand me the butterfly bandage."

I placed the white strip in her hand. "If they're going to name it after a butterfly, they should at least print butterflies on it."

Angie laughed while she stuck it over her cut, tightening the edges of her skin together. I could never work in the medical field. Even though Angie was a pain in my ass, she had my respect.

"That's all you needed me for?" I still held her hair, enjoying its silkiness far too much.

"Yep. I think it's dry."

"You could have told me I wouldn't have to touch it." We spoke to each other, facing the mirror.

"And lose an opportunity to make you suffer?" She quirked her eyebrow on her uninjured side. "No way."

"You have less than ten to be on your call." I pointed at the creepy kitty clock on the wall. "Why do you even have that clock?"

"It was my Grandma Anne's." She wiped the makeup off her eye and began reapplying. "That's always the answer. This house is a shrine to those who've lived here before us."

This dug at my soul ... at least it would have if I had one. I'd sacrificed it long ago after my first time buying land out from under ma and pop farmers.

"We need a bumper crop this year, or I'm going to lose it all."

Her soft words were slivers to my skin. My tongue felt heavy in my mouth. "Are you being forced to sell?"

"With Papa's medical bills ... and a couple of hard years of drought? It's going to be tough."

Now was my chance. I could throw my offer on the proverbial table and finish my charade. Something told me she'd say no and to go to 'H-E double hockey sticks.' And, I grudgingly admitted, part of me wasn't ready to leave Angie and this place forever.

"I don't want to talk about it."

I let the moment pass and cleared my throat. "The key is to act like you don't care if Smoot is in your life. It's the same dynamic as friends in high school. The more you act like you didn't care if they were your friends or not, the more they clambered to be one."

The mascara brush in Angie's grip stilled, and pained emotions flickered over her features. Took me less than a second to guess what kind of high school experience she'd had. I pictured Angie facing a crowd of her jeering peers. Nausea, having nothing to do with the sight of blood, settled in my stomach. Shit-for-brains kids. If I could time travel, I'd set her childhood bullies back a few paces.

"Well. I guess I can give it a try." She went back to applying her makeup, but a trace of a shadow remained.

Chapter 10

Angie

I paced in the sitting room off the front entry. We'd closed the glass French doors, shutting out the soft background noise of Mama and Papa's show. I leaned forward so I could see the faint glow of the television on their faces. They'd passed out on their La-Z-Boys like usual before Olivia Benson and Elliot Stabler found the perpetrator, which made this the perfect time for a FaceTime call.

I stood and adjusted the chair into the back corner and sat back down. Remi had removed the pastel kitty art and moved a plant into the corner. Now you couldn't tell I lived in a broken-down, old farmhouse riddled with the ghosts of my ancestors.

Remi had coached me in the field today while I helped him move the sprinkler pipe. I supervised him more than I helped.

My phone rang. *Go time.*

In one deep breath, I swiped up on the green telephone icon. In a split second between 'answering' and 'hello,' I panicked. What was I thinking? I couldn't do this. At the sound of his voice, I shoved the phone in the chair.

Hello, Angie? Daniel's muffled voice sounded from under my cushion.

"I can't do this." I mouthed to Remi.

Are you there?

An instant later, Remi's lips were next to my ear, his breath tickling goosebumps along the left side of my body. "Then give up and prove me right."

Remi leaned back, and I met the quirk of his lips with a determined glare. I yanked the phone out from under the cushion, softening my features. "Sorry, I dropped my phone. Hey, Daniel."

"Wow." Daniel opened his eyes wide behind his thick, black-rimmed glasses. "What happened to your head?"

I touched my forehead and looked at my fingers. Blood. I must have reopened the wound when I glared at Remi. "Oh, I hit it on ..." Remi held up his finger while he scribbled on a notebook with his Sharpie marker. He flipped the paper around, his face as pale as ever. I squinted my eyes and spoke as I read. "... a rock while I rappelled off a sick cliff this morning." My voice came out robotic. This was off to a great start.

Daniel must think I was such an imbecile. We should have thought this through better. Behind the phone screen, Remi slapped his hand on his forehead and started scribbling again, pausing only to pass me a tissue, strategically keeping his eyes down. It amazed me how much the sight of blood affected him, and I reveled in the fact I could hold this over him in the days to come. I pressed it to my wound.

"Ouch." Daniel's voice came out hesitant like he suspected a prank or something.

Remi flipped his notepad around. *Work on your acting skills.*

I held back the urge to flip him off. He didn't understand how good my acting skills were.

With Dan juxtaposed to Remi, I couldn't help but compare them. Poor Daniel was like a Remington on the sales rack, downgraded in every way. Though thick, his haircut and beard screamed middle-aged man working in the IT department. His features softened into a round face. I wouldn't call him ugly by any means, but I wouldn't notice his looks if he passed me in the street. His profile pic showcased his best qualities and was possibly photoshopped.

"Where'd you go rappelling?" Daniel asked.

"The Snake River Canyon." Boom. Easy question. Next. Remi pointed to his note. *Grand Canyon.* I continued, "It's no Grand Canyon, but it's local, so, you know?"

I leaned back into my chair, getting comfortable in my role, letting the tissue fall away from my head after dabbing off the droplet of blood.

"Bruh, no way!"

Bruh? My feelings for him curdled, but I kept my smile from faltering. Minor things like being talked to like a teenage boy wouldn't keep me away from a committed relationship. Not this time. Besides, my brother spoke like this too.

"I know Ted Martin," Daniel continued. "He legit wrote the book on back-country canyoneering trails in the Grand Canyon."

A slew of curse words flew through my mind. The gig was up. I might as well surrender. Why did this guy have to be not only into extreme sports but also an expert on everything?

"Oh really?" I acted impressed while Remi held his phone up to me so I could read the title of Ted's book. "Grand Canyoneering?" I tried my best to look like I wasn't reading a phone screen like this info already existed in the back of my brain. In actuality, I hadn't known canyoneering existed until this moment.

My performance must not have impressed Remi because he closed his eyes, shook his head, and went back to scribbling in his notebook.

"What trails have you done?"

Remi flipped up the paper, and I read it as I spoke, "Deer Creek Falls."

"Dude! No way!" Daniel's smile lit up his face, transferring his joy for the sport to me over the phone. "Some of the most beautiful scenery I've ever seen was on that hike. The first time I did it, I almost got caught in a storm, and we had to book it out of there to higher ground."

Another strike against him for calling me dude, however, his enthusiasm erased it immediately. Daniel continued to talk about his adventure in this backcountry I'd never been to, and I made a mental note to Google pictures as soon as this call ended. Not only did I want to experience a fraction of the adventure Dan described, but I also needed to be researched and prepared for the next time I met him.

Wading through gullies and rappelling down waterfalls? Camping under the stars, facing the elements in a wilderness out to basically kill you? Roughing it for me was staying at a Motel Six, but I could change.

Doubt crept into my resolve. Did I really have to go to these lengths to get a guy? No. But a guy like Dan would transform my world and was worth all the efforts I put into making this happen. Dan and I hit it off in our texts. Besides, with Remi's help, I'd be able to do all the extreme sports stuff.

And was it bad I needed someone's arms to hold me while I went through losing Papa?

The conversation veered onto safer paths. He asked about life on the farm, and I told him a few of my greatest hits about Papa and me.

"What about this Remi guy you talk about all the time? The guy who works for you?"

Shoot! I thought this conversation would be safe. I didn't talk about Remi with him all this time, did I?

Remi sat straight up, then shot me a sideways grin.

"He's still as incompetent as ever," I answered.

The grin didn't budge from Remi's face. He scribbled on his notebook and flipped it around. *At least now I know what you and Smoot are talking about all the time.*

Heat burned in my cheeks, but I resisted the urge to cover them with my hands.

"Well, it sounds like he's a good friend." Dan pressed his glasses back onto the bridge of his nose. "I'd love to meet him and your other friends."

This couldn't be happening.

Remi flashed his notebook at me. *I'm flattered.*

"S-sure." I kept most of the hesitancy out of my voice. "I don't think Remi will have much time to hang out."

Once again, I read Remi's scribbled words. *I'll make time.* My gaze moved from his notepad to his face. He controlled his laughter, but barely. As per the usual, life was a game for him.

I glowered at him, instantly regretting it as pain pulsed along my hairline.

"No worries. I was hoping to see you next weekend." Daniel ducked his head and peeked back at me through his glasses in a manner I found adorable. "Maybe we could meet? Like go on a date?"

"A date?" I repeated. This was exactly what I wanted. A fast relationship hopefully ending in a proposal. Then why did I feel pressure tightening my throat?

I glanced at Remi—my lifeline. He flipped his notebook around. I widened my eyes and slightly shook my head.

"Is that a no?" Daniel's lips tightened together. A telling sign of his disappointment.

"No." I focused on my screen. "My dog was getting into the plant." I didn't have a dog. Not since Kiba died. The lie slipped off my tongue fast. Pretty soon my life would be nothing but lies. "Sure. Let's meet. We could go to the Bearded Axe next Friday night. Meet you there at seven?"

"Yeah. That sounds great!" Daniel sat up straighter and gave me a bright-eyed look.

I resisted my normal blabbering about everything in one breath. Smoot didn't say anything either, so we sat in awkward silence until I broke. "Well, I have to go. The pipe on the farm won't move itself."

Remi silently laughed at me and shook his head. What had I done wrong this time? Next time we did something like this, I would avoid looking at him.

"Okay." Daniel leaned closer to his phone. "See you in a week."

Fireworks erupted inside me, only to be doused by a bucket of uncertainty. The last time I'd been to The Bearded Axe was senior year. I still remember Brady Vaus and his cronies singing the Jell-O theme song behind me after I'd thrown an axe. It hadn't made it to the target. I'd walked out without picking it up and never returned.

Thanks to Remi, I not only had to confront one of my high school demons, but I also had to learn to throw a fetching hatchet. I hung up and chucked my phone at Remi. "You jerk."

My phone caught him in his midsection, against his solid abs, then fell into his lap and skidded onto the rug.

"What did I do? I thought the call went well once you relaxed."

"I can't throw an axe to save my life."

"It's not that hard."

"For you." Thanks to Brady, all I could focus on when I threw anything was my jiggling underarms.

"Look," Remi picked up my phone and handed it to me with a smile, "throwing an axe is nowhere near as hard as jumping off a telephone pole or walking on a wire thirty feet in the air. You've done both of those."

"I'm going to embarrass myself."

"We'll practice beforehand. Don't worry."

Don't worry, he says to someone with chronic anxiety. I couldn't back out now. Maybe everything would be okay.

"So, you talk about me, huh?" He leaned forward on his knees, the pencil and notebook dangling from his hands.

"Only to complain about how annoying you are."

"That's not what Smoot said."

"Shut up." I touched my eyebrow, testing the bandage and questioning once again why I ever made a deal with a Loki. "Let's focus on how I'm going to survive axe throwing."

"Are you going to set up a guys' night?"

"No," I responded immediately, even though I knew I would.

I wasn't a liar. Most of the time.

Chapter 11

Angie

The orange juice shook in my hand, and I tried to hide it from my parents, who were both fixated on me. Cold scrambled eggs and a half-eaten piece of sausage remained on my plate. They often made breakfast for me for dinner since that was the real start of my day. I wanted nothing more than to crawl back into my bed and sleep for a week.

Medical bills kept arriving in the mail. We would drown in them. Papa had taken the risk of not insuring himself or my mother. He'd kept Jared and I insured while we were kids, and as an adult, I had coverage through the hospital. Of course, after the initial hit of his diagnosis, he'd gotten health insurance, but we still had to foot sixty percent of the cost.

If we didn't have a good harvest this year, we'd go bankrupt. It was the rhinoceros in the room we never discussed. I picked at the peeling, light-orange finish on our round oak table, a product of the early nineties. Like most of our furnishings in our hundred-year-old farmhouse; it was 'antique.'

"We're worried about you, dear," Mama said, continuing a conversation we had started before my nap. "You can't keep going like this. Let Remi help you more. Having him feed the chickens is great, but that's something I can manage."

She and I both knew she couldn't do anything aside from care for Papa. She'd given up running the grocery store, turning it over to one of her managers until she found a buyer. If she could make sacrifices, so could I. As independent as Papa desired to be, he couldn't be left alone.

Remi had proven to be my challenge the entire week and a half since he'd entered my life. He'd managed to let the cows out twice, given the pigs the chicken scratch and the chickens the pig feed, bent the truck's tailgate when hooking up the cow trailer, *and* he'd sunk the four-wheeler in the creek.

Even with me having to stop and save Remi from himself, I'd managed to get the last of the fields planted except the corn field. And not a moment too soon, as water was due to start running in a few days. Thankfully, corn didn't need watering for at least the first month it was in the ground. The hay and winter wheat had been planted last fall. Seed and fertilizer costs exceeded my expectations, but I didn't have any choice.

With all this on my shoulders, it was no wonder I hadn't had time to worry about my date with Dan. It was tomorrow, and I hadn't even had time to practice throwing axes. I got three hours of sleep on the days I worked at the hospital. In the mornings, I planted the fields, then I'd come in for a late lunch and nap before my shift at seven ... which didn't leave much time to do anything else.

"Would they let you go down to part-time, just during the farming season?" Papa asked.

He'd eaten less than usual tonight. Even with the fire raging, he wore his red flannel fleece. I missed Papa's large belly, as his willowy form seemed out of place at our table of two robust women. The red fabric drowned him. It had holes in it from burning weeds and snags from barbed wire, yet he wouldn't let us buy him a new one. The jacket was so old, I remembered holding onto it as a little girl while I trailed behind him moving pipe. I treasured those days.

"I'm sure they would, but we need the money." I stifled a yawn and waited to speak until it passed. "I'm doing okay. I wouldn't risk my patients' lives if I thought I was a hazard."

Mama stood and started clearing the table. "Okay. As long as you promise to take care of yourself, we'll let you keep working."

I ground my teeth together. *Let* me work. Although my parents' hearts were in the right place, they made comments like this all the time, as if I wasn't a grown woman. I only lived here with them because Papa needed my help to run the farm—and now I was the one running the whole crap-tastic operation. I threw the rest of the orange juice back down my throat, but it didn't burn like I wanted it to.

"Mama. What was the point of me going back to school if I don't work as a nurse?" Walking to the sink, I rinsed my cup and put it in the dishwasher. I started to do the same with my plate and froze.

"Here. Let me do that. I don't know where we would be without you, Angie darling." Mama grabbed the plate, but I didn't let it go.

My focus had shifted to the backyard, where Remi swung the splitting maul high above his head and slammed it down. The log split in two, and he retrieved the pieces, placing them back onto the stump.

The problem was—or possibly as luck would have it—he was doing this ... shirtless. The day had been atypically hot for early April. My jaw sagged as the water continued to flow in the sink.

"What are you lookin' at?" Mama bumped me over so she could see out the small window above the sink too. "Oh." She shut off the faucet but kept her eyes glued on Remi. "Holy bats." Mama's expletive exited her mouth with a soft rush of air, almost inaudible.

I raised her holy bats to holy guacamole ... then to a full-on holy *shit*. This guy actually worked for me? Cords of muscles flexed in unison with Remi's repeated motion. He surprised me by being proficient at splitting wood since he'd struggled with other simple chores on my list.

His skin glistened in the evening sun, and his muscles were as glorious as Thor's. If possible, he was even more beautiful than another hot Chris, Chris Hemsworth. Remi was real and in front of me—something I could touch, not just an over-the-top celebrity crush. Heaven only knew I had plenty of those.

I'd already determined Remi, and I could never have a future together with his distaste for marriage and how much he irritated me, but while I was stuck with him, I could still appreciate the view. As much as I hated to admit it, I'd come to admire far more than his looks. First: I respected his dogged determination. Second: his sense of humor, as I doubted he was ever serious. Third—Gah! He even had me making lists in my head.

I stood on my tiptoes to get as close to the window as possible. "Do you suppose I should tell him we have a hydraulic log splitter?"

Mama shook her head with wide eyes. "Why would we do a silly thing like that?"

Remi paused, wiping the back of his hand across his forehead, and glanced in our direction. We ducked to either side of the window, the plate crashing into the sink, cracking in two.

"What was that?" Papa asked from the table.

"Nothing," I said.

"I dropped a plate," Mama called to him at the same time.

And then we both peeked out the window at Remi one last time. He'd leaned the splitting maul against the stump, and much to my disappointment, he'd slipped back into his T-shirt. Mama cleaned up the plate while I walked back into the dining room, where Papa was still trying to eat.

He set down his fork and met my gaze. Mama walked into the room, wiping her hands on a towel.

"We've decided to hire a nurse to come by every day and take care of me," he said. "Our insurance will pay for forty percent of the expense, and we'll be able to pay off the rest with the harvest," he finished in a rush.

A dark cloud settled over me, and all thoughts of a shirtless Remi fled my mind. More dire issues pressed their way to the forefront.

Mama must not have told him about the other bills coming in. Otherwise, he wouldn't be doing something so stupid and unnecessary. Years of my life had been devoted to school so I could care for him, and he went and hired someone else anyway.

"I am a trained nurse." I took the chair opposite him, the words squeezing through the tightness in my chest. "I can take care of you. That's why I chose to go to nursing school."

"I won't have you dumping out my poo bag and emptying my urine any longer. Your mother doesn't need to be doing that either." He rubbed his thick white hair. His cancer meds hadn't made his hair fall out, but they hadn't saved his life either. "I'd like to go to my grave with a little dignity intact."

The dripping from the faucet in the kitchen plinked in the sudden quiet. We didn't talk about his death or his grave. It made it too real. Mama started breathing funny behind me, like she was crying, but I couldn't look at her, or my floodgates would open before I started my twelve-hour shift.

Runny mascara and red, puffy eyes weren't welcome in a delivery room. The muscles around my jaw tightened, and I glanced at my watch. One more hour and I'd start my commute to a place where I could make an impact instead of staring at an unconquerable mountain. Nothing I did would keep Papa here longer, yet a part of me still believed a miracle would happen. That he didn't have cancer.

"I better get going," I hedged.

"Hold on." Papa met Mama's eyes, communicating without words, a superpower gained by thirty-nine years of marriage.

Mama cleared Papa's plate.

"You're going to leave without challenging the reigning Farm Frenzy champion?"

Mama returned with a double deck of our custom-made cards. I'd forgotten. Thursday night was family game night, yet I fought the urge to escape the reality of my father's failing health this minute.

Papa shuffled the cards and gave me his characteristic smirk: eyebrows raised, smile wide, nose scrunched in his grin. "What do you say, Muffin? One game?"

Dagnabbit. I was going to miss him. Shoving the tears from my eyes and voice, I relaxed back in my chair. "Forty-five minutes."

"Deal." His grin widened.

Mama gave a little cheer and joined us at the table. The front door opened and closed. We all looked toward the sound.

"It's just me, Ms. Nora." Remi's thick Texas drawl reverberated in our house, sounding foreign. "I'm bringing y'all a stack of wood if you don't mind."

"Come on back. Fireplace is in here."

Our fully clothed, far too good-looking farmhand walked into the room less than a minute later with an armload of wood the size of a small calf, bringing the scent of the outdoors with him. He strode to our wood bin and managed a controlled descent of the logs. Hard as I tried, I couldn't resist watching his biceps strain against his sleeves.

"You should join us for game night." Mama's voice rang out from her mouth at a higher pitch than normal.

I focused my narrowed gaze at her.

"I'm all sweaty." He gestured to his midsection where sweat darkened his dirty white shirt.

"Nonsense. Deal him in, Tony." Mama tapped Papa's shoulder.

Papa stopped shuffling and began dealing four stacks of cards. "You got it." He lifted his eyebrows at me twice in rapid succession.

I dropped my forehead into my hands. I should have left for work when I had the chance.

Chapter 12

Remi

Fire crackling. Laughter in the air. Dinner dishes in the sink. Nora even brought out milk and homemade cookies. My cookie remained untouched and my milk next to it. I wanted to preserve it. I'd slipped into one of those too-perfect-to-be-real, moral-message-laden Disney shows. My whole life, I thought families like this were as real as unicorns, and I'd plunked myself into the middle of one.

I sat between Angie and Tony, holding cards with a cartoon horse, cow, rooster, goat, and pig plastered on the back, running wild with giant grins on their faces, and looking a bit frenzied. "So ... when two of the same cards are put onto the pile, I have to do some action, and if I'm the last one to do it, I get the pile. Right?"

I pulled at my shirt, sweat beading underneath. The sun shining through the windows, coupled with the blazing fireplace, made me wish I could take it right off again. Nora and Angie's faces flushed and glistened as well. Tony most likely couldn't keep his body temperature up, and they were doing their best to keep him comfortable.

"There are two exceptions. First, on the Farm cards you have to do the actions in the same order as the symbols on the card." Nora finished off her cookie and dusted crumbs from her hands.

"If a Farm *Frenzy* card hits the deck, you do all the actions forward as listed and then proceed to do them backward." Angie glanced at her watch and then at me again.

I guessed she'd be leaving for work soon, given she wore navy-blue scrubs. "And for the storm cloud, hand in the air. For the heart, hand to the chest. Pictures of the green plants, hit the table. Image of the sun, back of the hand to the forehead flick the sweat."

Tony fished a card with the bright red heart on it from the deck. "This card's my favorite. It takes a lot of heart to be a farmer." He nudged me and gave me the cutest little old man wink, topping it off with a nod toward his daughter.

As cross as a hog headed to slaughter, Angie narrowed her eyes at her dad and shook her head once. I grinned and wiggled my eyebrows at her, purposefully being peskier than a thorn in her side.

Angie cleared her throat. "If you're the last one to do the motion, you take the pile. Winner is the one who gets rid of all their cards first."

"You ready?" Tapping his deck on the table, Tony eyed me with a quirk of his lips.

I was about as ready as a hen in a hog hunt. I couldn't even remember playing a simple game of Uno. I tried to think of one board game in the big house ... Nothing. Not even chess.

Last time I'd held a deck of cards was at the high stakes table in Vegas.

I nodded, and Nora flipped the first card, Angie, me, then Tony. Round and round we went. The three Johnsons remained laser-focused on the revealed cards. Angie flipped her card. Competition must be genetic.

Farm Frenzy. I didn't stand a chance. Grass. Cloud. Heart. Forehead, flick. They slapped the table, ran through the motions, and tapped it again before I had my hand in the air. The three of them looked so ridiculous I couldn't help but laugh.

"Ha!" Tony shoved his pointer finger at me. "Remi gets the pile."

Nora joined in my laughter while Angie's cheeks pinkened.

"This game is a bit frenzied." I gathered my massive pile of cards from the center of the table. "Y'all look like you were struck by lightning."

A chorus of laughter erupted at my comment. I couldn't help but compare them to my family. We never laughed like this around the dinner table. We never spent time together. Ever.

"Don't worry. You'll get better at it." Flicking the cartoon-animal-covered cards like a professional poker Daniel Negreanu or a Phil Ivey wannabe, Angie met my eyes. "At least I hope you're capable of improvement," she mumbled under her breath.

Maybe she hadn't intended for me to hear it, but I had. Tony and Nora kept chatting like they hadn't caught her final comment. One mistake, maybe two ... definitely less than a dozen this week, and she neglected to appreciate all the work I did for her. Flashing, neon arrows in my mind pointed to the wood bin full to the brim. If I hadn't taken my shirt off, it surely would have pit stains and back sweat. Even still, it was damp from when I'd put it back on after chopping wood.

Card play resumed. It. Was. On.

Flip.

Flip.

No match.

The tension built with each card placed, the pile growing larger and—

Two suns! I slapped my forehead so hard I'd certainly have a red welt left over, then flicked aggressively enough to tweak my wrist.

Tony's hand flicked a millisecond after everyone else. He groaned and took the cards. "That was a bad one. Don't worry. I'll come back."

"Ow. That looks like it hurt," Angie said to me, while she exchanged a half-smile with Nora. "Your forehead okay?"

"It's fine as frog fur."

My answer sent the whole table into a fit.

"That's an interesting saying." Nora set down a heart card. "Does everyone from Texas speak like that?"

"I reckon so." The phrase slipped out before I realized how very Texas it was.

Once again, they all broke into hysterics. Not sure what made me so entertaining, I offered a curtesy chuckle, my focus remaining on the game.

Heart.

Cloud.

Plants.

Plants.

I slapped the table. A zinging sensation shot up my thumb and into my wrist. Milk sloshed over the rim of my mug onto the table. Game night at the Johnsons was as hazardous for my body as working their land.

"Oops." I picked up my cup and guzzled my milk.

"Easy there, I don't think this table can take another hit like that." Tony wiped his eyes. "I haven't laughed this hard in months."

Nora took his hand and looked at Tony with such loving adoration, I wondered if it was an act. It couldn't be. This home felt different. Like they all wanted to be with each other.

"So, Remi, what do you do for a living?" Tony met my eyes across the table while he sifted through his cards.

Dammit. I knew this was coming but thought I'd be better prepared when they asked. I kept my mouth shut, but I didn't look away.

"I assume you do have a career—aside from a BASE-jumping farm laborer," Nora said.

Angie remained quiet but hung on to every word.

I breathed in through my nose. "I'm on a sort of sabbatical right now. I want to live a different life from the one I was born into."

Angie gnawed at her thumbnail, then scrunched her mouth together. My answer hadn't satisfied her.

"Wait. That's all you're going to tell us? You're on sabbatical? From what?" Angie waited for someone to play a card on the one she'd flipped onto the table, but both her parents were focused on me.

I met Angie's analyzing stare. "I work in business. I was a ... am a ... cog in the machine of corporate America. Nothing too exciting about that."

Suits and dinners with potential clients, closing deals and finding new ones—always with the pressure of if I failed, I'd lose this unspoken competition between my brother and me. Combined with the constant threat that my father would take away my inheritance, severing my lavish lifestyle. It would all end once I closed this deal. With the payout my father promised, I could cut myself free of that life.

Come to think of it, my mother and I didn't see eye to eye either. I was a donkey born into a family of thoroughbreds. Despite my melancholic thoughts, I let out a soft chuckle.

"Your life has to be more exciting than farm life," Angie said.

Studying the Farm Frenzy cards in my hand, I became a little boy again—the one who did everything under the sun to get his parents' attention—guitar, basketball, debate team. The only thing getting any reaction was the time I went cliff jumping as a preteen. My mother hadn't liked how I'd risked my life, and it kind of sent me on a collision course with every extreme sport imaginable.

How much would simple things like family game nights have impacted me as a little boy?

Didn't matter. In extreme sports, I found a community where I belonged and a place where life became more than something to be endured. "Nothing is more exciting than farm life."

I earned another round of laughter from Tony and Nora with that comment. Angie didn't join them, but she didn't persist in questioning me either. I settled into the game. Despite trying my best, the cards in Angie's hand dwindled while I held most of the deck. I didn't care. This night was wish fulfillment for me.

Angie played her last card and rubbed her hands together while we continued. Unless she lost this round, she'd win. The cards thumped down, each of us drawing out the suspense. Taunting Angie.

Farm. Frenzy. This time, I reacted on instinct.

Ignoring Tony and Nora, I watched Angie. Quick as lightning, she slapped her chest, table, table, chest, forehead, and threw her hand on the air ... I matched her movements. My hand touched the table before hers.

I beat her. Breathing harder than I should, I sent her a triumphant look.

"Balderdash." Nora slapped the table again. "I missed my heart." She swooped up the cards.

Angie jumped to her feet and shoved her hands in the air. "I win." She smiled and became mesmerizing—a glimpse of who she must have been before layers of grief and responsibility chained her to the ground.

She walked over to Tony and placed a kiss on his cheek. "I gotta run." After squeezing Nora around her shoulders, she collected her purse and keys.

I squirmed in my seat and stared at my still-untouched cookie. The Disney-TV-family-ness of this moment soared past magnitude eight on my personal Richter scale. Angie was the one working around the clock, losing her father ... going bankrupt. Comparatively, I had everything, and yet, I was jealous of her.

"Oh, don't forget to feed the pigs their slop." She leaned onto the table toward me. "And mind your fingers. They might chomp them clean off." Her teeth clicked together in her overexaggerated biting motion.

Yeah. Right. I brushed off her words, made a show of not caring. But as she snorted like a pig then laughed as she walked down the hall, I clenched my fingers into a fist. The wild eyes of the pig graphic on the card at the top of the stack seemed to follow my movements.

Pigs wouldn't do that. Would they?

Chapter 13

Angie

Two more shifts and I had a few days off. I could do this.

The satisfaction of beating Remi in Frenzy wore off in the first fifteen minutes of my drive. The other thirty I spent fighting off images of Papa in his casket.

Pale and white.

Lifeless.

With my tires still rolling, I shoved my truck into park. It jolted to a stop. It was like I was trapped at the bottom of a cliff, watching a boulder crash toward me, powerless to prevent my impending doom. I smacked my steering wheel and leaned back into my seat. Yes, I couldn't stop cancer from killing Papa, but I could at least introduce him to the man who'd care for me the rest of my life, the way he cared for Mama if I redoubled my efforts with Dan.

Wiping at the track of a single tear on my cheek, I checked my reflection in the rearview mirror. Light from the parking streetlamp illuminated my truck's interior. Taking a few breaths, I spoke to my reflection, "Good to go, right?" I nodded and snapped a quick selfie before opening my truck door.

I sent it to Dan with the caption, *Headed into work. See you on the flip side.*

My phone buzzed almost immediately.

> *You look goood in scrubs.*

Emotionally spent, I couldn't think of a response, so I sent him a smiley emoji with blushing cheeks and shoved my phone into my purse.

Slamming my door shut, I marched through the evening light, past the hospital doors to the NICU on the second floor.

Papa was my example of how to work hard. Jared hadn't followed in our parents' footsteps, which was probably why he often referred to me as the chosen one. He'd hoofed it off the farm as soon as he'd graduated and bounced from job to job, avoiding the ones requiring regular drug screening.

Most recently, he landed a gig as a bass guitarist in a band called Taking Back Tuesdays. He fit better on the concert circuit than he did on the farm. I got postcards from all his destinations.

Gabby waited for me at the nurse's station. Her long, black hair was tied in its typical bun, and her flawless, perpetually tanned skin gleamed in the fluorescent light. I loved working shifts with Gabby. From day one on this unit, we'd been instant friends.

"Are you still talking to that Smoot guy on ExtremeSingles?" she asked before I had time to set down my purse.

I welcomed the change of subject in my life. No more cancer and funeral talk for the whole night. Letting my concerns for Papa fade, I focused on the few babies we had in our unit, hoping they would live with little to no complications—that it would be an easy night.

"Yeah," I answered Gabby. "I think he's still buying the whole extreme sports thing I'm—"

Ryan, another nurse, opened the door to the NICU in mid-conversation on his phone.

"Shh-shh." Gabby lowered her palms toward the floor, indicating I remain quiet. "I posted a free hens add on Craigslist and put Ryan's phone number as the contact," she whispered.

I laughed, and she shushed me again.

With his tatted arms bare, the one holding the phone flexed against his scrubs. As a Navy veteran, he was built like The Rock but handled these preemie babies with more expertise than the new moms. With his blond hair fading into a thicker, lighter-yellow beard, he was a strikingly handsome man. Initially, we'd tried our hand at a relationship, but it didn't work out. We belonged solidly in the friend zone. I couldn't count the times single mothers had left their numbers on their discharge paperwork and asked him to call them.

"How do I know you're going to care for my chicken like one of your own children?" Ryan's voice echoed to us.

We ducked behind the desk. I covered my mouth to keep from laughing out loud.

"Have you ever considered getting chicken health insurance? I have the number if you would like to—Hello? Hello?"

Both Gabby and I let our laughter loose. Gabby unabashedly pointed at Ryan.

He shoved his phone into his pocket. "You're in so much trouble. I am going to get you back for this, Gabby. You know how many calls I've gotten today? I had no idea chickens were such a hot item."

"Admit it. I'm frickin' hilarious," Gabby said.

"I think so," I added.

"I stopped telling them I don't have a chicken, and now I take them on grand chicken stories until they hang up." Ryan leaned over the desk and looked at Gabby. "Take the ad down."

"Only if you cover my shift next week." Gabby leaned against the nursing circulation desk.

"Okay. Fine. I'll take your shift." Ryan moved to start monitoring his babies' vitals. "You two better send me photos from the concert. I love *Imagine Dragons*." He slipped on a mask and walked to the babies in oxygen tents.

Oh, right. I'd forgotten about the concert that was in a few weeks.

I reached for the gloves. "I can't go to the concert with you, Gabs."

She shook her head. "Oh, no you don't. You can't bail on me now. We're being spontaneous."

"That was before Papa got worse and the planting season started. I thought I'd have more help."

"What about that hot guy your mom hired? What was his name again?" she asked.

"Remi." The man who was never far from my thoughts.

"Why don't you have him cover for you?"

"He can't even drive a tractor. How is he supposed to run a whole farm even for a few days?" I thought back on all his mishaps. How much damage could he do behind the wheel of a tractor? "Trust me. He's not ready."

"Why not? I don't want to go alone with Lili. She can't even drink right now. Teach him how." Gabby held her hands together in front of her. "Please. For me."

"I'll try." I gave in. "But I'm not making any promises. I mean the guy lives in the city. He's clueless." I thought about him very proficiently chopping wood. "The only reason Mama hired him was because she wants me to have his babies someday."

Gabby grabbed a mask. "I thought we were into Smoot."

"Yeah. Well. I am." I sat at my laptop and scrolled through everything that had been done to my little twins on the day shift.

"I don't care how popular dating apps are, meeting up with someone you don't know is a big risk. And he could be a serial killer." Gabby slipped the mask's elastic bands over her ears.

She acted like I was a novice at online dating. "I've done this plenty of times—"

"Every time I get nervous," Gabby interjected.

"He's not a murderer. I FaceTimed with him Friday."

"OMG. Shut up." Gabby shoved at my shoulder. "That's a huge step." She sat next to me and started typing on her computer.

"Our big date is tomorrow." I couldn't help being a bundle of nerves about it. What if he didn't like me in person. "What do you think?" I asked.

"What do we think about what?" Ryan walked back to the nurse's station and removed his gloves.

"She's meeting up with Smoot," Gabby said.

"The guy who could be a serial killer?" Ryan rubbed his thick beard.

Gabby lifted her hands toward Ryan, enunciating her words. "That's what I said."

"I don't know, Ang. My vote is to let the sexy farmhand have a go. He's real. You know him. That's a step up from any online dating app."

Ryan's mask dangled from one ear as he planted his hands on the shared desk.

What did they know? Gabby hardly dated because she was focused on her career, and Ryan could have any girl of his choosing. They didn't understand what it was like to be overlooked and overshadowed by practically every other woman in town. They didn't have to cope with the memories of the popular guys in high school calling them "porpoise." Yep. An aquatic animal similar to a dolphin but more closely related to belugas. They'd follow me around, barking at me like a seal. I bet Remi had been the same as my tormentors.

I kept that memory close to remind me never to try to be like those popular kids or to date anyone like them.

Ryan let his breath hiss through his teeth. "It's a big moment. The meeting."

"Bring pepper spray in case he wants to make a coat out of your skin," Gabby said.

Ryan looked down at Gabby with his eyebrows creased together, nodding in agreement.

"Gross. You need to stop watching horror movies." I finished reading the note on my twins from the day shift.

Gabby looked at the monitors. "Oh, shit." She pointed to the screen. "I better go check on Baby Reynolds. Her oxygen sensor probably slipped off."

The busy nature of our job took over, and the three of us had little time to sit. I loved how fast nights like these flew by. But the pressure of farming season hung over me, waiting for me at the end of my shift, with Remi-related disasters hiding around every corner.

Chapter 14

Angie

Once again, I doubted my choice of outfit.

I sat on a cold metal stool, listening to the thud of axes slamming into wooden planks. The hem of my black skirt only reached mid-thigh. Every time I bent over, no matter how many times I told myself to think positively about my body, I couldn't help but be self-conscious of the exposed cellulite on my upper legs. Plus, my thighs kept sticking to the stool. I'd paired the skirt with my cream blouse and hoop earrings, but I should have picked a more suitable pair of shoes other than my black wedge boots; they didn't help with stability when throwing a hatchet.

Remi had told me to wear something comfortable, jeans and a printed tee. He'd been overruled by Gabby. I never should have consulted her about my wardrobe. Maybe this was her sick, twisted payback for bailing on the *Imagine Dragons* concert.

Before she'd gotten involved, I'd followed most of Remi's advice and, according to her, put on an outfit that made me look like a lumberjack.

I'd responded I'd rather be Paul Bunion than be out of place dressed like a Kardashian. It fit the part. After she pointed out Paul Bunion lived alone in the forest with a big blue ox, I'd gone back into my closet and changed.

Remi walked in the door with a black bag slung over his shoulder, and his gaze scalded me from my toes to the tip of my head. He wore a fitted T-shirt, matching the lighter shade of brown in his eyes, paired with loose-fit jeans. After sliding cash to the teenager running the cash register, he walked to my lane.

"Well, you'll definitely get his attention." He quirked his lips into a half-smile. "It'll be difficult to throw axes in a miniskirt and those boots."

My half-smile froze in place, and I sagged a little. Though I hadn't admitted it to myself, I'd been waiting for his approval. Why? I had no idea. He'd proven on a daily basis his judgement couldn't be trusted.

"Gabby ..." My voice trailed off. I didn't have to explain myself to him. I was a grown woman. I glanced back at the place where, a decade and a half earlier, Brady had stood taunting me. No, not tonight. I wouldn't let him, or any man, affect my confidence. "I like what I'm wearing." I grabbed the hatchet with a duct-taped handle hanging on the wall and swung it toward him. "You're here to teach me how to stick this," I gestured with the axe to the wooden planks with a target painted on them, "—to that wall."

"Whoa." He held his hands up. "Put that thing away."

I clenched my teeth together and returned the weapon to its place. Walking back to the table where Remi had set his bag, I folded my arms and waited for further instruction.

"First, someone who does this regularly doesn't use the throwing axes provided. They bring their own." Remi pulled two brand new, sharp hatchets from his bag. He handed me a belt with a metal loop on it. "Here. Put this on."

I slid it around my waist and cinched it to fit. He then passed me an axe, which I placed in my belt, securing the snap over the protective holder. With it strapped on my hip, my nervous energy ebbed, replaced by a general feeling of badassery.

Remi took the second axe in his hand and toed the throwing line. "First lesson. Stand twelve feet back from the planks. Second. Hold your elbow in front of you, lining it up where you want to throw. Third. Throw with a smooth motion from your elbow and a little flick of your wrist." He threw the axe, and it landed with the blade centered on the bullseye.

My eyes moved from the target to him. I blinked. Who the hell was this guy? Some reincarnated Viking god?

Remi smirked. "Your turn."

I straightened my skirt and stepped to the line. Sliding my brand-new axe from its holster, I lifted my elbow in front of me like Remi had.

"Eh-hem." Remi cleared his throat loudly.

"What?"

"You might want to remove the protective cover before you throw."

I angled my head to get a better look at my blade. Sure enough, the leather cover was securely snapped into place. Heat burned from the base of my neck and into my cheeks. I yanked the sheathing off, marched it to the table, then stepped back in place. The wood handle grew warm in my sweaty palm. Without thinking or overanalyzing, I swung my arm back, closed my eyes, and let go.

A clank and a thud, like a blade sinking into the wood, echoed in the lane.

"Ahh! *Ye-ah!*"

I couldn't tell if Remi's exclamations were good or bad. Maybe I'd hit the target and shocked him.

Opening my eyes, I examined the boards and the floor in front of them but couldn't find where it'd landed.

"You almost hit me." Remi breathed hard.

I cringed and turned around, but still couldn't find it. I met Remi's gaze as his expression changed from startled to all-out laughter. He backed up, leaned on the counter-height table, and pointed up at the ceiling.

Grimacing, I peered upward, and there, stuck in the beam above my head, was my axe.

Remi wiped his eyes. "I'll pay you a thousand dollars if you can do that again."

Thankfully, we'd come early enough that only two other lanes were being used. The teenager at the counter tipped his head in my direction. Would they kick me out for hitting the beam above my lane?

"Stop laughing." I glared at Remi. "Quick. Help me get it down before anyone sees."

"It's too late for that."

Sure enough, the other four people in the lanes across from us pointed and whispered to each other. I jumped and tried grabbing the handle but missed and wobbled on my wedges once I hit the ground.

"Hold on." Remi chuckled and dragged a stool over to me.

He went to climb onto it, but I pushed him out of the way. I could get my own axe. Daniel would be here in less than an hour, and I hadn't even managed to throw the thing in the right direction.

I was doomed. Standing on my tippy toes on the stool to reach the handle, I yanked on it and tugged it in all directions. It didn't budge.

Putting all my weight into it, I flexed my arms and heaved. Both of my feet lifted off the stool, which teetered and fell, leaving me dangling for a split second. All at once, the axe slid free—a scream squeaked from me as I plummeted toward the floor with a sharp blade clutched in my hands.

This is how I'm going to die ... Angelina Johnson, the axe, on the concrete floor.

My journey to guaranteed pain ended almost as soon as it had begun, but instead of impacting concrete, Remi's sturdy arms wrapped around me, clutching me to his chest. The weight of the axe propelled my arms downward, and the shiny, lethal metal barely missed my temple and Remi's thigh. The wooden handle jerked against my grip.

Sounds of blood rushing through my ears quieted the calls of concern from the other patrons. The space between my face and Remi's was less than a thin slice of sandwich bread—

the cheap kind we ate during harvest.

His eyes met mine, and for an infinitesimal moment, his gaze warmed and touched my lips. Holy mother of pearl! I wanted to close the bread-width gap and mack on him, but my mind clung to Daniel and the future I'd built up in fantasy land with him.

Numbing tingles radiated into the tips of my fingers. I lost my grip on the axe. Remi's lips pinched together, a sheen coming over his eyes like he was about to cry.

Then he dropped me.

My backside hit the cold, unforgiving ground. A shockwave from the impact jolted through my spine. "Oof." I glared at Remi. How dare he drop me?

But he wasn't looking at me. He hobbled on one foot, rubbing the toes on the other. "Ow. That hurt. Ow. Ow. Ow," he repeated over and over. "Did you have to drop the butt end of your axe on my toe?"

He put his foot down and limped back and forth in our lane while I struggled to a standing position. I tugged my shirt and skirt into place and retrieved my axe.

"So, you dropped me?" Some hero he'd turn out to be. A little hit to his toe and the damsel would be plummeting down a cliff to her death.

"It hurts."

"And now, thanks to you, my butt will have a bruise the size of the Snake River Canyon on it."

But I knew it could have been much worse. Images of a compound fracture of my radius and ulna—the scan of my cracked skull—a gash on my head to match the one I already had—flashed through my mind. I was a blasted nurse. Pulling stunts like this was how trauma happened.

"Don't blame me. This whole situation was caused by you. I mean, you closed your eyes before you threw the axe." He gestured toward me with open palms, his fingers spread wide.

I shoved my axe into its holder and pointed my finger at him. "You're the one who set this whole night up. So, yeah, I might have thrown the axe and stuck it to the beam, but I wouldn't be here if it weren't for you ... and Daniel's going to be here in forty-five minutes. I still have no idea how to throw the axe down the lane, let alone hit the target." The longer I spoke the more animated I'd gotten. The worker behind the cash register had been walking toward us but then changed his mind and went back to his post—probably to call his manager.

Great. Now, they'd kick me out before my date had the chance to walk in the front door.

"Calm down." Remi held his hands in front of him like he surrendered. He stalked to his axe where it was still stuck in the bullseye and pulled it out in one decisive tug. The cords on his forearm remained tense the entire way back to my side. "I told you we should have done this two days ago."

"I didn't have time for that." Between work and farming, I barely scheduled enough time to eat and sleep.

Remi's breath hissed through his teeth, his upper body tense and rigid. "Stop arguing with me and get on the throw line."

I resisted the urge to stick my tongue out at him and stepped to the spot he indicated. My shoulders sagged, and I kept my mouth shut. There was no way he'd be able to make me proficient at this in time. I'd accepted I was going to make a fool of myself.

"We're going to try something different." Remi tucked his axe into his belt holder and came to my side. "Grab your axe."

"I don't see the point." Who was I kidding? My hands still shook from the last time I tried throwing the blasted thing.

"Just—" He reached around me and snagged the instrument of torture hanging at my waist and held the wooden handle to me. "Trust me."

Skeptical this would go any better than last time, I took the axe with my right hand.

Remi stepped behind me. "Hold it with both hands." His voice tickled my left ear. Chills raced along the side of my body, chasing away the remnants of my frustration. "Forget about everything. Your stress. Worries. They don't exist here." He softly gripped my forearms and lifted the axe above my head, his fingers running along my arms until their warm tips rested on my wrists. The heat from his body ebbed into the back of mine. "Focus on the target. Don't release your hold on the axe too soon or too late. Channel your frustrations at the center of that target. Take a deep breath. And throw."

His hands fell away from mine. I took a deep breath. The center of the target was Papa's cancer diagnosis, medical bills, and declining health. It was the countless hours it took me to maintain the farm. My lost sleep. The hours I spent at work trying to get the money to support my legacy. It was all my loss. My debilitating responsibilities. My pain.

And it deserved to be decimated.

I released my breath, steadied myself, and catapulted the axe at the wood panels. The blade buried into the dampened pine with a satisfying thunk.

My chest heaved up and down as if I'd run a mile. I didn't look at Remi, reveling instead in the victory of success.

"Yes!" Remi grabbed my shoulders and shook them. "You did it!"

I looked over my shoulder at him, and I couldn't stop the warmth generated by his praise from spreading through me. Remi whooped and did an overexaggerated fist pump, turning my smile into laughter. He came to my side, and, as if he'd been born with the axe in his hand, he threw it and hit the little blue dot on the upper left of the board.

We did this a few more times. Remi giving me tips when I missed, but by the time Daniel was set to arrive, I was throwing at a seventy-five percent success rate.

Nervous energy took hold of me. What if Dan rejected me? What if he liked how I looked with a few more pounds on my body?

As if reading my thoughts, Remi caught my hand and squeezed my fingers. "You'll be fine. Keep doing the double-handed throw, and you'll impress the hell out of him."

What he didn't know was throwing the axe was the least of my worries.

"Remember, I'll be in the lane right behind you, listening—"

"Oh, right." I yanked my AirPods free of my black, fringed purse, and tucked one into my ear, then let my long hair hide it from view.

Remi put in his own earbuds, then started scrolling through his phone. Mine buzzed from somewhere inside my purse. I tapped on my Airpod and answered.

"Can you hear me?" His real voice echoed in the ear without the mini-speaker in it, while also reverberating through the earpiece.

"Loud and clear."

At least I'd get through this night with the comfort and support of Remi.

Chapter 15

Angie

The front door flew open, and I snapped my head toward it. I thought it might be Dan, but instead, Blake, Chuck, Pedro, and Remi's friend, Myles, walked in. I swung around to Remi and raised an eyebrow in question.

True to form, Chuck wiggled his eyebrows at me. He'd been a pest throughout elementary and high school, always on his older brother John's heels, and he was still a pest. Pedro brushed his mustache and gave me a thumbs-up as he passed. Blake was more stoic than the others, and even though I didn't know Myles well, he cast me an overdone wink.

Somehow, I'd become this town's little sister. But did the three mechanic amigos and Myles have to come spy on me on my date? Come on. "Did you have to invite the whole posse?"

"I needed them to make this look like a bros' night. I couldn't exactly be in my lane alone, could I?" Remi's voice cut through the chatter of the guys greeting each other.

"Whatever," I said, too nervous to come up with anything else.

Tugging my phone from my purse, I flicked the ongoing call with Remi to the corner and texted Lili.

> Blake is at the Bearded Axe. Coincidence?

The dotted lines flickered back and forth on my screen as Lili formulated her response.

> *Someone has to make sure Smoot doesn't go all Hannibal Lecter on you.*

Clicking on the eye-roll emoji, I pressed send. Then texted her again.

> *He's not a murderer.*

The dots started cycling again. We'd been through this many times before with my other online heartthrobs. Which was probably why I'd stopped telling them whenever I scheduled an in-person date.

> *Rather be safe than sorry. Have fun!*

When Daniel entered the room, my eyes barely skimmed over her text. Although he was shorter than I expected, his fit build made up for it. His button-up, deep-blue shirt tapered into classic khakis, showing off his broad shoulders and narrow waist. Thick-framed glasses rested on the bridge of his nose, giving him the persona of the sexy, smart guy.

I shoved my phone into my bra and wiggled back and forth to make sure it remained secure. My shoulders tensed, and my smile faltered as I walked toward him. All my previous worries rushed to the forefront of my mind. What if I didn't understand him? What if he grew bored of me? What if he turned out to be a huge disappointment?

With each step, I drew closer to him, and I didn't know whether to go in for a hug or a solid handshake.

Hug. No. Handshake.

The gap closed, and I lifted my arms to move in for a quick embrace. *"Start off with a handshake."* Remi's voice came too late to save me.

Still, I shifted and stuck out my hand, but then Daniel went for a hug. I stayed firm in my position until he took my hand in his, almost crushing my fingers in his solid grip.

"That was awkward." Remi's mechanical voice sounded in my head once again.

Tempted to yank the earbud free, I flipped Remi the bird behind my back. His soft laughter mixed with Daniel's voice. I blocked out the masculine chuckle and listened to Daniel.

"Wow. You're even prettier in person." His smile grew, yet he remained focused on my face.

I breathed in his spiced cider cologne—it was applied a bit too strongly—and led him to our lane.

"Nice. He's looking at your ass," Remi said into my ear.

"Shut up." I glared over at Remi, who stood surrounded by his cronies, all of them shooting me sly glances.

"What?" Daniel came to my side.

"Tell him you were using shut up as an exclamation. Shut up! We have the same axe," Remi quickly said.

"I—uh—*shut up*, we have the same axe."

"Nice."

"Oh, yeah. Well, it is the official axe for competitions. Mine looks a little more worn than yours though."

"This one's brand new." I had a problem speaking without thinking. "My handle fell off my other one," I added in a rush.

Daniel only nodded, stepping to the line. "What do you say we start a game? Promise not to let you win." He winked at me over his shoulder.

I half smiled and twirled my finger in my hair. "Don't worry. I'll beat you all by myself tonight."

"Kinky." Remi's voice interrupted my conversation.

I'd forgotten I wasn't alone. "I mean, I'm gonna win."

Daniel raised one eyebrow at me and turned to face the target. I flipped around at Remi and held one finger over my mouth. With his constant commentary, I would never settle down and be able to focus on Daniel. I couldn't take him out of my ear either. He was a necessary evil ... for now.

Remi sat on the bench behind me with a scorecard and a pencil in his hand. *"I'll give you a tip. Make the axe go forward."* I watched his mouth move with the words flowing into my brain.

The thwack of Daniel's axe brought me back to my date, where my focus should be centered. His axe stuck halfway in the one-point ring on the outside of the board.

Daniel rubbed the back of his head. "I guess I'm a bit out of practice."

I laughed. "I haven't been able to come here much lately either."

He gestured for me to step in front of him and take my turn. I couldn't delay any longer. It was the moment of truth. Would I be able to pull off this catfishing scheme or should I call it a night and head back home—to Mama and Papa—where I'd live out the rest of my days caring for them and the farm?

Following Remi's instructions, I breathed in deeply through my nose and let the air flow through my lips. Both my hands gripped the axe. I lifted it above my head and brought it down in one decisive movement, letting it go.

It hit the target.

Just not the one I'd been aiming for.

It landed square in the center—in the target in front of Daniel, not me.

"Oops." I dropped my forehead into my hand.

"Don't admit when you do something wrong. Own it." Laughter tinged Remi's voice. I had to resist the urge to turn around and yell at him for poking fun at me.

"I mean ... I meant to do that."

I glanced at Remi, but his back was to me. He still sat on the stool at the table while his friends threw axes. Blake slid his eyes in my direction, narrowing them like an older brother would. I ignored his look, facing Daniel once again.

"Wow. You like the two-handed throw, huh?"

"Yeah." I followed him to the targets and yanked out my axe.

We threw a few more times, and I missed only once. Daniel managed to stay on the board, but his throws were everywhere.

"Dude. My arms are flamed." Daniel tugged his hatchet out of the wood and tucked it into his belt.

"The muscles in his forearms are tired because of climbing." Remi translated.

"You okay if we take a break? I'll get you a drink." Daniel tipped his head toward the drink fridge.

"Sure." I tucked my own weapon in its hook. "I'll take a Diet Coke."

"You got it." Daniel shot me with two finger guns and jogged to the counter.

I sagged into a stool.

"You're doing great." Remi laughed.

I swung around in the stool to see him facing me, and the other guys, save for Myles, rushed toward me.

"If he so much as tries anything, you let me know and I'll—" Blake started.

Chuck cut in. "I like this guy, but you should give me a go."

"She'd date a baboon before she tried dating you, Chuck." Pedro whacked Chuck in the back of the head.

"Incoming." Remi's voice cut through the chaos.

"Get back to your lane. I can handle this myself." I shooed them away.

"That's why Remi is over there with an earphone feeding you information." Blake jerked his thumb toward Remi as he walked away from me.

Every other night, I could handle being treated like the town's little sister. The one you hug and pat on the head but don't make out with. I didn't believe for a second Chuck actually meant what he offered. I supposed that was why I'd tried to date Troy. I wanted everyone to see me differently.

I wouldn't be the little sister anymore. No, tonight I'd be sexy, desirable, and a potential for a long-term relationship.

"Will you keep your friends under control?" I mumbled to Remi.

"They're more your friends than mine."

"Why did you bring them?" I asked louder this time.

"Because you said you wanted a diet."

I spun so my legs slid forward under the table. Daniel held the bottle to me, a question in his eyes. "Yeah. I did." I took the drink without further explanation, and Daniel sat beside me.

He opened his bottle of water and took a drink. I probably should have ordered water. Sports people didn't drink soda. Then again, I couldn't give up Diet Coke for a guy I loved, let alone a pretend hobby.

"Sorry." He set his bottle on the table and played with the condensation on the side. "I dogged a climb yesterday. It was a bit of a grovel. I had to garden with one hand while I held a chickenhead with the other.

I yo-yo'd it for a while, but my melon bucket saved me from the worst hit."

I blinked ... and hoped Remi caught all that.

Sure enough, the translation came in. "*He tried to climb a run multiple times, it was rough with dirt and plants. He had to clean it up while he held onto a rock protrusion. He fell a lot, but his helmet saved him from hitting his head.*"

Not that it helped much. What in the hell was I supposed to say to that? "Where did you go climbing?"

"Moab. I got back yesterday."

Sheesh. This man had more adventure in his pinky finger than I had in all of me. "I've always wanted to go there."

"You haven't been?" He held an incredulous note in his voice.

Remi chirped in my ear. "*Say in April.*"

"—In April."

"*It's too hot in June.*"

"It's hot in June," I repeated.

"I've jumped hundreds of times in Moab. I know the DZO and Rigger personally at the Canyonlands DZ. Have you BASE'd or skydived there?"

"*DZ. Drop Zone—it's where you go to skydive. Rigger checks your rig. Frickin' SkyGod.*"

"Frickin' SkyGod," I parroted, only catching the last thing out of Remi's mouth.

"*No—don't.*"

I jumped at Remi's urgent command and spilled my Diet Coke all over Daniel.

"Whoa." Daniel jumped up, causing his stool to tip and slam into the concrete.

"I'm sorry. I didn't mean to. Here." I grabbed the closest thing, my black, fringe purse, and rubbed at the brown stain growing on his blue shirt. "I can fix it. The stain stick that Mama makes gets anything out. Take off your shirt, leave it with me, and it'll be good as new tomorrow."

"Angie. You might want to stop rubbing the man and asking him to take his shirt off."

Daniel took my hands in his, and I finally stilled. "Are you calling me a SkyGod?"

"No. I mean ..."

He licked his lips. "Next thing you'll say is I'm a 100-jump wonder."

Everything coming out of his mouth may as well be the same language Mae spoke. I'd been trying to learn horse my whole life. True, I may not understand the exact intonations of her soft neighs, but I connected with her thoughts. Anytime I went on a ride, I couldn't carry my troubles along with me. As soon as I climbed in the saddle, I left every stressor behind. Nothing existed except me, Mae, and the ground flying beneath her feet.

Someday, I hoped to have this type of connection with another human. Preferably with the man, I chose to marry. So, although I didn't understand him now, I had no doubt I would be able to in the future.

While Daniel held my hands, I peeked over at Remi, waiting for his translation.

"Those are insults. Like he has a big ego, but a small d—"

"What do you think of this place?" I cut Remi off and pulled any question I could think of out of thin air. Immature nincompoop.

Why'd I leave my notecard of talking points on my dresser? They'd be helpful right about now.

"I'm not the best at throwing axes. I'm good. I beat most people, but I could improve."

"No, I meant how do you ... like this area, I guess?"

"It's not bad. Although, I've done the bridge, and it wasn't that epic ..."

Ignoring Remi's disgruntled noise, I continued to listen to Daniel as he picked up his stool and talked about all the places he'd BASE jumped. I interjected one word here and there in the conversation, which carried on for another thirty minutes.

"... my favorite is jumping from skyscrapers into the city lights below. Maybe we can do a tandem jump sometime."

His heated gaze zapped me like Superman's laser vision, microwaving my heart and leaving a pile of warm mush where muscle once existed. Sure, heights still made my toes curl, but being with a stable guy like Dan would be worth confronting my biggest fear.

"That means leaping of a building together."

"I know." The words flew out my mouth before I could stop them.

"You know what?"

"I know I like you."

Daniel leaned in close to my ear—the ear with the AirPod in it—and I jerked away. He quirked his eyebrows. "Listen, it's getting late. I better get going."

"That's code for I don't want a second date. Offer to walk him to his car."

"I'll walk you to your car." I stood and tugged my skirt into place.

"Good. Now make eye contact with him and bite your lower lip."

Daniel took a couple of steps in my direction. Tilting my head ever so slightly, I locked eyes with his and tucked my lip under my top teeth. Sure enough, his gaze trailed to my mouth.

He swallowed and fiddled with his glasses. "That'd be nice."

"*Well done. Now, find any excuse to touch him on your way to his car.*"

I placed my hand on Daniel's shoulder as he headed for the door; he paused mid-stride. Delectable shivers coursed through my veins. I'd always let the guy take the lead. This newfound power emboldened me to run my fingertips along Dan's arm and take his hand in mine. With an encouraging tug from me, he began walking once again.

He pushed the door open for me, and we moved into the chill spring evening. Leftover mist from the light rain from earlier in the day dusted my hair and face, coating my exposed skin. Dan led me to his car parallel parked across the street.

Of course, he chose to rent a pearl-gray Tesla.

"*Now tuck your hair behind your ear and step into his bubble. If he's interested, he'll do the rest.*"

How was Remi watching me right now? I didn't look back at the building to figure it out. The beat of my heart urged me forward. Desperate for a romantic connection, I pressed him back against his car.

Though our height difference wasn't as drastic as Remi towering over me, I still had to tilt my chin up to see his eyes. His pupils dilated in the darkness. As instructed, I tucked my hair behind my ear, waiting for him to do the rest.

The halo of the streetlamp illuminated half our bodies in the deserted street. Acting a bit tentative, his damp palms swept my hair away from my face, his thumbs tracing my cheekbones. His head dipped closer to mine; the warmth of his breath touched my lips.

Then it hit me. I was getting kissed. I held my breath. Time had been my enemy for too long. My lips had almost turned into dry husks during their extensive drought. Water was about to pour down from the sky.

His lips, wetter than I'd like, moved over mine. My body instinctually took over, and I opened my mouth and went with the flow. His hands dropped to my lower back, pulling my entire body closer to his, while mine tangled in his hair, knocking his glasses crooked.

My breaths shortened until I was gasping for air. I couldn't tell if this was because I didn't allow myself to come up for air or if the pressure from Daniel's arms stifled my ability to bring in more oxygen. He pulled back slightly and kissed my forehead.

"I had a nice night." He climbed into his car and winked at me. The Tesla chimed, and its screens woke up, accompanied by a soft hum. "Thanks for the awesome date. I'll be back." He did a poor imitation of Arnold Schwarzenegger and closed the door.

I stepped back from his car, and with one final wave, he rolled forward and turned around the corner.

Placing my hands on my scalding cheeks, I spoke through my grin, "Remi. It worked." But the masculine voice in my head I'd grown accustomed to didn't answer back. "Remi?"

I tugged my phone free from my bra and wiped the glistening sweat from its screen ... it was blank.

Remi had hung up.

Chapter 16

Remi

I collapsed on Blake's nursery floor next to the organized piles of screws and crib parts. "I am in deep shit."

Pedro couldn't come to the crib raising, as his kids had fevers, and Chuck had chosen to go to bed early since he was taking the opening shift at the garage tomorrow. It was Blake, me, and Myles ... discussing the impending disaster headed my way.

Myles shared a look with Blake and passed me an unopened beer, his own a quarter of the way gone. I took it but didn't open it and let it fall by my side, still clutched in my hand.

"Have you approached Tony and Nora yet?" Myles straddled the back of a chair, leaning his arms on its backrest.

I sat up and picked up a piece of Styrofoam, launching it at Myles. *What the hell are you thinking?* I mouthed and glared at Myles.

"What? Blake doesn't know?" Myles persisted like the dumb box of rocks he was.

If a duck had his brain, it'd fly north for the winter. I couldn't imagine the ramifications if Lili learned about me and the CDC. She'd go straight to Angie for sure.

"You want to approach them about what?" Blake looked over the instructions and grabbed the drill Myles held out to him.

I leaned my forearm on my bent knee, my beer still unopened, still dangling from my hand. "Um—"

"On giving him a raise," Myles finished.

Great, now I was begging for money from a man with terminal cancer.

Blake pressed the drill bit to the white finished wood, and slowly drilled a hole. "Stupid manufacturer didn't pre-drill these holes right," he muttered, blowing at the saw dust, then lined it up with another piece. "You want more money? From Tony and Nora?"

"That's not what's bugging me." No way would I let him believe I'd take more money from two people circling the bankruptcy drain.

"Then what's the problem?" After placing the screw, Blake grabbed the screwdriver and tightened it.

How could I describe my situation without lying to Blake and giving away too much information? He'd be the one who could help me. His wife was Angie's best friend, and I needed all the help I could get. Maybe he'd provide insight into the situation I'd gotten myself into.

Watching her and Smoot from the front window of the Bearded Axe had made me sick to my stomach ... the way his hands had possessively gripped her shoulders and how he'd dropped one to her lower back. I'd been tempted to go show her what it was like to be kissed by someone who knew what he was doing. Not by some guy as worthless as teats on a bull.

Crouching forward, I looked from side to side, listening for any noise in the quiet house. I pressed my index finger into the soft gray carpet, drawing smiley faces into the threads. "Where are Lili and Maddie?"

"They're having a movie night at Renee's."

Good. I leaned against the wall. "I'm starting to like Angie." My feelings were substantial enough that I didn't want to deny myself the opportunity to hold her, or to kiss her like a woman deserved to be kissed. "Like. I like, *like* her," I confessed, sounding identical to a middle schooler.

The assembly instructions floated to the floor. Blake analyzed me, then Myles. "Is this some sort of prank?"

Myles didn't say anything and took another sip of his beer. I knew his opinion: Women couldn't be trusted. Where I used to agree with him, lately, I'd started changing my mind. It all centered on Angie and why I couldn't get her out of my thoughts.

"No," I answered. "Not a prank. You have to promise not to tell Lili."

"You think I'm stupid. I value my marriage way too much. Lili and her hormones are like a hurricane. Right now, I'm enjoying being in the eye of the storm." He grinned from ear to ear.

I didn't expect the joy evident on Blake's face.

Myles pointed to me with his bottle. "You're happy about this?" he asked Blake.

"Are you kidding? Remi's not addicted to any illegal substances, and he's not unemployed living in his parents' basement or in jail. Plus—" Blake moved to a standing position. "I bet Lili you'd be head over heels for Angie in two months. She guessed six."

"What?" I held my hands up in surrender. "This is a crush. I'm trying to figure out how to get over it." Usually, it was simple. I'd take the girl back to my place, show her a good time, and we could both move on. With Angie, I couldn't risk tanking the deal for one night of fun.

Blake took my hand and pulled me to stand next to him. "You still have time." He set down the drill. "But while we're on the subject, do you see yourself falling in love with her?"

"Hell no."

I lowered my gaze to the carpet. Being asked this question point blank made me pause and look at my feelings for Angie with a critical eye. She was stubborn, determined, smart, drove me hella insane, challenged me at every turn, and all her fire was packaged in beautiful curves.

But I didn't love her, and I never would. She wanted marriage and the whole package, and I couldn't offer her that. "I've known her for less than two weeks."

"And I fell in love with Lili in two weeks. Time is relative." Blake went back to his instructions. "The piece marked A inserts into the corresponding board, but I can only find one board with an A on it."

"It's not that easy." I ran my thumb over the ridges on my bottle cap.

The screwdriver in Blake's hand paused mid-turn. "What do you mean?"

I wanted to yell, *I'm here to buy her farm.* The source of her happiness and joy, the thing which defined her, would be ripped from her only in a matter of time. I never failed. And I wouldn't this time.

"I'm not from here. At some point, I'll have to go back to my life in Dallas," I said instead.

Myles laughed, shook his head, and took another swig of his beer, an onlooker in this conversation rather than a participant. I shook my head at him, warning him with a look not to slip up.

If one person in town caught on to who I really was, it'd ruin everything. I'd been blackballed from my fair share of small towns.

"That's not a big deal. Lili left St. Louis to be with me. And I would have moved to St. Louis for her if she'd decided to stay." Blake skimmed over the instructions, twirling the Philips in his hand.

"I can't leave Dallas. I'm anchored there." More by my Bugatti and my parents' pool house, not by my family.

"Well, Angie will never move from her land. It means everything to her."

So, I'd noticed.

"If you're not willing to make concessions, you, my friend," Blake pointed the tip of the screwdriver at me, "are screwed." He looked away from the instruction manual. He dropped the papers to the floor. "I can't focus. What kind of relationship do you want with Angie, anyway?"

I'd never wanted a woman like I wanted Angie. Like a thirst I couldn't quench no matter how much water I drank, an itch not relieved by any kind of scratching, a deep hunger set to consume me if it continued to go unsatisfied. Do nothing, and I'd lose my mind—if I acted, I'd lose millions and the freedom I'd fought for my entire life.

Not to mention, I'd ruin Myles' dream as well.

I hadn't admitted this to myself until I saw her in Smoot's arms. More and more this past week, I'd found myself staring at her lips, her contours, imagining how our bodies would fit together. Thankfully, I'd had a day alone running errands to and from the farm store and mowing the lawn on top of the usual chores. For days, we moved and patched pipe, getting the irrigation set up for water.

True, two and a half weeks wasn't long, but I'd never spent this much time with a woman.

One taste of her, and surely, I'd go back to normal, back to my carefree lifestyle, where this woman didn't rule my thoughts.

I answered Blake's question, "I don't know. I just know I can't ignore this thing between us anymore."

"Then you stay away from her." The warning in his voice came out as loud and clear as a tornado siren. Older-brother, protective vibes came off him in waves. "Get your feelings solidly in the 'I love you' zone before you make a move on Angie, or I'll run you out of town. Don't touch her until you're ready to give her wedded bliss. She's not the one-night-stand type."

"I know." I dropped my unopened beer bottle onto the carpet and ran both my hands through my hair.

Myles let out a whistling breath and chortled. "Remi, married?" He drank more of his beer, nearly choking before he swallowed.

"Is that hard to imagine?" I asked.

"Yes," he responded without hesitation.

If I wanted to, I could make this work.

First thing to do: contact my asshat brother and tell him I refused to buy Angie's family farm.

Second: tell my greed-driven father I quit.

Third: beg my mother to allow me access to my inheritance, which wouldn't happen even if hell froze over.

Fourth: Use it to pay off Angie's farm.

Crazier things had happened. Right?

But was I ready to commit to one woman for the rest of my life? Not at all. My parents pretty much proved wedded bliss as a myth. Sure, Tony and Nora challenged that belief, but not enough for me to change the bro code I'd lived by since the age of ten.

In chick flicks, things like this worked out all the time. Not that I was a regular consumer of those romantic movies. For research into the women's psyche, I'd watched a couple of romantic comedies with a barf bag next to me, just in case. The unreal expectations set in those movies weren't possible to compete with.

Men simply didn't behave in that way.

Not in the real world.

The probability of all this working out wasn't in my favor. My mother would never let me have access to a cent, and Dad would cut me off and fire me without severance. Tenacious as ever, my brother would never leave a deal undone, especially one with this much potential for profit, and the land would get sold to him anyway.

Step one: Cut all association of joint ventures with Angie.

Step two: Let Smoot have her.

My throat tightened to the point where I had difficulty swallowing. I'd teach her enough about the lingo, and the sports Smoot seemed most interested in and then let her fly or fail.

Step three: No more caring, desire, or want.

I couldn't even think about how close we were as she'd leaned over me to shut off the tractor, about how her heartbeat pulsed into me, matching my own, the way her lips parted in anticipation of a kiss. I definitely couldn't think about her soft body in my arms after she'd fallen off the stool—or about the way I had to resist going outside, taking her from Smoot's arms, and giving her a thorough lesson of my own.

Stop it, Remi. I focused on the dull ache in my toe, still hurting from Angie dropping the butt of her axe on it. Feeding this attraction, even one kiss, would lead to a lot more pain.

I hit my head back on the wall. *I was in deep shit.*

Chapter 17

Angie

Twenty-seven days. I'd managed to keep my cool with Remi constantly in my way for almost a month. On top of working my shifts at the hospital, in the two weeks since axe throwing, I'd spent my time coming up with chores Remi deemed appropriate. And a lot of what he did, I had to go back over and redo anyway.

I'd also gone on three more dates with Dan—dinner and a movie, mini-golf, and an escape room. We didn't escape. He'd seemed disappointed in my non-extreme date night choices, so I'd promised him more adventurous options in the future, buying time for more lessons with Remi. Things were progressing just as I'd planned. Maybe a little too fast for what I'd normally prefer. Dan was already dropping hints about weddings and babies and such. Where I'd normally put on the breaks, I was on a timeline, and it was full steam ahead.

I tugged my Chevy baseball hat over my forehead until the brim touched my large sunglasses and ducked lower in the passenger seat of Lili's made-over Audi. The sun had set a half hour ago, leaving the car to be sheltered by darkness.

Remi had begun to act funny, started being nicer to me. His happy-go-lucky personality reminded me of hot Chris number three, Chris Pratt, especially in his role as Starlord. Hence, I was subjected to a man who constantly joked, fought to make every chore fun or turning it into a challenge, an extreme sport. If he sank the four-wheeler in the creek one more time ...

It was weird having someone else in the cracks of my life, aware of what I was doing minute by minute. I took care of myself. Remi turned out to be one observant little puppy dog. Like the other day, he'd brought lunch to me in the field, so I didn't skip it. He was an irritating trip hazard at times but also loyal, shadowing my every move and getting me what I needed before I even knew I needed it.

His behavior sent warning bells off in my head. And his phone conversation I'd overheard wouldn't leave me alone.

That was why Lili and I were here, in her car, waiting for him to leave my house. We'd both come prepared with snacks and sweatshirts. I'd insisted the car remain off, the chill outside making its way in. Although I'd wanted to keep Lili out of this, her involvement was necessary since Remi would recognize all my cars.

It was bros' night out at Tractor's Bar and Grille, providing me with the opportunity I'd been waiting for. I tipped my head back against my headrest, agitated with myself that I knew Remi's schedule.

Even Dan had made a special trip to Clear Springs for this guys' night. He wanted to get to know my friends and be a part of my life. Dan spared only a brief kiss and hello to me before he was off to the bar. Which was all fine and good, with the exception of Remi. If it weren't for our agreement, I was certain he'd do something to sabotage my relationship with Dan.

"What are we doing here, staring at your house again?" Lili whispered through her bite of peanut butter and sauerkraut sandwich.

Her large, pregnant belly brushed the base of the steering wheel. The rank smell of her choice of food hung in the air. I gagged and stared at my front door, tempted to give up and walk into my house.

But I didn't. I needed answers.

"A stake out. I'm telling you, there's something off about him." I'd plied Remi with questions, and the only other information I got out of him was that he lived in Dallas and loved extreme sports.

The cog in the corporate machine comment did nothing to give me a clue as to why he was here. Why my farm? Why this small town?

His knowledge of the inner workings of a man's mind and all things extreme had come in handy with Dan. Handsome, sweet, not boring Dan hadn't ghosted me yet like all other potential Mr. Angelina Johnsons. Dan had gone over several ideas for another extreme-sporting date, ranging from skydiving to cliff jumping. I'd done my best to talk him into a sport where I was at least tethered a secure surface. Dirt Biking. With my basic knowledge of riding a bicycle and a four-wheeler, surely Remi could handle teaching me the rest.

And I'd have to get over my acrophobia. Exposure therapy helped with paralyzing fears, and I was ready to be different, to let go of everything that'd been holding me back from being a part of a true relationship.

Lifting the binoculars, I aimed them at the front porch light and examined the front door. Mama's windchimes swayed and even with the car windows closed, their tinny sounds still made their way to my ears.

What was taking him so long?

My parents adored Remi, and they missed Jared. Papa's dream had been to pass down the farm to his only son. To work the land together. Jared had never been interested in farming, not like in the way I had. We'd lost Jared to the dream of becoming a world-famous musician back in high school. The last time I'd received a postcard from him, he'd been in Nashville.

Sure, we texted off and on. He'd tell me about his gigs. One day, I might even be able to travel and watch him play. Despite how my parents hated his choice, Jared possessed a true talent for guitar. His voice was one of the best I'd ever heard. And as his Irish twin, I had been his first fan.

My parents played house with Remi now, sending him off to the grocery store, inviting him to dinner, and running sandwiches out to the field for his lunch. It was sickening. Maddening, really.

They couldn't replace their biological child with a man who'd been a stranger to them less than a month and a half ago. But they ate up the flattery he laid out for them, buffet style, every day.

Lili shoved the last bite of her sandwich in her mouth. "Ooh. Ooh," she managed around the food in her mouth and tapped my shoulder. "The door."

I dropped the binoculars to my chest. Mr. GQ walked onto the porch, my mother hot on his heels. She waved, and he turned and responded to something she said and hopped into his truck. I suspected he'd bought his 1990s white F150 solely to bolster his role as the farmer, which was a strike against him.

We only drove Dodges in this family.

"Follow him." I nudged Lili into action. "But don't let him see you."

"That's kind of hard since we're the only two cars on the road." She shifted into gear and pulled onto the street.

We meandered to the back entrance of the Mountain Meadows neighborhood, my personal hell on Earth. He turned into the driveway of the model home and turned off his truck.

"What is he doing here?"

"He lives this close to you?" Lili asked at the same time. She drove past him and looped back to park across the street, in an inconspicuous location where we could continue our stake out.

We both ducked under the dash as he walked to his front door, spinning his keys in his hand.

"What do we do now?" Lili rested her hand on her oversized abdomen.

Remi disappeared inside his home. I had to get in there, search through his garbage, find any clue to indicate why he was here.

"We wait. When he leaves, we'll sneak inside."

"You're an expert in breaking and entering, are you?" Lili shook her head. "I don't know, Ang. Following him is one thing, but breaking into his house could get us thrown into jail. I could lose my medical license."

"Only if we get caught. I promise. We won't." I toyed with the binoculars' strap hanging around my neck. "And no one locks their doors here."

"Whatever." Lili leaned against her seat. "I'm in. But you owe me a dandelion crown. Plus, Blake has been annoyingly protective since I got knocked up."

"I don't blame him." Blake's protectiveness umbrellaed everyone he considered family, including me. "And deal."

Lili drummed her fingers against the steering wheel. "You—" she hesitated. "You must like this guy to go through all this trouble."

Like him? No, not even a little bit. A blush flushed up my neck, contradicting my thoughts. The fact was, I'd come to rely on him far too much in both my farm and personal life.

"BS." Lili pointed to the house. "I mean, have you noticed the muscles on him? And the way he treats your parents? Tell me you haven't fallen slightly in love with him."

I hadn't told Lili about seeing his text messages after the plane or about his admission to being a player. She didn't know about our deal. In any arrangement, I hated to be on lower ground than my opponent, which led me here, sitting across the street from Remi's house on a Friday night.

Something in his house would give me the edge in our arrangement. "I'm so far from in love with him I may as well be in Antarctica."

Lili's raised eyebrow, slight tilt to her head, and way she looked at me through her lowered lids told me she didn't believe me.

I turned on the radio and kept quiet. What was the point in talking if she wouldn't believe me. It didn't matter anyway. A few minutes later, Remi and Myles left the house. I couldn't help but appreciate his going-out look. He'd shoved his Stetson over his thick, dark hair. He wore fresh jeans and a tight blue shirt with the top buttons undone ... Yeah. Fantasies I'd gotten lost in the prior week resurfaced. I caged them in the back of my mind.

Maybe Lili had been right in calling BS, but attraction wasn't close to love.

They drove off in Myles' little car. We waited another few minutes. "Okay. Let's go."

I led the way across the miniscule, manicured lawn, regulating my pace so my pregnant friend could keep up.

She huffed up next to me in the alcove of the front door. "Woo, these babies take a lot out of me. That lawn felt like it was a mile long."

I kept a lookout around the corner in case they'd return for a forgotten item while Lili turned the knob.

"Crap dammit." She jiggled the door handle. "It's locked."

What? My heartbeat picked up its already racing pace. Who would go through the trouble of locking their door in small-town Idaho? The answer came to me before my question fully formed. Someone who'd spent their whole life in Dallas. Someone who had something to hide.

"Let's go around to the backyard and check for open windows." Glad I'd instructed Lili to wear dark apparel, I led the way to the back patio.

Testing out the first few windows with no success, I clenched my hands against my side.

"This place is Fort Knox." Lili stuck her hand in her pocket and pulled out a red Jolly Rancher. "I guess we can call it a night and head back home." She unwrapped the candy and popped it into her mouth.

"No. There's one more window." I pointed to the small bathroom window above our heads. "Here. Give me a boost."

"Why don't you boost me up there?"

"Are you serious? You look like you swallowed two watermelons. You wouldn't fit."

Lili folded her arms. "And I'm not supposed to lift anything heavier than a thing of paper towels. You should have thought about having a pregnant woman as an accessory to your crime."

"Here." Two patio chairs sat next to the solid sliding glass door. I dragged one over underneath the window. "Keep this stable for me."

I climbed onto the chair and tested the window. "It's open!" I whisper-shouted to Lili. "I'll climb through and let you in the front door."

"Roger that."

Shoving the window wide open, I braced my hands on the ledge and jumped. I straightened my elbows and leaned halfway through, shifting my arms in front of me.

"You good?" Lili's voice muffled through the window, currently plugged by my butt.

"I think so!" I hollered. "As long as I can get my hips through."

I scanned the area beneath me. A vanity was to my left, littered with various manly stuff, an electric razor, and beard trimmings. The bathtub and toilet were to my right. Maneuvering to the left, I shimmied further into the bathroom. As predicted, my butt lodged in the window frame.

My abs burned, but I still reached for the hand towel hanging on a ring over the sink. I pulled. The towel ring gave way as my bottom half zipped through the small opening. Curling my arms around my head, I crashed to the floor.

"Angie!"

I groaned and peeked back at the window.

"*Angie.*" Lili's fingertips appeared on the sill.

"I'm good," I called. "Meet me at the front."

Her fingertips vanished, and I stood, stretching my back. I pulled my phone from my bra and turned on its flashlight as I made my way to the front entry.

I opened the door for Lili. "Quick." I motioned her inside.

I closed the door and we both collapsed against it.

"Do you think anyone saw us?" Lili peeked out the side windows.

"No." I returned to the hall leading to the bathroom. Two bedrooms exited into the same hall, and one of them had to be Remi's. "You check that one, and I'll go through this one."

Lili nodded and took off. I walked into the room. The blankets on the bed lay jumbled in a mass. Clothes had been scattered on the floor, and several crumpled papers surrounded a small trash can underneath the desk. The Wranglers and stained white shirts gave him away.

"Lili." I poked my head back into the hallway. "This is his room."

She came to join me and searched through the garbage while I dug through his dresser. There was nothing in his underwear drawer, as I'd searched that one first. The other drawers proved just as fruitful.

"Password protected." Lili flicked the laptop closed.

I lay on my stomach and looked under the bed. The beam of my phone's flashlight caught the edge of a briefcase.

Yes.

I yanked it out from under the bed.

The sound of the front door opening echoed into the room. Hugging the briefcase to my chest, I met Lili's eyes and dove behind the bed after her.

Chapter 18

Remi

"I could've sworn I locked the door." I turned the knob and moved the door back and forth. I must be a couple sandwiches shy of a picnic.

"Weird." Myles flipped on the light switch and walked to the fridge.

I closed the door and followed in his wake. "I left my wallet and my phone on my nightstand. Be right back." We'd made it all the way to the bar and ordered drinks for the guys before I'd noticed.

Part of me wanted to stay home since Smoot joined this week's guys' night. His overuse of climbing slang made me want to shove cotton balls in my ears.

The layout of the model home was already familiar to me. I felt more at home in the three weeks I'd been here than I ever had at the big house in Dallas. I pushed the door wide to my cluttered room. For me, it was a luxury to be messy. Efficient maids invisible to me since they cleaned during work hours, did my laundry and made my bed everyday.

A luxury, yes, but it got old.

Turning on the light, I retrieved my wallet and phone and then turned to leave.

Wait a second.

A tennis shoe stuck out the end of my bed. One far too petite and feminine to be mine, and it was still laced onto a foot. In a couple of quiet strides, I stood over ... Angie?

She lay on her back, clutching my briefcase to her chest, and Lili was curled onto her side next to her. They both had their eyes closed like two naughty children. *If I can't see you, you can't see me.*

The moment she read any of those documents stored inside my case, my charade would be over. I placed my hands on my hips and glared down at them, madder than a snake in a hornet's nest. "What the hell are you doing here?"

Angie's eyes shot open, and she screamed. Lili joined in, piggybacking off Angie's reaction.

Myles ran into the room, wielding a frying pan above his head. Long strands of his hair had escaped the elastic he'd used to tie it back. "What's going on?"

"I caught these two burglarizing our place." I shoved my thumb toward the women.

Myles relaxed his stance and let the frying pan swing to his side. Really, a pan? Why hadn't he thought to grab a knife out of the block?

Angie scrambled to her feet and helped Lili up. "We weren't planning on taking anything." The handle to my case was still gripped in her fist.

"Is that right?" I inclined my head to my bag and tightened my lips into a flat line. I was going to jerk a knot into her tail!

I held my hand in front of me, waiting for her to slide the handle into my palm. She motioned like she'd do exactly that but then dug her shoulder into my stomach, knocking me off balance. My Stetson tumbled from my head to the floor. She sprinted past me and Myles.

Lili's mouth gaped open.

She stared at the spot her friend had vacated. As soon as I steadied myself, I tore after Angie.

She stood in the living room, the couch between us, wrestling with the clasp on my briefcase.

"Give it back!" I yelled.

"Not until you tell me what you're hiding!"

I lunged in one direction, only to pivot and roll over the top of the couch. Her reaction was a millisecond too slow. I snagged the briefcase. She didn't let go. We yanked the case back and forth between us like a tug of rope.

"You're so immature." I pulled her and the briefcase close to me.

She fought back, succeeding in jerking me toward the end table. My shin clipped the corner, and I clenched my teeth. With determination burning under her skirts, she was strong enough to make Samson look sensitive.

"Oh, I'm immature?" Her breaths came out in strained puffs. "This coming from a farmhand who can't even drive a *tractor*."

She braced her feet against the edge of the couch and heaved. My case slipped out of my sweaty palm. Angie fell backward onto the floor. I landed on my chest, half on the couch, half off. But my focus lasered onto the black, Italian leather briefcase given to me by my father. It hit the wall and flew open, spilling its contents everywhere.

Papers scattered onto the wood floor. Each one with a logo on it, condemning me. Not bothering to stand, Angie army crawled toward the papers. I dove and caught her foot, preventing her from going any further.

She kicked at my hands, but I hauled her, hand over hand, to me until I looped one arm around her midsection.

"Let me go!" She squirmed, hitting and kicking any part of me within range.

I managed to get to my feet, taking the irate woman with me. "Not a chance."

Myles and Lili stood next to the island in almost the exact same pose: hands over their mouths, heads tilted, and eyebrows raised.

"Lili!" Angie yelled. "Get the papers!"

Lili attempted to take a step toward the contents of my briefcase, but Myles stepped in front of her. "I think we should stay out of this. Can I get you something to drink?"

"Oh good." Her shoulders drooped over her pregnant belly. "I am sooo thirsty. I had no idea Angie planned to go this far. Otherwise, I would have packed a water bottle." Her large belly protruded much more than I'd expect for someone only seven months pregnant.

Must be the two babies in there, instead of one. Then again, I hadn't been around many pregnant women.

"Come on." Angie sagged in my arms as she watched this exchange.

Ha. I won.

She must have sensed me lowering my guard. At that precise moment, she grated her heels down my shin and bit into the fleshy part of my thumb.

"Ah-hh." I released her and waved my hand in the air, checking to see if she'd broken through my skin.

She sprinted to the pile. Not slowing, she scooped up some papers and ran to Lili's side at the kitchen table.

My chest heaved up and down with each of my labored breaths.

Angie dropped her eyes to the white sheets, briefly taking in their contents, then looked at me, her gaze clashing with mine. The air in my lungs vacated as if I'd had the wind knocked out of me.

I admired Angie's ability to be as open as a book, but now I wanted to shield myself from what I read in her eyes. Betrayal. Hatred. Anger, no *fury* ignited in her crystal-blue depths. I waited for the inevitable slew of heated words she'd sling at me. This wouldn't be the first time I'd been despised.

This job taught me how to have thick skin, but Angie pierced right through it like she had x-ray vision.

"You're with Cockrell Development." Her accusation burst out with a healthy dash of venom. "Remington James *Cockrell* the Third. Left something out there, didn't you, you lying son of a—this changes everything."

"It changes nothing. I still work for you." I grasped at the only leverage I had—my one chance to stay in Angie's life. "Or do you want me to go to the bar and tell Smoot all about our arrangement?"

Myles and Lili sat at the table, rubbernecking from Angie and back to me. Some friend Myles was. Not lifting a finger to help me.

"I'll find another Daniel. You're fired." She let the documents flutter to the ground and scowled at me. "Now it makes sense. The reason you've been so cagey about your life before you came here. You're not a cog in the corporate machine. You're the jerkoff making the cogs turn." She shook her head once and trudged past me toward the door. "Come on, Lili. Let's go."

Lili shoved a large chunk of muffin in her mouth, not moving. "Can't I finish my blueberry muffin first?"

"Take it with you." Angie paused, within reach, and turned to her friend.

"You know how finicky Blake is about food in cars."

"You ate sauerkraut and peanut butter in your car."

"That was an emergency." Lili sipped from her glass of iced tea.

Angie stomped her foot. "And this isn't?"

I wiped the sweat beading on my upper lip. This situation was spiraling out of control. I couldn't let Angie leave. This wasn't supposed to happen. I'd dealt with unexpected kinks in negotiations before, but it never felt like a red-hot poker had been shoved into my abs.

If she succeeded in firing me, I'd no longer get to look forward to bickering with her daily. Not to mention, my dreams with Myles would be a bust. Somehow, they came in second to never seeing Angie again. The power she held over me scared the shit out of me.

"Are you saying your feelings for Smoot aren't genuine?" I grabbed Angie's upper arm, and she filleted me with her eyes. "You'll have to keep up your charade all on your own." It was my one play before everything unraveled.

"I'll tell him the truth."

"Go ahead. And he'll split faster than a wet log."

"A wet log?" She rubbed her temple. "Where do you come up with ..."

Lili raised her hand like she was in a classroom. "Does a wet log split better than a dry one?"

"It does," Myles answered. "I read an article—"

"Enough!" Angie shouted and turned back to me. "My only other option is to let you keep working on the farm, hustling my parents into selling it to you."

"How 'bout we all calm down and share a glass of iced tea?" Myles held his hands out as if he stood in front of two live bombs.

"Shut up, Myles," Angie and I said in unison.

"Fine." Myles slunk back in his chair. "I'm only trying to help."

"Let this play out." Lili touched Myles' shoulder. "It's getting good." She took another bite of her muffin, settling back into her chair.

My hackles had risen at the mention of Tony and Nora. I cared for them and wanted only what was best. Selling the land would prevent bankruptcy. At this point, it was already lost. It'd be much better for someone who had their best interest at heart to ease them into the idea of off-loading rather than allowing some East Coast, faceless shark of a company take advantage of them.

I went on as if our friends hadn't spoken. "I haven't misled your parents at all."

"No?" She leaned toward me until we were nose to nose. "You're just weaseling your way into their good graces, biding your time like a snake in the grass, waiting for the perfect time to strike." She threaded her hands through her hair at her temples. "Ugh! Why won't you Cockrells leave us alone?"

And with her statement, she exposed her greatest weakness. I lowered my voice. "You can fire me. Tell your parents about me. Break it off with Smoot. But I'll never leave you alone. I'm not going anywhere. You won't have any peace until you, one," I held my pointer finger in front of her face, "sell me your farm. Or two," I lifted my second finger, "I die trying to buy it."

Sudden silence reverberated in my ears. The heat pump clicked on, and the sound of air rushing through the vents filled the void. Our eyes battled each other until she backed up a step.

"If I let you do real work, option two will come quicker than you think. 'Don't take it too hard on me.'" She air-quoted, imitating a whiny toddler.

I folded my arms and glared at her. "I can take whatever you throw at me." Wait ... What did I just say? If only I could shove my words back down my gullet.

She straightened. "Oh really? How about we amend our deal then?"

Not able to back out now without walking away with my testicles in my palm, I pressed forward. "Sure. What do you have in mind?"

"No work restrictions. I can make you do whatever I want. If you don't last until the harvest, you and your company leave us alone forever."

Gauntlet thrown, she stared me down, making a hornet look cuddly. My father should have offered Angie my job, and yet I was still better at it. I pretended to mull over her offer. She'd given me the window I'd been waiting for.

"Fine. But you can't tell your parents. And if I do make it to harvest, you sell to me without a fight." I stuck out my hand to her.

"Hold on, Ang," Lili broke in. "This has gone too far."

Angie glanced at her friend then locked onto me with her steely irises. "Do you think I'm stupid? My name isn't even on the deed."

"We both know your parents will do whatever you ask—"

"Papa will never sell—"

"Fine." I flicked my hands apart, slicing through the air and cutting her off. "How about this? If I make it to harvest, you talk to Tony in support of selling to the CD ... I mean Cockrell Development Company."

"What were you going to say?" Angie took a step toward me. "The CD what?"

I could ignore her, yet once she wanted to know something, she latched onto it, like a lion to its prey, until she was satisfied. Case in point: her, standing in my living room, dressed like a ninja.

I rolled my head, slinking it to the side before I answered. She was going to give me hell for this. "The CDC."

Angie broke into laughter, though I would call it more of a cackle.

"You nicknamed your company the CDC?" She hooted some more before continuing. "I bet you have all sorts of communicable diseases in your *business*." She inclined her head toward my crotch with a smirk.

She had to go there. And I was supposed to be the immature one in this relationship. Both Myles and Lili tittered in the background, but I remained focused on Angie.

"Do we have a deal?" I shoved my hand out to her.

She threw her hands in the air like she surrendered. "I don't know if I can make a deal with the CDC."

"How certain are you that Tony won't sell?" I challenged.

Her laughter cut short, and she narrowed her eyes. "You and your company will stop bugging us if you can't hack it? Like, never ever again?"

"Promise." I didn't falter.

"And you'll still help me with Daniel?"

"Yes." Bile rose in my throat with my short response. I choked it back down. By any means necessary. Focus on Texas Bros and my goals for the future. Even if the people I was helping along went together about as good as sardines and ice cream.

With one final glance at Lili, she firmly grasped my hand and shook it. "Then you—my useless farmhand—have a deal."

Inside, I cheered. I was one summer away from everything I'd ever dreamed of. But Angie's lack of hesitation in taking my deal castrated my excitement.

"Meet at the North field. Five a.m. Tomorrow."

"Tomorrow's Saturday. We don't work weekends."

"I do. And from now on, you do too."

Working seven days a week didn't scare me. I'd been employed since my mom took away my binky. If Angie wanted me gone, she'd have to try harder.

Still holding her hand firmly, I tugged her to me until our foreheads almost touched. "Bring it."

Her answer was a simple grin so evil it could be on the poster for the horror film *Smile*. A chill spread through my heart.

What had I gotten myself into?

Chapter 19

Remi

P ool balls clacked together behind me. Karaoke night was in full swing. The bar was packed with a ton of Swifties. Songs from her latest album were being belted into the microphone by far less than Emmy winning voices.

"Bro. If you scratch, you have to stay in the kitchen." Chuck rubbed chalk on the tip of his pool stick. He leaned against the pool table next to Pedro, pointing and making comments in Spanish.

"Haven't you ever played this before, amigo?" Pedro smoothed his mustache and scratched the side of his head.

He didn't always come with us to the bar on our at least bi-weekly bro nights. His five kids and wife took up most of his free time.

Smoot waved his hand in front of him. "Yeah, I play by different rules, though." He went to set the cue ball down, hesitated, then said, "I don't see a kitchen on this table."

All of us broke out into a round of drunken giggles. Except Blake's were non-drunken. He'd ordered his usual Coke.

Chuck grabbed his beer and took a swig. "Dude. It's behind this dot." He pressed his finger into the pearl circle in line with the headstring.

"Oh. Yeah. I knew that." Smoot adjusted his glasses, set his ball down, and took his shot. Bad move buddy. He'd make his shot, but ... Smoot tapped the cue ball, sending it sailing. It ricocheted off the three-ball and into the side pocket.

I threw my scotch back. I needed to be drunker to survive this night. What did Angie see in him? More importantly, why had I agreed to hang out with him? "Sam!" I hollered across the counter and got the bartender's attention. "Can I get another?"

He nodded but finished serving the mayor and his wife, plus all the friends I'd made from the farm store.

"Hey, Remi!" Agnus hollered while Mitch and Joe tipped their beers to me.

Sam set a full tumbler in front of me. "Rough night?"

I raised my scotch to my farm store friends and answered him, "An unexpected bend in the road, but I'll get it figured out." Tonight, Angie emerged the victor, or so she thought. If I could have picked this outcome, I would have. I had a clear path set before me to achieve all my goals. Yet, looking at Smoot fumble with his cue stick, I didn't revel in the victory like usual.

She picked this whirlie over me?

Blake twisted toward me in his stool. He narrowed his eyes. "You didn't tell me about your job," he hedged.

Oh, great. Lili must have texted him. "It's just business."

"You know it'll crush her to lose her land?"

I slumped backward until the bar pressed into my spine, my elbows edging onto the counter, my scotch clutched in my right hand. "I have no doubt she'll land on her feet."

Pedro cheered as Chuck sank the eight ball in the corner pocket. Game over. I let out a short puff of air. Smoot still had five balls on the table.

"You could have told me at the crib raising." Blake finished off his Coke, slammed his glass on the bar, and stood. "You're even more screwed than I imagined." He directed a sympathetic grimace my way.

I didn't respond to him, and he didn't wait for me to.

Blake checked his watch then sauntered to Chuck and Pedro. "One more game, and I've got to get home."

Smoot handed him his stick and loped toward me. Swiveling my head to the right and then to the left, I couldn't find an escape hatch. I wasn't drunk enough for this conversation.

"Hey." Smoot sat on the seat Blake had vacated. "Thanks for this. I'm having an epic time."

Everything he said felt forced, like he was an actor on a stage. Nerves, maybe? "No problem." I drained my drink, caught Sam's eye, and pointed at my empty glass.

"So, uh, I was wondering if you knew any of Angie's favorite places. Other than her farm, of course."

Even in my foggy state, I recalled the details I'd cataloged about Angie. "City of the Rocks. She and her dad used to go camping there."

"Perfect. Thanks."

"What are you planning?" I asked while Sam traded my empty glass for a full one.

Blake, Pedro, and Chuck burst out in simultaneous cheers and groans. By the looks of it, Blake was cleaning house. Being sober gave him an unfair advantage.

Smoot leaned close to me. Fermented barley and yeast clung to his breath. "Can I tell you a secret?"

No. Please don't, my mind pleaded, my mouth too slow to respond before Smoot continued talking.

"I want to propose to Angie."

My elbows slipped off the bar, and I nearly fell from my stool, my drink sloshing over the edge. "Hold on. What?"

"I know I've only known her for a month—"

Not quite a month.

"—but from the first time I chatted with her, I just knew she's the one. Why wait when you know, you know?"

"Because it's the rest of your life you're talking about." I wiped at the liquid I'd spilled on my shirt. "Don't you think you should wait a little longer? At least a couple months?"

"Oh yeah, man. I'm in the planning stage. Make sure everything is good to go, you know. Not going to propose for another month, probably two."

My throat went dry. If he said *you know,* one more time, I'd tell him just what I knew. I struggled to swallow. Propose? He didn't understand Angie, not half as well as I did. Yet, after what she'd discovered tonight, I doubted I'd be able to get any closer to her.

What did I care? This was good for me. The sooner Smoot proposed, the sooner I'd have my freedom. This fit right into my three-step plan. Step two: Let Smoot have her. "Congratulations. This calls for some celebrating. Next rounds on me!" I shouted above the music. Everyone cheered and clambered to the bar.

I slapped Smoot on the back. "Now. Let's get you up on that stage."

Keeping my hand on his shoulder, I propelled a less-than-enthusiastic Smoot forward with Blake, Pedro, and Chuck trailing behind.

Chapter 20

Angie

My jaw cracked with my third consecutive yawn. Dark clouds on the horizon hid the rising sunshine and mimicked my mood. Until the cancer made it impossible for him to work, Papa had often taken care of the early chores and let me sleep in until eight.

Eight o'clock mornings became the standard with the responsibilities around this place resting entirely in my hands. I much preferred working into the night rather than waking before dawn—and I hadn't considered when making the deal with Remi, in torturing him, I'd also included myself.

The glowing face of my watch showed fifteen after five. My eye twitched. Remi was late. Maybe he wouldn't show up at all, and I'd already rid myself of his presence. Relief, combined with a sense of disappointment, swirled together within me.

His leaving would solve so many of my problems, but he'd also take with him my newfound excitement. The adventures would end, and I'd return to normal life's monotony. Plus, I'd kiss my chances with Dan goodbye. I should have been more disappointed at the thought of Daniel exiting my life, but I was simply numb to everything—everything except the burning fury of seven suns I directed through a magnifying glass at Remi.

How could I have been so blind? I'd gotten myself tangled up with the one man bent on my destruction.

I turned my shoulder into a frigid gust of wind, stepping forward to prevent it from knocking me over. The brief warm spell in the last couple of weeks of April plummeted into near-winter temperatures in early May. Pebbles of dirt stung my exposed cheek. Roller-coaster Idaho weather, much like Remi, came with the job, and they couldn't be fired. I couldn't be happier about how it behaved right now. Remi would be sandblasted by this wind all day.

Before last night, I'd started looking forward to the time I'd spent working with him. He had a kindness in him I couldn't ignore. Life with him in it was never boring.

The knife in my back still stung. He'd lied to me. The bastard.

I tucked my chin further into my jacket, wishing I'd brought my truck and not the tractor without a cab. It'd be worth it. An inconvenience for me now meant the preservation of my farm. My security blanket. The only thing keeping me upright in my lopsided world. By the end of this summer, CDC would never send another representative to harass us again.

My eye twitched again, and I rubbed at it. Dagnabbit! He'd given me eye spasms. If he stayed here much longer, my whole body would be convulsing soon.

Remi's headlights became visible through the swirling dust, bouncing along the canal road. He hadn't left town in the night. Darn. Rays of sun broke through the clouds as he stopped next to the oldest tractor we owned.

He shut his truck door, pointing behind me. "What is that?" he shouted over the wind.

I didn't respond until he came close enough for me to communicate without shouting. He hadn't bothered shaving. His pale skin and bags under his eyes showed how much fun he'd had last night at Tractor's Grille. Using his body as a wind block, I gestured to the old Case tractor I'd nicknamed Oscar the Grouch. The budding daylight illuminated its creamy white hood. Surface rust peeked out from the worn orange loader arms and wheel wells. Rust covered the entire bucket with the occasional speck of paint. The thought of the uncomfortable hours I'd spent as a child in the metal tractor seat with no back almost caused the muscles in my butt to cramp.

I couldn't stop my lips from curling into a wicked smile. "I'd like to introduce you to Oscar. Oscar, meet Remi."

"It's ancient."

"He still runs."

"It doesn't have a cab."

"Precisely," I sang in a bubbly voice.

Though his face was shadowed in the pre-dawn light, I easily read the displeasure he attempted to disguise with a half-grin.

"Great." His over-the-top fake enthusiasm made it obvious his true intent was sarcasm. "What am I doing today?" He rubbed his gloved hands together, and I almost felt bad for him. Almost.

"You, my heartless destroyer of farmland—"

"Cute." He raised one eyebrow and shook his head at me.

"—are going to pick rock," I announced like I held a megaphone.

He waited as if he expected me to continue. "Pick which rock?"

"All of it." I giggled, taking way too much pleasure in this.

Picking rock haunted the dreams of every single kid who'd ever worked on a farm in this valley. Each year, the rock floated to the surface and had to be removed by hand before the field could be planted. Countless hours of my life had been spent sweeping from one end of the field to the other until I cleared it. An endless battle in a valley once covered in lava.

I walked over to the tractor's bucket and hefted a jagged rock the size of a watermelon. "You take this." My voice strained. "And put it into here." I dropped the chunk of basalt into the bucket. It landed with a loud gong against the metal.

"That's not a rock. It's a boulder."

My laugh turned almost maniacal, much like Angelina Jolie when she played Maleficent. "Yes. It is. And they're everywhere." The tractor's headlights illuminated the varying mounds speckling the entire field. "Good luck." I sent him a mock salute.

Remi turned full circle; his arms spread wide.

"Keys?" I held my palm to him, with the key to the tractor in it. Remi went to grab it, but I pulled it away. "I'll exchange it for the key to your truck ... Orrr ... would you like to give up and save yourself months of pain? In that case, I'll drive Oscar home."

"Where are you going?"

I yawned again. "Back to bed," I lied.

Farmers didn't have the luxury of sleep during the season. As much as my bed called to me, I'd be discing the pasture up until I met with the irrigation guy about replacing the pivot tire and sprucing up the same pivot's engine, then I'd rush home for a nap before I headed to the hospital. But I preferred to make Remi think of me curled up in my down comforter while he faced this wind.

He tugged the hood of his jacket tighter around his ears and rubbed at his upper arms.

"Once you finish this field, you can start on the next one. Get it done by tonight. We'll be planting corn tomorrow. Oh, and Mae's stall has been neglected, the chicken coop is also due to be cleaned again, and the haystack fell over. It'll need fixing. You've got a full day ahead of you. I don't think you'll be leaving at your usual time."

I patted his shoulder. Leverage was power, and I loved having it.

His grin tightened almost into a grimace, but he handed over his keys, taking the ones to the tractor. "Any trick to getting it started?"

"Prayer. A lot of prayer." I smirked, not willing to give him any more help.

He'd have to figure things out by himself from here on out. Easy button privileges had been revoked the moment I saw the watermark of his company on the pages in his briefcase.

How many times did we have to tell them no for them to get the hint? We were never going to sell. My kids and grandkids would play on this soil, the ground their great-grandparents had homesteaded when this valley had been settled.

Now the power to toy with an executive in their ranks fell into my lap, and I'd have way too much fun running him off the property. I wasn't going to tell him to put the tractor in neutral and let it roll next to him while he threw in the rock. Let him figure that out by himself.

"Sounds good." He stretched his arms; the wind buffeted his thick coat sleeves. "This is just the workout I needed." Jogging in place, he did a couple of tuck jumps and started in on the rock.

I laughed at his optimism, knowing by noon, it'd give way to despair. Chuckling all the way to the truck, I climbed in, only to be enveloped by his scent. Minty cedar and the mountain air. My mind instantly went back to my chest pressed against his, his breath tickling my lips, and the heat in his eyes consuming me.

No longer chilled, my body warmed from the inside out.

I shoved the truck in reverse. Slamming my foot on the gas, I propelled backward, spitting chunks of dirt and small rocks into the undercarriage.

This was war. A war I couldn't afford to lose. The trenches were dug, barbed wire strung, weapons primed and ready to be fired, trained on Remington James Cockrell the Third. My nemesis. My adversary.

My enemy.

Chapter 21

Remi

Several hours after the sun had set, with my arms as weak as twigs, I set the last rock in Oscar's bucket. My head still pounded from the remnants of last night's hangover. After Smoot dropped his wedding plans bombshell, I'd stayed way too late and had way too much to drink. I might have still been buzzed this morning when I met Angie.

The buzz left soon after she had, and the ensuing headache made me determined never to touch liquor again. Morning winds had only gained in strength throughout the day. Summer would be in full swing back at home. By this time of year, I'd be lounging by the pool. I missed the Texas sun. True, it burned hotter than a honeymoon hotel, but I missed the consistency it provided me. Once I returned, I'd never complain about it again.

The temptation to return to the ease of the life I'd been born into—the parties. The fun. The leisure. The ability to set my own schedule. Most of all, the *rest*—became almost irresistible. My old life hung before me like a mirage in a desert wasteland.

Within the first hour of becoming acquainted with the Case tractor, I understood Angie's nickname for it. It was the grouchiest farm equipment on Earth. It only worked after I cussed at it and beat the steering wheel until the palms of my hands stung.

The one bright spot in my day had been when I took a small break to share a home-cooked lunch with Tony and Nora. Even that was short-lived. Angie had walked downstairs, dressed in her nursing scrubs, and rushed me outside to get the chicken coop and stable cleaned, along with feeding all the animals, including the pigs and the devil rooster—who'd managed to draw blood during this encounter.

And damned if, even in the midst of my misery, I didn't feel drawn to Angie. Her dark-blue hospital scrubs triggered all my hospital fantasies. In an instant, my mind threw me into a supply closet with her, boxes of bandages and whatnot falling around our bodies. Her legs locked around my waist.

It didn't matter how many times I reminded my body she was the source of my torture ... it still responded to her. However, the longer I spent shoveling shit, the more my fantasies turned to dump a whole wheelbarrow full of animal excrement over her.

Once I'd finished the animal chores, I forced myself to return to the field where the rocks waited. I had no idea what time it was. I'd been working in the beam of the tractor's headlights for the past few hours at least.

I trudged to the maddening machine, shoved it into gear, and chugged into the massive mound of rocks I'd collected throughout the day. It took all my body weight to shove the lever forward and get the bucket to dump the rock.

Each bump I hit jarred the length of my spine. I intended on downing a whole bottle of ibuprofen and soaking in an Epsom salt bath the moment I walked into the model home.

Turning the tractor in the direction of the farmhouse, I jolted forward. I probably could walk faster than this thing drove. As I slammed my foot onto the rusty pedal, the engine revved into high gear only to sputter and die.

"Damn, piece of *shit!*" I threw my head back and screamed at the top of my lungs.

I jumped to the ground and gave the tractor a solid kick to the front tire. Pain exploded in my foot and up into my shin. I continued along the canal road. Hobbling now, I cursed Angie, the land, my family—anything and everyone who'd brought me to this moment in my life.

Fifteen minutes later, I hugged my bright white truck which basked in the light of the front porch. The rest of the house was dark, and the ever-present ring of the windchimes reverberated around me. Both Nora and Tony were probably in bed, and, with the absence of their red and white beast, Angie had taken their ancient Dodge to work. I couldn't be more grateful. If she were still here, I couldn't guarantee her safety from me.

With my strength waning, I drove to the model home and parked my truck in the driveway, my frozen fingers fumbling with the shifter. The brilliant stars shined in the dark sky as I wobbled through the front door and collapsed on the living room floor. Finally, out of the blasting wind, the relative quiet of the house hummed against my wind-burnt ears.

"What happened to *you?*" Myles paused the show he was watching and set his can of beer on the end table.

It was no wonder I'd caught his attention so fully. Dirt and shit of the chicken, horse, and pig variety covered me, and straw and hay poked at me under all my clothing and were sure to be in my hair. The scratch on my cheek still oozed blood where the rooster had attacked me. Aside from visibly being hashed, my body ached all over.

"Angie." I rubbed my hands over my face, grimacing when I thought about what could possibly be on them.

Willing energy into my leg muscles, I stood and moved toward the bathroom, focused on nothing but the hot water of my shower. Too dirty to think of the Epsom salt bath I'd contemplated on the way here, I walked behind Myles as I peeled off my jacket, dropping it on the floor.

"Told you you'd regret ever making that deal with her." He laughed.

I closed my eyes and listed again the reasons for this torture. "You know what's at stake. I'll be able to start the business we dreamed of with the money from this sale. Once I close this deal, I can rid myself of both my father and my brother. I don't have to be the bad guy anymore. All I have to do is survive for the next few months."

I swallowed hard. I couldn't think about returning to the farm tomorrow morning, let alone going back for months of this. Real tears stung the base of my eyes.

"And Kathryn?"

Kathryn. As determined as a she-bear in satin, she still hadn't stopped texting me. Her messages had slowed to once a day instead of two to three times a day, though, without much encouragement from me.

I didn't respond to Myles' taunting and groaned at the pain involved in the motions of removing my shirt.

Myles laughed again. "Why don't you quit and find another way?"

"And let her win?" My frustration renewed my strength as I marched into the bathroom and turned on the shower. I stomped back into my room to get a towel from my closet. "No."

Myles stood by the bathroom door. "Come on, man." He shook his head as he glanced at my once-new Wranglers. "You're working harder for this deal than you ever have in the past. Do you really think you can keep this up until November?"

"November? I thought harvest ended in September."

"I talked to Chuck and Pedro. Some farmers don't harvest corn until mid-November."

May. June. July ... I counted on my fingers as I ran through the months. Six and a half months. My confidence deflated.

"Maybe you could approach Tony and Nora. They have the final say on the sale, after all."

Though Myles had a point, my gut told me Nora and Tony wouldn't sell without Angie's approval. Plus, I enjoyed the relationship I'd established with them. Angie may hate me, but her parents loved me. So, I might be reveling in love from stable parents for the first time in my life. I didn't have my parents' respect, let alone love.

"It's not the right time." I pushed past him, walked into the bathroom, and stripped to my boxers. "If I bring it up now, then everything I've done up to this point would have been for nothing."

Steam billowed against the glass shower doors and filtered into the bathroom, beginning to fog the mirror. I breathed in the steam, the memory of my sauna and hot pool etching intense longing into my soul. I forced the ache back into the netherworld of my mind. I never considered myself lazy, but compared to my new workload, my life in Dallas was filled with ease.

"I know what I'm doing," I said more to my blurry reflection than to Myles. I couldn't help counting the short hours I had left before I returned to the farm. I groaned again.

At least, I hoped I knew what I was doing.

Chapter 22

Remi

Although I'd adapted to my increased workload, my entire body still ached from the tips of my hair to the tail end of my pinky toe. Not to mention the bruise healing from another nip Mae gave me. That horse disagreed with everything I did and made my life on this farm as difficult as she possibly could—much like her owner.

It'd been a month since Angie found me out and became my unleashed taskmaster. A month of hauling bags of pig and chicken feed, plus fifty-pound bags of grain and bucking hay, caused a knot in my shoulders that wouldn't go away. At least the fields had all been planted, and I was no longer subjected to picking rock.

I was beginning to understand the true meaning of manual labor.

The chill days of May eased into the warmer temperatures of June. The midday sun beat down on the brim of my Stetson. Nothing hindered it. No clouds. No trees. Cows grazed on bright green grass on the other side of the creek.

A creek I couldn't manage to get across.

I stood on the footboards of the four-wheeler, which was currently submerged in water. Twisting on the throttle, I attempted to dislodge the tires from the mud. It sank deeper until half the tailpipe gurgled and hissed beneath the surface. I'd driven dirt bikes up steep, shaly passes, yet I couldn't get this ATV to jump a simple stream.

The first time, I'd gotten distracted by the challenge of the creek when I was moving the cows from the north pasture to the one on the western side of the property. Today was no different ... except I should have known better. I'd approached it at the right angle but hadn't given the ATV enough throttle and ended up short of the bank on the far side.

If I hadn't hit the throttle hard as I arched downward, I could have been crushed by the four-wheeler. As it was, I remained seated, but my mechanical steed needed pulling out.

Angie was going to give me an earful for this, but I reveled in the possibility of seeing her face all scrunched in irritation. Anytime I managed to get under her skin was a victory for me. Gone was the Angie who explained the things I did wrong, like I was a toddler learning to ride a bike, replaced by a more vocal, demanding woman. Her obvious underlying frustration at my ineptitude gave me immeasurable pleasure, considering the torture she put me through.

How had I ever been attracted to someone so domineering, controlling, and bent on seeing me fail? Well, I would show her how we Texans were more stubborn than the long summer days our state was famous for.

Mud, flicked from my irrigation boot, smeared on the black leather seat as I looped my leg over it and hopped into the creek. It was deeper than I'd anticipated, and water gushed over the edge of my boot, soaking my jeans and my socks.

Damnation. I sucked so bad at being a farmer, and I wasn't used to sucking at anything.

My phone buzzed in my pocket as I walked into the pasture where the cows still ogled me. Wind buffeted against my wet jeans, and goosebumps rose on my arms despite the rising afternoon heat.

I tucked my gloves in my back pocket and answered the FaceTime call. My brother—calling to check in. Happy day.

"Hey, bro. What're you up to?" I answered in an overly chipper way that I knew annoyed the shit out of him. The wind picked up, nearly blowing off my cowboy hat I'd come to appreciate for more than its looks. I placed my hand on the top of it until the gust of wind died down.

"Remi?" Matthew, never Matt, leaned closer to the camera on his phone. His thick mahogany brown hair and brown eyes matched mine, but the similarities ended there. "What the hell are you wearing?"

My brother was so contrary, he floated upstream. I held my phone at a distance so he could get the full effect of my mud-splattered jeans, and my now-stained white shirt with my pecks and biceps stretching against the fabric. My muscles had bulked up with Nora's lunches and Angie's workload.

Not a bad side effect. "My new work clothes. I could still kill it at the club wearing this, don't you think?"

Matthew put his forehead in his hand and shook his head. "Have you made any progress?"

Ah, right, my real job. They called me 'The Finisher' back at the office, like some sort of superhero name. I almost had a costume made with a big 'F' sewn on the front, but then I figured that would get misconstrued.

"These things take time, but I think I'll convince Angie to let me drive the bigger tractors soon." I laughed but grimaced when I looked back at the ATV. Maybe not.

"You been there for over two months. The Johnsons haven't even been informed of our offer. Stop playing farmer and do your job."

The engine noise of a tractor sounded from over the rise. How did Angie always know when I'd made an ass of myself? I swore she spied on me. "If I tell them about my real job and my offer right now, then I'll be as successful as you and Pop were. You told me I could take as much time as I needed to get it done. This one's going to take months. I'm working my angle."

"Your angle gets you into trouble. That Kathryn girl showed up asking about you couple weeks back." He raised his eyebrow and tipped his head forward, making his recently acquired double chin quite apparent.

"You didn't tell her anything, did you?"

"I try to stay out of your soap operas."

"What are you talking about? I'm as wholesome as they come." For the past two months, I'd been the star of my own small-town romance. My wardrobe, truck, and Stetson were spot on. If only I had a dog, a closet full of flannel, and a tragic past ...

"How many months are you talking?" Matthew ignored my joke, steering the conversation back on track. "Give me some parameters. I already have a waiting list ready to buy the lots when they become available."

Dust whipped into my eye, and I rubbed at it. "I'm not sure. Two, if a miracle happens, but more likely six months." If I could survive that long. I thought of my store and being freed from my family's business. One last paycheck, one last job, and I'd have it. Had I known then what I knew now, would I have still taken my father's deal?

Without a doubt, yes. I couldn't stand being the man who ripped properties from families who'd farmed them for one hundred years. Sure, I was good at it, but it was such a downer.

The engine noise grew louder. Even with Angie in on my double life, I wasn't ready to subject her to my older brother. He'd ruin everything I'd worked for.

"Get it down closer to two. I believe in miracles." His flat tone indicated otherwise. The wind made it hard to hear Matthew's response. "And answer Kathryn's messages, so I don't have to be the one doing your dirty work."

My nocturnal activities nettled my brother, which gave me a good reason to continue with the status quo. Sometimes I opted to take girls back to my parents' mansion and surrounding grounds. My brother lived in the guest house on the property, while I preferred to crash in the pool house.

These were our buildings by unspoken agreement, which suited me fine. More often than not, the women I took home swung by a day or two later and ended up finding Matthew. Considering my job, I should be good at hard conversations, at break ups. Where I could handle them, I didn't like the tears, so my brother provided the perfect solution.

I made it clear before starting up with any woman I wasn't looking for commitment. This didn't slow down the gold-diggers and the hopeless romantics. For those women looking for love yet determined to warm my bed, I'd tried to make it abundantly clear I wasn't a good guy. I neither deserved to be loved nor did I want to be tied down by it. The pool house arrangement was exceptionally convenient in my book.

"I'll do my best."

Angie parked the tractor next to me.

"I gotta go," I said without looking at my brother and hung up on him while he was mid-sentence.

Angie wore her typical button-up plaid shirt with jeans and her cowboy boots. She was as hot as a two-dollar pistol on that tractor, and how I loathed her.

She placed one hand on her waist and shoved a finger at the stuck four-wheeler. Her hip jutted out, accentuating her figure with all the curves and softness I appreciated. I blinked and narrowed my eyes, refocusing my mind on the true nature of my taskmaster. She'd made my life hell, and I'd had enough.

"How did you manage to do it again?" A strand of her hair slipped loose from her ponytail and fluttered in front of her narrowed eyes.

"I was going after a calf," I lied, but it sounded like a legit reason to go crashing into a creek.

"And last week when this happened?"

"That calf's a sneaky little bastard." I shot her a humorless smile, but she saw through my lie.

"You don't have to do anything with the calves. They're with their mamas."

I shrugged. She got me.

"Son of a monkey!" she shouted and shoved her hands in her hair. I found her tendency to swear like an old man cute. "You do more damage than good."

As cute as a spine on a cactus. That comment was all the opening I needed. In two strides, I covered the ground between us, so I stood right in front of her, forcing her to look up at me, the shadow from my brim covering half her face. "Don't give me that. You have been working me so hard I barely have time to get everything done. It's no wonder I make a few mistakes trying to keep up."

"A teenager could do the work I ask you to do."

"A teenager wouldn't last a minute. I doubt anyone could hold up to your standard," I said loud enough to ensure she heard me over the wind gusts. "I mean, I'm working until midnight with a headlamp most nights to finish the shit you have on your lists, and all you do is criticize me when I slip up. If this farm had an HR department, I'd report you." I folded my arms and leaned to the side.

Her lips twitched upward. "HR is in the kitchen having an early dinner. Be my guest." She gestured toward the house. "Though the severance package they offer will be in the form of baked goods." The spark in her eyes jumped like hot grease on a skillet.

Oh, she thought I was giving up, the frustrating little porcupine. I dropped my hands to my sides and leaned within inches of her face. "You won't get rid of me that easy."

Her characteristic tropical aroma filled my nose, and in an instant, my anger fled, replaced by a strong desire to pull her to me and shut her up with my lips. Frustrating woman. How could I want to throw her into the creek and kiss her all at the same moment?

In my weakness, I brushed the stray hair back behind her ear, and she stiffened, stepping back from me. But her distance didn't stop the heat or the current of anticipation encasing us.

Consequences be damned, I lifted my hand to—to do I didn't know what. Possibly pull her to me and kiss her senseless so she'd see me as more than a farmhand hired by her parents to torment. More than the man sent here to buy her farm. More than the tool she used in her attempt to date Smoot. Her phone pinged, and I never got the chance to figure out what my hand would have done as she stepped even further from me. Which left me with my arm lifted in the air. I raised my hat and brushed my hand through my hair before setting it back in place, hoping she didn't notice my awkwardness.

I didn't need to worry. Her eyes were glued to her phone, thumbs typing rapidly.

"Him again?"

She nodded. "I have another date with Dan. A big one. He wants to go dirt biking in a couple of weeks." She walked back to the tractor, retrieving the chains.

So, it was Dan now. Not Smoot, or Daniel. Just Dan. I guess that was good for me, considering I'd been put in charge of this catfishing operation. Over the past three weeks, he'd been a pain in my side. Boise wasn't far enough away. Smoot would show up at the most inconvenient times. I'd walk in with an armload of wood and there they'd be, cozying up playing cards.

At what point had he met the parents? Game night was *mine*. Smoot needed to back on out of my way, or I'd ... do absolutely nothing because this was the plan all along! I took a deep breath. Okay. I might as well admit it. I was jealous of not only the time he spent with Angie but also of the time he spent with Tony and Nora. At what point had I become so possessive of the Johnsons?

"Have you even ridden a dirt bike? A motorcycle? Anything on two wheels except for a bicycle? And have you forgotten your fear of heights?" My questions came out more intense than I intended. "You'll be driving that dirt bike on mountain roads that have cliffs."

She walked past me to the creek. "I *used* to have a fear of heights."

I pushed the brim of my cowboy hat up, tilted my head, and raised my eyebrows at her.

With one look at my expression, she quickly pressed on. "I'll get over it. And I can learn to ride a dirt bike. Besides, isn't it part of the deal for you to prepare me for that?" She hooked a chain around the hitch of the ATV.

"You could barely make it up a telephone pole, and now you think you're ready to ride a dirt bike up shaly mountain passes?" I straightened the length of the chain and secured it to the tractor, a hard edge in my response.

The longer Smoot was in her life, the more he'd grow to annoy me until he surpassed my brother on that front. I couldn't let Angie be collateral when that 100-jump wonder's stupidity caused an accident. Land deal or not.

"I can manage." The waiver in her voice betrayed her confidence. "You want me to give up, so you win. Spoiler alert. I'm *not* giving in. I'm *not* selling my land."

Oh, she was going to sell. She just didn't know it yet. I ground out a breath, harnessing the tension in my fingertips. Why did this have to be so difficult? "What do you want me to do this time?"

"Isn't it obvious?" She threw her arms out in front of her once again. "Teach me to ride a dirt bike. I can do it." She made her way back to the tractor with a stiff, determined stride.

She'd be led along an abandoned mountain path by a man she'd lied to from day one. A man she memorized lists of terms to even understand what he was saying. A man so conceited he couldn't take enough time to spot the lies Angie told him. The enigma she presented.

I'd interacted with my share of girls and not one of them was as intriguing as her. Even if she made my life as difficult as putting socks on her devil rooster.

One of the reasons I couldn't rid myself entirely of my attraction to Angie was, despite being handed one of the hardest challenges life had to offer—watching someone she loved dearly carved away by cancer—her view on the world remained positive. She believed the best in everyone, albeit naively. Re: her blind trust in Smoot.

"I like that about you. You're optimistic." The words slipped from my mouth before I had a chance to swallow them.

She paused with her foot propped on her tractor and crinkled her eyebrows together. "Like it's that hard to ride a dirt bike. I'll definitely be better at it than you, Mr. I-can't-forge-a-creek."

I was almost relieved she interpreted my comment with a sarcastic lens. Upon straightening my shoulders, new life sparked into me. I'd much rather fight with Angie than delve into my true and impossible feelings for her. "Whatever. The first time you tip your bike, you'll cry like a nanny goat for its mama."

She laughed. "You say the strangest things. A goat? I remind you of a goat? And a baby goat is a kid, by the way."

"Nanny goat sounds better."

"Are all Texans as weird as you?"

"Yes, ma'am. But not as stubborn as you. And that's saying something. Bless your heart." I hooked my thumbs in my belt loop and put every ounce of Southern twang I had into my voice.

"Don't call me ma'am."

"What's wrong with calling you ma'am? Just trying to be polite." I'd been programmed to speak like this since birth. Yes, sir. No, sir. Yes, ma'am. No, ma'am. A bit of a cold relationship with my parents, but at the very least it was respectful.

"Do I look like I'm old enough to be your mama?"

"No."

"Then don't call me ma'am."

"Why are you hell-bent on winning over Smoot anyway?" I veered the subject back to the real thorn in her life. "You shouldn't have to pretend to be something you're not to get a man. Not a man worth having."

"Like you never lie to the *many* women you date?"

"Nope. I'm so honest you could play poker with me over the phone." I quirked my lips into a half smile.

"Do you ever think you could find one woman to settle down with? Spend forever with?"

My parents' open-door relationship destroyed the lies I'd been told about true love. Plato's theory that we were all down here searching for our other half was full of bull honky. I'd chosen not to waste my life on a futile search for my soulmate.

Angie didn't compute in this declared bachelor lifestyle. If any guy treated her like I treated the women I took back to the pool house, I'd be tempted to punch them in the gut.

Why? I didn't know. One thing I did know—"Nothing lasts forever," I said aloud, my thoughts once again escaping from my head.

"Love does. Look at my parents."

Tony and Nora. The one exception to my theory, and yet their love was still ending in heartbreak.

"For every one of them, there are hundreds of others like my parents." I tried to pass my comment off as a joke with a nudge. "You have more faith in the world than I have."

She didn't bite and pulled herself back onto her seat. Her lips tugged into a slight frown. "How sad your life must be—but of course you're an evil overlord, so it makes sense."

Starting the diesel engine, she slammed the glass cab door before I had a chance to respond.

"You still owe me tractor lessons. And don't think Oscar counts!" I shouted at her, but she made a motion like she couldn't hear me.

I took out my phone and texted her. *No dirt bike lessons until you teach me to drive the big tractor.*

In every negotiation, always keep the upper hand.

Chapter 23

Remi

The green, hulking, metal machine stood in front of me, waiting to be tamed. I'd driven every recreational machine under the sun, but I hadn't branched into heavy equipment. Angie kicked at the soil beside me and chewed on her nails.

The dirt rose in the air and blew away in the stiff breeze. A few months before I came here, Myles complained often about the winds. I found them refreshing, not stagnant and filled with car exhaust or heavy fast-food byproducts. My eyes focused past the dissipating dust to the ground, still mostly brown, but it was broken up by tiny bright-green sprigs of—corn? The only way I could identify the plants pushing out of the ground was the location of the fields and the direct connection to helping Angie load the planter with the kernels.

Corn I'd help plant. I left the tractor behind me and crouched near my baby plants. "Look, Angie." I peeked up at her with what I was sure was a goofy grin and her face softened into a smile. "The little baby corns. They're *growing*."

I couldn't describe the pride washing over me as I looked down the rows of green fledgling sprouts. I had a part in their existence. Leaning onto all fours, I put my face right next to the row and brushed my fingers over their delicate leaves. I'd never experienced anything like this.

Angie let a funny laugh out her nose. I was surprised I even got that much of a reaction from her. She tried to stay cold and indifferent with me since seeing the letterhead, but the chemistry between us didn't budge.

I sat back onto my knees. "What? I had to touch them. They're so cute."

Squatting with her elbows on her knees, she joined me. "It never gets old. Watching the miracle of life every season." She took the delicate leaf between her fingers.

Our knuckles touched, and she jerked her hand away as if she'd been burned. I'd spent more time with this woman than any other, even possibly, my own mother. Yet she'd taken to treating me like a prickly cactus.

I stared into her eyes and licked my lips. Slowly. Deliberately. For the briefest second, she focused on my moistened lips. Yeah. She still wanted me. "I understand why you love doing this. It's hard work but with such a great reward. I mean you can see your work grow. Not many career fields are like that."

My eyes followed the arch of her eyebrow. What would it be like to trace its subtle curve with my finger and brush my thumb along her high cheekbones, flushed pink by the wind. My hand would then move to the back of her neck and then I'd pull her close and solve the mystery of what it'd be like to feel the warmth of her full lips beneath mine.

I shook my head. I was a masochist. She literally tortured me from dawn until dusk, and I kept coming back. The only thing I wanted from Angie was her land. Smoot could have her.

"Remi?" She tilted her head, and I recentered my focus, doing my best to ignore her parted lips. "What's it like to travel?"

I stood and dusted off my knees. My jeans no longer looked new and were now spotted with oil stains and small rips where they'd caught on barbed wire. I turned to go back to the tractor. "Magical. And exhausting."

Angie caught up to me, placing her hand at my elbow. I paused and stared at where her palm rested on me. The hair on my forearm stood up, chills raised by her simple touch.

"Wait. You have to give me more than that." Her hand fell away from my arm. "You see. I've never left Idaho."

"For reals?"

"Yeah. Why is that such a surprise? I'm a farmer. I can't leave." She folded her arms over her abdomen.

"You want your life to be this way?" Even with the miracle of the plants I'd grown, the desire of owning a massive farm like this flared out within the first twenty minutes of working it. Yet, Angie didn't know anything different. Life could be so much more than pigpens and chicken coops, or day after day spent dealing with all forms of excrement.

"Yes."

I believed her answer about as far as I could spit. "Sure, you do. Sounds more like a prison to me."

"Not all of us have the luxury of being a nomad with a helmet on our backpack."

I paced toward the tractor but then spun back to face her, ready to call her on her bluff. "If you're so satisfied with your life, why did you lie to Smoot?"

Her mouth opened and closed without any words coming out. I had her in checkmate.

"And you're the expert in honesty, huh?"

So, she wanted to go down that road. *Okay, Angie. I'll see your argument and raise you one.* "And you're looking for meaningless sex? I'm sure there are a lot of guys around here you could put a lot less effort into, and they'd give you what you want."

"You're awful." She left me by the tractor and marched back to the truck.

But I wasn't about to let her off that easily. "What about my tractor lesson? You can forget about dirt biking ..."

She stopped. I had her trapped. In a few more weeks, I'd have her maneuvered into a corner, begging me to buy her land. This thought didn't give me the pleasure it should have. Tearing Angie's entire life apart was never my intention. Would I be willing to destroy her to make my dreams come true?

"Fine." She shoved me toward the tractor. "Get in."

I climbed into the cab. Dirt puffed into the air as I sat on the cloth seat.

"Make sure that level is pulled to the N—that means neutral."

I laughed. I'd driven a Formula One race car, and here I was being told what the big N meant on the gear shifter. Angie continued to describe all the nobs and symbols to me, taking pleasure in treating me like my brain was a piece of leather not even big enough to saddle a flea.

But when she sat in the small cab on the armrest next to me, I couldn't focus on anything but my arm grazing her thigh anytime the tractor bounced. Doing her best to avoid all contact, she was coiled as tight as a rattler about to strike. Formula One or not, I kept mixing up the forward and back pedals, giving us both whiplash.

My abysmal driving couldn't be blamed on me; it was Angie's fault. Her and her distracting softness, smell-goodness—her absolute lack of patience. She wouldn't stop talking. Telling me to watch out for this and watch out for that. We traveled at a breakneck speed of five miles per hour, in danger of premature death.

She told me about her expectations of how the tractor was to be parked. Bucket flat on the ground. Gear in neutral. Implement lever on zero. Key off. Words constantly spilled from Angie's mouth, a habit I'd become accustomed to. Usually, it indicated she was uncomfortable. I took my hand off the wheel, brushing it across her thigh in the process of reaching for the lever that lifted the attachment being drug behind the tractor.

Instead of slowing down her instructions, more words poured from her. "... you'll want to be comfortable raising the implements behind the tractor while you keep forward progress. The more you keep the tractor moving ahead, the more you get done in a day. I always listen to the radio or something while I'm doing tractor work. Of course, you don't have to ... You can do what you want. As long as it's not reading ... we don't have those radar automatic ..."

She spoke ten words a second with gusts up to fifty. Yet another piece of the Angie puzzle I'd figured out. The tractor bumped back and forth, causing my hand to shift to a higher position on her thigh.

She jerked from me, and our heads cracked together in a particular jostling turn.

"I think I'm done." Angie pinched the bridge of her nose. "Shut it off."

I rubbed the side of my head, which had connected with her forehead. I cut the engine and lifted Angie's chin to see if I'd caused another wound on her eye, praying at the same time there wouldn't be blood. "Sorry. I didn't mean to hurt you."

Why did I feel like I'd be saying that again on a much grander scale? The hard edges around her eyes softened under my scrutiny. I carefully shifted her hair from her eyebrow, checking the cut and for any other damage. My rough, tan fingers stood out against her porcelain skin, near flawless in complexion.

The cab grew smaller as I ran my fingers along her forehead and down her cheek. The pulse in her neck picked up pace. It was all I could do not to tilt her head back and ... her breaths shortening into smaller gasps gave her away, no matter how she tried to pretend she wasn't affected by me, no matter how much she pretended to be pissed at me.

Her mouth dropped open, and I couldn't resist the pull between us any longer. I tugged her close to me and dipped my lips toward her.

But she stopped me with a hand to my chest. "Remi. I ... uh ... I ..." She stammered but didn't attempt to move.

My lips hovered an inch from hers. Her breath fluttered against my skin. "Am I good to help with cutting the hayfield next week?" I whispered.

"Oh." She shoved me against the opposite window, snatched the keys, and climbed out of the cab.

"I take that as a yes!" I hollered after her, laughing as she ignored me and stomped the entire way to her truck. Guess I'd be walking back to the house again.

Chapter 24

Angie

The truck door clicking shut startled me awake. My flailing arms knocked against Remi's empty bottle of Dr. Pepper Cream Soda. He'd parked his far-too-clean truck to a stop in a small dirt patch at the mouth of what looked like an overgrown trail. Between working four nights in a row, squeezing in a last-minute movie night with Dan, and finally getting the last of the crops planted this morning, I hadn't had much time for sleep this past week. Mama and Papa still hadn't warmed up to Dan. Not in the same way they had to Remi.

This morning, Remi had loaded two dirt bikes—where he'd gotten them, I didn't know—tossed some gear in his backseat and told me it was now or never.

Of course, any time I came to a seated position, and I wasn't driving, I passed out. No matter how much I slept, my sleep piggy bank never filled up. I would be in a perpetual deficit. My jaw cracked as I yawned and climbed to the ground, shutting my door behind me.

Damp mountain air rushed into my lungs, soothing me the instant I breathed in. How long had it been since I'd taken the time to go to the mountains? Not since Papa got sick the first time. We used to come up here in our old Cummins with a mattress in the bed and two sleeping bags. Not bothering to set up a tent, we'd sleep under the stars. I remembered my eyes drifting closed as Papa pointed out all the constellations.

Usually, we'd only get a couple of overnighters since the farm never quit demanding his attention. I understood if he neglected the crops we wouldn't get any money, but as a little girl wanting nothing more than more time with her Papa, I may have been a tiny bit jealous too.

I arched my back and stretched my legs. Green grass speckled with bright yellow, white, and sparse red wildflowers carpeted the rolling mountains. End of June temperatures had climbed into the nineties the past week, but at this elevation, the air was always cooler. I needed this. A break from farming, my day job, and my parents pretend happiness, as they were never able to rid themselves of the underlying grief. The pressure built inside me like a teapot ready to release steam. Only I never allowed myself to unload the pent-up pressure.

I walked to Remi, careful not to step on any wildflowers with my boots. He opened the tailgate and pulled the ramp to the edge of the bed. His pecs and biceps flexed against his shirt as he pushed the ramp into place behind the blue bike's tire.

I'd noticed his muscles were growing more defined with the amount of work I'd laid on top of him. Over the past month his citified look had all but disappeared, with his Wranglers now spotted with stains, white shirts no longer crisp, and his gloves needing replaced. The days he worked with his shirt off challenged my ability to focus. He never detected how I ogled him from my tractor or paused in the Dodge while driving along irrigation lines. Maybe, on occasion, I checked him out more than I checked on the crops.

One of the greatest tragedies of life was the waste of a good body on a man who didn't know how to treat women. It'd be like Excalibur falling into the wrong hands in medieval times. They wielded their weapon without care of the broken hearts and embittered women they left in their path, wreaking havoc and devastation wherever they passed. If only Merlin could save me now.

My heart was safe. Even if I admired Remi's body, and maybe his determination and work ethic, the kindness he showed my parents ... I still would never fall prey to him.

Today, he matched the part of a bicycle racer, but with motorcycles—whatever they were called. Long sleeves protected his arms, the neon green and blue accented his matching gray and black clothes. A big FOX was tagged his chest along with the shape of a fox's head. I tilted my head to read the block lettering on his arm ... RACECO?

He'd been more prepared for this outing than I imagined. When was Remi not prepared? His habit of analyzing and being ready for all possible scenarios irritated me to no end.

"Here." He handed me an outfit almost identical to his. "I got this gear for you."

The tags had been removed, yet I was almost certain these items were new. My focus bounced from the clothes to the bikes tied down in his truck. Knobby tires, no mud—blue plastic, no scratches—shiny chrome spokes ... I thought when I asked him to teach me how to ride dirt bikes, he would borrow some bikes from the following he'd accrued in town, not buy brand new ones, complete with all the safety equipment.

He might be as wealthy as Elon Musk, but I couldn't help but inflate a little bit at all he'd done for me.

"Oh, and give me your phone."

I held up my armload of stuff. "It's in my front pocket."

Without hesitating, he reached into my pants pocket and gripped my phone. His eyes flashed to mine, his hand lingering longer than necessary. Goosebumps spread from his point of contact through the thin fabric throughout the rest of my body.

He freed my phone and unlocked it. Maybe I should have set more personal boundaries with him.

"I'm installing the Find My Phone app. In case we get separated." With one final click, he slipped it back from where he'd retrieved it.

"There's nowhere to change." And I wasn't about to strip in front of him.

He pointed to the scrubby bushes on the edge of a quaky grove. "You can get dressed over there while I unload the truck." He pushed some boots, other random pads, and what looked like a chest plate into my overloaded arms. "Put these on as well."

Padded sleeves slipped from the mound of stuff I held. "What, no bubble wrap?"

As I bent to grab the two things I dropped, he tucked them under my chin. "I thought about it."

A snicker escaped me before I managed to stop it. I didn't need to encourage him. As my nemesis, he wasn't allowed to make me laugh. In less than a minute, I traversed the meadow and walked into the protection of the trees.

High-pitched engines revved to life as I removed my clothes, the cold air chasing chills over my skin. Laying my jeans on the ground to keep my socks clean, I tried on everything Remi bought for me.

With all the things he'd been helping me with, it was surprising how much he knew about me. Everything fit perfectly, down to the boot size. I gathered the shoes and clothes, shaking the dirt off my jeans. I walked to

Remi, where the two bikes idled, struggling in the stiff white and green plastic boots which climbed to my upper calf.

What other details about me had he'd filed away in his mind?

His gaze roamed from the top of my head to my feet, a smile softening his face. With all the padding in place, I felt like the Stay Puft Marshmallow Man, my arms not even able to touch my sides, dropping me to the bottom rung of the attractiveness totem pole, which I didn't mind. It'd be even better if I had a big pimple on my nose. The less appealing I was to Remi, the safer I'd be.

He handed me a vibrant pink helmet with gloves and goggles tucked inside. "I hope these fit. I did my best."

How much time had he spent at the store gathering all these things? When had he managed to find the time and still get everything done? He wasn't kidding about the headlamp and midnight.

Putting on the gloves first, I slid the helmet over my ears, and where it would work, it wiggled when I shook my head side to side. I fumbled with the black straps and buckles, my gloves hampering my dexterity. Remi moved to help me.

"I've got it." His fingers ... *touching my neck?* Not if I could help it. I leaned away and swallowed.

"Stop being so stubborn and let me help." This time, he didn't allow me to push him away.

He tilted my chin up and drew one finger along the length of my neck, looping the tip of his index in the two metal rings on the left strap. I held my breath and bit my lip. A burning kindled in my core, and I closed my eyes, afraid to look at him. He took his time with the other strap too, his fingers lingering on my skin far longer than necessary.

Goosebumps engulfed me, my body warming more with each pass of the shuddering waves. The click of a snap resonated through the helmet.

"There. That wasn't difficult, was it?" His voice was soft and husky.

He no longer touched me, yet the path of his fingers branded my skin. I lifted my lids, gathering the courage to look at him. He didn't attempt to hide his desire ... and he knew exactly what he was doing to me.

No. Uh-uh. No way. I would not be seduced by him. I stepped back and shoved my goggles into place, grateful for the layers protecting my lips from his. His smile grew wider, taking on a wicked tilt.

By refusing him, was I becoming his Everest? An irresistible challenge he couldn't help but conquer. Well, this was one mountain he wouldn't climb. I crossed my arms and angled my shoulders away from him. He turned his back to me and grabbed the rest of his safety equipment.

That's right. Take the hint, Remi. Read my sign. No vacancy.

Placing his helmet under his arm, he moved the side of the smaller of the two bikes. "This is the one you'll be riding."

I ran my hand along the length of the seat, then looped my leg over it, my toes barely touching the ground. "Are you sure it's not too big for me?"

"Nope. Fits fine." Remi pressed a lever on the left of the bike. "This is your clutch, and this—" He fiddled with the chrome lever on the right. "—is your front brake. Your back one is the pedal by your right foot. If you're ever in trouble, hit the clutch, and then the brake."

The small engine rumbled below me, rattling my nerve endings, sending sparks of life to areas of my body long dead, killed off by extended grief and stress. Tinted yellow by the goggles, details in the world around me sharpened. Hummingbirds circled each other, dancing into the sky and parting ways fast as bullets. Butterflies and buttermoths moved from flower to flower, creating a moving tapestry for me to enjoy.

Was this why I persisted in dating Dan? Life surged inside me with each new adventure I contemplated.

"Remember, take it slow. It's easier to go fast and much more difficult to control the bike at lower speeds."

I gnawed on my bottom lip. I should have probably been listening to his instructions. It couldn't be that much different than the four-wheel-er. Mama and Papa spent years telling horror stories of accidents on ATVs and made me promise to be responsible. Anything motorized on two wheels had been straight-up banned, put in the same camp as rock climbing, skydiving, or any other extreme sport.

"Ready?"

I nodded once.

"Okay. Put up your kickstand and try a couple of loops in this clearing before we try the trail. Practice your starts and stops." Remi's voice was gentle yet patronizing.

The smirk on his face told me he couldn't pass up the opportunity to treat me as I'd treated him when I'd taught him how to operate the tractor. Like a baby taking my first steps. Didn't matter. *I'll show him just how capable I am.*

Letting my breath ease out, I flipped the kickstand back and twisted the throttle. The bike wobbled and took off. Remi hollered something behind me. I ignored him. The inner daredevil in me took the reins, and I shifted into second, then third gear, increasing my speed on the straight away. Air rushed under the lip of my goggles, causing my eyes to tear.

Slowing in time to loop around in a semi-controlled manner, I turned back to Remi. I came to a quick stop next to him, skidding a bit on the gravelly soil. "How was that?"

Remi's smile grew. "You don't know how to start slow, do you?"

"Nope. Can we go now?"

I made a couple more loops while Remi suited up, in much less gear than I had on. He only wore a helmet and gloves. No elbow pads, chest plate, or knee pads. Did he think I was going to drive off a cliff?

Once again, I drove to Remi, now seated and ready. "You go first. I'll follow you. Only go as fast as you're comfortable."

I nodded. My helmet shifted again, knocking my goggles more askew. Not bothering to fix them, I took off. The wind rushed under my protective layers, fluttering against my eyelashes.

Narrowing my eyes, I kept them locked on the front tire. The trail became rockier the further we went along. Each small bump jostled me, clacking my teeth together, the shocks of the bike not taking enough of the impact out of the hits.

Cold sweat washed over me, my heart racing faster the higher I climbed. I managed every bump and every challenge, looking ahead to the next. Each obstacle I successfully overcame built my confidence. The tensing in my muscles relaxed, which translated into my fingers, lessening my death grip. Every now and then, I even had the courage to—

Something hit my eyebrow, followed by a buzz echoing inside my helmet.

Zzzz ... zzz ... ZZZZ ...

Sounding like—a—*wasp!* My anxiety rebounded, hitting me in full force. My muscles shook, constricting back into their original tight ball. I lost focus on the road, my eyes following the blurry black and yellow spawn of Satan, its movements frantic as it fought against the wind current the gap between my goggles and helmet created. It hit the plastic, my nose, lashes, and upper cheek.

Get it out. *Get it out!*

I screamed and jerked on my handlebars.

Chapter 25

Remi

Mere minutes ago, I'd made the mistake of thinking, *Angie's a natural*. I'd followed her for a couple miles, letting her choose the path of least resistance to the viewpoint awaiting us. Myles and I had made a predawn ride to make sure this route was appropriate for an amateur.

She'd taken off faster than a sneeze through a screen door. Her previous experience with tractors and other ATVs proved an asset in taking on two wheels. The pure joy I'd seen in her eyes after her first loop gave me a high better than any drug. It challenged me to a new mission in life: search out anything and everything to make Angie look like she'd harnessed the rays of the sun.

I'd done my legwork to make ensure the most successful outcome—and all my work had been paying off ... until Angie lost her mind. Her tires bobbed and weaved with the motion of her head, which she kept shaking back and forth.

Twisting the throttle, I accelerated to her position just in time for her bike to tip onto its side at full speed.

I hit the brakes.

Shit. Shit. Shit!

Angie propelled forward, rolling well beyond where her motorcycle got hung up in a grove of trees. Not bothering to kill my engine or put the kickstand down, I dropped my handlebars. I barely registered the plastics scraping against the ground, running to where Angie lay.

As soon as her momentum slowed, she hopped up and slapped at her helmet. "*Get it out!*" She flicked her goggles off and kept messing with her helmet. "Wasp!"

Understanding hit me. But how had a wasp managed to get inside her helmet?

I grabbed her shoulders, forcing her to remain still. As fast as I could, I undid the clasp around her neck, and she threw the helmet from her head. Once freed, she tossed her hair back and forth, undoing her braid and slapping at its ends.

"Is it gone?" she asked, still smacking at her head.

"I think so." I checked the inside of the helmet and went to retrieve her goggles.

My bike chugged on its side. I jogged back to it and hit the kill switch, then stood it up. A wasp? She'd wrecked her bike because of a tiny insect. What if she'd severely injured herself? This could have happened in a much more pivotal spot along the trail, and she would have ended up rolling down a steep ravine.

I turned on her. "What the hell were you thinking?" Images of her beautiful body tumbling down a cliff tore at me, sharpening my anger at myself. I took off my gloves and threw them to the ground.

"Uh. Fighting for my *life*. That beast could have stung me."

"A tiny insect bite? So you wreck your bike at full speed? Remember clutch, brake? Clutch. Brake!" I stepped closer to her and removed her elbow pads, checking for possible injuries. "You can't take risks like that."

"It was in my *goggles*! It got sucked in by my face current." She jerked her arm from me and pointed at her eyes. "Its nasty body touched my iris. It could have given me wasp herpes! I'm going to go blind."

"Do you even hear yourself?" I rolled up her sleeve, watching for bruising. "Wasp herpes," I scoffed under my breath.

"It's a real thing," she mumbled.

Even though she and I both knew it'd come from her overactive imagination. I unclicked her chest protector and slipped my fingertips under its bottom edge.

She took a couple of steps away from me until she'd backed into a tree. "What *are* you doing?"

"Checking you for injuries." Her bike lay silent on its side, the handlebar possibly bent, the engine probably flooded since it no longer ran. I'd spent thousands of dollars on her bike on this outing, and I'd be furious at myself if that money resulted in her getting hurt.

This had to stop. My attempt to buy her land could put her in the hospital. Where I usually believed in any means necessary to close a deal, especially this one, I'd never forgive myself if my actions got Angie paralyzed or worse, killed.

It didn't take long, being a part of the extreme sports circuit, to see horrific accidents. Once on a BASE jump, the guy right in front of me fell to his death when his canopy didn't open. All of us knew the risks you took to be part of these sports, but never thought we'd be one of the stats.

When I'd agreed to this plan to take Angie on these extreme-sporting outings, I never considered how badly she could get hurt. I also never envisioned I wouldn't want her to be with another man.

I never dreamed how I would come to care for her. To want her all to myself. I wanted to be a part of every one of her adventures.

"I feel fine." Her hesitant, shaky voice brought me back to the present. "I-I can take it off myself."

I stood with my hand still on her. This close to her, the almost tangible chemical reaction between us rose in temperature until it scalded me, making it impossible to ignore.

The further down this road I walked, the more complicated my life became. Getting involved with her would shake my resolve to manipulate her into a position where I'd go in for the kill shot and force her to sign over her land.

Even in a town as small as Clear Springs, I had plenty of women to choose from. Tonight, I could go to the bar and have my pick of them. My options were endless. But somewhere between shoveling manure and growing corn, Angie had become the only one who would satisfy me.

"No. Let me." Why did she—the one woman I needed to stay away from—have to be the most tempting creature on Earth?

With little fight she released her grip on her shoulder straps. Angling my eyes down to her, I lifted the chest protector over her head, never releasing her from my gaze. Her hair caught on it, then released to pool around her face and shoulders. Our bodies were mere inches apart. Stripping her of her protective gear strained the desire I'd managed to keep in check to its breaking point.

Without it, her soft curves became exposed for my perusal. Under the guise of inspecting for injuries, I allowed myself to examine the shape of her thighs, the narrowing of her waist, and the curve of her perfectly shaped breasts. My eyes lingered on the spot on her neck, where I'd imagined placing my lips countless times.

How could she see herself as anything less than perfect?

I ran my hands along her shoulders and her upper arms. "Does this hurt?"

She shook her head. Her lips parted, and she brushed them with her tongue, leaving behind an irresistible sheen. I moved my hands to her waist, slipping them under her silky shirt to her smooth skin underneath.

Dipping my head just enough that my mouth brushed her ear, I whispered, "What about here?"

Birds sang from the trees. The mountain stream gurgled in its tract along the road. Leaves rustled together in the breeze, which cooled the warmth in my face. All these forest sounds faded into the background as the beat of Angie's heart pounding in rhythm with mine took center stage.

She stiffened, tense as a rabbit preparing to run from a fox, yet she stayed. Shifting my hands from her waist to her back, I pulled her against me, tracing from her shoulder blades to the base of her spine.

I stretched my fingers until my hands encompassed her lower back, slipping ever so slightly onto the upper roundness of her bottom. "And what about here?"

My breath set the blonde strands of her hair near her ear along her neck to motion. Visible goosebumps rose where it brushed against her. Her chest lifted and fell against me as she took in shorter and shorter breaths, yet her arms remained straight as sticks by her sides.

I could think of a half billion reasons why I should stop myself from rubbing circles on her back, from taking control of her mouth, delving my tongue into that forbidden vault, tasting, testing, savoring everything it had to offer. Five hundred million excuses why I should move away from her and backpedal our relationship to the bickering one of employer and employee.

She tilted her head, yielding me access to the length of her neck where her pulse thudded against her skin. Caution flags ignited and disintegrated like ash in the wind, and my desire consumed me.

I pressed my lips gently to her velvety skin. One taste was all it took for me to hunger for more. Freeing one hand from her shirt, I threaded it into her hair and nudged her head back further.

Trailing kisses to the hollow of her clavicle, I teased her with my tongue. Relishing every touch, I snaked my way back to her chin, growing ever closer to the lips that'd taunted and tortured me for more than two months.

And I was more than ready to return the favor.

Chapter 26

Angie

Few experiences in life came around in which the very ground beneath my feet was swept away, leaving me floating without a tether. The first contact from Remi's lips topped the charts for one of these events. Whiskers from his trimmed beard stimulated my skin, magnifying the effect of his kisses, simultaneously tickling and arousing me.

I hung in the air as if detached, plunged into a new experimental world where nothing but pleasure existed.

All growing up, Mama and I made homemade jam—raspberry, strawberry, and apricot. While stirring the thickening liquid, big bubbles built up over and over again, boiling and popping to the surface. It'd entertained me until one of the blasted things landed a thick glob of goo on my skin. It was molten lava. Pain spiked through my arm. I licked at the semi-cooled filling, and it tasted like heaven.

This same feeling overtook me now. My body ached from impacting the ground, and it ached from the sweet, blessed magic emanating from Remi's mouth. My insides were a melting glob of sugary, gelatinous berry goodness. Large bubbles heated in my core, growing bigger with each flick of Remi's tongue. The feel of his hot breath on my skin brought them near to bursting any time he came close to my mouth. The pressure on my back increased and I melted against him.

He massaged the back of my scalp, his fingers toying with my hair, adding to the chills cascading through my body. I closed my eyes, focusing my whole being on him and the torrent he stirred inside me.

What was I thinking?

I couldn't make out with the destroyer of all things holy. He'd kiss me one minute and rip my childhood home from me the next. This had to stop. I made up my mind to tell him exactly that.

"Uh ... oh ..." My failed attempt at making words exhaled out of me more like a sigh.

He kissed his way back to my ear. "What was that?" He let out one of the most dratted sensual laughs I'd ever heard as he tormented my earlobe with his teeth.

Fiery waves licked their way down my left side, and with that, my womanhood whipped my mind back into its cage. Brains were only useful at work in the hospital or on the farm, not in situations where a man held me captive in his embrace.

Pure carnal instincts took over. Cautiously at first, I wrapped my arms around his lower back still trying to resist the magnetism pulling me toward him. But after two more expertly executed kisses, I clutched at the fabric of his shirt, fighting to remain upright.

"Please ..." I opened my eyes, and my breaths heaved in and out of me as I struggled to draw in air. I wasn't sure how I planned on finishing that sentence.

Please stop?

Please put your lips on mine already before I lose my ever-living mind?

Remi paused and met my eyes. The brown in them was barely visible, overtaken by his inky-black pupils. They were glazed in an intense longing which spoke directly to the instinctual half of me. The part of me that understood too well his restraint.

Whatever he saw in my gaze caused him to nod. "Okay." His whisper hung on his exhale.

Wait. I didn't mean—Did I? I wasn't ready ... Not yet. Don't stop. I couldn't—

His lips descended on mine, halting any possibility of cohesive thoughts.

This ... happening—now.

An adventure-seeking, bridge-jumping, perfect ten—pain in my pa-tootie, freakin' hot farmhand turned evilest of all land buyers—was kissing *me*. Boring old—never-left-Idaho, tractor-driving, horse is my closest friend—me.

He tasted heavenly.

And holy cow, he was a good kisser. His lips were basically demi-gods tasked with the sole purpose of pleasuring mere mortals. I didn't know what I imagined when I kissed Remi—and I thought of this moment plenty of times—it wasn't this gentle, patient lesson of mastering passion.

His body movements spoke to me. The way his lips slanted tenderly over mine, they were punctuated by ... a question? Testing for my response? Almost like with each shift of his mouth, combined with the havoc he wreaked with his wandering hands, he found new parts of me to savor.

Thorough in everything he did, he took his time exploring every inch of me, yet I sensed he held back ... waiting on—me.

Curious, I lifted my arm and weaved my fingers in his black hair at the base of his neck and pressed him to me, opening my mouth further to his oh-so-talented tongue. My simple response seemed to shatter whatever control he was maintaining.

He dropped his grip to my hips and pinned me to the tree. With the added leverage the trunk provided, I curved into him until our bodies fit like puzzle pieces. His hands traveled upward, toying with the edge of my bra. The warmth of his palms seeped through the thin piece of lacy lingerie—chosen more for lack of options due to laundry day than for today's activities.

Spreading his fingers, he used them to tease, tantalize, and taunt, scorching me from the inside out, driving me to heights I'd never escalated to before in one simple kiss. I lost my grip on reality. Nothing existed aside from the constant thumping of Remi's heart, his touch, the feel of his beard on my skin, and the pressure of his weight against me. I tasted hints of the Dr. Pepper he'd finished on the drive; his familiar smell cocooned around me.

I reached behind me to find something, *anything* to cling to.

My hands met a damp pile of leaves and pine needles on the forest floor. Somehow, Remi had maneuvered me onto my back without me realizing it. Yet my body remembered the feel of one of his arms wrapping around my middle, lifting, and guiding me to the ground. With a hand braced behind my head, he pulled up my shirt. Sun broke from the canopy, highlighting Remi's form above me, sprinkling my face with light.

Tracking kisses down my body—neck, shoulder, chest—he turned his attention to my abdomen. I closed my eyes, relinquishing myself to the waves of absolute bliss crashing steadily over me.

I wanted this. I *needed* this.

Nothing else mattered more than Remi and his solid body on top of me. Pressing his knee between my legs, he spread them wide, inching his hand toward my waistband—

Almost literal brake lights lit up in my mind. Somehow my brain broke free from the temporary prison I'd placed it in and took control once again.

What was I doing?

This man manipulated people—women in particular—for a living, and I was about to give myself to him.

I grabbed his wrist, halting the progression of his hand. "No."

Ragged breaths shuddered from him. He rested his forehead against mine.

My former conviction came back to me. I would not be seduced by him—okay ... I would only be halfway seduced. I shoved against his shoulders, severing our connection. "I can't do this."

Yes, you can, the other half of me screamed, but I didn't allow these thoughts to slip out.

Remi immediately stilled and pushed up from me, dragging his palm along my bare skin as if resistant to relinquishing his hold over me. Currents of mountain air replaced the heat of his body, cooling me and further clearing my mind.

"You're right. We can't do this." His chest heaved with each breath, and he leaned back to rest against the tree, looping an arm over his bent knee.

I lifted myself onto my elbows, wanting nothing more than to pull him back on top of me and beg him to finish what he started.

But how could I let a professional player have his way with me on the side of an abandoned dirt bike trail? I'd be chalked up as another one of his conquests and he'd leave me after claiming my land.

I fought to get to my feet, cursing the stiff boots Remi had insisted I wear.

I'd chosen Dan. Dan was my future. He wanted kids, a wife, a family. We were planning a future together, and I was one button and a zipper away from ruining everything. As it sat, I wasn't sure how Dan would react if he found out about this. Long-lasting relationships didn't start with cheating. And that was what I was. The cheating-est cheater of all time. Damn Remi. Damn him for risking my entire future for one kiss.

What a kiss it had been. I closed my eyes and licked my lips, remembering his touch.

But Remi'd given me no hint he ever wanted to settle down. I'd be no different from any other woman he'd roll around naked under a tree with.

Was this part of his sick, twisted plan? Sex me up enough to sign his purchase agreement?

"Angie—" Remi stood and took one step toward me. "I'm sorry. I didn't mean for it to go this far."

I angrily brushed at the leaves clinging to my hair and jerked my shirt back into place. "Sure. You must have fallen, and your lips locked onto mine." I turned my back to him and walked to my bike.

"Oh, no you don't." He shoved his way between me and my downed metal pony, breaking into my inner bubble once again, he whispered, "You wanted that as much as I did."

While I didn't verbally respond to his suggestion, my body gave him all the clues he needed. From my goosebump paralysis the warmth of his breath against my ear caused, to my soft exhale and slight tilt in his direction, my body—the two-faced hussy—all but begged him for the soft kiss he planted on me before he righted my bike and rolled it to the center of the trail.

My mind broke through my temporary immobility. I dug my toe into the dirt and cleared my throat. "Promise you won't kiss me again."

He shot me a half smile and winked. How was I supposed to interpret that?

"Is that a yes?"

"What are we, two?" He pressed on the bike's starter button, and it chugged. "I'm not going to promise you that. What I *will* promise is you'll want me to kiss you when I do it again."

How could I have let this happen? He was my declared super villain. The one person on this planet I was destined to beat. It'd be like Supergirl kissing Lex Luther. Like the coolest members of the X-Men, Storm or Rogue, macking on Magneto.

Like Batman seducing Catwom—wait. Never mind.

"That's where you're wrong." I marched to him, shoving him with my pointer finger. "I'll never respond like that again. I can't do that to Dan."

"What you have with Smoot's not real, and you know it." He took hold of my wrist and tugged me to him until we were chest to chest. "This. You and me. This is very real."

My heartbeat intensified and escalated at the same time. His gaze met mine before it dropped to my moistened mouth, and before I could douse my body's reaction, I leaned ever so slightly toward him. He lowered his head until he once again claimed my swollen lips with his. This time he toyed with my bottom lip, sending shivers tumbling down my body until I—Wait. No. Not again.

I elbowed him hard enough that he grunted and jerked away from me.

His soft chuckle shredded my nerves worse than Grandmama's antique cheese grater. He raised one eyebrow at me and quirked his mouth into a crooked smile.

"Dadgummit, Remi." I tugged on my helmet, more to hide my flaming face than for protection.

Remi burst out laughing. "Don't you dadgum me," he said in between his guffaws. "You're adorable when you're upset."

I didn't bother to respond and latched my strap around my chin. I, after all, was the grown-up in this relationship. Finding my goggles, chest padding, elbow and knee pads, and my pair of gloves, I hoisted my leg over the blue and black vinyl seat. Two solid kicks, and my bike roared to life. The handlebars were bent, so I aimed the tire in the right direction and rocketed forward, my back tire spitting gravel and dirt behind me.

Chapter 27

Remi

I pushed the wooden farmhouse door open and stepped into the foyer. The lamp on the side table illuminated the piles of stacked mail, its green lampshade casting a garish hue on the papers. Without central air, the house had begun to warm with the rising afternoon temperatures.

Dust gathered in the corners, and seldom-used coats fell from the overloaded hooks onto the white shoe bench. Shoes, which had been stuffed under the bench spilled into the walkway, the dirt clods clinging to irrigation boots haphazardly dropped on the floor. Opposite the professionally cleaned house I'd grown up in, as sterile emotionally as it'd been clean, this place had become more of a home for me than the big house.

Voices echoed down the hall to me. Tony and Nora must not have heard the door. I tiptoed closer to better hear what they were saying.

"... should speak to him ..." Nora's worry carried into her voice.

"Out of options ... Angie ... love won't ..." Tony's words rose and fell in and out of my hearing.

"What about Angie?"

"She'll have to accept his offer," Tony said, more adamantly this time, making it easy for me to hear him.

They both fell silent. The mantle clock next to the lamp ticked in the quiet.

Offer? What offer?

My mind immediately went to the conversation Smoot had with me about his plans for proposing. Plus, he kept showing up in the evenings and watching movies with her late into the night. Had she slept with him?

After the way she'd kissed me, how could she be placated by Smoot? I couldn't stop thinking about our escapade in the mountains. It came with me everywhere—the shower, the grocery store. Memories of our kiss edged their way into my mind even when I was hanging out with the guys.

Myles hadn't asked about the bike ride, and I hadn't offered any information to him. How could I tell him I was screwing up our dreams by screwing around with the farmer's daughter?

I threaded a hand through my hair. Smoot must have proposed. Angie had been working for a serious, committed partner, what I promised to help her accomplish. I should be elated. This meant I was one step closer to the freedom I'd fought for, yet it made me about as comfortable as a pimp at confession.

Tony apparently didn't think she loved Smoot, but in the end it didn't matter. Obviously, her parents thought she needed someone to take care of her after Tony was gone. Both monetarily and emotionally.

But they both underestimated their daughter. While it'd be nice for her to have companionship after her parents passed, she didn't need anyone. Even if she got stuck in hell, she'd kick the devil out and tell him what was what.

Sneaking back to the front door, I opened it and closed it, loudly this time.

"I'm back," I called into the home, a bit less enthusiastic than usual after overhearing their conversation.

"We're still in the kitchen." Nora's voice echoed down the hall into the entryway. "Did the hardware store have all the parts we need?"

"Yep," I called.

The pipes under the kitchen sink had started leaking, and under Tony's guidance, I was fixing them.

The scent of fresh bread drew me down the hallway, through the living room, and on into the kitchen. Two hours had passed since lunch, and with my new workload, that meant I needed another meal. The heat of the ovens made the back of the house more unbearable than the front.

Papers, opened envelopes, Farm Frenzy and Skip-Bo playing cards piled on the table in front of Tony, where he'd parked his wheelchair. He scanned a piece of mail as I passed him, heading to the sink. Though he tried to disguise his discouragement, it was clear what he read wasn't good news.

"You know anything about this Smoot fellow who keeps coming around here?" Tony asked.

Bitter gall burned my throat. They really had been talking about Smoot and Angie. "Not really," I lied. I knew far too much about him. "He comes to our guys' nights sometimes. Nice enough, I guess, but I don't really trust him."

For some reason, my answer had both Tony and Nora fighting smiles.

"Well, she seems mighty fond of him." Nora let her lips split wide into a grin and opened the oven to check on the bread.

My mind spiraled. Angie marrying Smoot? After the way she responded to my kiss, she couldn't be this sure about another man. The thought sliced through my peace of mind, and I swallowed the bile burning my throat. Yet, I wasn't exactly a fan of until death do you part. Was I?

More and more, I'd begun to yearn for something ... different. Something like what Tony and Nora had. But a relationship like theirs was as likely as a cowboy riding a bucking unicorn.

With her face glistening, Nora fumbled the full bread pans while I got things situated under the sink. The metal pans clanked on the speckled, cream laminate counter, golden-topped loafs tipping onto their sides.

"Ah! Fart nuggets!" She shoved her oven-mitted hands on her hips, then set about righting the loaves and flipping them onto the cooling racks.

I couldn't stop my short snort of laughter. Like mother, like daughter. Nora didn't react to my laughter and continued to fuss over the dent in her freshly baked loaves. I lost sight of her as I maneuvered into the cramped space under the sink. Cleaning supplies and odds and ends littered the floor around me.

I'd thought about convincing them to call a plumber since I had absolutely no experience, but then fixing a sink sounded way more appealing than spending the afternoon in the fields.

"Don't forget to put the crimp ring on the pipe before you connect it!" Tony yelled from the table; his voice less boisterous than it'd been a week ago. "Also, shut off the water supply before you start removing the broken fitting."

"And when you're ready for a break, I'll have hot, buttered bread and jam waiting for you." Nora ducked to look at me as she wiped her hands on her apron, which had a picture of two eggs as eyes and a slice of bacon for a smile on it.

"Hey, Papa. How're you feeling today?" Angie's voice reached me.

My hands stilled with the pipe cutters clutched in them. Hidden by the bar counter, I remained tucked under the sink, unabashedly eaves-dropping.

I missed Tony's response but hung on Angie's. "Don't worry over these bills. I have a good feeling about this harvest. We'll manage like we always have."

Maybe Smoot had only asked for permission to marry her and hadn't popped the question.

"It's sure been nice with Remi's help around here." Nora giggled and tapped my foot with hers.

I briefly closed my eyes and then returned to what I was doing.

The fridge door opened and closed. "He's about as helpful as a foxtail in my sock."

The hell I was. I did everything she asked me and more. This was the appreciation I got ... she compared me to a sticker weed in her shoe? Infuriating woman. Whatever, Angie. Be my guest. Marry Smoot and pop out a gaggle of Smoot babies for all I cared. I clamped the pipe between the cutter.

"But I wouldn't be able to manage without him. He's turned into a decent farmer."

What? She said something positive about me? Doubters, mainly my family, could keep hating on me, but Angie believed I made a good farmer. Bolstered by her admission, I snipped the blue plastic pipe clear through, releasing the water it'd contained. A lot of water. It sprayed at my face, onto my shirt, and flooded the floor. I'd expected a few drops to come out of the pipe, not this deluge.

"Oh, shh—" I cut off my expletive, not wanting to curse around Angie's parents. I'd forgotten to shut off the main valve. I blocked the pressurized stream with one hand and twisted the valve closed with the other. Relaxing my head and upper back on the bottom of the cabinet, I took a couple of breaths.

Way to go, Remi. I ducked out from the cabinet and sat in the puddle around my waist.

Angie stood above me with her eyes wide. She'd dressed in her work jeans and a ratty *Nirvana* T-shirt. She must not be on shift at the hospital tonight. Two golden ringlets slipped free of her elastic band and framed her face.

"Hey, Angie," I said, likely looking like a drowned rat. I rubbed at the water on my face and flicked it to the ground.

"Hi." She chuckled once ... twice ... then let her laughter flowed down on me as fast as the water stream.

"What happened?" Tony asked from the table. "He forgot to shut off the water supply, didn't he?" Though I couldn't see him, I imagined him doing a solid facepalm.

"Oh dear. I'm gonna go get a bath towel." Nora rushed from the room.

I should be humiliated, but hearing Angie's laugh again satisfied me immensely. "I've got everything under control."

"Sure, you do." She tilted the glass of lemonade in her hand to her smile, and I couldn't help but follow this movement with my eyes. The glass pressed against her full lips as she drew in the liquid, licking the leftover droplets after she swallowed.

Did it get hotter in here? Nora returned and dropped the towel on me. Grateful I had it to cover my flushed cheeks, I wiped the water off my face and neck, then used it to sop up the mess I'd made.

It'd been two weeks since Angie and I'd kissed. Sightings of her had become rare. Instead of giving a rundown of what she expected throughout the day, she'd taken to leaving lists of things needing to be done on the counter for me to find, with instructions if I had any questions to ask Tony. My time with her had been limited to watching her do tractor work from a distance.

I stood and padded at the water on my ass, sending Angie into another fit of giggles.

Her creative ways of torturing me had increased tenfold since the day on the trail. Though I still had access to Oscar, she never gave me a job where I could use him. Instead, I'd spent the last two weeks hoeing miles of burs in the beet and bean fields. It took me a week to finish the beets and then another to tackle the beans. Sunup to sundown, I took out weeds that'd grown up to my armpits, only to have the ones in the first field already grown back as if I hadn't done any of it.

It was psychological anguish.

There had to be a more efficient way to farm. Maybe they didn't have the money to pay for weed killer, or they were going for certified organic produce. Either way, I tried to flag down the crop duster planes whenever they buzzed overhead.

Please drop some of your magic dust from the sky and put an end to my misery.

Even with the intensity of the monotonous mind-mushing chore, that kiss had been worth it. I'd go back and do it all over again. The true agony came from the long hours spent in the fields where I had nothing to distract me from reliving it. Her delicate skin, the feel of her body under me, her response which had totally undone me.

I'd never lost control like that, and I couldn't think of the last time a simple kiss took over my senses so completely.

It'd crossed a boundary, a turning point in our relationship, and Angie had made it clear she wasn't interested in any sort of intimacy where I was concerned. With this deal hinging on Angie's acceptance, sleeping with her would make buying her land trickier than bagging flies—nearly impossible.

Therefore, the only way forward was backward. If only I could get Angie to go back to the teasing, argumentative, talkative women I enjoyed sparing with, maybe I could forge a friendship between us.

Anything was better than this awkward silence.

"Well, as fun as this has been, the tractor's waitin' on me." Walking to the dining table, she crouched next to Tony and placed a kiss on his forehead, resting her hands on his bony ones. Tony's weight loss had snowballed the past couple of weeks.

"Bye, Papa. I'll come back and finish our round of Skip-Bo in a couple of hours." Knocking two stacks of mail together that her father had been sorting, she moved swiftly toward the front door.

Not caring what her parents thought, I jogged after her. As I passed the table, a bright-red foreclosure notice caught my eye, along with a couple of past dues stamped on the bottom of what looked like medical bills.

If the Johnsons weren't so stubborn, I could make all that go away.

"Wait."

"I don't have time right now. That hay's not going to bale itself."

Much of farming was repetitive. Alfalfa growth, followed by cutting, letting it dry, raking, then baling and stacking. It felt like we'd barely finished that job and now we were well into the second go 'round.

I lowered my voice. "You can't avoid me forever."

She tilted her head. "Hmm ... actually I can."

She retrieved her truck keys from the dish and went to open the doorknob.

I caught her elbow and turned her around to face me. "Look ... about the kiss."

"I don't want to talk about it."

"We need to—"

"No, we don't." She cut me off. "All I need to do right now is get back in the tractor. And you ..." She looked me up and down. "... need to go change your shirt." She smirked.

"Fine," I conceded. We wouldn't talk about the obvious energy snapping between us, but I wouldn't let her out of my sight until I got one promise out of her. "You can't go dirt biking with Smoot. You'll hurt yourself. Do something else, like go-carting. Something in a controlled environment."

"Are you trying to act like my father now? My brother?" She rolled her eyes and shook her head. "I can handle myself."

"Please, Angie." I dropped my gaze to study the wood grains in the floor. Slowly releasing my breath, I lifted my eyes to meet hers. "I wouldn't be able to forgive myself if you got hurt."

The smirk dropped from her face. Her brief glance down at my mouth told me I wasn't the only one thinking about our time under the tree. She gave me a short nod. "Okay. I'll ask him if we can do something else. He rescheduled anyway. Something came up."

Code for 'I forgot about my daughter's recital, and now I have to spend time with my wife and kids.' Or code for 'my girlfriend surprised me with a weekend away.' Being a player myself, I spoke their language, and this guy was playing Angie hardcore. I wish I could make her see it. Smoot didn't give off the cheater vibes, but his over-the-top use of climbing lingo made me think he was a pretender.

I pressed my lips into a flat line. This wasn't exactly the assurance I wanted, but it was better than I expected.

"You bale that hay like it's never been baled before. Give that field hell." My attempted banter came out of left field. Awkward and gangly. It didn't fit with the tense emotions I kept in check.

Still, Angie rewarded me with a grin. I returned her smile, then headed back toward the kitchen and my half-assed attempt at plumbing.

"Um, Remi?"

I stopped midstride and faced her again, my hopes rising slightly. Why? I didn't know. I'd already gone over the reasons why getting involved with Angie was the worst idea ever. "Yeah?"

"I was wondering ..." She tucked the loose strand of her wavy hair behind her ear.

My hope ballooned.

"What's a burble? Dan mentioned when he was talking about a sky-dive he went on. He also said whirlie. I couldn't remember either from the vocab sheet you gave me."

Insert pin to inflated hopes. "Whirlie is a newbie climber."

"Oh. Huh." Her brows furrowed together, and her mouth puckered and tucked to one side.

If only I could decipher the look on her face. Was it good or bad? Had Smoot insulted her? "Burble is essentially dead air," I continued.

"It happens when you fly directly over another skydiver. You become unstable and sometimes drop."

This was exactly how she'd made me feel. Unstable like I'd freefallen over twenty feet. She took the rules I'd established from childhood, almost infancy, and jumbled them until I couldn't decipher the code I lived by.

Marriage to one woman. Kids. White picket fence. Maybe a cow or two. Mae even fit in the picture I painted in my mind of life with Angie. But it wouldn't last. Just like paint faded and cracked, inevitably we'd grow bored of each other and end up divorced or like my parents, glorified roommates living two separate lives.

I couldn't marry Angie, but I still wanted to revel in the nirvana I'd gotten a taste of in the mountains. Blake's warning came back to me. 'Get your feelings solidly in the "I love you zone" before you make a move on her ...'

Well, shucks, I hadn't listened to him. Love. Such an overinflated term that got in the way of good times. A feeling which took a rational woman and turned her into a she-cat.

I didn't have any interest in it.

"Thanks, Remi." She offered me a half-hearted wave, already focused on her phone as she texted her way out the door.

I nearly ran over Nora when I turned the corner into the kitchen.

"Oh, my stars. Sorry." She fiddled with her apron. "I was just ... uhh ... straightening this picture."

Bullshit. She'd been caught listening to our conversation. I didn't openly call her out on it. Instead, I reached over and tapped the indicated picture until it was level, smiling at her the whole time.

"Okay. Fine. My ears are as hot as a chili pepper. You caught me." She walked to Tony's side.

He'd also moved more toward the entrance to the living room, where our voices would have easily echoed to them.

"Look." Tony grimaced up at me. "Angie's been real cagey with us lately. She's usually not too good at lying to us, but ..." He straightened. "You've been taking her on some sort of dangerous adventures, haven't you?"

"I wouldn't say dangerous ..."

"She had a cut on her eye. And bruises on her arms." Nora pointed her finger at me.

"The cut was from her hitting it on the bathroom counter. I—"

"You keepin' our girl safe?" Tony grilled me.

"Yes, sir."

"Then carry-on doing whatever you're doing," he continued.

"We've never seen Angie more alive. After Tony's cancer came back, she kind of withdrew from life. Until you came along."

"We want to thank you. And ..." Tony wheeled himself back to his stack of papers. "I want you to take me whitewater rafting before I die."

"Antonio Marcus Johnson." Nora turned her attention away from me and glared at Tony. "Are you determined to leave me sooner than the good Lord says? You know I was just reading that article about how Idaho has the most deaths on our rivers. More than any—"

"Call it my final wish. I want to do something more exciting than bumping over rocks in a tractor. I dreamed of going to the Highlands, but that's not going to be possible, so the least I can do is float down the river on a raft."

Nora's rigid posture relaxed the more Tony went on. "Fine, you old goat." Her voice got all wobbly and she wiped at the base of her eyes.

"So, what do you say?" Tony asked.

It wasn't enough; I had to keep their rather clutzy daughter alive after she'd basically forced me into helping her. No, now I'd either have to say no to a dying man's wish or take on the responsibility of getting him on and off a raft without further damaging him.

Why the hell not? "Let's do it."

Tony let out the cutest old man whoop at my answer.

"But you have to finish helping me get these pipes put back together."

"Lead the way." Tony gestured with his hand toward the sink. "You better be better at white water rafting than plumbing, or we're all gonna die."

Chapter 28

Angie

Food. I needed food. Only an hour into my shift, my stomach gurgled like an active volcano. I'd managed to avoid running into Remi for a few more days, but it was getting difficult with him practically living at the farm. He was everywhere. The stable. The garden. The pasture. The fields. The toilet. Remi. Remi. Remi. Remi. Remi. Fracking man was going to drive me batty.

Gabby sat next to me, twirling in her office chair. I'd taken over for her, but like usual, she stayed behind to catch up on the happenings in my life before she went home. She lived alone and only had the hospital as a social life. Lili lounged next to Gabby in a rollie chair while Ryan and I filled in our notes about the babies we'd examined. All of us had our blue medical masks covering our chins.

My phone buzzed on the counter next to my laptop. It was Dan.

> *Fourteen days can't go by fast enough. I hate that work gets in the way of me seeing you.*

We'd discussed marriage several times, but I couldn't let myself think about the possibility of a proposal. We'd talked of our future, about how many kids we wanted, our ideal home ... of his goal to be married by his fortieth birthday this fall. He wanted kids and didn't want to be too old to play football with them in high school.

We'd been together for almost three months, he'd met my parents a few times, and still, I hadn't slept with him. Dan only knew the person I pretended to be. How could I be intimate with him without confessing everything? If I came clean, he would surely abandon me, and I could kiss his possible marriage proposal goodbye. I couldn't tolerate liars. Why should he?

Our relationship was disjointed. It was too serious too fast, yet he was my only viable option for making Papa's dream come true, so I pressed forward.

I gnawed on my lip. Dan was on a work trip, taking some execs on a skydiving tour. We'd had to postpone our next grand adventure for another two weeks. Dan had something big and secret in mind after I'd told him my dirt bike was out of commission after a gnarly wreck, which was true. He'd immediately suggested BASE jumping the bridge. When I'd made up that lie, I hadn't understood the hundreds of skydives you had to accomplish before even qualifying to attempt your first BASE jump. I'd assumed all you had to do was strap on a parachute and go for it.

Thankfully, I got Dan to back off that train easily enough, but he mentioned we could go canyoneering since I enjoyed it so much. I couldn't exactly tell him I'd lied about Deer Creek Falls. Whatever he had planned would have something to do with heights. If anything went wrong while hanging from a rock ledge ... I could die. I thought back to my failed dirt biking attempt. I'd only sustained a few bumps and bruises, a scratch here and there after wrecking, nothing serious.

The pain of my crash was nothing compared to the ecstasy of Remi's kiss. Anytime I had a quiet moment to myself, I'd find myself reliving that moment. Dan's kisses paled in comparison to the way, with one touch, Remi lit me on fire.

Remi's plea for me to be safe came back to me. It was one of the first times he'd looked at me without a selfish thought. He hadn't wanted to take advantage of me or find a way to buy my land. He looked straight into me, genuinely worried about my wellbeing. Not because of some land-deal falling through.

No. He cared for me.

And yet, he'd still find any way to get his hands on my land. Plus, he didn't believe in monogamy. He couldn't give me or Papa what we wanted most, what I'd been dreaming about since childhood. Finding someone to spend the rest of my life with. Someone who would love me like Papa loved Mama.

Therefore, Remi's attention, no matter how sincere, couldn't be trusted. True, I didn't love *love* Smoot yet, but those feelings would grow even after marriage.

I texted Smoot back.

> I can't wait.

My finger hovered over the send arrow a second before I pressed it. The pressure of my tangled lies tightened my chest.

His response came quickly.

> Are you at work?

Yep.

Thinking of you in your nursing outfit turns me on.

My nursing outfit? I glanced down at my bland hospital-issued scrubs.

"Is that Smoot?" Lili snatched my phone. I wouldn't expect a pregnant woman to be so fast.

"Give it back," I whined like a two-year-old.

Lili's pregnant belly had reached epic proportions. She had a month and a half to go, but if her belly button was any indication, those turkeys were well past done. I couldn't believe she managed to keep working. Most moms pregnant with twins were on bed rest at this point, not in operating rooms.

Sometimes, she snuck into the quiet of the NICU after surgeries. I think the hospital let her do whatever she wanted. They were too afraid to lose her.

Gabby huddled with Lili. "You're such a turn on," she teased and laughed.

"Scrubs are so hot," Lili chimed in, tucking her chin and lifting her eyebrows at me.

"*Daniel* is excited to see me again." I gave up trying to get my phone.

"Yeah. After he canceled on you two weeks ago?" Gabby swiveled on her chair to face me.

"What if the guy is a closet criminal?" Ryan paused and looked at me. "I've heard so many app dating horror stories."

"I already met him and kissed him, remember?" I'd told them about locking lips with Dan but not about doing the same with Remi. Given how much time my brain focused on the two, Remi's performance far more impressed me than Dan's. Not that Dan wasn't a good kisser; he just wasn't ... Remi. "Besides, we all know you'll find his social security number and take him out," I continued.

Ryan gave me a non-committal grunt. His Ex-Navy Seal background had never left him. He could be intimidating when he wanted to be, but it all melted away when he took care of his babies.

"Look, I like Daniel. He could be the one." I slouched back into my seat. Ironically, a few months ago, Lili was egging me on to swipe right on every profile on my screen. Now, she was the one waving the biggest caution flag.

"Are you two going to make a big deal about deleting the app from your phone together?" Gabby became more animated. "I think that's kinda romantic."

I shook my head and rolled my eyes. After her break-up of blockbuster proportions at the end of February, she'd sworn off dating altogether. That'd lasted three months, and she was back to her hopeless romantic self.

Lili splayed her feet apart and leaned back in her chair, still looking unbearably uncomfortable.

"When are you going to start maternity leave?" I deliberately changed the subject. I finished up the note, pressed submit, and focused on my best friend.

"Once the babies are born. Blake thinks I'm crazy, but I want to work until I go into labor or until Dr. Rusk puts me on bed rest."

I couldn't stop the wave of jealousy that hit me. Loving husband. Not one but two babies on the way ... after all Lili had been through, she deserved this level of happiness. It was just ... I did too. Didn't I?

"Can't wait to meet these two." Gabby leaned toward Lili's belly and scrunched her face.

"As long as they're not guests in our wing for too long. Hopefully, not at all," Ryan mumbled while his fingers moved across his keyboard.

My phone buzzed again in Lili's hand. She glanced at the screen, and her eyes widened.

"What?" I asked. "Whatever he said, it's confidential, and you're not allowed to tease me about it."

"It's not Smoot. It's Remi. You gave him your number too?" Lili asked. She tugged at her mask. "My my ... Look who's love life has exploded."

"Who's Remi, again?" Ryan asked, and my other two friends shushed him.

As if he needed shushing for a text.

"He's Angie's drop-dead gorgeous employee she hired to help her with the farm," Gabby answered while not looking away from my phone.

"My parents hired him," I pointed out and focused back on Lili. "You call *two* men an explosion? I was tired of communicating through Papa. It's easier this way." But Remi and I had done more texting since I'd started avoiding him.

Our all-out battles we'd waged against each other in person had moved into texts. I asked him to move pipe to the dry section of the cornfield. He told me he'd get around to it in two millennia when he finished hoeing the beets.

Fun times like that.

"You've been talking about Remi a lot lately. And I've never seen you look happier than you have this past week." Lili leaned back in her chair.

Even relegated to only using Oscar, Remi had taken over a lot of the responsibilities at the farm. Which meant he must be sneaking into the other tractors without me knowing, but I didn't care as much as I once would have.

This round of hay harvest had been the easiest in history. More than half the field had been baled by the time I'd napped and gone out to the tractor. I couldn't figure out how Remi managed to do it all. It was like he was three people. One step ahead of me and done with my check lists before I could make them.

Lili tapped her thumbs rapidly over my screen.

"Wait. What are you texting him?" I moved to take my phone, but Gabby held me back. I looked to Ryan for assistance, but his eyes simply crinkled at the corners as he smiled and went back to typing his notes. "You two are going to get us in trouble with Janice. She doesn't like cell phones out on shift."

"You and I both know Janice never checks in on the night shift." Gabby allowed me to sidestep her.

Lili tossed me my phone. "He's outside. He brought you food."

My stomach gurgled loudly as if sensing its torture was nearing a close. "What? Me? Food?" I gestured dumbly to my chest. I couldn't form sentences.

"I told him to meet you at the main entrance." Lili shifted to the front of her chair. "I'll come with you."

Of course, she would come.

"I might as well leave now too. My shift ended over an hour ago. And I need to feed my fish." Gabby stood and walked into the breakroom.

Ryan froze, and his eyes laser-locked on the door Gabby had gone through. Not one minute later, she marched out to Ryan and threw a handful of leftover hole punch confetti at his scrub top.

"You filled my purse. It'll take me forever to get these out." She hit him on his shoulder with her bag, and little, round, white pieces of paper fluttered to the floor.

Being an immovable wall of muscle, Ryan didn't budge with the impact. "Payback for the chickens," he said.

I laughed and helped Lili stand as we followed in Gabby's furious footsteps. She paused at the door to the washroom and flipped her middle finger at Ryan as she pushed through.

With a laugh, Ryan looked at me. "Take as long as you want. I'll cover for you."

I held the door open for Lili. "You know her revenge isn't going to be pretty."

The crinkles around his eyes grew. "I'm planning on it."

Chapter 29

Remi

"Be right back." I closed the door to Myles' compact car.

"Sure." He shook his head at me like I was a lost cause.

With the stress of his job, I'd forced Myles to take a Friday night off. On our way into town, we'd stopped for burgers, and without thinking, I'd also placed an order for Angie. She'd become a part of my daily routine and had me trained like one of Pavlov's dogs.

No, I wasn't trained. I just couldn't let her go hungry.

Pine needles littered the sidewalk, and the scent of evergreen permeated the dry air. Harsh evening light warmed my back as I faced the main entrance to the hospital. If the sun could get this hot in the first couple of days of July, then working in the fields would be brutal come August.

Weather this far north wasn't supposed to compete with the Texan summer. Of course, I spent most of my days in an air-conditioned office or a cool pool house.

The sliding doors opened, and I stopped pacing by the banner that read *Heroes Work Here*, nearly dropping the bag I held. Angie walked out in her scrubs and slipped the mask first off one ear and then another. Her blonde hair flowed in soft curls around her navy-scrub-clad shoulders, and I couldn't stop staring.

The pull I felt for her magnified tenfold. She saved lives for a living, tiny baby lives ... what could be more attractive than that?

I exited my trance and took a few steps to meet her under the awning. Lili and another nurse flanked her sides.

"Hey, Remi." Lili waved, looking all nine months pregnant and wearing oversized scrubs.

"Hello, Lili." I forced myself to look away from Angie and focus on her. "Did Blake get those cribs built?"

"He's gotten one up. But the other one is giving him fits. I've heard more cuss words coming from the nursery than I do from his mechanic's shop."

I laughed and turned to the other woman standing with Angie.

"This is my co-worker, Gabby." Angie motioned towards the other woman but betrayed herself and eyed the to-go bag I still held.

"Nice to meet you." I nodded at Gabby, whose Latin heritage showed in her deep-brown eyes, black hair, and tanned skin.

"See you later." Lili waved and walked into the parking lot.

"Until tomorrow," Gabby said, walking alongside Lili—with round flecks of white paper floating behind her.

I looked from Gabby's purse to Angie. She laughed. "It's a long story."

I handed the fast-food bag over to her. "I thought you'd be hungry since you didn't have a chance to eat before you left."

Walking to the bench situated under a large pine tree, she sat as she dug through the bag of food I brought. She pulled out the wrapped burger and gasped when she opened it. She took a bite without saying anything.

"I got you the bacon cheeseburger, but I know you don't like the calories in fries, so I ordered you the sweet potato ones," I chattered on and on while she took bites, chewed, and swallowed.

"Mmm ... This is the best thing I've eaten all year," she said between bites. "Thank you."

"You're welcome."

I sat with her while she finished her burger, telling her about the day and the rooster attack I'd barely avoided. All at once, the desire to do this every day filled me. To come visit Angie at work or wait until she walked in the door and fill her in about the happenings on the farm.

My eyes constantly dropped to her lips. The longer I went without, the more I wanted to kiss her, yet I resisted the urge to tuck her under my arm and plant one on her. Why? Because friends didn't kiss, and I needed to prove to myself I could be friends with a woman. I'd never successfully had a platonic relationship with one, and the challenge of it pushed me to try harder. Plus, Myles told me he didn't think it was possible. What he didn't understand was having Angie in my life as a friend would be way more tolerable than living without her.

This life was fiction, and as much as I wanted to act out *Leave it to Beaver* with her, how did I think it would end? I fell silent as she told me all about the feud between her co-workers until she'd finished the last fry.

"Well, I better get back inside. I left Ryan alone in there." She crumpled the burger wrapper and stood.

I followed her to the garbage and walked her to the front door. My hand itched to hold hers. Fisting my hands, I kept them by my sides.

"Have a great night saving those babies." I moved in to hug her but paused when I got close. Our eyes met, and for the briefest second, she leaned toward me, her eyes half-lidded and glazed. I smiled and ran my tongue over my bottom lip. So, I wasn't the only one still stuck in the memory of what happened on the side of that mountain trail.

She straightened and took a breath. "What's in it for you?"

In it for me? "I didn't want you to go hungry ... I don't know what I could gain—"

"No. Buying our property." She spoke softly, but we still stood close enough I heard her words fine. "You're putting a lot of effort into this. What do you get?"

My first instinct was to lie and say something like profit for the company meant profit for me. A friend wouldn't do that, so I told her the truth. "I don't like what I do. I'm good at it, though, which is why my father has made it nearly impossible for me to leave. He's promised that if I make this deal happen, he'll let me leave the company and give me enough startup money for mine and Myles' business."

I expected Angie to react in anger, but she became more contemplative. "What business idea do you have?"

"We want to open an extreme sports store called Texas Bros."

I waited for her reaction, but a slight crinkle on her forehead and a nibble on her fingernail were the only indications she repressed her feelings.

I went on, "We're working on the name. But if we open it here, we could also offer tandem jumps off the bridge."

Her eyebrows shot up. "You're thinking of staying here and not going back to Dallas?"

Shuffling a step closer to her, I took one of her hands and rubbed my thumb on her palm, never dropping my gaze from hers. "I can think of a few good reasons to stay. One in particular."

Stiffening her posture, she tugged her hand from mine. "Well, thanks for the burger."

The automatic doors whooshed open, and she rushed back inside. I'd rattled her. She couldn't only think of me as the big bad wolf coming to blow her house down if I had goals and dreams.

Wandering back to where Myles was parked, I got in with a slight smile on my face.

"That took longer than you said." Myles backed out of his spot. "I'll never believe you again. 'I'm going to drop off this burger. Be back in two minutes.'" He air-quoted and did a sad imitation of my voice.

"She had a few things to go over with me. You know, farm stuff."

Myles out right laughed at me. "You mean the stuff you've been hiring our crew to do?"

"Shhh ... if you don't say anything, no one will find out."

The workload Angie laid on top of me had become unbearable, and I remembered ... *I have money*. So, I cheated.

New construction in the neighborhood had slowed with the supply chain, and it'd been a headache trying to get the houses built without destroying the budget. Myles needed to keep his full attention on being CDC's lead foreman, but still, I pulled him away to help get my list done, taking on Angie's work as well as mine so she could get the sleep she needed.

A few times this week, I'd even tasked guys from landscaping to get the hay bales off the fields and hoe the beet field. Angie had no idea since I only employed the extra workforce during her shifts at the hospital and put in sixteen-hour days when she didn't.

Tonight, I took great pleasure in the fact that the pea field harvest was getting finished while Myles and I went to the climbing gym. Some things were worth paying for.

"You're so far gone with this girl you can't tell up from down." Myles pulled out of the parking lot into traffic.

"We're friends." If I could even call us that. When she wasn't avoiding me, we still argued. Fighting Angie sparked more life in me than jumping out of a plane.

"You're telling me you haven't made a move on her?" He stopped at the red light and turned to look at me with one skeptical eyebrow raised.

I shrugged and half-smiled, unable to hide the truth from my oldest friend.

"Remi." He shook his head, faced forward, and slammed on the accelerator when the light turned green. "What are you thinking?"

I scrubbed my right hand down the side of my face. "I don't know. She's so amazing and—"

"Has a vagina?"

I glared at him. "Not fair. Last time I checked, you like vaginas too."

"Not ones that could cost me my lifetime goals and dreams." He flipped on his blinker and turned toward old-town Twin Falls. "We're this close to being free to open our store—"

"You think I would jeopardize that?"

"With your track record ... I'm not sure. Angie isn't your usual type."

I wasn't aware I had a usual type. "Meaning?"

"She's a girl who wants commitment. Remember what Blake said." He turned the wheel and swerved into a parking spot facing the gym. The car jerked to a stop as he shifted into park before coming to a complete stop.

"Of course, I remember."

"She's the first woman who hasn't cowered to you or worshipped you, and you're not one to back down from a challenge. That's all this is. She's another Katie Carlenti."

College. Junior year. Katie wore her principles on her shoulders like a cape. It took me a while, but eventually, she gave in to my persuasive powers ... like they all did. It didn't end well for Katie and me. She wanted more than I was willing to give, so when she presented me with an ultimatum, I left.

Every time I thought of a woman` in my past, I imagined a guy treating Angie that way. I squirmed in my seat, uncomfortable with the nause-ating guilt settling in my stomach. I'd used Katie horribly. How could I have been so unfeeling, self-centered, and ... wrong?

"Angie's not Katie. I've never felt this way—"

"You know what's going to happen once you buy her land. She's never going to get over it. A relationship with her is impossible."

He echoed my relentless thoughts. "Who said I'm looking for a rela-tionship?"

Myles leaned his head onto the headrest and hit me with an I-don't-believe-you look. "Sure. And you brought her a burger and spent twenty minutes talking with her while she ate it, without so much as a peck. You're hooked."

"Are you kidding? You're talking about a woman who's punished me from sunup to sundown for the last three months."

"Pigs get fat; hogs get slaughtered. Make sure you stay the pig." Myles opened his door and got out.

I always thought that saying was dumb. Pigs get slaughtered too, in the end.

Looping an arm over the top of his open door, Myles leaned back into the car. "You're setting both you and Angie up for a whole lot of pain."

He closed his door and popped the trunk to retrieve our gear.

Chapter 30

Angie

Water rushed over a rock, jutting out in the middle of the river. It amazed me how clear it could be, yet the river became murky, a deep olive-green color, when looking at it in its entirety. As if the sediments dumping into it took away its clarity.

Oh, how I could relate. Normally, I didn't struggle with sleeping; however, the last couple of nights, I'd found myself waking up and staring at my bedroom ceiling. Debt. The farm. Papa's illness. Family. What would Mama do when the cancer took Papa from us? Loneliness. Dan. My job. Remi. My feelings for him ... All these sediments weighed on me and robbed me of direction. I wandered the meandering paths of possibilities at night.

If Remi didn't work for CDC and I didn't own the land they wouldn't rest trying to buy until it was theirs, then what would our relationship look like? If he believed in marriage then maybe, just maybe, I'd be with him instead of Dan.

All the pebbles weighing me down lifted for an infinitesimal moment. Remi lifted my worries. He'd find solutions to my problems and be there to wrap his arms around me, let me cry on his chest when they couldn't be solved. Like Papa's cancer.

I yearned for Remi to be a possibility. But he said himself, he'd never marry. What he wanted from me was to scratch the itch he couldn't ignore until another one came along. Tears gathered in the base of my eyes. I blinked them away.

A breeze rustled the leaves and wispy branches of the willow tree next to me. Today was the Fourth of July, and for the first time, I skipped the parade in town, which usually consisted of a shiz-ton of tractors, livestock, and classic cars. Papa didn't feel up to going this morning, and I didn't want to field the pitying looks or condolences given as if Papa had already died. In lieu of festivities, I'd gone out and worked the fields with Remi before dawn.

Then, at Remi's insistence that the holiday needed celebrated, we'd changed into swimming suits and come here.

The crackling heat between us had only grown since the taste we'd had of each other. An appetizer that hadn't fully satisfied either of us. Props to Remi, though. I'd clarified that I wanted him to stay away from me, and he'd kept his distance.

He was as good as the fourth and final hot Chris, Chris Evans. On and off-screen, Chris not only had the looks, but he also had the sensitivity and generosity to go with it. Over the course of the past few months, Remi had proven he possessed attributes of all the Chris's.

My eyelids sagged, and I leaned my head against the rough bark of the willow tree behind me. I drifted in and out of sleep. I was in the bubble bath, ear buds in place, and sounds of nature, the rushing river, resounded in my head. Steam clouded the mirror. Strong hands rubbed the tight knots in my neck, then dipped beneath the water, following my spine to my lower back and the upper curve of my bottom. The touch of his fingertips on my shoulders replaced by his lips.

Bubbles clung to my arm as I lifted it and curved it around my husband's neck. I angled my head back and met the dark irises, deep and rich golden-brown eyes of ... Remi.

I jerked upright, fully awake.

Crab nuggets! Remi'd invaded my fantasies like a computer virus. Too bad I couldn't shut down, reboot myself, and get rid of him. I grudgingly admitted I'd miss him. He made my life so much more complicated, yet interesting, messy, and thrilling ... And, blast it; he wasn't easy to deny.

Remi came to sit next to me on the bank of the river, wearing a green and grey swimming suit. He kept his top-half covered with a T-shirt, much to my disappointment.

No! Not disappointed. Thrilled. Couldn't be more pleased. Ecstatic, in fact, that he wore a shirt. The more he remained covered, the easier I'd be able to regain control of my imagination.

Considering our attire, I already guessed we'd be doing something in the water, but he didn't remove anything from his truck bed.

Which left ... cliff jumping? Oh dang—I hoped not.

"What's in store for today?" Resisting the temptation to shield myself from him, I lounged back against a rock in my one-piece, navy-blue bathing suit, grateful for the shorts covering more of my body from his view. Still, considering where my mind wandered during my brief nap, I felt naked.

"It's a surprise. Just waiting on a couple of people, and we'll be ready." He bent his knees and leaned his elbows on them. Grabbing a twig, he drew designs in the dirt.

His beard, trimmed shorter with the hotter temperatures, framed his chin, tempting me to touch it—to rub my cheek on it and remind myself how it felt on my skin. That was definitely on the 'not allowed to do with Remi' list.

Mid-morning sunshine crested the canyon rim and chased me further into the shade of the willow tree, the temperatures creeping into the eighties. Slight breezes carried smells of sagebrush, occasional wafts of stagnant water, and scents of Remi's fresh-cut-cedar deodorant mixed with his sweat. Somehow, Remi'd become a proficient farmer, and repeatedly surprised me with his work ethic.

Although, I suspected he hired a workforce, I couldn't prove it, but what he accomplished would be impossible alone. I couldn't break him. The closer to harvest we got, with Remi hurdling every obstacle I threw at him, I began to panic.

Would I sell my childhood memories, a hundred years of family history, over some bet?

I couldn't. It sickened me to think of backing out of an agreement, but I had to. I couldn't handle losing Papa and my land. Every square inch of the property had been plowed, fertilized, planted, watered, and maintained by me, forming an unbreakable bond.

And then there was the conflict of Remi to consider. I wanted him gone. I wanted him to stay forever.

"Why don't you believe in marriage?" The question spewed from my mouth before the thought of it had fully formed.

He lifted his gaze to meet mine for a millisecond, then he went back to contemplating his drawing in the dirt. Seconds stretched to minutes.

"I was five ..."

His response was so soft I had to strain to hear him over the water.

"... when I first walked in on my dad having an affair with another woman. Didn't take much longer before I figured out my mother had a string of lovers too. My home wasn't like yours. Sure, my parents spoiled me with stuff, but love was lacking."

I remained silent, afraid that if I spoke, he'd stop. Since our kiss, I sensed a shift in him. Of course, I'd been staying away from him as much as possible. It seemed like he manufactured reasons to be with me, like that blessed burger on my last shift, but he hadn't tried to kiss me again.

My body hated him for it, but I couldn't be the one to break first. I had to stay strong. Okay, maybe those sleepless nights had been caused by my subconscious wandering to that moment—his hand traveling to my waistband—only in my dream, I didn't stop him ...

"I guess I don't see the point of getting married. At least I didn't." He stopped sifting the twig through the dirt and locked eyes with mine.

Words weren't necessary to communicate what I saw in his deep-brown eyes. The breeze picked up, tugging a strand of my hair free. Remi brushed it back into place, moving his hand to cup my chin and tipping my head further up. I froze, and while I appeared to have halted all movement, my insides became a percussion section in a middle school band.

"Since being here, I can see the appeal of being with one woman for the rest of my life," he whispered in my ear.

I couldn't look away from him, and yet doubts seeped in. Why would this amazing, charismatic, caring man—who happened to be a million-aire—choose me?

I enjoyed the feel of his body next to me and despite the warm air, chills flowed from where our bare thighs touched. Sounds of the gurgling river and calls from meadowlarks and killdeer receded as all my senses fixated on him.

My chest expanded with my deep breath, and I savored our contact.

"Angie, I—" He stopped, even though I waited to hear what he had to say.

His thumb traced the line of my jaw, my bottom lip, and my cheek. I closed my eyes, savoring his touch, anticipating the pressure of his lips on mine—alarmed by how much I yearned for it.

Why, oh, *why* did I always fall for the wrong guy?

Tires crunching against gravel pulled me out of the cocoon Remi had woven around me. My eyes flicked open. Remi's breaths still fluttered against my face as he slowly dropped his hand, allowing me to drift further from him.

Daniel, I reminded myself. I would see Daniel in a few days, and his goals matched mine. He wanted a family. It wouldn't be good to be hung up on Remi the entire time I was with Dan.

Disappointment and longing collided in every one of Remi's non-verbal cues. The slight sag in his shoulders, the way he didn't relinquish his hand immediately, and his eyes spoke volumes. It almost made me sad as I stood and pushed the willowy branches aside to see better who'd joined us.

"Myles?" Remi's friend towed a trailer with a raft in it, and next to him, in the cab were ... my parents. I turned back to Remi. "Why are they here?"

I hadn't told Mama or Papa about my 'adventures with Remi' as I liked to call them. Mama would have a heart attack, and Papa would lecture me on unnecessary risk.

"Believe it or not, your dad asked to do this." Remi walked past me to assist Papa from the truck.

With as much care as if Papa was his own father, Remi gently gripped Papa's forearm and waited for Mama to come to his other side. Once again, my eyes clouded with tears. Over the last couple of weeks, Papa had become much weaker, a constant reminder we would be forced to say goodbye sooner than I ever planned.

I swallowed around the lump in my throat and forced a smile. For the remainder of the time we had, come hell or high water, I would make the most of it.

Myles opened a reclining camp chair near the spot where Remi and I had been sitting, and Mama and Remi deposited Papa in the chair. Remi must have bought that specific chair to allow my father the most comfort. I walked to Mama, who rested a hand on Papa's shoulder while Myles and Remi unloaded the raft.

Life vests were then retrieved from the trailer, and Remi handed a bright pink one with black accents to me. Despite my best efforts, I wiped at the tears that slid along my cheek, attempting to hide it by slipping my arms into the vest. But of course, Remi noticed, in tune with me as ever.

He moved to me and helped me zip it closed, giving me a reassuring squeeze on my shoulder. Myles assisted Papa into his, first taking off his ratty flannel, carefully laying it on the back of the chair, then making sure his straps were tightened. They chit chatted around me while I struggled to get ahold of my emotions.

I hadn't seen Papa this happy since his cancer had come out of remission. Nothing made him look forward to another day as time marched forward. How many times this week had I begged the clock to stop to allow me more time with my Papa? But it never listened. Dawn would come, followed by night, taking another precious day with it.

Myles pushed the raft into the water and called to us. Nerves overtook my melancholic thoughts. I didn't like water, especially water in Snake River with its hidden eddies and dangerous currents.

Hiding my fear, I let my feet carry me to the water's edge. I looked back at Papa. "Are you sure about this?"

His face brightened with his smile. "I haven't been this excited in years. This has always been on my bucket list."

"Then why haven't we gone sooner? I thought you were afraid of doing anything remotely dangerous." I looked from him to Mama, who stood on the water's edge, clutching her vest in a white-knuckled grip.

"The farm kept me busy, and your mother isn't a fan of water ..." He cupped one hand around the side of his mouth and leaned toward me. "Or anything not safe," he finished in a loud whisper.

Mama whapped Papa gently on his shoulder. "Hey, nothing wrong with a good dose of fear. Keeps me from doing dumb things like this." She gestured to the swirling current.

"It'll be okay. We're in good hands." Papa rubbed Mama's arm that still rested on his shoulder.

Remi helped Papa stand and slowly walk toward the small raft. Handing us both a paddle, Myles instructed me and my mother to straddle the raft. Flinching, I looped a leg over the blue rubber and dipped my sandaled foot into the opaque water. For Papa, I would float the river and keep my terror under control.

I looked at Mama. She sat across from me, her lips in a tight line, and she hugged the paddle to her chest.

Myles helped Remi situate Papa in the center, causing the raft to bob up and down.

"I'll meet you at the end of the run," Myles said.

"Thanks," Remi called to him as Myles jogged to the truck.

After showing Mama and me how to paddle in sync and teaching us how to sit properly, Remi moved to the back and pushed us into the current.

Frigid water rushed over my submerged sandal as we glided over its swirling depths.

"You okay, Mama?" I asked. My own heart thudded in my throat.

She let out her breath and nodded, a smile wavering on her lips.

"I'm going to need you to paddle through this first set of rapids. Remember if you fall off, keep your legs straight, relax, and go with the flow of the river. Don't fight it."

"*Rapids?*" I asked in a high-pitched screech.

We rounded a bend, and the now-visible white caps almost made me drop my paddle.

"Oh, hell no." I paddled backward, causing the boat to spin.

"Forward paddle. We don't want to hit these sideways." An urgency hung in Remi's words that terrified me.

"Angie ..." Mama's scared voice carried to me over the sound of the river.

"It's okay." Papa touched my shoulder. "You're tougher than this river."

When I glanced at him, it was as if his illness had left him. New life had been breathed into him. His face split into a wide grin; he was ready to take on what lay ahead ... even if I wasn't.

Trembling and holding my breath, I put my full force into the paddle, bringing the nose around. We hit the first rapid. The raft lifted and fell, jarring my leg inside the boat free. I lost grip on the paddle and fell into the churning water. I sucked in a deep breath.

Cold and darkness engulfed me.

For the millionth time since Remi had come into my life, a single thought stabbed through my brain: *I'm going to die.*

I AM GOING TO EFFING DIE.

I rammed against a rock, which sent me rolling in the churning water.

My lungs burned.

I couldn't breathe.

Reaching in any direction, I tried to find something to pull me to the surface.

Nothing.

I'm going to die.

The strong current tossed me about like a rag doll.

Remi's voice came to me. Calm and steady. *Relax. Keep your legs straight. Don't fight.*

Then my Papa's. *You're tougher than this river.*

Closing my eyes, I stabilized my mind, stiffened my legs, and grabbed the shoulder straps of my life vest.

Then, I submitted to the chaos around me, trusting it to bring me above water. The world around me grew lighter. I broke the surface and gasped for air.

"Angie!" Two strong hands gripped my life vest and pulled me into the boat. "Are you okay?"

I coughed and fell back onto the plastic base of the raft next to my father. The sun blinded me as I continued gulping in air. I wanted to yell, *Get me out of here!* But then Papa leaned over me, blocking the sun. I couldn't ruin this for him.

"Never been better," I croaked. Leaning on Remi, I made it back to my position on the edge. I checked on Mama. Her hair was still dry, but she held the paddle like her life depended on it. Thank goodness she hadn't gone in with me.

Remi maneuvered the raft to where my paddle floated in an eddy. We retrieved it in time to face off with the next gauntlet. Rivulets of water trailed down my body, cooling me in the bright sunshine. I'd already survived falling off the boat. Holding my chin up, I challenged the rapids.

"Bring it on," I whispered.

At the same time, Remi hollered, "Forward paddle!"

Chapter 31

Remi

Double checking the straps on the rafts, I waved to Myles in his rearview mirrors. After picking us all up at the end of the run, he'd given Angie and me a ride back to where I'd parked my vehicle.

"Thanks for your help!" I yelled.

Myles leaned out his window. "No problem. I'll make sure these two get home safe. See you later." With one final wave, he let off the brakes and drove forward.

The back truck tires spun on the gravel until they leveled out on the paved road. Checking the surrounding area for anything we might have left, I walked to where Angie sat with a towel wrapped around her in the passenger seat of my Ford.

With each step, the last of my stress left me. Tony and Nora were alive and well. Angie too. As a bonus, Tony had loved every minute of it once his nerves had settled. His smile had lit up his whole face, making everything worth it.

I'd chosen the rafting run because everyone around here talked about the mild rapids. With the low water levels, some had been bigger than I'd anticipated, and when Angie had disappeared under the water, my heart had stopped. The experienced rafter in me expected she'd surface like everyone usually did. The key word being *usually*. I'd never been present when someone had died on a rafting trip, but I'd heard horror stories. My mind went to those worst-case scenarios the longer Angie stayed underwater.

What if she never came up? What if she drowned? What if Angie wasn't a part of my life anymore?

What if? What if? *What if?*

In less than two minutes, my feelings for Angie had become clear.

I loved her.

At least, I thought this feeling of 'I can't live without her' meant the big L-word. I'd sacrifice anything to guarantee her happiness. I'd never felt this way for a woman; hell, I never planned on ever feeling this way. It'd snuck up on me like a rattlesnake in the brush and bit me.

What the hell was I supposed to do now? Confess my undying love for her? That sounded so corny I almost vomited in my mouth. Instead, I'd rather do the most unromantic thing possible.

I climbed into the truck and shut my door. Starting the engine, I shifted into drive and followed Myles's route out of here. "I heard about an event in town and kind of sort of signed us up."

She shivered even though it was as hot as a billy goat in a pepper patch in my cab. "I don't know if I'm feeling up for it."

Her statement presented a conundrum. First option: listen to her and run into the possibility of dropping the L-bomb on her. Second option: proceed forward as if she hadn't said she didn't want to go and get her in a horn-tossing mood.

Arguing was much safer than being nice. Rather than teasing her about falling in the river, I'd give her a break now, seeing as how her eyes were already half-lidded.

Angie leaned her head against the seat and dozed while I drove the thirty minutes into town, to the high school soccer fields. I'd parked at the back of the full parking lot and slipped the white T-shirts I'd custom ordered in the over-sized pockets of my swim trunks. The entire town gathered in the bleachers, though I was too far away to spot anyone I knew.

"Where are we?" Angie stretched and yawned, dropping the towel to the seat. She looked around her as the distant crowd erupted in a cheer loud enough for us to hear over the still running air-conditioning. "What exactly does 'I don't feel up for it' mean to you?"

"What?" I jiggled my earlobe and turned the key in the ignition. Sliding it out, I put it in the cup holder. "Got water in my ears. I can't hear you." I shoved my door open.

She huffed out a breath and let out a little growl—perfect. Hopping to the ground, I waited for her tirade to begin.

"How could you have water in your ears? You never went in the ri—"

I shut the door on her words, knowing this would drive her crazy enough to get out of the car and tell me exactly what a terrible human being I was. She didn't disappoint. Quicker than a scalded cat, she came up next to me.

"First, you dump me in a river, then you ignore me and expect me to take part in this barbaric ..."

Barbaric? Angie trailed on. I started walking toward the crowd of people. Everyone cheered on what was happening in the pen in the center of the field. A circle of feeder panels had been erected, and as I drew closer, it'd been filled with mud up to the edge of the slits ... making the puddle about two feet deep.

I came to stand at the side of the bleachers, waving to Agnes, Joe, and Mitch, my friends from the farm store. They cheered on their coworkers, dressed in matching Country Store shirts, although the three in the ring were now completely brown. A timer ran on the clock while they dodged and dipped, falling face-first into the slop.

Chuck and Pedro called to me, surrounded by Pedro's posse of kids. One kid hung on Pedro's arm, and another sat on top of Chuck's shoulders.

In a matter of a few months, I'd been accepted in this town. I had actual friends who knew nothing of my family or my fortune. I'd never experienced this phenomenon.

A squeal cut through the air as one of them caught hold of the animal's back leg.

"... most low-down country thing we do. Pig wrestling? Seriously, Remi. You couldn't have warned me?"

Pig wrestling. It qualified as the most unromantic thing possible. And I didn't like how much the stub-nosed, curly tailed beasts scared me. Against my better judgment, I'd Googled the story of the pigs and old man Peterson. What I'd read could never be unread.

Today, I'd face my fear head-on.

"If I would have told you, you wouldn't have done anything but mope around your house and work yourself past the point of exhaustion on your farm. It's the fricking Fourth of July. Let's celebrate."

"By traumatizing a pig?" She put her hands on her hips. "No, thank you. And I thought pigs terrified you."

"Angie!"

I was saved from answering by Blake's little girl.

She came running down the bleachers and launched into Angie's arms. "You've been busy. I missed you."

"Hey, Maddie. Your mom here?" Angie turned her back to me and looped an arm around the girl, knocking the headphones on Maddie's head askew.

"No. She's at home with Daddy." Maddie pointed into the stands to a woman with short, gray hair who looked like an older version of Lili. She lifted a hand at us, mid-conversation with Chuck and Pedro. "I'm here with Renee. The Bennies are making Mommy tired and sick." She straightened her headphones and peeked up at me, then stiffened and leaned closer to Angie. "Who's this human you're always with? He comes over to my house sometimes."

I laughed and walked to stand in front of them. I stuck out my hand. "Remington James the Third."

Maddie eyed my hand, tilting her head back and forth, not budging from Angie's side. "Do you like him?" She jutted a thumb in my direction. "This human."

Angie looked at me. "He's tolerable."

"Okay. Nice to meet you *tall*er-rable Remington."

I laughed as she finally took my hand but grimaced when the pig squealed again. "I don't like it when the piggy is upset."

I turned my attention to the mud-covered men carrying the whining animal. They managed to place the pig in the barrel and a cheer went through the crowd. I tended to agree with Maddie, I felt for the pig. "It'll be our turn soon." I nudged Angie. "Maddie, want to join our team?"

"No." She didn't hesitate, then tugged on Angie's arm. "Are you going to go in there? With him?"

"He thinks I'm going to, but I'm so *not* going in there to get all muddy and chase around a pig for sport. I'm in my swimming suit, and I've had a rough morning ..."

The longer Angie went on, the more emphatic Maddie's nod became. Without hesitation, she joined the force against me. It appeared I had to win over more than Angie.

"Might I remind you of condition number three?" I held three fingers in Angie's face. "You have to do ..." Motioning to her, I waited for her to finish my sentence.

"Everything you say," she mumbled. "But this doesn't count—"

"Bup-bup-bup." I put my index finger over her full lips. She narrowed her eyes, and for a split second, I thought she would open her mouth and bite my finger. Didn't know why, but I found this to be a bit erotic. "I picked up every single rock from one side of your farm to the other, because you told me to. It goes both ways ..."

"I also pay you," she said around my finger.

"Is this the weird human who has been working on your farm? Nora says Mae doesn't like him." Maddie folded her arms and jutted her hips out like a teen. I guessed her to be under ten. I caught sight of a scar slanting across her cheek and couldn't help but wonder what happened.

I let my hand fall to my side once again. "You and I both know I don't need your money," I whispered, making sure the super-observant kid didn't overhear. "I have other motivations for staying." I raised my eyebrows suggestively at her.

She stiffened. "No."

Rex Southerland, the mayor of this small-town, announced Angie and me over the loudspeaker, followed by the name of our team ... The Bacon Bandits. Capitalizing on this opportunity, I whipped out our shirts. An image of a pig with a mask and a cape sneaking off with a bag of money centered on the shirt.

"You're not joking." Angie put a hand to her forehead. "When did you have time to get these made?"

"Do you have one for me?" Maddie pointed at the logo.

"You can have mine." After all, I matched them well enough already with my plain white shirt. I winked at the little girl. "Or I can get one made in your size."

"I'll take it." Maddie snatched my shirt and pulled it over her head. "And I'll be on your team. But I'm not going in there." She pointed to the pen.

The men working the ring, thankfully, switched the much larger pig to one that could be managed by two people. If I'd been pitted against that other beast, I would have lost my nerve and run screaming back to my truck. "Okay, Maddie. Go over there and wait for my signal." I pointed to the pens where the other pigs were being held and gave her the rest of her marching orders.

"Angie? Remi? I see you over there. Stop making eyes at each other and go catch yourself a pig." Rex's mechanical voice boomed over the loudspeaker.

The stands erupted in laughter.

"We're coming, Rex. Give us another minute!" I shouted toward the announcer's booth.

"One minute. Convince her quick." Another laugh came from the bleachers. *"Can we get sixty seconds on the clock?"*

The scoreboard lit up with one minute on the clock and began ticking down.

60 ... 59 ... 58 ...

"Are you going to make me wrestle a pig by myself?" I leveled one of my smiles on her I knew to be effective on other women.

"Don't forget about me." Maddie's adult large shirt hung well past her knees.

47 ... 46 ... 45 ...

"Stop looking at me like that." Angie folded her arms and glared at me. "The whole town is watching."

"I'll stop once you agree."

34 ... 33 ... 32 ...

After a few more terse words emitted from Angie's mouth, she took her shirt and yanked it on while she marched to the mud pit. I did an over-the-top fist pump, sending the town into another round of cheers.

Maddie took off to the pens at a run while Angie and I made it to the edge. The circular structure had no gate. By the time I'd figured that out, Angie had gotten in quicker than a whip. I followed, landing in mud well above my ankles.

The black and white spotted pig about the size of the bacon bits faced us on the opposite side of the pen. I'd grown attached to the tiny monsters capable of ingesting my bones and instantly pitied the creature.

In the background, a horn blared, and the crowd shouted with it.

Sorry little guy. I promise this is for your own good. I dove for the pig. Angie must have had the same idea. We collided mid-air and slid into the mess. I fell backward while her entire body disappeared under the surface.

The pig scampered to the other side of the pen as Angie came up, gasping for air. She scrubbed the back of her hand across her mouth.

"Ugh." She wiped at her forearms, flicking her fingertips toward the cesspool. Mud splattered in tiny specks around her. Slop glopped from the previously white shirt now bunched at her midsection, exposing her navy-blue swimming suit.

I stood and laughed. "Well, you can't get any dirtier now."

"Are you just going to stand there laughing at me, or are you going to help me catch this pig?" Angie pointed to our black-and-white, spotted prey quivering in the corner.

The pig followed us with its eyes. It remained where it stood, its belly brushing the surface of the mud pit as if waiting for us to make a move first, ready to bolt at any moment.

"You come around that way and force the piglet to me. Don't let it circle around you."

I straightened and gave her a mock salute. "Yes, ma'am."

"Don't call me ma'am." She bent her knees and widened her stance, preparing to catch the pig as I shoved it her way.

Following her precise instructions, I waved my arms and hollered at the pig. It pivoted in a quick circle looking for a window of escape. I did my best to hop in front of its face and force it in the direction I wanted it to go. It darted past Angie, and she dove for it, missing it by mere inches. It bolted toward me. I laid out my entire six-foot-three-inch body, belly-flopping face first.

The cool, oversaturated dirt contrasted with the heat I'd been subjected to all day. How much of this was mud, and how much of it was feces? Surely the pig peed and pooped with how many times he'd been scared today. Still, it felt like a spa day. Some people, my mother included, spent a fortune soaking in mud baths like this one.

Honestly, they should charge extra for adding in the natural element of pig urine and pig feces. I wrinkled my nose and gagged. Since being on the farm, I could decisively say, pig manure was by far the most stinky.

Once again, Angie and I regained our feet. I glanced at the clock, and we only had two minutes remaining to catch the pig before someone else would take our place. It was now or never.

Forgetting all strategy, I charged the animal. It squealed and bolted in the opposite direction. I predicted its movements, and as it ran past Angie, dodging her attempt to grab it, I jumped on it and wrapped my arms around its middle.

The stewed mixture splattered into my mouth, and I did my best to spit out what I could, but I swallowed the rest, not relinquishing my hold on the pig.

The poor animal bucked and kicked against my chest, screaming as if I was about to strangle it.

"Help me!" Its snout hit my jaw. "He's getting away from me."

Angie came to my side and contained the squirming animal's front legs. She jerked it toward the barrel, but I shook my head.

"This way." I tipped my chin toward the nearest fence. "Trust me."

Awkwardly, we made our way to the edge. The feisty little pig almost caused us to drop him twice. The mud, combined with his slick hair, made him harder to hold than a than a potato covered in KY jelly.

I led the way, leaning over the top of the panel. Angie followed suit. The crowd's murmur grew louder as I met Angie's eyes and, with a nod, released the pig. The animal's hind legs hit the ground before Angie completely relinquished her hold. It kicked free of her slackened grip and sprinted toward the other caged and wailing pigs.

I gripped the brown panels and jumped over the top. My sandaled feet hit the ground at a run. Covered from head to toe in mud, I channeled my best imitation of Mel Gibson and lifted my arm and yelled, "FREEEEDOMMM!"

With her lips set in a firm line of determination, Maddie scampered to the other five gates and threw them open. The remaining pigs joined my squealing friend, forming a mass which moved together as one.

Chaos erupted. People poured from the stands, chasing the wayward pigs, while the mayor garbled words into the loudspeaker. I came to a stop by Maddie.

"That was fun." She looked like a nymph with her mischievous grin.

I turned to find Angie, covered in mud, by my side.

"I had no idea this is what you had planned. Those farmers are going to be so mad." She rubbed the drying mud from her eyes and cheeks, creating a pale mask in the dark sludge. "What good is it to release pigs into the soccer field?"

"To make a statement. Maybe after this debacle, they won't do pig wrestling next year."

The corners of her mouth lifted into a smile, and she laughed. The late afternoon sun descended closer to the horizon, and the breeze picked up, sending goosebumps all over my body, whether from the cooling air or from the fact that I made her laugh, I didn't know.

Maddie pointed at something beyond the field. "Uh–oh."

Following her gaze, I saw Renee, Chuck, and Pedro headed our way. Though Renee looked less than pleased, she had a smirk on her face, which gave me the impression she'd go easy on Maddie.

I pushed the little girl toward her guardian, leaving a muddy handprint on her otherwise clean, oversized white shirt. "If you get into too much trouble, I'll come over and beg for your freedom."

Maddie started toward Renee, paused, then ran back to me. Slowing to a stop about two feet in front of me, she wrinkled her nose. "I was thinking about hugging you, but you're dirty. Thank you for helping the pigs, Remington James the Third." With her proclamation finished, she returned to Renee.

Angie let out a low whistle next to my ear. "Wow, that's impressive. Nobody has gained Maddie's trust quite that quickly—except maybe Lili."

"It's all for the shared love of pigs." I placed a hand melodramatically over my heart. The mud dried unevenly over my skin, giving me a camo appearance. And she looked the same, her blonde hair now dirt colored.

"Speaking of the pigs we just freed." She tapped my shoulder and pointed to someone behind me. "That is one angry mayor headed our way."

Rex towered over the crowd, his deep-mahogany bald head glinting in the sun. He sliced through the chaos, keeping his fixed stare on us.

Seeing him made me feel a little bad for what I'd done, though not enough to regret it. "Do you suppose we should help get the pigs into the trailer?"

"Nope."

She grabbed my hand, and though dirt rubbed between our palms, I reveled in the warmth of her soft hand in mine.

"I suggest we leave. Right now." She tugged me toward the truck.

Pushing through the crowd, we practically sprinted the rest of the way, leaving behind the soccer fields and the churning mass of people accompanied by the occasional squeal from the herd of pigs.

I climbed in and started my truck. "The little guys will be okay, won't they?" My back tires peeled against the gravel in the parking lot.

"They'll be fine. Marv will get them wrangled back in his trailer, or they'll make it to the Russian olive forest and live as wild free pigs." She leaned her head on the headrest, chuckled, and closed her eyes. She sniffed at the air. "We stink. Turn right here, and we can hose off at the fairgrounds."

I left the engine running while we sprayed as much of the pig excrement and mud off our clothes. We shrieked like kids at a water park, spraying each other until most of the filth was removed. I wrapped a towel around Angie and opened her door. She hopped in, and I climbed behind the wheel, reticent for our day together to come to a close.

Clouds painted orange and pink by the setting sun stretched before us for miles. Wind flowed through my open window and buffeted my wet shirt as we drove along the fields I'd become well acquainted with. Knee-high corn plants flashed past the truck, and the air smelled of the freshly cut hayfield on the right. A sense of accomplishment filled me—one like I'd never experienced before.

Each of those corn plants had been put there by Angie and me, the hay I harvested. If only I could make a living as a farmer, then I'd tell my family to get lost and keep doing this with Angie daily. But as evidenced by Tony, family farms couldn't compete against the corporate farms controlling crop prices, or the tempting offers of land developers.

"Did pig wrestling help you feel better ... after ... you know ...?" I looked over to Angie, my words coming out in a jumbled mess. Her damp, white shirt clung to her body, showing the outline of her navy swimming suit underneath. Somehow, this was even more alluring than when she'd stood before me with just her swimming suit on.

She turned to me. "I thought I was going to die in that river." Then, she brushed off her dark words with a laugh. "But I didn't. Although, I might have a new fear of water."

"You mean respect, not fear, right? Like with wasps?" I continued without giving her a chance to say anything. "Having a healthy respect for something keeps you alive but doesn't keep you from enjoying life."

Her only response was a soft sigh or a long exhale. I let the quiet settle in around us as the last rays of the sun illuminated the horizon. I turned into the neighborhood, taking the route to my model home.

Angie shot me a questioning glance.

"I forgot some tools in my garage. I thought I'd stop by and pick them up before I dropped you off at your house."

"Thank you," she said as my house came into view.

She spoke so quietly that I had to lean closer to hear her.

"What you did today meant the world to Papa."

Tony loved every minute he was on the water. Life bled back into him, but it'd also exhausted him. Still, a tired yet satisfied smile was on Tony's face when he'd left with Myles.

"You're welcome." I brushed a hand through my drying hair. "You're lucky to have a dad like him."

"Yeah." I caught the waver in her voice and wanted to fold her into my arms and take away her pain.

To hell with mortality. Some people should be allowed to live forever. "I'm sorry. For what you're going through."

"You have nothing to apologize for." She smiled through the wet sheen in her eyes.

"Are you expecting someone?" she asked.

I shook my head. "No."

But then I saw a familiar figure under my porchlight. The glimmer of twilight highlighted her stilettos, designer clothes, and Chanel purse dangling from her artificially tanned arm.

Kathryn.

How had she found me? This took stalking to a whole new level.

I clenched my jaw and shoved the truck into park, heat rising from the pit of my stomach to my face. Rushing to get out of the truck before Angie, I slammed my door and met Kathryn on my sidewalk.

She threw her arms around my neck. Her abnormally long nails stabbed into the skin next to my spine. She kissed me everywhere. My lips. My cheeks. My neck. Not giving a care my clothes were still quite soaked.

"I've ... missed you ..." she said between kisses. "Your brother ... told me ... where to find you ... Why didn't you ... answer my calls? ... It doesn't matter ... We are together now ..."

Matthew. How dare he manipulate my life like this?

I grabbed her shoulders and pushed her away from me. Angie stepped into view, and for a split-second, heartbreak reflected in her eyes. With one shake of her head, she took off toward her land.

"Angie, wait!"

But she didn't pause or turn back to me; she ran faster.

"Who's that? Don't tell me she thought you would ever be interested in someone like her. It looks like she lives in a shack like a feral woman."

"Kathryn, I look just like her."

Her over-plumped lips drooped downward. I didn't have time to feel sorry for her. Or feel sorry for the way I treated her. I couldn't afford to waste another second and risk the chance of losing Angie.

"Here." I shoved my keys into her hand. "Go inside. I'll be back later. To talk."

"No. You can't do this to me." She chucked my keys at me, hitting me square in the chest. "After everything. How can you leave me? I know you said you didn't want anything serious, but I thought ..."

I tried not to think about how far ahead Angie was getting. "Look. You're an amazing woman and you deserve someone to treat you better than I treated you."

Tears tracked down her cheeks and she arranged her features into a practiced pout. "I came all this way. To show you I love you. You're good enough for me. Really, you are."

I was lower than the dirt growing my corn. Lower than the lowest life form on earth. How many guys had treated Angie this way? Discarded her like I was abandoning Kathryn? I needed to be better. To change.

But I still wasn't meant to be with Kathryn. I took her hands in mine and placed a kiss on the back of them. "I'm sorry." I dropped her hands, and, without a backward glance, I sprinted into the fields.

Chapter 32

Remi

Bright green leaves, sharp as razor blades, tore at my arms. I broke through the edge of the cornfield and skimmed the yard. No sign of Angie. Myles's truck and trailer still sat in the driveway. It took me a while to spot Nora and Myles sitting in camp chairs on the front lawn. They both sipped iced tea or lemonade. I couldn't tell in the darkening twilight.

Nora pointed to the back. "She went that way."

I sprinted toward the barn. Knowing exactly where Angie would be, I opened the barn door, barely making out her figure. As my eyes acclimated, her movements became more refined. She rubbed her horse's nose and leaned into Mae's forehead. Soft noises like ... crying? ... sounded in the dark barn.

I was as dumb as a box of rocks. In fact, if my brains were dynamite, I wouldn't be able to blow my nose. Locating the light switch, I flipped it on before I walked toward her.

"Stop." She didn't look at me. Her hand paused on Mae's nose. "Don't come any closer."

"No." I approached her as I would a doe primed to bolt, forcing her to turn her attention to me. "I'm sorry, but I can't stay away. Not from you."

She dropped her hands from Mae and focused on me with a glare hotter than all the fires of hell. "You don't make any sense. With all your Texas sayings and how you're kind and treat me like I matter—but that's not important. Men never change. *You'll* never change. You'll never—"

"Angie, you don't need to run away from me."

She rubbed at the tears which had cut lines in the leftover mud on her face. "What about that girl on your porch?"

"Kathryn."

"Whatever her name is. You've done this before with a bajillion women."

"I don't know any man with the stamina for that many women."

"You know what?" She threw her hands in the air and walked to the back of the barn, which suited me fine. The further from Mae, the better. I followed her while she kept talking, "I don't even know why I am asking. I don't know why I'm crying. You're not worth it."

"I told Kathryn she deserves better than I treated her. *And*," I pointed at her, "you're crying because you care," I shoved my thumb to my chest, "about me."

"No, I don't. I would never fall for a … d-dirty man-whore like you." More silent tears fell, telling me the opposite was true. She stomped outside into the early night, and I continued to trail her.

Ignoring the dirty man-whore part, I smiled, and the clamp around my heart eased. Had she fallen for me? Could a miracle like that be possible? She came to a stop by the haystack and folded in on herself.

I stepped in front of her and ran my hand along her cheek to her chin. I tilted her head up until the moon glinted in her eyes and lost myself in their depths. "I didn't know you existed when I was with Kathryn."

Her stance softened a little. Mae whinnied and knickered inside the barn, but Angie didn't approach her. Taking her wrists in my hands, I drew her close to my chest. I slid my hands along Angie's forearm to her upper arm, rubbing circles with my thumb on her skin. I moved my hands onto her shoulders, mimicking the same movement, and as if drawn in by a magnet, she leaned closer to me.

Finally, I'd broken through whatever wall she'd built between us. I'd anticipated this kiss since the mountain trail, dreamed of it. The promise of this moment had robbed me of my focus. It took me ten times longer to do tasks I'd grown used to doing.

With the barest of pressure from my fingertips, she molded her body to mine. I dropped my grip to her lower back, pressing her into me. I reveled in the contact.

Angie didn't resist as I tugged her toward the haystack—one step, two—until my back was firm against the tarped bales. The stars had become visible at night, carpeting the ceiling above us.

Not capable of holding back any longer, the control I'd exhibited in the past weeks crumbled. I covered her lips with mine. With this kiss, I tried to show more restraint and play with her body gently. But once I made contact, a frenzy ignited inside me. I couldn't get enough of her.

Tangling one of my hands in her hair, I tugged and tilted her chin up to give me better access to her throat. My other hand gripped her bottom, pressing her into me.

I moved my lips back onto hers. In all my experiences with women, I'd never come close to the sensation. My tongue delved into her mouth, and she responded, challenging me with the same level of hunger.

Fireworks erupted overhead. I lifted my lips from her and tilted my head to watch the colors dance across her face. Her lips were swollen, her hair matted and in disarray, and yet I'd never seen a more beautiful woman. Nothing mattered to me more than her happiness. I wanted to be with her—to see her and make love to her—every day for the rest of my life.

More fireworks exploded in the sky, reflecting in her dark pupils, which were nearly as wide as her irises. She ran her tongue along her lips, her breath tickling my neck. I dipped my head and kissed her again, tugging her bottom lip with my teeth. I traced my lips along her cheekbone to her ear.

"Angie," I whispered. "I love you." My heartbeat grew as loud as the crashing fireworks in the sky.

Immediately, she stopped moving against me and put a hand on my chest. She pushed off me. "No."

"I love you," I said it louder this time and willed her to look at me, to see the sincerity in my eyes. Her head remained tilted down. I'd never said those three words to anyone before, and this wasn't how I'd imagined the woman I loved responding.

She shook her head. "I'm such a fool." Then she darted into the night.

The last of the sparks faded to oblivion on their crash course to Earth.

Chapter 33

Angie

Blue balloons bounced on their tethers, and the last of the binky-topped cupcakes disappeared from the tower. I sat in one of the extra chairs we'd put up in Renee's living room. Lili smiled and waved at each of her departing guests. The dandelion crown I'd made her now sagged to the side of her head.

Tucking my feet under my seat, I studied the wood grain in Renee's floors. I might as well be a wax statue for how much I contributed to the conversation.

Angie ... I love you.

Those four words in Remi's deep, sexy, and frustrating voice kept puncturing my focus. Sadly, I couldn't just forget he'd said it. Nope. Something like this embedded itself into my short and long-memory stores.

Ugh! How could I let myself become wound up in Remi? How many girls had he dropped the big L-word on? He'd probably told that poor girl on his porch he loved her, then he wrung her dry, sucked everything he wanted from her, and abandoned her.

No wonder she'd shown up on his doorstep on the Fourth of July and begged him to give her another chance. I could see myself doing the same thing if I had the willpower the size of an ant.

The closing door snapped me from my thoughts. Renee, Lili, and Gabby all stared at me.

"All right." Lili placed her hands on her hips, her large belly protruding over her shoes. She pulled the wilted dandelions from her head and swung them in front of my face. "Out with it."

"You've been off in La-La Land this whole shower." Gabby collected the torn wrapping paper and shoved it into a leftover box. She set the box filled with paper down and sat next to Renee. "Is it your dad?"

Papa. He only moved from his TV chair to his bed. Since the rafting trip, he'd taken a turn for the worse. How he struggled. Papa never spent much time indoors even in the winter. He was built to roam his land.

Keeping my gaze locked on the floor, I rubbed at my nose and the sudden pressure behind my eyes. I'd spent so much time running the farm, working, infatuated with Remi, obsessed with Dan, I hadn't capitalized on my time with Papa.

Papa understood. Yet, as time with him became a measurable thing, I couldn't help regretting every minute I didn't spend by his side.

If I ever let myself stop and think about Papa and the evidence of his time running short, I would cease to function. I'd turn into a useless heap, a ball of paralyzing emotions in a puddle on the ground.

There had to be a miracle. Something to fix the brokenness in my life.

"No, Papa isn't doing the best, but he's had bouts like this, and he's bounced back," I finally answered Gabby and looked at her. Deep inside, I knew this was a lie. He would never bounce back from this, and soon I'd say goodbye to him.

Renee stopped stacking the disposable dishes on her coffee table. She leaned over the arm of the couch, placed a hand on my shoulder, and squeezed. She'd been through this before. Both she and Lili had parted with way too many loved ones. I admired Lili for having the courage to love Blake and Maddie and pop out more babies after losing her first family.

If I'd been placed in an identical situation, I wasn't sure I'd come out of it similarly.

See the pile of emotional goop ... oh yeah, that once was Angie.

"I call bullshit." Renee dropped her hand to her side.

So much for Renee being sympathetic.

Lili set her crown on the table, stood before me, and spread her legs as if to balance the extra weight of the twins. "You can't be hunky dory with everything going on."

"I think there's something more." Gabby leaned onto her knees, focusing all her friend's psychic abilities on me. "Spill it."

I could count on Gabby being all practical, almost callus, with emotion. It was something as a nurse you had to do to survive ... turn off emotion, or you'd drown.

"We're in the circle of trust." Lili sat in between Gabby and Renee.

All three of them stared at me, their eyes burning holes in my resistance. Sweat beaded on the back of my neck. I folded my lips together, doing my best to keep this nuke to myself.

"Remi told me he loves me," I blurted, then buried my face in my hands. I'd never been good at keeping secrets anyway. The words spilled out of me like water from a broken pitcher.

I peeked through my fingers. As if on a puppet string, all three leaned away from me, like I'd dropped a stink bomb in the middle of the room.

"What—" Lili's eyes were as wide as her mouth.

"Who's Remi again?" Renee asked.

"The hot farmhand who's been working for her," Gabby filled in.

"Oh him. He's been hanging out a bit with Blake. If Remi's got Blake's approval, he's got my approval."

"What did you do?" Gabby asked.

At the same time, Lili said, "I thought you hated him." Her half smile told me she knew I'd kissed him and liked it.

What I didn't say I gave away. Mama always told me I was an open book, my pages legible on my expressive face. Right now, I'd love to have an ounce of Remi's deceptive capabilities.

"Remi isn't an option. A poor girl, one of his women, showed up on his porch last night. Only she looked normal, like we'd be friends, and she'd let herself get taken in by his lies. She was broken. I can't let that be me."

"But did Remi tell her he loved her?" Renee posed the question that haunted me for three days.

"I bet he did." I couldn't shake the broken look on the woman's face when she'd seen me with Remi. I couldn't turn into her and be the next shattered woman on his porch asking for a speck of affection.

Gabby and Lili both spoke.

"He brought you dinner."

"Maddie likes him."

How could they choose to defend him? "Doesn't matter." I slapped my hands on my thighs. "I'm dating Dan and not Remi. In fact, I'm meeting Dan at City of the Rocks this evening. He's planned something special."

"Is Remi going to be there just in case?" Lili tucked her hair behind her ear.

"I don't need Remi to babysit me."

"What're you going to be doing?" Gabby shifted toward Lili.

"Wait a minute. Who's Dan? Why have I been kept out of the loop?" Renee whined. "You promised to keep me in the loop with your dating life." She wiggled her finger at me.

She'd forced a promise out of me after my breakup with Troy. Thankfully, an ocean separated me from him. The problem with telling Renee everything was she tended to want to fix things. And I couldn't be fixed.

"I met Dan on a dating app," I told Renee. Without giving her a chance to formulate the 'he-could-be-a-killer' response, I continued, "We're going rappelling. It's going to be epic."

"Your fear of heights is magically gone?" Lili arched her back. She constantly shifted in her struggle to get comfortable.

"Exposure therapy. Remi has been helping me with it."

Angie ... I love you. Instantly, I regretted mentioning him. But how could I not? He'd been involved in my day-to-day life since April.

"I'll be fine." I clamped down the urge to bounce my feet or tap my fingers. "Trust me."

I hated how much I sounded like Remi.

Chapter 34

Remi

"Let me get this straight." Myles leaned against the handle of the broom in his hand. "You're confronted with a woman who was obsessed with you enough to fly here and surprise you on a holiday, and you throw the keys at her and say make yourself at home, then you run after another woman?"

"Sounds about right." I gripped the black trash bag tighter and shoved the fluffy stuff from my gutted pillows into it.

With the demands of the neighborhood and the farm, I hadn't had time to clean my room after Kathryn destroyed it. We'd managed to repair the tornado in the living room and kitchen. She'd broken all our dishes and cut holes in our couch cushions. The TV hadn't even been spared from her rage. She'd taken one of our tractor seat stools and pummeled the hell out of it.

In an amazing show of strength, the Samsung screen hadn't broken, just the pixels behind it. The only image that came on were vertical line shards connected like a puzzle. Sure, the TV would never function again, but if left on, it could be viewed like a digital Jackson Pollock.

"I deserve everything she did to me." After Angie had left me in the barn, her awful words *I'm such a fool* tainting the air like a week-old carcass, I'd done some introspection.

I'd returned to find the house trashed and ...

"She stole your truck."

... my truck gone. Maybe Kathryn had gone a little overboard. Still, I should never have treated her like an object.

"Have you filed a stolen vehicle report?" Myles swept his pile into the dustpan.

"I can buy a new truck."

He shook his head and walked out of the room without responding. I could send the police after Kathryn, but why ruin her life when I had plenty of money to pay for the damages? Of course, all expenses would be put on my business account.

This time, I'd buy myself a brand-new truck.

The first thing I did after discovering the mess Kathryn had left was call Matthew. He hadn't answered, the coward.

But nothing hurt more than Angie's rejection. Through all my mind-numbing cultivating—I straight-up ignored her refusal to let me use the tractors now, at Tony's request—I hadn't been able to keep myself from reliving what went down in the barn.

I'd told her I loved her; then she'd called herself a fool. I hated this feeling. *If this is what love is, how do I turn it off?*

Myles walked back into the room sans broom. "Are you sure you're in love with Angie?"

I dropped the bag and leaned back onto my mattress. "We've been over this."

"But you've never been in love before. This is foreign territory for our friendship. You're usually the one in my position, helping me piece together my shredded heart."

His latest love of his life, Samantha, had nearly destroyed him when she left him. I'd be no better off if Angie cut all ties with me. Which was where our relationship was headed? On a one-way collision course with a bull whose nut-sack had been shot with a paintball gun.

"You could have influenza, maybe COVID?" Myles persisted. "I hear the brain fog can cause all sorts of problems."

"I'm not sick. Just in love." Hearing my own words made me want to gag, and yet I couldn't keep the goofy grin off my face. *Who am I?* Did I fully transform into a small-town romance groupie?

It'd be a lot easier if I didn't love Angie. I wouldn't hesitate to buy their land out from under them. Now with my feelings involved, I lost my killer instinct. For days, I did nothing but try and find scenarios in which I took Angie's land from her, and she still ended up with me. Not Smoot.

Myles leaned against the broom handle. "Measles can cause hallucinations! You have the measles."

"Nope. Sorry. I love her." The more I said it, the more I knew it to be true.

"I think I should report you to the CDC. You've got all the symptoms." Myles kept going as if I hadn't spoken.

"Ha. Which CDC are we talking about here?"

"The most annoying one, of course." Myles scratched the back of his head and took a couple swipes at the floor with the broom. "Look. I know I've put a lot of pressure on you with our Texas Bros dream, but if you love Angie, I'll support you in whatever you decide to do. We'll figure it out."

I knew Angie well enough now to come up with the basic equation: CDC buys land equals Angie hating me forever. I'd forfeit any chance

I had at winning her over. If I didn't buy it, the dream Myles and I had been working on since grade school went up in smoke. My phone buzzed in my pocket. I looked at my screen, and my far-too-sentimental response froze in my throat.

Matthew.

"You might want to leave the room," I said to Myles instead.

"He finally called back, huh? Took him a while to grow some balls." He walked into the living room.

With a tense swipe of my finger, I answered the FaceTime call. "What the hell were you thinking, sending her here?"

"You need to focus. That farmer's daughter has made you soft."

"The hell she has. You've jeopardized everything, you asshole."

Matthew adjusted his glasses. He might not show much emotion, but I'd figured out his tells over the years. Any time he touched his glasses, he was pissed. Point for me.

"Stooping to name-calling? And we're not even two minutes into the call."

"What did you expect when you pull a dick move like that?" I paced the room, now clean of debris thanks to Myles. "She stole my truck and trashed the model home."

"Then you shouldn't leave me to do your dirty work."

"I'm not buying their land." I stopped moving, my unfocused world becoming clear. "And I'll make for damn sure you won't be able to buy it either."

Money, goals, and dreams didn't matter if Angie wasn't in my life.

"You can't do that." Matthew's normally pale complexion flushed red.

I'd always been a burr in his coat, and now I had an opportunity to really hurt him, and my father.

"Oh?" I leaned close to the screen. "I'm the one who's formed a relationship with Tony and Nora. I'm the one who's been with them every day. You don't think I know how to do my job well enough to manipulate them to exactly where I want them to be?"

"Don't do this." He rubbed his forehead and temples, just like he'd done when I'd filled his suit pockets with gravel. "Not because of a girl. She's not worth it."

"That's where you're wrong." I held the phone back and placed my free hand over my heart. "She's worth everything I have."

"That won't be much once I cut off your magical business credit card. You won't have access to the big pot of money at the end of the rainbow."

"So, you're a leprechaun now?"

"Shut up." Matthew sounded too much like a teenager, not a business tycoon. "You and I both know you'll come crawling back. Without money, you can kiss all your extreme-sports hobbies goodbye. I won't fund them anymore."

Matthew couldn't handle being in the spotlight. He didn't like crowds, press interviews, or dealing with people, which was another reason the company needed me. Maybe they'd replaced me, but at this point, I didn't care.

Tony and Nora were far happier than my parents and lived on next to nothing for most of their lives. I'd much rather live like they had, than own multiple properties, marbled mansions with gold fixtures as cold and unwelcoming as stone, or even my Bugatti ... Okay, I had to admit, that one would be hard to give up. Maybe someday I could eke out enough of a living to buy a Corvette.

For the first time in my life, I didn't feel lost. I had a place, and that was here with Angie. If only she'd look past Smoot and see me—the real me.

"Your threats don't scare me." I hung up the phone, the bright call screen replaced by the wallpaper I'd taken of my baby corn.

No more skydiving, BASE jumping on the Greek Isles, no more rappelling down the world's tallest building in Dubai. I tightened my grip on the edge of the bed, my dark-blue comforter bunching in my hands. Somehow, even without the financial backing of my family, I'd figure out a way to take Angie on as many adventures as possible. I wanted to share everything with her—experience all that life offered.

Almost instantly, my phone started buzzing again. Although tempted to ignore it, I picked it up, ready with a fresh wave of anger. But that all eased out of me when I saw who the caller was.

I answered and held the phone to my ear. "Lili?"

She didn't bother with a greeting. "Angie just left my house. She's going rappelling with Smoot. I'm worried."

Of course, she'd keep going with Smoot. Even after I told her I loved her. With Smoot being the Darwin-in-action he was, I didn't trust him with Angie's life.

"Where are they at?"

"City of the Rocks. She said he has something special planned."

"City of the Rocks?"

My conversation with Smoot at the bar.

Her favorite place.

My vision swam, and my head dizzied like it did when I saw blood.

Smoot was going to propose.

And maybe get her hurt in the process. I jumped into action. Without properly saying goodbye, I hung up. I pulled out my phone and opened the locator app, hoping Angie hadn't uninstalled it.

A small dot pinged on my digital map. I looked heavenward. Thank the heavenly angels.

"Myles," I called into the next room. "I need the keys to your car."

Chapter 35

Angie

I fiddled with my shirt and double-checked that my shoes were tied with the laces safely tucked in. The last thing I wanted to happen would be to trip and fall off a cliff. I kicked at the dirt and desert plants at my feet. Most of the June wildflowers had faded, and now only sunflowers and white milkweed had popped through the brush.

Dan and I stood on a large overhang, taller than the boulders around us. The harness he'd handed me dangled in my grip while he looped the rope in the anchor bolted into the rock. Thankfully, we'd been able to drive to the edge of this cliff; if I'd had to climb the face of it, I may have given up already. The sun had begun its descent and beat down on me, warming my skin under the layer of sunscreen I'd applied. Other rocks jutted out of the ground, creating an alien city landscape.

City of the Rocks. I couldn't think of a place more aptly named.

The farm demanded a lot of our family, but when we got a spare weekend, Papa would take me here. Yes, I didn't like sleeping on the ground; however, sitting next to a campfire with Papa, the noise of the world eased, and I found peace. This was one of the only other locations on Earth I'd been able to feel ... quiet.

In lieu of dirt biking, we both agreed to rappel, skipping the effort of scaling the boulders.

But how did Dan know about my favorite place?

I kept my arms rigid by my side to disguise my nerves. I was about to drop off the edge of a cliff, and despite the confidence I'd spat at Remi, I'd lied. I was still afraid of heights. Dan's hands shook as he handled the rope and peeked over the cliff's edge. He looked as scared as I felt, which struck me as odd. You'd think a sky-diving instructor wouldn't have a fear of heights.

Maybe he was nervous for a different reason. My mind latched on to our recent conversations. About future plans. Dreams. My ideal wedding ...

Son of a sock monkey!

Smoot—Dan was going to propose. What the hell was I supposed to do? Did I want to say yes?

Of course, I would. No. Maybe. This was for Papa and his dream. Dan and I could be happy if we worked at it. But I'd been working my patootie off my whole life—did I want to spend the rest of it fighting upstream in a lukewarm marriage?

The thought made my stomach sour.

"I'm sure you've done this before." Dan weaved the rope between his fingers.

I nodded and swallowed. No sense giving up yet.

Dan shoved his glasses back onto the bridge of his nose. "I got you a helmet and gloves since you came from a baby shower." He dug through the tote and handed me the mentioned items.

"Thanks." I took the helmet with gloves shoved inside.

In slow, methodical movements, I looped one foot into the harness, followed by the other.

How had I gotten here?

Sure, at the beginning of this relationship, I'd thought this was the best course of action. Could a long-term relationship be built on lies?

Yet in all our conversations not involving extreme sports, I could see a stable guy in Dan. He almost hedged on boring. I'd put all my eggs into this basket. The only hope I had of Papa being at my wedding stood before me with pit stains and shaking hands.

I snapped into my harness and slid my helmet into place, putting on my gloves after I'd clicked the chin strap. "You ready?"

"Yes. Just—ah—give me a moment." Dan sat on a smooth rock and adjusted his harness for the tenth time. "It's hot out here today."

He slid from the rock and knelt on one knee in front of me. He tilted his head up. Oh! Ready or not, here it came. My heartbeat as fast as a Jackrabbit's foot. He couldn't propose yet. I hadn't figured out my answer!

But then he dropped his focus to his hiking boot and tied his shoe. Placing a hand over my heart, I took a deep breath. Bullet dodged.

"Yeah. It is." I stood awkwardly above him. Lifting my hand toward my mouth, I attempted to chew my nails, but my gloves thwarted me. I let my hand fall back to my side.

Dan coughed, clearing his throat. "So, I guess, uh, you ... Do you want to go first?"

"Sure," I drawled out my response. No, I didn't want to go first! What was wrong with me? "Yippee-Ki-Yay. Am I right?"

I meandered toward the cliff's edge and began shoving the rope through the metal loops attached to my harness. Inch by inch it slid through my gloves.

The tips of my tennis shoes touched the edge. Tiny bits of gravel cascaded over and were carried away in the wind.

Holy daisies in a handbasket!

The bottom of the cliff was so far away. It blurred in the glaring sunlight. Panicked breaths shoved their way in and out of me.

I didn't want to do this. Couldn't do it. I dropped the rope and unclipped the carabiner attached to the metal circle I'd looped the rope through. "I'm sorry. I can't do this anymore." My ears rang. My mouth had already gone dry with the potential of a proposal and the added stress of being on an outcropping of a tall boulder.

"What do you mean?" Visible sweat beaded on Dan's forehead as he leaned one hand against the rock.

One careful step at a time, I backed away from the edge until I stood beside him. I took his hand in an almost desperate grip. The leather of our gloves bunched in my palm. I needed to come clean. I'd taken this too far.

I took a deep breath. "I've been lying to you this whole time."

"*You've* been lying to *me*?" Dan cringed and leaned away from me with each word.

"Yes." With my admission, my inner word dam broke. "When I saw your profile picture, I thought I needed to find a different sort of guy. Change up where I looked for matches. Change myself. I'd tried everything for a year and was desperate to find someone to connect with." I gulped in air. "I'm terrified of heights. I wanted to pretend to be someone else. And I thought I could make it work. Become a person you'd be interested in. The truth is, I've never been off my farm. I've never jumped off a bridge. I've never been to the Grand Canyon, let alone canyoneered in the back country—"

"Shh. It's okay." He cut me off. "I sort of don't do extreme sports either."

"Hold up." I held up a finger. "You're not a BASE jumper?"

Had I wasted the past three months? Still holding his hand, I sat on the rock, and he followed my lead. This entire spring and summer, we were *both* lying? Maniacal laughter bubbled inside me. What were the odds of two people semi-catfishing each other? The only thing we didn't lie about was what we looked like. I couldn't contain my laughter anymore, and it spilled from me. We were perfect for each other, except, maybe not. This summer had changed me. Before it, I would have been completely content with a man like Dan. Now I wanted ... more.

Dan's eyebrows wrinkled as he tried to make sense of my laughter. "No. I'm also terrified of heights. I thought maybe if I investigated dating in a completely different group, I'd find more success, you know?"

"Oh, do I ever," I mumbled.

He went on as if he hadn't heard me. "I don't run a skydiving business or have a cabin in Pine. I'm an accountant. I love Excel sheets and data. And for the love of Pete, I like being safe. I didn't lie about Ted Martin. He's my idiot friend who helped me hatch this scheme."

I let his words die in the wind and listened to nothing but the sound of my heart and our rough breaths. All this time, I'd been trying to catch a guy by lying and, *plot twist*, he was doing the same thing to me.

Had I wasted the last three months of my life forcing my square self into a circular mold? Even before I finished asking myself the question, my mind responded. No. Without this spring and summer, I never would have known how much I craved excitement or how much I needed to live my own life.

It was odd how in pretending to be someone else, I'd discovered myself.

At the start of this, I'd had no interest in BASE jumping. Now, I wasn't so sure. What would it be like to have Remi with me and feel the weightlessness, the thrill of falling through the vast emptiness of air?

"You weren't skydiving with execs for the past two weeks?"

"Nope. I was working on a budget for a client, and then I went to a seminar to get my CPE's. Not nearly as exciting."

"You could have told me the truth."

Dan shook his head and sagged against the rock. "We're kind of perfect for each other. Aren't we?" He let out a laugh. "Are you still interested in being with me? Like possibly marrying me?" He dipped his head away and looked at me from the corner of his eye, his Adam's apple bobbing more than ever.

There it was. I'd been waiting through part of winter, all of spring, and the beginning of summer for this moment. I could beg him to marry me tomorrow, and Papa would be there on my wedding day. He would be by my side to hold me as I said goodbye to Papa. But in the split second I thought about Papa leaving me, it wasn't Dan standing next to me, comforting me in my fantasy.

Crap. Everything around me spun.

Dan turned to grip both my hands. His eyes locked on his target, and he moved in.

Remi's voice broke through.

Angie ... I love you.

Along with his declaration, memories of the antics we'd gotten into since the start of the growing season poured into my mind. Tractors, corn, high wires and axes, game nights and dirt bikes ... and his kisses. I licked my lips, remembering his touch, how it'd branded my skin and leeched into my soul.

Which was what happened ... when you fell in love. Flaming hell in a handbasket! I'd fallen in love with the enemy.

Dan's breath fluttered against my chin. His lips pressed against mine.

"Wait." I broke contact and pushed him back. "I can't."

He stiffened and sat up. "I thought you wanted to get married. You said—"

"I know. And I meant all those things when I said them, but then ..." I let my voice trail off, not sure what I would say.

Dan's shoulders slumped, and his features softened into a defeated frown. "Remi."

"No, he has nothing to do with this." I sounded like a preschooler caught with red finger paint on her hands. Being willing to admit my love to my innermost thoughts was one thing but speaking it into existence was entirely another.

"For someone who can keep up a lie for months, you're not very good at lying to yourself. You talk about him all the time—"

"That's because we're always working—"

"Why do you think I went to guys' night with him and Myles and the others? I asked him about where I should propose, and he immediately knew your favorite place."

I should have guessed Remi was the one who'd told him. He remembered the tiniest details about me.

Dan kept talking. "He's a threat. One I lost to. I've been dumped enough times to know this is an I'm-in-love-with-someone-else scenario."

Shaking my head, I said nothing. I didn't want to lie to him anymore, but I wasn't brave enough to admit the truth.

I loved Remi, like the once in a lifetime, ugly-crying-into-your-popcorn-at-midnight kind of stuff. I loved the way he challenged me. I loved the way he supported me. Before he came into my life, I was barely surviving on adrenaline and dread. I was a black-and-white photo, and he injected color back into my life. Most of all, I loved that I didn't have to earn his love or change myself for him. He'd fallen in love with me ... the real me.

"Look, Daniel, I'm not the right girl for you. Even if it weren't for ..."

"Yeah. I get it." He nudged me with his shoulder. "I really wanted you to be my soulmate. I guess I'm going back to square one. No hope of getting married before forty."

"You never know. It just takes meeting the right person." Remi had come out of left field. I'd been so stubborn. "And getting married after forty wouldn't be a bad thing."

"I guess so." He dusted off his pants and got to his feet.

"Angie!" A distant voice echoed from the bottom of the outcropping.

It sounded like ... I scrambled to my feet and peeked over the edge. Remi? How had he found me? The question barely escaped my thoughts before I locked on the answer: the app. My phone.

"You should go to him."

Without hesitation, I marched to my previous positions and re-clipped the carabiner to my harness. Before I took another breath, I gripped the rope, one hand above me and one behind, and dropped over the edge.

Chapter 36

Remi

My heart stopped beating in my chest the moment Angie slid from the top of the cliff. I waited for her to plummet to the ground. But she didn't. Instead, the rope glided through her gloved hand with the calm assurance of an expert.

The tension in my jaw relaxed and my mouth sagged open. Athena couldn't be more extraordinary than Angie rappelling this sheer ravine. Her feet hit the ground. The powdered dirt clouded into the air.

I opened my arms, ready to wrap her in a tight embrace.

"You." She shoved me back. "You ruined everything." She pommeled my chest with her balled up fists. "He was the one. A decent guy who had a stable job who treated me well. He wanted a family and kids ... Yeah. He lied to me, but we could have worked it out." Her hits became weaker as her sniffles grew louder.

"He lied?"

"Yes." She sniffed. "He's an accountant and doesn't like extreme sports. His friend Ted Martin—"

"Ha!" I cut Angie off. "I knew there was something off about him."

She growled and stomped away from me, but I captured her wrists before she walked out of my reach. I tugged her back to me and held her hands to my chest, covering my pounding heart. "How exactly did I ruin everything?"

"You confuse me." She tilted her chin up. Her eyes shimmered with tears.

She didn't explain anymore. Could it be possible she had feelings for me? Substantial enough that she turned down Smoot? "I get that. And this is a bad thing?"

Her lips quivered. "A person like you can't possibly understand having a dream of a house with your kids with someone who treasures you above all else—there for you no matter what crap life throws at you—maybe even a dog and enough land for Mae, with trees lining the drive, and white fencing around the pastures." Everything jumbled together as her thoughts poured from her. "The hospice nurse said Papa has weeks left. Weeks can be measured in days, and Papa is going to be gone, and my last hope to having him be with me on my wedding day is up there, and I'm down here ..."

She kept going but my mind stuck on one word. Wedding. In my line of work, I provided solutions to problems at the negotiation table, and right now—her one problem—I was fully equipped to fix.

"Marry me." The words slipped out faster than a prairie fire with a tailwind. Bless my heart. I'd just proposed marriage. To a girl. To Angie. As in one-person-for-the-rest-of-your-life-until-death-do-we-part kind of thing.

When negotiating terms of agreement, I relied on instinct, and right now, they hollered at me that this was the most important deal I'd ever closed in my life. I needed Angie like a door needed hinges. Without her, I had no purpose.

She stared at me, slack jawed. "What did you say?"

I said it again with more confidence. "Marry me."

She blew air out of her mouth making her lips flap together. "You? Your second day working for me, you said, and I quote 'I'll never get married.' When the next pair of tan, long legs pass by, you'll be saying sayonara, babe. Good luck with raisin' our kids on your own."

Kids? Everything inside me froze. I could be a dad to Angie's kids. "I was wrong. I didn't know you existed when I made those decisions about marriage."

She gave one more tug against my hands, and this time, she slipped free of my slackened grip. "You're going to take my land and desecrate it with your cheap homes."

"I won't buy it. I already told my brother—"

"The problem is, I don't trust you." She took a couple steps away from me into the shadow of the overhang, still tethered to the rope.

"Why? Haven't I proven myself to you? I've kept your farm running. I could farm next to you for the rest of my life and be happy. Kids, dog, white picket fence ... you name it, and I'll make it happen. *And* your parents love me."

"My parents don't know who you are." She took another step back.

I followed until we were only inches apart. Taking hold of her harness, I hauled her toward me and unclipped her carabiner. "You have no other options."

She laughed. "This is the best proposal ever. Marry me. I'm your only option."

I placed my hands on her hips, pulling her against me and halting her retreat. I leaned closer to her. "Does that mean you say yes?"

She touched her bottom lip briefly with her tongue; then she nibbled on it with her upper teeth. Without even trying, she had me tied in knots.

I held on to a thread of patience for her answer, wanting nothing more than to give her lips the same treatment with my own tongue.

"I'll think about it," she whispered.

My smile filled my whole body. "I couldn't ask for more."

Wrapping my arms around her once again, I lowered my lips to hers, giving in to my previous temptation.

Chapter 37

Angie

In the next couple of weeks, Papa declined far faster than the hospice nurse had expected. He didn't have enough strength to leave his bed, now relying on Mama and me to get him to the bathroom and around the house. Gabby and Ryan made sure my shifts got covered and forced me to take a break.

Papa dozed off and on as his pain ebbed and flowed with his med schedule.

On the rare occasions he requested to leave the confines of his room, we helped him into his La-Z-Boy, where he'd stay for the rest of the day, sometimes opting to sleep there where we could keep the fire stoked at night. Even with the summer heat, his body couldn't produce enough of it to keep him warm, and nothing made Papa happier than sitting in his home next to his fire.

Lili, Blake, and Maddie had stopped by a few days ago. He'd said hi to the babies coming closer to their due date, reminding the boys of how much their Papa Tony loved them. But then Lili had been put on bed rest. That didn't stop Renee from checking in every day. Rumors all but confirmed she was the giving angel in our town, the one leaving money in mailboxes and paying off bills for those with money troubles. I had no doubt she was the reason we were still financially afloat. But even Renee didn't have enough money to keep our ship from sinking.

For the most part, Papa remained lucid, but as the cancer took over more of his body, he crept back in time. Sometimes, he recognized both me and Mama. Sometimes only Mama.

I'd moved our green-velvet wingback chair into his room. I sat in it next to Papa. The TV flashed against their log pole bed in the dark room. Night had descended in the middle of the old Clint Eastwood Western we'd been watching. Mama's perfume and Papa's aftershave still hung in their room, now underlying scents to medicine and sickness.

A young Eastwood's face squinted against the sun, beads of sweat on his forehead, but my mind didn't follow the dialogue. It cycled back to Dan's attempted proposal. I should be more upset about losing him. Now all hope was lost. Without Remi's mask of lies, I went back to being a boring Idaho farm girl. Too insignificant to love.

Which made me suspicious of proposal number two, Remi's. However, his heart seemed to be in the right place. He'd taken over running the farm, providing me and Mama the ability to sit with Papa.

I still hadn't given him an answer. True, he knew the real me and didn't balk at my oddities. But his love, his proposal, couldn't be trusted. No matter what he said, he'd do anything to own this land, even get himself locked in a monotonous, loveless marriage.

Would the trade-off be worth it? Do I risk losing my land and potential happiness to give Papa his dream? Marriages could be annulled, and Papa would go to his grave believing I'd found my match.

I shoved my fingers through my hair and leaned my head against the chair. Making a decision of this magnitude in my emotional state wasn't the wisest choice. Yet each day drew me closer to the biggest loss I'd ever faced. If I hesitated too long, I'd lose my chance.

Light from the TV illuminated the patched hole where I'd shoved the doorknob through the sheetrock in a teenage fit—Mama hadn't let me go to a New Year's Eve party because she'd wanted me to stay home and be with the family on the last New Year's before Jared went to college.

If only I'd known then what I do now. Time always ran out, and past moments could never be recaptured. I'd stayed in that night, but I pouted in my room, not even coming out to do the countdown with Jared, Mama, and Papa.

Now this December, I'd celebrate the end of this year without Papa. I choked on the tears in my throat, blinking at the water along the base of my eyes. I'd been so caught up in saving the farm, in Remi and Smoot ... how many moments with Papa had I let slip by?

I usually couldn't stand boredom, and now I wished I could have it as my constant companion.

Boredom implied the absence of something. Absence of grief, absence of big life changes like a parent dying, selling your childhood home, welcoming new lives into the world. Not to mention, Remi dropped a missile in the middle of my life by telling me he loved me and proposing to me.

Yes, I could use a dose of boredom in my life.

Holding onto Papa's hand, I leaned over on the white down comforter. The sounds of Mama cooking in the kitchen echoed in the room. I closed my eyes ...

The smell of the barn, Mae, the haystack in the warm night, fireworks exploding in the sky. *Angie ... I love you.*

Rappelling. A wall of rock behind me. Arid dirt clouding into the air. Remi's bass voice resonating in my chest. *Marry me.*

The lid from a tin can peeled back, and I looked inside to see my life unfold as if I'd accepted his proposal. A white house on my land, and a couple of children playing with us and our puppy in the yard, all the while Mae trotted in a pasture covered in bright green grass. Remi stood in the front yard. *Angie.*

"Angie ..." Remi's voice morphed into someone else's.

My world moved back and forth.

"Angie." Another sharp whisper cut through my mind.

I opened my eyes and shot up, hitting something solid with my head on the way.

"Ow!"

My eyes locked on the owner of the voice.

"Dude, I think you broke my jaw." Jared rubbed his chin, opening and closing his mouth. Decked out in a black leather jacket with chains hanging from his pockets, thick eyeliner, and painted, black nails. Dark leather draped over his Nine Inch Nails T-shirt, half tucked into his torn, acid-washed jeans.

Ignoring the soft pain thrumming in my own head, I smiled. Some things never changed, and Jared was one of them. I threw my arms around him and squeezed. "You came."

His gaze locked onto Papa's sleeping form. "Mama called. I found a couple of days to come home and say my goodbyes." His voice broke on the last word, and he wiped his palms along his bottom eyelids.

More tears gathered in my eyes and ran down my cheeks. I hated that word. Goodbye. I never wanted to say it again.

"What about your career? You've fought so hard for this." He barely scraped by making a living on his music. This tour was their first big-ish break, playing covers for concerts nationwide.

Papa and Jared hadn't always agreed. They used to get into epic fights once Jared finally told Papa he wouldn't be taking over the farm or going to college.

Rifts once created were mended at the onset of Papa's first battle with cancer. "I'll have other tours, but I only have one dad." He ruffled my hair like he used to, and I batted his hand away. "How's he doing?"

"He's in a lot of pain. On the days I can convince him to take his meds, he sleeps a lot."

A knock sounded, and Remi shoved the door open. He wore leather gloves, and his hair was disheveled; he hadn't even bothered to remove his muddy boots. "Angie." His whisper was insistent. "Blake called and—"

He stopped midsentence, looking from Papa to me to Jared. I gestured toward the exit, and Jared followed me, closing the door behind him. It didn't latch and rebounded open, leaving the door slightly ajar.

Energy buzzed around Remi, an urgency in how he looked at me. "They're taking Lili to the hospital. She's in labor."

"Crap dammit." I used Lili's custom phrase and paced in front of Remi, trying to gain control of my breathing. "It's too soon." I couldn't get the worst-case scenarios of the babies I'd lost born at thirty weeks. "Why wouldn't Blake message me directly?" I patted my pockets in search of my phone. But I didn't find it. "Maybe they'll be able to administer a tocolytic to stop her labor."

"He tried. When you didn't answer, he called me. I hopped on the four-wheeler and came straight here."

Jared stepped in between us, forcing his way into my visual field. "Wait. Lili's having her babies! Uncle Jared can't wait to meet them."

He had no idea how dire this situation was. In our sparse conversations over the past year, I'd told him about Lili's pregnancy. He'd been present at Blake and Lili's wedding and been gone ever since. I didn't think that qualified him to be considered an uncle, no matter what his brother-like relationship with Lili looked like in high school.

I should stay with Papa, as I didn't want to miss his potential last moments in this life, but Lili needed me. Long ago, I promised her I'd be there for her babies when they were born. These babies would for sure be admitted to the NICU.

Their lungs weren't ready yet.

I had to be there.

Mama came into the family room from the kitchen. "Go on. I'll stay here with Tony. You make sure those boys are all good." She must have read my inner conflict. Mama stepped forward and interlocked her elbow with Remi and glanced at Jared. "Remi, Jared, and I will take care of anything here. You have nothing to worry about. Your Papa should be fine until you get home, and we'll call if anything changes."

I gave her a trembling smile and darted upstairs into my room, throwing off my clothes, grabbing my scrubs, and yanking them on. I slipped on my white tennis shoes and sprinted down the stairs. Remi and Jared stood by the door, Jared with keys in his hands.

"I'm driving." He opened the door and held out his hand, waiting for me to lead the way. "By the sounds of it, you haven't been getting enough sleep. Remi and I both decided we wouldn't let you get behind the wheel. Besides, Uncle Jared has to be there for his nephews."

Apparently, they'd taken care of introductions. However, it wouldn't be hard for Remi to identify my musician brother with all the pictures we have of him in the house.

"Fine." I glared over my shoulder at Remi who stood in the illuminated doorway. I continued down the front steps to Jared's beat-up, black 5.0 Mustang. "As long as Uncle Jared stops referring to himself in the third person."

Fast food bags and soda cups spilled out of the door when I opened it. The interior light reflected off the McDonald's, Chick-fil-A, and Wendy's bags. An unmistakable scent of pot wafted into the air, now freed from his Mustang's interior.

"Ugh. Jared, you're a pig." My gaze automatically went to the pigpen. Calling Jared a pig was an insult to them. "Promise me you're not high."

"Sorry, bruh. I live in my car, okay." He shoved his foot on the accelerator before he closed his door. "And of course I'm sober, you ninny." He started the ignition, the back tires spinning in the gravel as we shot out of the driveway.

Chapter 38

Remi

I closed the door and took the time to remove my boots. Before Blake called me in an absolute panic, I'd been working on a broken irrigation pipe that had flooded the road. Stars had covered the jet-black sky before I'd managed to fix the damage. My body was exhausted.

As the adrenaline from Blake's call left me, a sick, shaky feeling replaced it.

"Have you eaten, Remi?" Nora asked from the family room by the kitchen. "Come get a warm slice of bread."

Ever since Tony's illness took a turn for the worse, Nora's baking had increased. The freezer at the model home was stuffed full of loaves of bread, muffins, and cookies. Myles and I couldn't keep up.

I made my way to Nora. She left the kitchen with a heavily buttered slice of homemade wheat bread. If I ever had to leave and Angie turned me down, I sure was going to miss this.

"I'm certain Angie will make sure those babies are okay. She's very good at her job." Nora patted my shoulder.

"She's good at everything she does." Except scaling rock walls, or riding dirt bikes, or jumping from the top of a telephone pole. Even then, I had no doubt, with her stubbornness, she'd gain expertise in anything she desired to do. Taking the plate from Nora, I moved to sit on the sofa.

"Remi? Nora? That you?" Tony's weak voice came from the cracked open door.

I tightened my grip on the dish in my hand. My heartrate picked up tenfold. I'd been waiting for this moment—for a time when I could talk to Tony and Nora alone. Over the past couple of weeks, Angie hadn't left Tony's side, and I couldn't blame her.

"Yes," Nora answered him.

We both walked into the room. I sat in the bombin' vintage green chair, and Nora leaned onto the end of the bed. My sore body eased into the chair.

Bliss.

Pure bliss.

After working an entire day and pushing my muscles to the limit, the moment they got to relax was sweeter than stolen honey. I took a bite of the bread and couldn't help but think *this is what heaven would be like.* If only death weren't staring me in the face. If only I'd known Tony for more than one growing season. How many treasures of knowledge would he have passed on to me?

Closing my eyes, reveling in the quiet, I let out an audible sigh. "This chair is the most comfortable thing on Earth."

"Remi ..." The hesitancy in Tony's haggard voice had me sitting up and looking at him.

"What is it? Do you need your pillows fixed?" I set down my plate on the nightstand, which was packed full of pills and papers.

Lifting Tony's skeletal body, I adjusted the pillow beneath his neck. Nora picked up the controls for their bed and raised him to a sitting position.

Fiddling with the remote at his side, Tony pressed a button, and the TV went dark. "I think it's time we told him, hun." He spoke to Nora even though he'd just said my name.

Told me what? Did Angie and Smoot get back together? Impossible.

"You sure?" Nora creased her eyebrows together, studying Tony's face.

Tony met her eyes and gave her one slow, deliberate nod. Each of his calculated movements took up his much-needed energy stores. I'd looked at Tony's battle against cancer from all different angles, but there just wasn't a solution to this problem.

"Okay." Nora placed her husband's other hand in hers and gave it a slight squeeze. "I'm with you. Always."

"Tell me what?" I voiced the question, spinning circles in my head.

"We know." Nora's gaze bored into me.

"What do you mean, you know?"

Tony ducked his head. "We know you're with Cockrell Development, and you're here to buy the farm."

I fell back into the velvet chair. They'd known this whole time, and still they'd hired me? Tony's breaths rattled in the quiet until I found my voice. "W-why didn't you say anything? Why did you give me the job?"

The smell of the buttered bread covered the hospital scent that had taken root in this room. I picked the slice up and took another bite. Before I came here, I'd never known the joy of homemade anything. My mother was always watching her carb intake and made sure the chefs followed her various fad diets. As a result, I'd been raised on mostly vegetables, some fruit, and a little dash of protein.

I couldn't imagine what my mother would say about my Idaho diet, which incorporated meat with every meal—including breakfast—carbs galore, and potatoes—glorious, giant potatoes.

Dammit. I didn't want to leave.

"We hired you because we liked you—had a good feeling about you." Tony's Adam's apple bobbed as he paused to swallow.

"And," Nora took over, "Angie took a shine to you at the airport. Who do you think told Wendy to send you our way when you came sniffing around?" She winked at me.

"Keep your enemies closer." Tony's breathy words were so soft I almost missed them.

Were they at the same airport as me? Angie's shine was about as bright as an oxidized penny. I shoved the last of the bread into my mouth and dusted my hands off over my plate. This was the strangest negotiation I'd ever been a part of, almost like I was the pawn in Tony and Nora's plans, not the other way around.

"Okay. Start from the beginning."

Tony flinched, whether from pain or the conversation, I couldn't tell.

Tony cleared his throat. "We—"

"You," Nora interrupted. "You looked."

"I ..." Tony shot his wife a crooked grin. "... took a gander in your briefcase when you went to the bathroom on the plane."

"What?" My briefcase. I usually wasn't so careless. But at that point, I hadn't known Tony and Nora were my targets.

"Okay. I may have encouraged him." Nora patted the back of Tony's hand. "You're so kind, handsome, and appeared to be quite wealthy with that Italian leather bag. You were perfect for our baby girl. I just had to know a bit more about you ..." She let her voice trail off.

They'd known since the beginning, and yet ... "Why didn't you chase me off like you did the other representatives we've sent?" I pressed my hands against my thighs, not quite comfortable being outplayed at my own game.

"I'd already been toying with the idea of selling. Nora isn't too happy about it, but she's come around. We didn't know what company would give me the best offer."

Nora gestured to me with her outstretched hand. "And we figured if you could handle the workload Angie shelled out, your company might be worth a second chance."

"We both thought you wouldn't last a week." A raspy chuckle escaped Tony's parched lips.

"But I stayed ... and suffered." I almost laughed.

"Payback's a bitch." Tony's soft voice cracked.

I couldn't help but laugh. The conversation I'd overheard, the one I'd fretted over for weeks, came to mind ... They weren't talking about Smoot. They'd been talking about accepting CDC's offer to buy the land. All those days picking rock, taking on the devil rooster, hoeing beets, fearing for my life feeding the pigs ... had all been part of *their* game. I'd met my match.

"Watching that horse take a chunk out of your ass was the most we'd laughed in years," Nora said through her own laughter.

"You saw that?" I cringed. Mae and I were on better terms now, but I still didn't trust the beast enough to turn my back on her.

"Yep. I thought you'd leave when you saw how hard it is to work this land. Instead, you stayed and became a pretty good farmer. I don't know what we'd do without you right now. Muffin, and my sweet Nora." Tony regarded Nora with nothing short of true love.

How could I be envious of a dying man?

Tears shuddered down his cheeks. "They'll both need you to help them through this."

"Don't you worry, none." Nora wiped at her own shining cheeks. "As long as you find us a nice spot in heaven and wait for me there. We'll meet again. Someday."

My heart ached like it was bruised. If I had the power, I'd give up all the money in the world to save this man. They communicated without words, then Tony angled his head back to me.

"We want you to buy the farm. First thing tomorrow."

"Tomorrow?" I leaned away from Tony and rubbed the back of my neck. This was what I wanted. What I'd been planning for. Then why did it feel like someone had dropped an anvil down my gullet?

"Yes. This ticker of mine won't last much longer."

"Does Angie know?"

"I've tried, but she changes the subject and won't listen. I was going to today, but Lili and her babies ..." Tony jerked his head toward the pile on his nightstand. "I don't want her drowning in all my debt. I won't let this place sink her. You saw what she was like a few months ago. This place will kill her, even if she can't see it."

"But I want to marry her," I blurted.

"I knew it!" Nora pumped her fist in the air. "Told you, Tony. We didn't have to worry none about the Smoot boy. Remi loves her."

Tony's eyes widened, and his lips curved upward. He looked straight at me. "*Do* you love her?"

"Yes, sir." Warmth, emanating from my center, trickled to my fingertips and into my toes. Heat burned my cheeks. I'd never been more sure of anything in my life. "I promise I will do my damnedest to make her happier than a hog at an all-you-can-eat buffet."

"Good. I couldn't stand Daniel." Tony let go of Nora's hand and eased higher onto his pillows. "Nice enough kid, just—"

"Not for our Angie," Nora finished for him.

Ha! They liked me more than Smoot. I'd feel even more triumphant if it weren't for Tony's hollowed-out cheeks, made even more apparent in the dim lamplight.

"Does Angie feel the same?" Tony asked.

"She hasn't given me her answer yet. But she sure does love kissing me." I smirked.

Tony lifted his hands at his wrists. "I don't need the details—"

"Speak for yourself." Nora cut in.

Tony went on with a sense of urgency in his voice. "And I know she doesn't need my permission, but ..." He shifted his hand closer to me. I took it in a firm grip, careful not to bruise him. "... I'll give you my blessing to marry my daughter if—" Deep-rooted coughs overtook him. Each hacking sound jolted through him, making my body ache while listening to it.

I swallowed past the sudden tightness in my throat. How had I come to care for this man so much? I respected him far more than I ever would my own father. The coughing fit passed, and Nora held his water straw to his mouth.

He took a couple of sips then continued. "If you promise to buy our farm," he finished.

In a rare show of strength, Tony knocked his forearm against the stack of papers. My plate clattered to the ground, foreclosure notices and medical bills scattering on top of it. "Make this all go away."

He rested back on the bed. The sleeve of his red flannel jacket brushed against my forearm. I would never forget this image, the picture of an old, withered, stubborn farmer in John Deere pajamas and his red flannel.

Nora gently held onto Tony's shoulder. The fingers of her free hand shook against her mouth while tears silently escaped her eyes.

The warmth I'd felt at declaring my love for Angie fled, replaced by an ice-cold brick. "I promised Angie I wouldn't buy her land."

"We're out of time, and she won't listen." He coughed. "Angie's true calling is being a baby nurse, not running this place. Between the two she hardly finds time to sleep. And Nora only moved here because she loves me. She's never taken to farm life, not like me." He rested more fully into his pillows. "No. It's time to let it go."

I rubbed my chin, my soft beard brushing against my fingertips.

Tony took hold of my wrist, squeezing it without much strength. "Promise me." He locked eyes with me. "Promise me."

I couldn't ignore his desperation. Not in his last moments on this Earth. "I promise. I'll get the paperwork ready."

"Have it ready with a notary in the morning."

"Tomorrow morning. I'll be here."

And Angie would never forgive me.

Chapter 39

Angie

I stared at one of Lili's perfect boys. Smooshing his tiny lips together, he squinted one eye open only to close it again. Everything in the delivery had gone as best as we could've hoped for. Their lungs were underdeveloped, and they couldn't maintain their body temperature independently. As anticipated, they'd been admitted to the NICU.

We'll know in the next few hours... The pediatric intensivist's words ate at my resolve and probably haunted Lili and Blake. I'd fought through those hours with my everything. The scale tipped ever so slightly in their favor.

While I'd assured Lili everything was going to be fine, her little boys were precariously balanced between life and death. Chorioamnionitis: infection of the amniotic fluid. Lili had been leaking fluid from a small rupture for possibly days. Bacteria got in. The babies had been swimming in putrid soup.

Fifty percent. The pediatric specialist had given them the same probability of living as flipping a coin. Lili blamed herself, saying stuff like, 'A doctor should have recognized a premature rupture.' She couldn't accept the fault. With a leak that small, it would be easily confused with urine, even for a medical professional.

Jared left immediately following the delivery, promising to come get me after my shift.

All night long, I'd managed to keep their oxygen saturation above dangerous levels.

Braden Thomas to my right weighed only four pounds two ounces, and Benjamin Jorge to my left weighed four pounds four ounces. Relatively large babies for the NICU, both were perfect, and both were my responsibility to keep alive.

I stood between their oxygen beds. "Hello, little buddies. You're going to be the most treasured boys on this planet. You just have to fight for it."

We had three other babies in the NICU. Gabby managed their care. Her soft phone conversation carried to me even though she kept her voice hushed. I couldn't decipher her words, but I wasn't really trying. She put the phone down and went about her work.

I double and triple-checked the doctor's orders for Brady and Benny. Administering their meds, checking their vitals, and watching their breathing rate like a hawk. I'd worked here long enough to know Papa wouldn't get to meet these babies.

The monitor grew blurry, and I wiped at my eyes.

Depending on how they responded to the IV antibiotics, they'd be here for at least four weeks, give or take.

Papa wouldn't last that long. Brady and Benny would never be held in their Papa Tony's arms.

If it weren't for Papa, I'd set up camp at the hospital until these little ones were discharged. I wasn't about to let someone else I loved leave me.

Not when I could control it.

Blake had been the only one allowed to visit. He'd followed his boys here as soon as the doctors had let him. Now he was back in Lili's recovery room. Waiting with her. Wondering. Praying.

Hopefully, Maddie would get to meet the new members of her family tomorrow. I checked my watch and huffed an exhausted chuckle. It was already tomorrow. Three o'clock in the morning, to be exact. Which meant I hadn't slept in over twenty-four hours. I had been up the night before with Papa and hadn't been able to get my mind settled enough to nap during the day.

Even if provided the opportunity to sleep, would I be able to?

The doors to the NICU opened, and Ryan walked in. He wasn't supposed to be on shift until seven a.m. "What are you doing here?"

Gabby set down her chart and came to stand shoulder-to-shoulder with Ryan.

"I'm here to tell you to go home."

Gabby placed both her hands on my shoulders. "You need sleep."

"But ... the babies. I can't ..."

"We'll take care of the boys," Ryan said.

Looping her arm behind my back, Gabby guided me to the doors. She pressed the button and waited for our path to clear. Ryan stood behind us, an effective barricade to my retreat.

Remi stood on the other side of the open doors. "Hey. How's she holding up?"

"Not well," Ryan answered.

"She needs to go to bed ASAP," Gabby said simultaneously.

Great. My nemesis and would-be fiancé had enlisted my friends to spy on me. "*She* is standing right here and can answer for herself." I pushed out of Gabby's arms and moved away from all of them. "What is this?"

"An interventi—" The doors closed on Ryan, cutting his response short.

"We asked for Remi's help." Gabby leaned her hip against the door button. "Go home. Take care of yourself. We're all worried for you."

She left me. I stood there in the hall alone with Remi until the doors had fully closed. Without saying a word, I marched past him into the main foyer and out into the night. I kept going.

How dare Remi presume he had the right to handle me?

I was strong. Capable. Smart. I could manage my own life without a man doing it for me. And Gabby and Ryan, the traitors, wouldn't have even let me in the hospital to keep Lili's babies alive. Yes, I trusted them to do as good of a job as me, but relinquishing control sent me spiraling into the what-if game.

What if one of the monitors malfunctioned and Gabby didn't notice?

What if another baby crashed, and Ryan tunneled in on them and neglected to watch Brady's or Benny's oxygen saturation?

What if the power went out, the backup generators failed, and they couldn't get power to the beds?

What if a category five tornado hit the hospital, and I wasn't there to get the twins to safety?

Sure, a category five tornado had never touched ground in Idaho. Most of ours were small and puny compared to the ones in the Midwest. But there could always be a first.

Stopping, I looked around. A tall lamp post lit up the halo of light encircling me. I'd walked to the far edge of the parking lot. I turned a full 360 degrees. Cripes. I didn't know what Remi's new truck looked like.

He came to the edge of the light. "I parked back there." He clicked a button on the key fob in his hand, and orange lights flashed near the hospital entrance.

I grumbled and turned back the way I came. "You could have mentioned that sooner."

"I'm not dumb enough to tease a pissed-off rattlesnake." He followed behind me and spoke so quietly that I almost didn't hear him.

A snake? Did he just compare me to a snake? I didn't want pity or to be treated like a fragile butterfly, but a little respect would be nice, especially considering all the garbage going down in my life.

Clamping my mouth shut, I successfully bottled my outrage and got into his truck. He started the engine and pulled out of the lot. Mesmerized by the blanket of darkness around us, I stared out the window, at the way the headlight beam rolled seamlessly over the grass.

Soothing country music drifted from the speakers at low volume. His radio switched from song to song. Thirty minutes flew by until one of my favorites came on: Taylor Swift's "Fearless." The name of her record-breaking album and a song about love, driving in a car, first kisses, and being fearless.

In the cab of Remi's truck, I could almost forget about the storm that raged outside, waiting to consume me.

In here, I could be fearless. Give him an answer. Say yes.

In here, I could also be furious. Kind of like a pissed-off rattlesnake.

"I remind you of a snake?" I took the second option. "What about me says scaly, deadly beast?" I turned from the peace of the window and glared at him.

"Ah, there's the venom I've missed so much." He shot me a quirky half smile.

320

"Now, not only am I a snake, but I'm a venomous one?"

"In the most adorable way."

"Gah!" I yelled and pressed the palms of my hands to my temples. "You are the most infuriating—Why did you have to come pick me up? I'm handling things fine on my own?"

"From where I'm sitting, you're half a bubble off a plum." He made the right turn, taking us into downtown Clear Springs. One blink, and you'd miss it.

"What does the even mean?" I took a breath. "You make no sense."

"What I mean, dear Angie, is that you are one loose wire away from exploding. I talked to your mom. You haven't been sleeping or eating much, and this was before Lili's delivery."

"I'm doing fine."

"Would you stop saying fine? I hate that word. Stop lying to me."

"What? You want me to say instead that Papa means everything to me. Without him in my life I'm going to be so lost—tell you that I'm the failure who walked this farm right up to bankruptcy's door and knocked—that Lili's beautiful babies, the ones she and Maddie and Blake have been praying for, have only a fifty percent chance of surviving the week?" The wall I'd held in place since the reality of hospice care entered my world began crumbling. Tears spilled over the edge of my bottom lid, and I could do nothing to stop them. "You want me to confide in you about how I want to get married so badly before my dad dies? That I invested three months into a complete lie? Instead of spending more time with my papa?"

Remi approached my lane.

I pressed my arm to his chest. "Don't." Air. I couldn't get enough air. "I can't—I can't let Mama see me like this."

"It's okay. Breathe."

Passing my driveway, he turned into Mountain Meadows, heading to his house.

I pulled on my seatbelt and on the collar of my scrubs. Everything was too tight. Suffocating me. The edges of my vision blurred, and I felt for the handle. "I need to get out. I need to get out of this truck now."

"Hold on." Remi slammed on the gas and drifted into his driveway.

I pulled on the handle and threw the door open once he stopped. The cold night air washed over me. I tried to get out, but something yanked me back in my seat. Again and again, I tried.

Remi materialized in front of me. Reaching around me, he unlatched the belt which kept me captive. Like a dope, I hadn't freed myself from my seat belt. His hands were on my upper arms, guiding me to the ground.

"Focus on me. And take deep breaths. In and out." He helped me into the house—into his bedroom.

I couldn't fight him. Couldn't listen to him and gain control of myself. My breaths still came in short gasps. My head dizzied. The fire propelling me through this nightmare went out. Doused by the torrent of tears, I couldn't stop.

The door latch clicked, cutting off the light from the living room and sending us into darkness. He took my stethoscope and placed it on his dresser.

He pulled me onto the bed and wrapped his arms around me. "I'm so sorry."

No wonder he was sorry for me. I was a nothing. Had nothing. No money. Still terrified of heights. Useless in a raft. Soon to be fatherless.

Even with all my schooling, I hadn't been able to save Papa or manage to drive the probability of those precious babies living any higher.

I was a worthless, powerless loser.

Pressing me to his chest, he massaged my head, running his fingers over my scalp and along my spine, sending soothing, calming chills chasing through my body.

"I'm not ready, Remi." I balled my fists against his chest and cried into his shirt. "I can't say goodbye. It's not fair."

"I'm so sorry." His voice cracked.

I didn't need to hear anything else. I didn't want advice or for someone to say it was okay. Nothing about Papa dying was *okay*. With him gone, my life wouldn't be *okay* for a long time.

Remi's soft words, packed with emotion, sabotaged the rest of my strength.

I let go of my pain, of my fear, my anger, and jealousy of anyone who had a healthy papa. I let it all out, while he simply held me.

Chapter 40

Remi

The clear part of the eggs started turning white as I sprinkled salt, pepper, and a handful of cheese over them. Breaking the yolks, I stirred it all together with my favorite bamboo spatula.

I'd already eaten my first breakfast, checked on the crops, made sure my repair still held water, gave the re-tasked construction crew their orders for the day, and returned here to find Angie still sleeping ... at one p.m.

For all I cared, she could sleep until tomorrow. Heaven only knew she needed it.

I made another breakfast, so she would wake up to the smell of bacon, a glass of fresh orange juice—well, as fresh as I could get it at Nora's grocery—and scrambled eggs. I liked good food, and sometimes the fancy chef my mother hired cooked such weird things like duck liver and haggis, that I'd to learn to cook to allow my tastebuds to live to fight another day.

This morning, after I'd woken up beside her, I'd watched Angie sleep. It convinced me more than ever that I wanted to wake up next to her every morning for the rest of my life. It was a first for me. Sleeping with a woman without having sex. It created a tender, unbreakable bond between us, more intimate than intercourse.

My door creaked open. I smiled. The last of the liquid solidified into golden clumps in the pan. Perfect timing.

Grabbing the handle, I turned to face Angie. Her low ponytail was mussed into a lopsided, tangled mess, and her scrubs were wrinkled.

She yawned and walked toward me with sleep still in her eyes. "What time is it?"

"One fifteen."

Her eyes came fully awake. "I've been here that long? I've got to get home. Papa—"

"Is doing fine. No change from when you left. Jared's been with him, and I think they've appreciated the alone time."

Her shoulders relaxed, and she dropped her gaze to the table. "What's all this?"

"I thought you'd be hungry. So, I made you breakfast ... well ... two breakfasts. I had to eat the first by myself." I set the eggs on the table and pulled a chair out for her.

She stood, frozen in the awkward space between the living room and the kitchen, looking at me like she saw me for the first time. Admiration. Wonder. Love. All present in her eyes.

I wasn't a good guy. Every single woman in my past would treat me the same as Kathryn had, and I deserved it.

With yesterday's events, I'd betrayed Angie with a notary and a stack of papers. Tony had said he'd talk to her when she returned home from the hospital. Thinking he'd be able to spare me from blame, he'd asked me to keep quiet until then.

So far, I'd kept my mouth shut. Part of me didn't agree this was the greatest move; the other part was plumb chicken. Ironically, after a summer helping her lie, I understood that Angie appreciated blunt honesty.

I squirmed under her scrutiny. "Sit down. Eat."

Placing two slices of bacon, a healthy serving of eggs, and a full glass of OJ in front of her, I sat across from her and began eating.

She took her first bite. "Mmm ... these eggs are good."

"You sound surprised."

"Well, I thought you would have had a chef growing up."

"Confession." I set my fork on my plate and wiped my mouth with the napkins I'd folded into triangles. "What you see here is the extent of my cooking abilities."

She laughed. I'd never get tired of hearing her laughter. We finished the rest of the meal with her quizzing me on what it'd been like to grow up as a spoiled rich boy. I kept my responses light, but to sum it all up in three words ... isolated, stifling, and cold. The antithesis of Tony and Nora's home.

Her smile took on a more playful lilt to it, yet her eyes grew serious. "Hypothetically, if I were to say yes to your proposal ..."

My heart stopped. Yes. Did she say yes? I pressed my hands to the table, fingers spread wide, not daring to say anything or interrupt.

"... Papa can't leave his bed. Would you be opposed to getting married in his room tonight?"

I jerked my head toward her. "Tonight?" From single to married in one day. Sure, I could man up and do this for her. But tonight? I forced myself to swallow, to take a breath. Certain my neck would be sore from the whiplash I'd given myself, I continued, "You're sure. You don't have to make this decision right now."

If she didn't find out about the sale until after our marriage ... it'd be annulled. I couldn't go into this marriage with a big lie hanging between us.

"I want to marry you, Remington James *Cockrell* the Third." She leaned over our breakfast and kissed me.

She tasted of oranges. Her teeth toyed with my bottom lip; then she pressed her lips against mine once again. Allowing her tongue to delve into my mouth, tentatively exploring and growing bolder the longer the kiss went on, I reveled in every detail of her: sweet, strong, courageous, smart, talented, determined Angie. And she wanted to spend her life with me.

But all for the wrong reasons.

I broke free from her lips. "Maybe we should wait to make this big of a decision."

"Wait?" She fell back into her chair.

"Why do you want to marry me? Because you love me or because Tony is dying?"

Leaning her elbow on the table, she dropped her head into her hand. Not a good sign for me.

"If I marry you ... when I marry you ... I want it to be for the right reasons. I don't want to have the marriage that my parents have. Two strangers living separate lives, used for the political and financial benefits, but not the intimacy of it."

Birds sang outside on the sapling tree that'd been placed in the center of the green lawn, caught in the quiet. Shafts of sunlight cut across the table, glaring off my fork.

"So, you won't do it?" Angie finally asked.

I flinched at the pain in her voice. I'd do anything for her. "Is this that important to you? You'd risk marrying me so your father can be there?" I tried to pass it off as a joke, giving a half laugh and lightening the mood.

"You're not half bad. I mean, you're no Hemsworth ..." She raised her eyebrow at me and smiled in the most seductive way, then grew serious. "Please, Remi," she whispered.

Who the hell cared about the reasons she wanted to marry me anyway? This was the biggest risk I'd ever taken, but even if I had a one percent chance of a happy outcome with Angie, I'd take it.

"Well then, after serious reconsideration, I've decided to accept your proposition," I said in my best business voice. "See my man on your way out, and he'll fill you in with the details."

She tilted her head back and laughed. "I have a feeling I'll be laughing a lot more with you as my husband." Grabbing her empty cup and mine, she walked toward the fridge. "And yelling a lot more." She smirked. "You want some orange juice?"

"Sure."

Husband? I pushed down my rising panic. I loved Angie and I thought she loved me. We wouldn't have the same relationship my parents had. It wouldn't happen to us.

"What's this?" Angie pulled the manila folder with a single slip of paper peeking out from the front cover off the counter.

Shit. I'd been checking over Tony's closing documents when Ryan and Gabby had called. I hadn't planned on bringing Angie back here. I'd slipped them under the couch. Myles must have 'cleaned up' last night and put the folder there.

"Nothing." I stood and rushed forward to grab it from her, but she snatched it out of my reach.

"Then why do you want them so bad?" She peeled open the front cover.

Before she could read very far, I told her what I should have told her the moment she walked into my living room. "It's the closing documents for buying a parcel on five hundred and forty acres belonging to Tony and Nora Johnson." Each word pounded the nail in my coffin.

"These are signed." She flipped through a couple more pages. "And notarized."

The folder slipped from her fingers and papers flapped onto the floor, scattering at our feet. I couldn't meet her accusing glare. Couldn't bear the way the light in her eyes faded into dim betrayal.

"What?" She croaked. "What happened to 'marry me and I won't buy your farm'? Did you mean anything you said? Or were you playing me from day one?" Her voice rose until she all out shouted at me.

A vice clamped around my lungs. I couldn't breathe. I was going to lose her. How could I make her see? "No. I didn't lie about loving you." I held my hands up like I would around a live bomb. "Tony's going to talk to you about his decision. It's your father's dying wish. How can I deny him his last wish?"

"A dying man's wish that fits so conveniently into your agenda."

I couldn't think of anything to say to defend myself.

She shook her head and kicked the papers on her way to the door. "I'm not going to let this happen. You sick son of a bitch. You manipulated my father, who is not in a clear frame of mind, to get what you want."

"It's not like that. He's doing this for you." I took a step toward her.

"For me?" Gripping the doorknob, she slapped her hand against her chest. "Only I know what's best for me. Not you. Not Mama. Not even Papa."

"Don't leave. We can sit down and talk about this and figure it out."

"So you can lie to me some more? Yeah, right." She yanked open the door. "You knew about this last night, and you didn't tell me. You let me cry in your arms. And in a crazy turn of events, you're still the bad guy."

"You needed sleep. And Tony asked me to wait to tell you until he had a chance to talk to you."

"I was so stupid for trusting you. Forget about me, forget about my family, and leave us alone." She stepped outside, slamming the door behind her.

I followed after her only to stop at the edge of my lawn and watch her disappear into the corn, which was now taller than me.

Chapter 41

Angie

Swiping at my eyes, I tore open my front door. Dagnabbit. I thought I'd cried all my tears the night before.

"Mama!" I hollered down the hall. "Is Papa awake?" Still wearing my scrubs from almost two days ago and my hair a webbed mess, I beelined it to Papa's room.

"He just ate lunch." Mama stood at the sink and dropped a couple of dishes in the dishwasher.

I pushed open Papa's door. The curtains had been pulled open, brightening the typically dim room. Papa must not have a migraine today.

He laid on the propped-up bed, wearing his favorite red flannel jacket, his stare boring into me. Usually, we were so in tune with our opinions, Papa could read my thoughts. Ever so slightly his eyes flinched and shifted from me to the floor. I had no doubt he knew that I knew.

"Where's Jared?"

Mama came up behind me. "He's in bed. He spent all night with Tony."

"Told my boy—not to waste his one chance to achieve his dreams on me," Papa said, his voice even weaker than before I'd left for Lili's delivery. "He's going back on tour. He can join that Zoom thing ... for the funeral."

"Oh, so now you know what's best for Jared too?" I stomped up next to his bed.

"I won't have you ruining your lives because of me." Each breath he took labored in and out of him.

I slumped into the chair. "Papa. Why did you sell our land? Our home? It's not enough I have to say goodbye to you. I have to lose my home. My land. Mae ..." Without a place to put her, I'd have to sell my one friend who'd always been there for me, the only living thing who understood me. Words weren't needed to communicate with her. She sensed my every need. Without this farm, I was a boat without water, a cheese grater without any cheese. Useless.

I looked to Mama. Her cheeks shined in wet tears. "Did you know?"

She nodded. Tears streamed down her cheeks. "I don't know how to tell you this." She placed a hand on my shoulder.

"Mama, I—"

"Remington works for Cockrell Development Company."

"I know. I've known for a long time. What do you think I was doing this whole summer?" I glanced over my shoulder at her. "I was trying to chase him off."

Papa's body started shaking. My heart pounded in my throat. Was he having a seizure? I relaxed as the first of his wispy laughs became audible. "Some job you did. You made the boy fall in love with you."

I shook my head. If Remi loved me, he wouldn't have done this. "What did he tell you?"

"He loves you. Asked for my permission. To marry you." Papa coughed, his voice growing weaker, each phrase proceeded by a rattling breath. "You going to tell him—yes?"

"Hell no. He's taking everything from me." I gripped the sides of my head. "I spent the entire summer trying to get Dan to propose so you could be at my wedding. He did. And I turned him down. I want to make you happy, but I just don't think I can marry either of them." I threw my hands in the air then let them fall to the mattress.

Papa pressed his lips together and ran his tongue over their cracked surface. "Nora? Would you mind. Give us time alone?"

"I'll be right outside the door if you need anything." Mama rubbed his legs which were draped in blankets.

"Oh, and Nora?"

"Yes?" Mama paused mid-step.

"I love you … Always and forever."

Life sucked. It was so unfair. Love didn't prevent tragedy. It enhanced it. My parents had just celebrated their thirty-ninth wedding anniversary. They'd made such plans for forty, but Papa wouldn't make it.

I swallowed past the lump in my throat. My tears turned back on like a switch had been flipped.

Mama's chin quivered. "Always and forever," she repeated and left the room.

"I didn't mean to put so much pressure on you. About being at your wedding." Papa took a raspy breath. "My greatest wish is for you to find happiness. With or without a man in your life."

"I want what you and Mama have—"

"You will." Patting my hand, Papa lifted his head from his pillow, his neck barely able to support it. "Don't rush it. A wedding isn't all that important. My greatest dream was for you to find a love like your Mama and I have. And you did that. We both know you're in love with Remi."

"I do not love him." If I said it loudly and with enough authority, it became truth.

"Now you're lying to me on my deathbed," Papa quipped and laughed softly.

"I'm so afraid. What if it all goes bad?"

"Don't be. Afraid." He rubbed the back of my hand with his thumb. "Remi's a good guy. His better qualities came out this growing season. He's your other half, and it'll work out." He fell back into his pillow. "But if not, focus on making your dreams come true, not mine. You can't keep pushing yourself like you have. Nursing and farming. Too much. You're killing yourself off." He took a rattling breath and briefly closed his eyes. "The farm was my adventure. It's time you go and find yours. We both know your calling is to save babies."

He was right. Remi had actually shown it to me. He'd gotten so excited about the emerging corn, but I hadn't. Not like I used to. Each plant bogged my spirits down with more work. In the NICU, I couldn't describe the feeling of saving a baby's life. It. Was. Magic. Even with the few tragic losses, my work there fulfilled me. And Papa knew it. He'd always understood me better than myself.

"I don't understand," I began, my voice cracking.

"What don't you ... understand?"

"Why do you have to die? And now you're taking all our memories away from me too. I can't. I can't do this without you. Without my safe place." I wiped my eyes and nose with my sleeve, too angry and hurt to look at the man I'd idolized my entire life.

"Muffin."

Muffin, my lifelong, terrible nickname. What I wouldn't give to have Papa around to make up awful nicknames for my children. I looked into his eyes, memorized the flecks of green in their hazel depths, wishing I could reverse time and keep everything the same.

"You ever wonder why I call you Muffin?" His voice weakened to a whisper.

I shook my head, unable to form an audible response.

"You're the smell of your Mama's baking. You're mornings sitting around the breakfast table. You. Are. My happiness."

My sobs came out in uncontrolled spasms. Maybe my nickname wasn't so bad after all. "I can't. I can't—" *I can't stop time. I can't cure cancer. I can't make money appear out of thin air.* Can'ts piled on top of me, threatening to suffocate me.

"I'm not leaving you. Not really. I'll be there. Right by your side. You just won't be able to see me."

Or be enfolded into a big Papa hug. Or talk to him about the crops or the stresses at work. Or celebrate all the things. He *was* leaving and he wasn't being given a choice.

The withered skin on his arm trembled in time with his muscles as he lifted his hand and pointed to my temple. "Memories live here," he then pointed to my heart, "and here. That's where I'll be. With you. Forever."

I kissed the back of his hand and pressed it to my cheek. "I'll miss you so much."

"I'll get a plot for us in heaven." He smiled and rubbed his thumb over one of my tears. "Land paved in gold."

A laugh escaped through my soft sobs. "That wouldn't grow potatoes very well."

His cheeks shook against his smile as he nodded. He closed his eyes and relaxed further against his pillow. "You're right," he whispered.

I laid his hand on his sheets, letting him doze for as long as his pain would let him. Resting my forehead next to him, I let my cries continue. At some point, Mama walked in, wrapped her arms around me, and bawled right along with me.

Days later, I still sat next to his bed. Mama and I had both taken to sleeping in this room. Jared had left to meet up with his tour. We FaceTimed Lili so she could show Papa Tony her boys. They'd made it out of the danger zone and were able to keep their sats up with only a low level of oxygen.

I took over his hospice care while Mama busied herself with making all of Papa's favorite things even though he wasn't able to eat any of them. Remi still managed the farm, ignoring my request that he leave. I refused to acknowledge the hurt I saw on his face. The grief he felt at losing the friend he'd found in my Papa.

Mama worked side by side with Remi, setting up the farm auction, while my heart continued to grow hard against him. No matter what Papa said, I had no desire to forgive him.

A week after the sale of the farm was finalized, I held Papa's hand as his breaths grew further and further apart, telling him stories of our adventures in farming. His hands, once strong enough to plow thousands upon thousands of acres, carry a mountain worth of boulders, move endless rows of irrigation pipe, grow enough food to feed the entire state of Idaho—strong enough to carry me through my life—now hung limp in my own.

Sapped of their strength.

Stripped by cancer down to nothing but veins, skin, and bone.

I told him of the first time I'd helped him deliver a baby calf. About the time he'd rescued me when I'd gotten stuck upside down from a bin of baby chicks.

About the day he brought home my beautiful Mae. The first time I drove Oscar, the tractor he'd first taught me to drive, into the ditch. The time I'd won my first beauty pageant, and the trophies from rodeo.

He'd been at every competition.

I talked about when I'd helped with planting and crouched next to him, feeling the excitement of the tiny plants emerging, and the time he comforted me in high school after Brock Cooper broke my heart.

He fell asleep listening to our stories with Mama lying beside him, holding him in her arms. A smile on his face.

Never to wake up again.

Chapter 42

Remi

The last of the people from the funeral left the parlor. I'd made sure all Tony's funeral expenses were paid for, even if I had to do so from a distance. It'd been professionally catered with Tony's favorite food, smoked ribs and tri-tip, corn on the cob, and hot chocolate with mini marshmallows.

My heart ached from watching Angie spread her Papa's ashes over the field they'd cultivated since she was a little girl. She'd stood right in front of me, drenched in the worst pain, and I couldn't do anything to comfort her.

I'd never been so helpless.

Tony's wish had been to become a part of the land he'd loved so much. I'd make sure the place where his ashes lay would be made into a grassy field. I'd preserve the maple tree on the edge of the field and install a bench under it with an inscription dedicated to Tony.

I walked to Nora, who sat in her recliner, gripping the arm of Tony's matching chair, empty from now on. I crept to her side and wordlessly gave her a big hug. My last goodbye to the woman who'd shown me how a real mother cared for her kid.

Taking the envelope from my jacket pocket, I pressed it into her hand. "Remember, this is what Tony wanted."

She wiped her eyes with her handkerchief and opened it, numbly pulling the check out far enough to read it.

Her eyes widened. "This is a fortune."

"I promised I'd give you the best offer my company could manage." Matthew railed at me when he found out what I'd paid for the property. A small win I gained in this whole affair. "Your debts are paid."

"This is what's leftover?" Her arms fell into her lap, and she started crying once again.

"Tony didn't want you to worry about anything for the rest of your life. I can only hope to love a woman as much as he loved you." And to have her love me too.

"The dope. Knew me better than I know myself. I'm going to miss him." She brushed at her tears. "When do you leave?"

"Tomorrow, after the auction."

She nodded, and, giving her hand one final squeeze, I walked toward the door, my heart heavier with each step. The happiest I'd ever been in this life had been in this house.

"She's in the barn," Nora called to me.

I turned with my hand on the doorknob. I couldn't see her. "Thank you," I spoke to the quiet house. "For everything."

Evening glowed orange as I made my way along my well-beaten path. The gravel eased into the hardened dirt of the barn, and I raised my head, my eyes locking on Angie.

Angie hadn't noticed my entrance. The image she presented would be something I'd never forget. Still wearing her black funeral dress, her feet bare, and strands of hair falling loose in her updo, she leaned her head against Mae and sobbed.

Each sound breaking from her became an arrow to my heart.

I lost my courage and ducked behind a post, yet I was still unable to keep myself from peeking around the beam at her.

"Don't forget me." She threw her arms around her horse's neck, burying her face in her mane.

Opening the stable, she led Mae to stand by her side. In one fluid movement, she leapt onto her back. Mae was already in motion; her hooves thundered out of the barn into the pasture and fields.

I chased after them. Angie's braid came loose. Horse and rider moved as one. Mae predicted her movements; they were two halves to a whole. I'd never seen a stronger connection between human and animal. With Angie's hair now flowing free behind her, she threw her head back and unleashed an almost feral scream at the distant thunderclouds illuminated by the now-red glow of the sun.

The lump in my throat made it hard to breathe and even harder to swallow. My breath shuddered in and out of my lungs while I studied the now-familiar land around me. The setting sun added to the picturesque painting of patchwork fields and rolling green pastures. I dropped my gaze to the grass tamped down by my feet. I'd never be able to forget this view, soon to be overtaken by homes. From the moment I arrived here, I'd been hell bent on taming this land, and, lo and behold, it'd ended up taming *me*.

I covered my face with my palm. I'd made the biggest mistake of my life. Funny how love worked. I wanted nothing but to ensure her happiness, and I'd been the root cause of her sorrow.

I swiped at the wetness on my cheeks and left, heading straight to the bar.

"Whisky." I slapped a wad of cash on the slick counter and unbuttoned the top two buttons of my tux. "And keep them coming." Sliding the black tie off my neck, I tossed it to the bartender. "Here, Sam. Have a tie."

"Thanks." He caught it midair and shoved it in his apron pocket. "I've been thinking about my future, like you told me to."

Sam told me his ideas, feeding me drinks the whole time.

Four tumblers in, and the door swung open. I glared at the blinding light. Once it closed, the outline of a man turned into Myles.

"Myles!" I shouted. "Friend! Come join me."

"When you didn't come home, I thought I'd find you here."

I kicked out a stool for him. This early in the evening, the bar remained mostly empty.

"Why not?" He sat down, and Sam filled a glass for him and slid it in front of him.

"Thanks." I downed a drink, praying for the numb I-don't-give-a-damn feeling it would bring. "Sam has been telling me about all his ideas for a start-up." I wrapped my arm around Myles, bumping him enough that he spilled his drink a bit. "Picture this. Hatching rubber duckies. You put an egg in your bath water and out comes a rubber duck. I think we should invest."

"Kids would go crazy over them." Sam dried a cup behind the counter.

"Solid idea. You know who I think would really like them?" Myles tossed another drink down his gullet.

"Who?"

"Angie."

"Awww. Why'd you go and mention her?" My words slurred now I'd almost reached an optimal alcohol intake. "We were having a good time."

"She gave you the cold shoulder today. I take it you weren't successful in getting her to see your side of things." Myles set his glass down, and I slid another one to him. "I'm good."

"Drink."

"Two is enough for me." Myles held his hand up to Sam, indicating he wanted him to stop filling the empty shot glasses lining the counter.

"The woman I love will never talk to me again, and you refused to get smashed with me?"

Myles closed his eyes and rubbed the bridge of his nose. "Here we go." He took the glass and gulped down the contents. "At least you have enough money to break away from your family. Texas Bros: a place for all your extreme sporting needs, here we come!"

We clinked our glasses together and downed the liquor. The usual excitement at the mention of our store didn't fill me. Without Angie, any dream was hollow.

"We need music." I went to the jukebox and pushed some buttons.

The next few hours blurred together. Lots of singing. Myles and I performed a duet on the table. Somehow, the tie I'd given Sam ended up strapped around my forehead. I leaned my head on the cold bar and closed my eyes for ten seconds.

Someone tapped me on the shoulder. I rolled my head to see Myles snoring with his head leaning on the bar. I swiveled around on the stool. "What?" I blinked my eyes. "Blake?"

"Myles. Blake's here." I shook my friend awake. "Hey! New daddy. Have a drink on me. Drinks all around for the Richardson twins!" I shouted.

The patrons in the now-full bar cheered.

"I don't need a drink. Just had to come see for myself how pathetic you are."

Flapping my lips together, I waved my hand at him. "I'm not pathetic."

"You're going to give up?" Blake towered over me with his hands on his hips.

I jumped to my feet, causing my head to spin. "Whoa." I held my palm to my forehead. "I tried everything! She. Hates. Me. With a capital H."

"With how much time and energy you invested in buying Angie's farm ..."

I slumped lower with every word Blake said. My treacherous mind went back to our dirt bike kiss. To my hands holding her, teasing her, my lips on her neck, her abdomen. Then it moved to holding her while she sobbed, cradling her while she slept.

If only I could have more kissing. More cuddling. More of her.

"I thought you'd fight harder for her," Blake finished.

"We're leaving tomorrow." Myles looked at his watch. "Oh shit. Our plane leaves in five hours." He rubbed his eyes. "What is he going to do? Buy her farm back? His cut wouldn't even come close to being able to do that."

My mind started whirring, fighting against the alcohol in my system. Buy it back. It was impossible. My father and Matthew were very specific about owning the entire property, including the house. They didn't want the aged farmhouse affecting sales. But what if I used my money to buy something else?

Jolting upward in my stool like a lightning bolt struck me, I slammed my hand on the bar. All three of my friends jumped.

I jerked Myles to his feet and kissed him. "You're a genius."

Chapter 43

Angie

We hadn't been allowed time to wallow in our grief. The farm auction had rolled ahead the day after the funeral. All my beloved animals, the equipment we'd struggled to make the massive monthly payments on, were bought and carted off.

I'd stayed inside that day, hiding from my animals' calls and the auctioneer's incessant droning. Immediately, we both dove into packing up the house. The hardest was going through Papa's things. Touching his favorite shirt that he'd never wear again and smelling his aftershave and cologne; I could almost pretend he'd walk in the front door and holler at me to come help him change the water.

The insurmountable was surmounted. We packed everything we owned and hauled it to a storage unit. Sure, Remi had indicated we could stay as long as we needed, but with his company paying cash, our house was sold before the funeral. Both Mama and I didn't want to live on charity.

Any way to keep ourselves busy was good. In the quiet moments, the gaping hole Papa left in our family couldn't be ignored. In the quiet moments, I couldn't keep thoughts of Remi from invading.

Towers of boxes surrounded Mama and me. The last of our stuff had been delivered to the apartment Mama had purchased.

"I don't think all this will fit." She pushed boxes around and read the labels, the wood floor creaking beneath her feet.

Using my box cutter, I sliced through a line of clear tape. "I think these are the last of our books."

"Did we really have that many?" Mama shrugged. "Oh well, I guess I need to buy a bookshelf."

She'd purchased this apartment along with the empty commercial space beneath it. Space we'd spent the last couple of months cleaning, painting, purchasing ovens, tables, and chairs, and prepping for the grand opening, less than a week away.

Mama owned a bakery. Nora's Bakery.

I'd expected her to go back to running the grocery store, now being renamed Ivy's. She'd surprised me when she'd shown me the building she'd purchased and drawings with plans for the future.

"You know what? I feel like buying one right now. Get your shoes on," Mama ordered me around like a drill sergeant.

"I'm coming?"

"I'll need your second opinion."

"Fine." Slipping on my shoes and jacket, I followed her down the stairs and into the car.

We'd sold both of our unreliable vehicles at the auction and now had a brand-new Jeep. I'd never seen Mama so excited about a vehicle in all my life. Considering she'd married Papa at nineteen, she'd never experienced the life of an independent woman.

Driving through town, we headed down the one street I chose never to take. It wound right by our farm. Holding my breath, I rolled down the window as we passed. Golden stalks of corn rustled in the wind. A combine moved slowly through the field, harvesting the dried kernels that Remi and I had planted together.

Remi's voice was as deep and resonating as if he sat next to me. *"Look, Angie. The little baby corns. They're growing."* He'd bent down to his hands and knees, putting his face right up to the emerging plants.

I breathed in the fall air. It smelled of wet earth and fresh cut plants ... the scents of harvest. An overpowering wave of homesickness hit me, and I choked back tears. As happy as I was Mama had gone after her dream, being in an apartment for a couple of months had me pacing the 1200 square feet, restless as a caged lion.

What I wouldn't give to hop on Mae's back and ride to my favorite spot on my land where a tall maple blanketed the green grassy knoll in shade, next to where we'd spread Papa's ashes. The place where I sat with him and could see our fields knitted together like a great patchwork quilt.

I needed to stop using the words "my" and "our." It wasn't mine anymore. I'd lost the war. Soon, the pastures would be covered in houses. Thankfully, Remi had flown back to Dallas.

That man was single-handedly responsible for this deep, wrenching pain I carried with me. The longing. The homesickness. I was a boat adrift on an unfamiliar sea with no place to dock. I couldn't imagine if he'd moved to town, and I'd be forced to face him every day.

My body betrayed me at the thought of him—with his thick, dark hair, matched by his deep-brown eyes, his muscles rippling as he chopped wood, his kisses, and marriage proposals. My abdomen tightened against the anticipation at the mere thought of him.

Criminy. I couldn't get him out of my mind. He still had power over me.

"You know who I've been thinking about?" Mama broke the silence heavy in the car once we'd passed the only home I'd ever known.

"Who? Don't say—"

"Remi." Mama turned away from Twin Falls, in the opposite direction of any bookshelves.

"Where are we going?"

She didn't miss a beat. "There's an antique store out this way. It just opened. I thought we'd give it a try."

Antique store? That I hadn't heard about? Unlikely.

"Given our financial situation, we would have lost the farm anyway. Remi made it as painless as possible if you think about it."

"I can't trust him." I gripped my thighs. "Besides, he moved back to Texas."

"Maybe you should give him a second chance. Tony loved him like a son. He can't be all bad."

She turned down the most beautiful lane. Maple trees lined either side of the driveway. Bright white wood panel fences bordered green pastures. A horse galloped along with our car, almost looking like—

"Mae!" I tapped Mama's shoulder. "Look, it's Mae! Did you find the people who bought her?" I rolled the window down and leaned out to get a better view of my horse.

Mama slowed as she approached the house. The lane widened to a two-story white farmhouse placed in the center of sprawling fields and rolling hills of pasture. It had a wraparound porch with a swing on it, swaying in the wind. Windchimes, sounding just like Mama's, danced in the breeze, their melodic sound carrying to me through my open window, followed by the call of a rooster.

We came to a stop.

Remi was at the bottom of the stairs, wearing his typical white shirt and blue jeans, minus his cowboy hat, holding a ... puppy?

"This is where I leave. Get out. And go easy on him. That man is more in love with you than you know," Mama said.

I didn't want to get out. Remi could hold a hundred puppies in front of a thousand dream homes, but I wouldn't move from this seat.

When I didn't move, Mama reached over and opened the door for me. She unlatched my seat belt. "Out."

Woodenly, I unfolded myself from the car and closed the door. If it weren't for Mae, I would have refused. Mama sped back the way she'd come. I stood rooted in place, staring at my dreamlike surroundings. Stables matching the house rose to the south, and a detached garage and a quaint chicken coop with my chickens milling about underneath a large willow tree stood to the north. A creek gurgled somewhere near enough I could hear it.

I spun 360 degrees until I faced Remi once again. "What's going on?" I did my best to melt him with my stare, but the wonder of this place took some of the venom out of it.

He took a few cautious steps toward me, the puppy whimpering and squirming in his arms. "I got it right, didn't I? White farmhouse. Land to call your own. A large, healthy pasture for Mae. And a," he held the puppy out to me, "dog."

I allowed myself to examine the puppy, taking in his curly coat with a white stripe in the middle of his forehead, leading to his white nose and chest. Black patches with two brown spots looped around his droopy eyes. He was the cutest darn puppy I'd ever seen.

"I didn't know what kind of dog you wanted, so I projected and picked one I would have loved to have as a kid. A Bernese Mountain Dog.

Turns out they're not only loveable and gentle; they also make good livestock guardian dogs." He rubbed the puppy's head while it licked his nose.

I opened and closed my mouth a few times before I found words. "What do you mean, you got it right?" I gestured to the area around me. "Why are we here? What are you doing back in Idaho, holding the cutest puppy in the world? Why is Mae in the pasture? And is that?" Marching past him, I focused on the metal structure at the end of a gravel path I hadn't noticed. "Is that Oscar parked next to the shop?"

Remi shrugged. "Even Booster the Rooster is here."

"Explain," I insisted. My patience ran out.

He set the puppy on the lawn next to his feet. "Remember the money my brother and dad promised me if I bought your farm?"

"Yes, you planned on using it to open your extreme sports store."

"I used every penny to buy this place and most of your stuff at auction. Some of the tractors I had to let go because they were just too expensive and too big."

I covered my mouth with my hands and didn't say anything.

"Sorry, I didn't tell you sooner. I tried. But I'm pretty sure you blocked my number."

I had, in fact, blocked him the morning I'd seen the closing documents.

"And I had to put a lot of work into it before it was ready for you." Remi kicked at the gravel. "It's not as big as your old place. Only eighty acres. Something you could manage while still working at the hospital ..." His voice trailed off.

I gaped at him. He'd bought me a house. Not just any house. My dream home. He'd given Mae back to me. Tears shuttered down my cheeks. He stepped forward with his arms outstretched, but I stopped him. "Why?"

His Adam's apple bobbed. "There are several reasons why I bought this place for you." He tapped his index finger. "One: you need a place to stay now that some jack-ass company bought your old one out from under you. Two: it's a peaceful spot. Three—"

Still covering my mouth, I started laughing through my tears. He touched his second and third finger as he ticked off his list and paced in front of me, the puppy chasing at his heels.

"... Mae has plenty of room to roam. Once I fixed the fences, those were a mess. And four: the year-round creek on the property will make it easy to get water to the cows. Five: a puppy needs a quiet place in the country to live."

"Remi—"

"Six ..." He kept going as if I hadn't spoken. "I love you so much." He dropped his hands to his side.

"What about your dream? With you and Myles?"

"You are my new dream, Angie. Nothing else matters more to me than your happiness." He started pacing again. "And working with my family for a while longer might give me an opportunity to improve my relationship with them. Seven ..."

My cheeks lifted into a shaky smile. Only one reason mattered to me. I didn't have to give up any part of myself, work my butt off, or become someone else to earn Remi's love. I was enough. Boring, Idaho, and all.

Taking hold of his shirt, I yanked him to me and stopped his list with my mouth. His arms lifted to encircle me. He pressed me tightly to him. The feel of his heart matching rhythm with mine, the taste of him—fresh air, fall leaves, and spearmint—the way his hands spread warming tingles everywhere they touched—these all told me emphatically that I was home.

"Of course," he whispered against my lips. "If you'll be needing a farmhand, I know someone who comes highly recommended. Used to be a high-rolling playboy in Dallas. Then came to Idaho and fell in love."

He kissed me again. Gripping the curve of my bottom, he lifted me off the ground. I wrapped my legs around his waist. Tilting my head, I continued to match the movement of his lips. He spun me in a circle, then, relaxing his hold on me, he let me slide down his body until my feet once again touched the ground.

"He'll have to submit an application to HR." I trailed kisses along his neck. "And agree to work for sex."

Remi laughed and pushed me back, forcing me to look up at him. "You might not want to be so loose with those terms."

"I can be as loose as I want with the man I love."

"Who, Myles?" He widened his eyes in mocking shock. "Does he know about your feelings?"

I let out a hoot of laughter and slugged him on the shoulder.

He caught my hand and held it against his chest. The beat of his heart thudded softly against my fingertips.

"Say it again." All joking left him. He dipped his forehead to mine.

"I love you, Remington James Cockrell the Third." Some of the weight pressing me down, giving gravity more power over me, left. I'd found the man I'd been searching for. Someone who'd love me as much as Papa loved Mama.

"Then I believe," he kissed my forehead, "Miss Angelina Johnson, we have a deal."

Epilogue

Angie

"Are you sure you're ready for this?" Remi checked the strap around my waist for the fiftieth time.

Cold steel steadied me. I gripped the railing and peered into the depths of the Snake River Canyon, cloaked in the glow of leftover spring rains and bathed in early sunlight. Waterfalls crashed over the edge of cliffs. The hem of my white gown flapped against my calves in rhythm with the edge of Papa's red flannel jacket.

It still carried hints of wood smoke and lavender laundry detergent of fresh rain and soil. Wrapped in the warmth of his jacket, its worn fabric soft against my skin, and cocooned by his smell, Papa was here with me—not to walk me down the aisle but to take a leap with me.

"It looks a lot higher from up here," I mumbled through gritted teeth. My toes curled in my white tennis shoes, tingling and growing numb. The only comfort I had was strapped to me.

Remi.

He'd BASE jumped hundreds of times and was certified to do the tandem jump we were about to attempt.

"One word from you, and I can tell all these people to go away," Remi whispered against my ear.

My gaze strayed to the pavement where flashing lights blocked and rerouted traffic. All our guests sat in chairs draped in satin with white balloons tied to them. Pedro and his wife with their kids, Rex and Wendy, the entire staff of the farm store, and most of the town of Clear Springs crowded onto the asphalt. Lili, Blake, Maddie, and Renee sat next to Mama and Jared in the front row, Maddie clutching a leash that kept our energetic Roscoe from running off.

Lili held little Benny, and Blake held baby Brady. The boys sat in their laps, happily playing with the white rattles I'd given them before the ceremony. It was crazy how much they'd grown in six months and how much they'd changed in that time.

Remi's family sat next to mine—Matthew and his parents—looking less than enthused by their surroundings.

My gaze faltered on the empty seat next to Mama. "You were right, Papa," I whispered to myself, my grip tightening on the flannel cuff.

I'd found my own adventure.

"Do you, Remington James Cockrell the Third, take Angelina Johnson to be your lawfully wedded wife?" Chuck asked. He stood opposite us on the safe side of the railing wearing a pearl snap, plaid shirt, and jeans. It turned out he had a license to wed and had agreed to marry us on the edge of the Perrine bridge. All the other pastors were too afraid of heights.

"Last chance," Remi whispered. Louder and toward our guests he said, "I do."

I gave him a nod, reassuring him this was my choice. And I'd continue to choose him from this moment until forever caught us.

"Then let's do this."

Carefully, he helped me climb over the rail with him. We stood on a metal platform suspended over the abyss.

"Do you, Angelina Johnson," Leaning into his role, Chuck paused, adding dramatic effect. "Take Remington James the Third to be your lawfully wedded husband?"

My heart raced; the back of my neck broke out in a cold sweat. Two words were the only things standing between me and the greatest leap of my life. I reached behind me and gripped Remi's waist.

Without a doubt, I wanted my every adventure to begin and end with Remi. His muscles tightened against my back, anticipating my answer.

"I ... do."

"Then I pronounce you husband and wife," Chuck proclaimed.

Remi launched us off the platform, and I screamed. Our canopy opened, slowing our descent, but I continued to scream—all 486 feet to the ground.

The End

Acknowledgements

As always, I'd like to thank my husband, Richard. You are the reason I know what it's like to be truly loved. I'm so grateful for my oldest daughter, Emma Jo, for being a constant help, for being mommy number two, and allowing me more time to write. To William, for being so entertaining and making me laugh every day. Olivia, I'm grateful for your tender heart and your talent for writing. Dream big just like your mommy. Genevieve, I love watching you play in the imaginary worlds you create. Keep believing.

I wouldn't have been able to produce such high-quality work without my editors, Alex and Tina! Your detailed eye makes my work shine. Thank you to my proofreaders for catching all the typos and inconsistencies! And, Nat, this cover is even more stellar than the first!

This story first and foremost wouldn't have happened if my friend, Kristin Pete, hadn't told me about the man she met at the airport with a helmet strapped to his backpack, brimming with excitement to BASE jump the Perrine Bridge. Thank you for sharing. And to that man, wherever you are, thank you for being larger than life.

You all can't imagine how amazing my in-laws are! My father and mother in-law (Ken and Polly), my brothers and sisters-in-law (Spencer and Shonnie, Katie and Nathan, Lisa and Kelly, Amy and Lance, Danae and LeGrande), aunts and uncles, and cousins in-law, you are more supportive than I could've ever dreamed. Amy, you and Lance have bailed me out more times than I can count. Thank you for always being there, for coming and sitting with me when I needed you most. Christine, Elizabeth, and Marcie, I'm certain your hearts are made of gold.

I also couldn't do this without the "sisters' gambit." I give my heartfelt thanks to my consistently honest sisters, Kayla, Kelsey, and Marci. You don't let me get away with anything less than excellent. I'm grateful for the rest of my family, my parents, sisters (including Tamara), and brother, for being pillars of support for me in my writing career, and for simply being the absolute best when my family needed you. Your love and strength given in our time of need still brings me to tears.

Thanks to my Florida mom, Felicia, and thanks to Jerry who loves her, for always letting me crash at your place whenever I'm in Boise for writing conferences, and more.

I'm also so grateful for and humbled by the support, Marina Bartsch, has given me from all the way in Switzerland. I'm so glad for the foreign exchange program and that we had the opportunity to become friends in high school. Thank you. So much.

A big thank you to Sherry Briscoe for helping me with the development of the story and Remi's very Texan character. I'm also grateful for all the websites that took the effort to compile the plethora of Texan sayings, especially texasmonthly.com.

My writing groups keep me going when I want to give up. Thanks to The Sisters Prim/Grim, my SP writing group, my RWA CBC Boise writing group, and my romance writing group on twitter, Amanda, Lisa Marie, Megan, Hannah, and Lindsay, for taking the time to read snippets of this book and offer me feedback. Hannah, in particular, thank you for reading this book as a draft and for believing in me always, and helping me become better. I'm also grateful for my Storymakers friends who are always there when I need a boost.

To my Virginia friends, thank you for the deep, abiding friendships we developed in the years I spent there. You will always have a piece of my heart.

I'm grateful for my buoying community, for my church, for helping me when I didn't even think to ask for help. Small towns are the best!

To all the bookstagrammers, bookstores owners, and reviewers, thank you for championing my book and taking the time to share it with the world.

I can't forget to give a shout out to my volleyball family! You keep me mentally sane. Volleyball for life!

Most of all, I'm grateful for my God, for uplifting me and sustaining me throughout life's challenges. And for you, for picking up my novel and opening your heart to Angie and Remi and their love story.

Now go out and find your adventure.

Yours Truly,

Bonnie Jo Pierson

About the Author

Gifted with a short attention span, American romance author, Bonnie Jo Pierson, wants to experience and do as much as she can. As a member of Romance Writers of America, the Storymakers Guild, Idaho Sisters in Crime, Idaho Writers Guild, and Manuscript Academy, she's won the Heart of Denver's Molly contest, placed third in the Orange Rose contest, was a finalist in the Shiela and Four Seasons contest, and placed multiple times in the contest at Storymakers. She also earned a spot in the RAMP mentorship program. She and her Navy veteran husband have four children and spent several years as military nomads. Now she's made her home in small-town Idaho, where she's attempting to resurrect her great-grandparent's one-hundred year-old farm. What Happens in Idaho was her first novel. Her third, book club fiction Barefoot in Flames, is releasing February 2026.